Cattle, Cards, Barbed Wire & Gold

By

Wiley Joiner

Shalako Press

Cattle, Cards, Barbed Wire & Gold

For information contact: Shalako Press

P.O. Box 371, Oakdale, CA 95361-0371

http://www.shalakopress.com

ISBN: 978-0-9961748-3-1

Cover design: Karen Borrelli

Editor: Judith Mitchell

PRINTED IN THE UNITED STATES OF AMERICA

Historical Note

The Mississippi River in the early days formed a borderline between savage and civilized life. West of the Mississippi the unsettled conditions attracted, fostered and harbored the lawless and the reckless.

Much of the violence and romance of the country was exaggerated by writers of the day. This is not to say there was no violence. There was---the worst kind we can imagine.

As ranchers acquired thousands of acres, their cattle freely roamed the land. In time it became necessary to fence the lines between ranches to define ownership.

Some ranchers were never satisfied with what they had and they would go to any length to acquire more of the same.

Acknowledgements

This is a work of Historical Fiction. Characters and events portrayed in these stories are fictional. Resemblances to real people are purely coincidental.

The story *Andrea* in Book 1 is based on an actual event that took place in the Arizona Territory in late 1880s through early 1900s.

The story *Bacon. Beans, & Coffee, A Sierra Gold Adventure*, is based on an event the author experienced in his younger years while camping and mining in the mountains surrounding the old mining town of Downieville, California.

A loving thanks to my wife Glory Ann, for her patience and understanding with me spending so much time closeted in my little office and for the meals she served me there.

A thank you to those readers of my previous books:

Oakdale California, Early Days & Modern Times
California's Golden Glory Days
Black Bart, the Search is Over
Black Bart's Resting Place, in Everlasting Sleep

FUTURE BOOKS

Connected History
Where the Sun Sets

BOOK ONE

Corral of Western Stories

Andrea

As a little girl, I remember Dad was always tending the cattle. It seemed he was never home, but of course he was. Most times I was already in bed when Dad came in. He would tiptoe into my room to kiss me goodnight and I would keep my eyes closed until he bent over to kiss me. I would then reach up to hug him. We played that game for a number of years.

When my little brother Tom was born, Dad took a different roll toward me. I knew Dad was hoping for a son to carry on the family name. I didn't mind. I knew he was a loving Dad and that was good enough for me.

When Tom turned seven years old, Dad taught him to milk the two milk cows. Tom enjoyed doing that and the family cat also enjoyed it, as she always got a squirt or two in the face from Tom's milking. Tom didn't afterwards enjoy hand-churning the milk to make butter.

Dad and Tom were always together. Dad gave Tom a horse when he was nine years old and they would ride together when Dad made his rounds.

We didn't have a nearby school in those days so Mom and Dad did the best they could to teach little brother and me how to read and write. Actually Dad was better at it than Mom was.

One summer evening in 1900, after little brother had gone to bed, Mom and Dad sat with me at the dinner table and Dad began telling me about a time in 1888.

While riding with a group of men, they came upon the scene where the Indians had attacked a wagon and killed the man and woman driving the team. After chasing the Indians away, the men began digging graves to bury the couple, when they heard a faint cry. Upon searching inside the wagon they found a small infant girl of about four months among the loose clothing.

The men buried the couple there on the high desert and marked the site with wood crosses. Dad brought the infant girl home to raise as his own.

I sat for some time with tears running down my cheeks. I was surprised and hurt. Both Mom and Dad wrapped their arms around me. I knew they loved me as they had proven so over the years.

Dad said they were unable to identify the man and woman or where they came from. The old wagon Dad kept in the barn was the one in which he found me.

Gathering myself, I asked Dad if he would take me to the grave site. He answered he would. Early the next morning we saddled horses and rode out. We didn't talk much during our ride. I had things going through my mind about the situation. Arriving at the site, Dad was surprised the crosses were still upright. I told Dad I wanted to be alone for a few minutes. He understood and took a walk.

Being there gave me a strange feeling. Under those crosses were my Mom and Dad. Yet I was living with my Mom and Dad. I wanted to talk to them, but didn't know what to say. I thought about Dad mentioning about finding me in the wagon and taking me home to be his little girl. I was unhappy and joyful at the same time.

During our ride home, Dad reached over and took my hand. With his usual warm smile he said, "I have never felt you were other than my little girl." I suddenly felt a warmness run through my body. After that day, I have never doubted I was Daddy's little girl.

In May 1901, Brother Tom turned ten years old. Dad was in the barn doctoring a sick cow when Tom walked in. Tom suddenly slipped and fell back against the stall wall. The plow mule was startled and kicked, hitting Tom in the head. Dad quickly gathered Tom up and rushed to the house to   doctor his head wound. Dad began talking to Tom, telling him he was going to be alright. Tom never opened his eyes and he lived only a few hours.

I never saw dad cry before. It broke my heart to see him holding Tom in his arms and suffering as he was. Dad had lost his little buddy.

Tom was buried next to Grandma there on the ranch. Dad visited Tom's grave every day for a long time. Twice more I saw Dad cry and it broke my heart. Then one day, Dad didn't go to the grave. We never asked why.

I turned fourteen in 1902, and dad gave me a hand gun for my birthday. I practiced shooting until I could hit a moving target at forty feet. Dad was pleased and told me I was as good as he had ever seen with the revolver. Dad had a revolver, but he didn't care for it. His choice was the shotgun.

Dad often mentioned, "You can't hardly miss with a 12-guage."

Our ranch was considered small for a cattle ranch in that part of the country. Dad said 975 acres was about the best he could handle without having to hire fulltime help. Dad did most of the work himself. He would on occasion hire help when help was needed. Dad was tight with the buck and would trade off labor when he could.

Our nearest neighbor was a widow named Jessie Youngblood. She was a sweet lady who would on occasion come to the house to visit Mom. They became good friends and would exchange ideas and talk about the latest fashions the ladies were wearing in the nearest town.

Jessie's ranch of 1,250 acres bordered our ranch. She was having trouble keeping ranch hands. She was deciding if she should marry a gentleman she met over in Phoenix by the name of Frank Barnes. Jessie asked Mom what she thought.

Mom asked where he was from and did he have any experience running a cattle ranch? Jessie answered that Frank was from New Mexico and lived on a cattle ranch for a number of years, but was now living in Phoenix and working at the stock yards. He was seven years younger than her and seemed to be a right good person.

3

Mom questioned Jessie, "When did Frank begin showing an interest in you?"

Jessie replied, "Shortly after we talked about him working for me on the ranch."

Mother thought about Jessie's remarks and commented. "Be careful Jessie, it's not often a man wants to marry a woman that's older then him without a motive of some kind."

It was shortly after Jessie's visit when she married Frank. Before long, Jessie stopped coming to the house for a visit.

Mother decided to visit Jessie. When she arrived at the house, Frank met her on the front porch. "You can't come in, Jessie is sick with something. I'm waiting for the doctor to come take a look."

Almost one year to the day after their marriage, Jessie mysteriously died. Frank became sole owner of the ranch as Jessie had no living relatives.

Later, when Dad went to town he asked the doctor what Jessie had that killed her. The doctor replied, "I don't know, I never knew she was sick until I was informed she died."

Frank lied to Mother about him waiting for the doctor to arrive when Jessie was sick. Dad informed Sheriff Yancy Brandt about that situation. Sheriff went to see Frank. He claimed he lied to mother because he didn't want her to catch whatever virus Jessie had.

Yancy didn't completely swallow Frank's explanation. Frank buried Jessie without a service and without announcing she died. Mom and Dad were upset, but there was nothing they could do.

Dad made it clear, "We need to keep an eye on Frank. He can't be trusted."

Shortly after Jessie died Frank began coming to our house, sweet talking Mom about selling the ranch to him. Mom told Frank he was to stop coming around when Dad was not home. "It just don't look right."

Mom hesitated to tell Dad about Frank for she knew if she did Dad would make a visit to Frank.

Dad stood six-feet-two inches and hefted out at two hundred and twenty pounds. Folks thereabouts said Dad was strong as an ox.

When I turned sixteen I wanted to help out on the ranch. I told Dad I was going to plow the family garden area. I soon realized, sixteen year old girls could not do man's work. Dad saw me struggling and told me he would finish. Dad kidded me about that, but he did it with kindness.

On my eighteenth birthday, Dad announced it was time for me to take on more responsibility. He took me to town and added my name to the ranch deed as a full three-way partnership. It was me, Mom and Dad.

Ranch life was fun most of the time. Dad taught me to ride and take care of my horse, how to hunt and how to spot a sick cow.

Dad often mentioned, "You need to learn these things for someday this ranch will be yours."

Mom and Dad worked hard through the next few years. Dad set himself to work from just before sun-up to sun-down and he no longer came into my room to kiss me goodnight as he used to do. Before going to bed I would hug both Mom and Dad and kiss them goodnight.

One evening, Dad came into the house and asked if we had seen his new steel plow blade anywhere. Of course we hadn't. Soon a few other items were missing from the barn. Dad knew someone was prowling around the yard, but he had not seen or heard anyone. He told me and Mom to keep an eye out and told me to keep my revolver close at hand.

Dad turned twelve head of cattle into a special grassy area to graze for a few days. After the third day, three of the cattle came up missing. Dad rode all over the ranch looking for them. He rode over to Frank's and asked him if he had seen the cattle anywhere on his land. Frank became defensive and claimed Dad was calling him a cattle rustler. Dad never said anything of the sort. Dad never did find the cattle.

From time to time strange people were seen in the area of both ranches. Every so often one of those people would stop at our ranch and ask for water from the well.

On one occasion when Mom gave her permission to drink at the well, she heard noise from the house and went to investigate. Another lady was going through the kitchen cabinets and ran out the back door with Mom's favorite frying pan. Mom ran around the other side of the house to head her off and discovered the lady at the well was also gone, along with the bucket, the drinking cup, the bucket rope and towel. Mom was furious.

When Dad came in Mom told him what had happened. Dad saddled his horse and went into town to inform the sheriff and to inquire if he knew who these people were. Dad was gone most of the day and I stayed close to Mom with my revolver. When Dad got home he told us sheriff Yancy was going to ask around about the people and inquire about where they came from and why they were here.

On my twenty-first birthday, I was upstairs getting dressed. Suddenly I heard a loud pop. I rushed to go down and found Mom lying at the foot of the stairs. She was moving, but I could see she was badly hurt. Dad rushed in from outside and cradled Mom in his arms. She was bleeding from a bullet hole in her chest.

"Martha, who did this?"

Mom opened her eyes for a moment and said, "Fra, Fra, Frank." Mom closed her eyes and died.

Dad began to cry as he cradled Mom to him. I got my revolver and told Dad I was going after Frank and headed for the barn to saddle my horse. Frank was going to pay with his life for this.

Through his sobbing, Dad called out, "No! Go after the sheriff; Frank will hang and it will be legal."

I finished saddling my horse, holding back the tears that swelled within me and left for town. I explained to sheriff Yancy about my Mom and he left with me to the ranch. When we got to the ranch, Dad was still holding Mom in his arms. He was completely lost in his surroundings. The sheriff tried to console Dad and Dad refused to separate himself from Mom. Yancy asked me if I was up to riding with him to Frank's to cover his back. He knew I could handle a revolver.

Frank wasn't home. His housekeeper replied he was over in Phoenix and had been there for three days. Sheriff Yancy rode back to town and telegraphed the Phoenix sheriff, asking him to verify Frank's presence there. Word came back that Frank was indeed in Phoenix and had been there a few days.

We knew Mother would not have accused anyone of shooting her if it were not true.

Dad told Yancy, "Something here doesn't make sense; there is a skunk working the wood pile somewhere."

Sheriff spread word around town and throughout the county about Mom's death. Folks for miles around came to the ranch for the service. It was the worst day of my life.

Mom was buried next to her son Tom. Dad sat for hours at Mom's grave. After that and to begin each day, Dad would visit Mom's grave and talk to her before beginning the day's chores. He never missed a day for many weeks. Then suddenly, just as he did with Tom, Dad stopped going to the grave.

My heart was broken for Dad, but also for me losing my Mom. We were the only females, other than Frank's housekeeper, for miles around. Female companionship was important and now I was alone. It was just me and Dad to run the ranch.

Dad made it known that he was sure Frank was involved in Mother's murder. Every time Dad was in town he would talk up the possibility that Frank was involved. Frank heard about Dad talking about him and filed a complaint against Dad.

Sheriff Yancy had no choice but to serve papers on Dad to silence him. Dad told the sheriff, "Paper don't mean anything; its facts that count."

The sheriff told Dad he understood how he felt, but he must lay low where Frank was concerned. Somewhere down the line if Frank is guilty, he will get all that's coming to him, I'll make sure of that."

One day when Dad was riding fence his path crossed Frank's. Frank attempted to tell Dad he was sorry about everything that had happened lately. Dad told him he was not half as sorry as he would be when he was proven guilty of Mother's death and when that happened, Dad would kill him with his bare hands.

Again Frank went to the sheriff about Dad's threat. Dad made it clear. "If Frank was not guilty, he had nothing to worry about. He must be guilty for why else would he be worried and go to the sheriff?" Sheriff Yancy agreed with Dad, but there was nothing he could do without proof.

Things did calm down for a while until one day a group of about fifty people were seen camping on Frank's land. It was about then when Dad again discovered things missing from around the house and barn. He was sure those people were the culprits and he informed the sheriff.

The sheriff rode to Frank's and inquired about those people camping on his land and why they were there. Frank reminded the sheriff that the land was his. Those people were friends and they were allowed to camp on his land anytime for as long as they wanted.

The sheriff told Frank there was a lot of strange things happening lately. If any of those people were found to be involved he would arrest them and Frank as an accessories to the crime. Frank was beside himself. He ordered the Sheriff off his land and told him. "The next time you come on my ranch you better have a warrant allowing you to do so."

The sheriff told Frank, "When I come with a warrant it will be to arrest you for murder." Frank lost it. He reached for his revolver as the sheriff landed a punch right between his eyes. Frank went down and stayed there as the sheriff left.

Often times when Dad was away from the house, Frank would appear in the yard and sweet talk me like he did with Mom, about selling the place. He was so brazen that one time he even told me that if anything happened to my Dad, he would propose to me and combine the two ranches. That was when I told him to leave the property and not to come back.

Sheriff Yancy rode throughout the county talking with people and everyone he talked to had about the same thing to say. There were many strange people wondering around the county the last two years and things of value began to disappear. Those same strange people disappeared after that tragic night for about five months. Sheriff didn't think that a coincidence. Then suddenly, overnight, they reappeared and were camped on Frank's land. It was shortly after their reappearance that items again went missing.

Sheriff questioned a few of the campers about their reason for being there and about the death of my Mother. They told the sheriff they knew nothing. Dad came across two of the people while out riding fence one day and asked what they were doing there. They told Dad they had permission from Frank to camp on his property whenever and for as long as they wanted.

Folks in town were saying these people were from a tribe of Gypsies. Every time they were around, it was necessary to keep a sharp eye. They would suddenly appear, ask for water from the well and sometimes ask for something to eat. When they left, things would always be missing.

Dad decided to talk to Frank about the people, but all Frank would say was, "It's my property and I can do with it as I please. Those people are welcome here anytime. If you sold your place to me I would tell them to leave the country and both our problems would be over." Dad took Frank's answer as somewhat a threat, for by not selling the ranch, he should expect more trouble.

While out hanging the wash one day I was surprised by a stranger suddenly appearing in the yard. I was frightened. I thought it was Frank, as the person looked like Frank. This person wanted permission to use our ranch for a short cut and I gave him permission to get rid of him. I didn't know he was asking for the whole group of campers. As they came through they stopped for water at the well.

I could tell Dad was put out by my decision. As usual, after they passed through, Dad discovered a few items were missing from the barn. It wasn't often me and dad had a disagreement. I can think of no other time Dad ever let it be known that he wasn't pleased with my decision.

Once again things settled down after the campers left the area. I was learning to do the things Mom always did when Dad was in the field. We were enjoying ranch life and often shared coffee together.

On my twenty-second birthday we were sitting at the dinner table when Dad heard a commotion from the barn and thought it was a critter of sorts. He took his shotgun and went to investigate.

Dad was gone for some time, and I began to wonder. I then heard Dad's voice, "You there, stop where you are!" I then heard a shot and knew it wasn't Dad's shotgun.

I grabbed my pistol and rushed outside to find Dad lying in front of the entrance to the horse barn. He was motionless. I turned him over to face me. Dad was dead.

My emotions were such that I couldn't think straight. Both my Mom and Dad were dead. Tears filled my eyes and I couldn't see. I cannot recall ever feeling such hatred, loneliness and fear. I had to somehow get Dad into the house. I removed a throw rug and rolled Dad onto it and drug him to the porch of the house. I couldn't lift him onto the porch and had to leave him there. I sat a few moments to gather myself. I knew the next few hours were going to be critical.

I saddled my horse and rode to town for the sheriff. My grief, mixed with tears, began to burden me. I do not recall arriving at the sheriff's office. I was sitting my horse at the hitching rail when deputy sheriff Tom Andrews found me. Sheriff Yancy wasn't in town, so Deputy Tom rode to the ranch with me.

The deputy examined Dad and found he had been shot directly into the heart. Deputy Tom searched the area and found a spent cartridge from a Winchester .44 rifle. I cried out, "Frank owns a Winchester .44 rifle!"

Tom rode to Frank's ranch to question him but Frank was in New Mexico, visiting with his brother. His housekeeper showed the deputy the Winchester rifle. It had not been fired.

The next few days were the worst in my life. I couldn't seem to get things straight in my mind on what to do next. Sheriff Yancy came out to the house leading a number of town citizens who knew Dad. While Dad's grave was being dug, a few ladies prepared his body for burial. The church preacher said the usual and they lowered Dad into the ground. I was sick with an awful feeling.

I was alone on the ranch and I was frightened. I knew I could not do all that needed to be done and I could not protect myself as Dad did. I needed help but had no funds to pay for help.

Sheriff Yancy deputized two men to stay in the bunkhouse as protection for me and to help out where needed until I could find my own help.

The sheriff spread word around town about my situation and before long two young men approached me about moving into my bunkhouse and helping out. They mentioned they knew my money problem, but for a place to sleep and a little food, they would do what they could to help me.

Chico Martinez and Felix Young informed me they were both familiar with hand guns and rifles and would protect me at all cost. I informed them that I would pay them if and when I could. That was satisfactory with them for it was the best offer they had had in some time.

They then surprised me. They asked if I could spare twenty head of stock to sell at the stock yards in town. I would need cash from time to time to run the place. I stalled to think. Here are two strangers, asking me for some of my cattle to sell. Could I trust them? I realized I had no choice, for they were right, I would need cash. I told them they could cut twenty head for the market. The boys returned from town the next day and handed me the cash they received for the cattle.

Both those boys were true to their word. They worked hard and I did all that I could to feed them well. My trust in them built within me and I invited them to take their meals with me in the house and they were grateful for it.

We had settled into a routine when, while riding fence, the boys found a large section of fence had been cut. My cattle were grazing on Frank's property. Frank was furious and demanded we remove our cattle at once or he would begin shooting them. I told Frank that if he shot even one of my cows, I would kill him. We of course drove them back across the cut fence and made repairs.

A few days later the boys burst into the house and informed me that the fence and fence posts were all gone and the cattle were grazing in the marsh area. I saddled and rode with them and we drove them back and pastured them in a temporary area.

I told the boys, "I am determined to hold this ranch at all cost, regardless of what Frank may do. That is what my Mom and Dad would want me to do." The boys began cutting new fence posts and I went into town to purchase wire.

It took a few days to replace the posts and wire and when it was finished, the boys took a day in town to relax. I gave them each twenty dollars and received big smiles from them both. I was hoping they wouldn't get themselves into any trouble while in town.

I thought them to be steady minded men and I was right as they both returned that evening completely sober and ready to go back to work. They both handed me their winnings from a poker game they got into, asking me to hold it for them and to use any part of it I needed. I took a second look at the money and asked, "Just how much is here?" They both smiled and Chico said his share was the same as

Felix. It came to $350. I told them the total amount would be theirs when they were ready for it.

For the next couple of months things went along normally. I realized that on occasion when the boys were out working the cattle or mending fence, certain things needed to be done around the barn and house which I just was not able to do. I thought perhaps the hand of another young man would be just the answer. I mentioned this to the boys that evening at the dinner table and they said there was a young Indian boy about sixteen or so that was hanging around town looking for work. He seemed to have some education and was clean cut. I asked, but they didn't know his name.

I took a ride into town later in the week for a few supplies and as I was talking with sheriff Yancy, I mentioned the Indian boy the fellows told me about. The sheriff said he was helping out at the blacksmith shop when extra help was needed He mentioned that he would check around.

As I was loading the wagon the sheriff came over to inform me the Indian boy was camped outside town. "If you want to talk with him, I'll ride out with you."

As we approached the camp, he came forward to greet us and extended his hand. The sheriff took it and introduced me. His name was Dark Cloud. He said, "Most people call me Cloudy." He was from New Mexico where his folks lived. He attended a white man's school for three years and could read and write a little. He mentioned he didn't need much, just a place to camp and a little food. He was willing to work for that.

I explained the situation at the ranch and he replied that would do just fine for him. He put what gear he had in the wagon, mounted his horse and followed me to the ranch.

I introduced him to the boys and they showed him around. Evening was coming on and it was near dinner time. The boys washed up and came into the house to eat and Cloudy announced that though he attended the white man's school he had never eaten at a white man's table. It was soon obvious, his manners went lacking. Chico and Felix said they would take care of that and they did.

Cloudy was a good worker and he always completed ever job he started. It took a while for him to understand everything that needed to be done around the barn and house, but once he understood, he did a good job.

As we sat around the dinner table one evening, we each began to tell of situations we had been involved in over the years. Cloudy began talking. What he was saying sounded familiar to me. Somewhere in this world he had a sister, but she disappeared sometime before he was born.

A white man and his wife were living near the Mesa and the white man was very friendly with his mother. She gave birth to his daughter. The white man and his wife took the infant and left the area. His mother grieved for her daughter and wanted her back. A group of Mesa Indians left in search of the white man and they soon caught up with him two days ride from the Mesa. The white man refused to give up the infant girl and was killed along with his wife. A group of riders came upon the scene and chased the Mesa's away. From a distant hiding place the Mesa's watched as the riders discovered the infant girl in the wagon. The riders buried the white man and his wife. They took the infant girl and wagon and rode away.

Cloudy continued to speak. His mother was soon taken as a wife and in time he was born. "When I heard the story as a young boy, I decided to someday find my half-sister. I have been searching for two years now."

As I listened to his story I became very nervous and called it a day. The boys then went to the bunk house. I could not sleep that night; it was obvious Cloudy was my half-brother.

A few days later while sitting around the table, I asked Cloudy to tell me about his mother. He described her as very pretty, almost like a white woman and many of the tribe males wanted her for a wife before she finally gave herself as wife to his father.

I asked Cloudy if his mother ever mentioned the white man's name. He replied she only knew him as Fargo. I decided to wait for the appropriate time to tell Cloudy I was his missing half-sister.

One day two ladies came into the yard asking for something to eat. I served them leftovers out on the porch. While they were eating I heard noise coming from the house and rushed inside to find a third lady going through my things. She had my best dresses and some under things in her arms. She ran out the back door, dropping the clothes on the ground. I then remembered the two women eating on the front porch. They were gone and so were the dishes, forks and spoons. I went into the house, strapped on my hand gun and gathered up the clothes dropped on the ground.

Cloudy came in from the garden area and asked what happened. That night the boys slept on the porch to give me extra protection. The next day Chico suggested the three of them take turns walking the area at night for a few days until things settled down again.

On the third night, Cloudy was walking the area when he heard a noise near the barn and went to investigate. Suddenly a shot rang out. It woke everyone. We found Cloudy on the ground and in a bad way. He was bleeding from a nasty shoulder wound and was in a lot of pain. Felix rigged the horse to the wagon and we loaded Cloudy. Chico mounted the wagon and headed to town for the doctor.

Felix took a turn around the area and found a .44 spent cartridge out by the hay barn. Again I thought of Frank. Late that morning, Sheriff Yancy came into the yard with Chico and told us Cloudy was going to be alright, but it would take a while. We went over everything that had taken place. Sheriff Yancy rode over to question Frank.

Frank was furious and asked Yancy if he had a warrant to come on his property.

Yancy replied, "I sure do, its strapped to my waist. Now show me your .44." Frank did so and it had not been fired. He then told Frank, "I am sure you are involved in all that has been going on lately and when I prove it I will do all I can to see you hang."

Frank pointed at Yancy. "You can't come on my property and threaten me without proof."

"Proof is not required when making a promise," replied Yancy.

As I sit here almost fifty years later writing this story, thoughts of those day's still haunt me. My father was shot down one year to the day after my mother was killed. I then thought perhaps the killer was following a plan and I was to be his next victim. Things were much different then than they are now. Sheriffs and police detectives are better educated and are better equipped. What was gotten away with back then would never happen in this day and age.

Cloudy was going to be laid up for a spell so I had to find someone that could do small jobs around the yard and at the same time look after me and my interest, no matter what.

I talked to a few men, but none fit the pattern I was looking for. One day when I was in town talking with Sheriff Yancy in his office, a fellow walked in to ask the sheriff if he could pick out a spot on the edge of town to camp for a couple of days; he had no money for a room and very little cash for food.

The sheriff asked him who he was and he said his name was "Fargo Travis" from down Tombstone way. I looked him over carefully. He was about 48 years old and he looked like he could handle himself. The sheriff asked him if he had ever been on the wrong side of the law.

He uttered, "Just minor stuff. As a young man I was associated with the likes of the Earp brothers and Doc Holiday, but I never took things as far as they did."

I suddenly remembered, Cloudy said his mother remembered the father of his missing sister was named Fargo. I developed a strange feeling in the pit of my stomach.

I introduced myself. "Do you know anything about cattle ranching?"

He replied, "Miss Andrea Hamrick, I don't know what all you are asking questions for, but whatever it is, you can count on me to have done it before and if it's within the law I'll do it again."

That was good enough for me. I explained my needs at the ranch and the money situation. Sheriff Yancy pointed out what had been happening at the ranch. Fargo said he could handle most any situation as long as he had two squares a day. I invited him to join us at the ranch and if after one month he was not happy with the situation he could leave without questions.

"That's a fair offer; let's do it," he replied.

I was no longer afraid to stay at the ranch. My next concern was making it a paying cattle ranch. I wanted to make enough money to pay my hands and keep us in grub. I hired a lady named Cathleena, who moved from town to the ranch, to do the cooking for the crew as I was never very good in the kitchen. All hands took their meals at my table, including Cloudy. He had limited motion with his wounded shoulder and we had to watch him. He was always trying to do things to help which he should not be doing.

One day to my utter surprise, Frank rode into the yard and dismounted. He walked up and began to talk. "Miss Andrea, I'm not sure these are the right words, but I want you to know I'm sorry for the things that have happened around here. I assure you I'm not behind anything you think I may be responsible for. I don't know how I can help you, but if you ever need anything special, you call on me." I was so surprised I couldn't speak for a moment.

I was finally able to say, "Frank, because of the trouble between you and my father, I don't want be friends with you. I don't even like you. Regardless of your denial, I believe you are behind all my troubles. I'll take care of my business and you take care of yours. You can leave now. I don't want you here."

Frank made no further comment as he tipped his hat and mounted his horse. Some weeks later I looked out the window and saw Frank again approaching the ranch house. As I walked outside, Fargo was right beside me. This time he wanted to know if I would sell the ranch to him.

I gave him the same answer my dad gave him, "This ranch is not for sale at any price, especially to you. I'm doing just fine here."

Suddenly Frank was like a little boy, he began lightly kicking the dust with his boot and spoke, "I was thinking something more. You have a nice little ranch here and we could combine it if we were married. It would be the finest ranch in these parts."

I was stunned without words. Fargo turned to me, waiting for my response. I replied, "Frank, if having the finest ranch in these parts required me to marry you, I would rather have no ranch at all. I would rather burn the place down. People in these parts would think me as loco as you are. I told you before, I don't like you. Please leave." Frank suddenly got a very nasty and ugly look on his face as I turned and walked back into the house.

"Did you notice the look on Frank's face?" inquired Fargo.

"Yes I did, "maybe now he will stay away," I answered.

One evening after dinner, the boys were sitting on the front porch enjoying coffee when Cloudy suddenly jumped to his feet and shouted. "I smell smoke."

Everyone went to the front yard and saw smoke rising in the sky. "The hay barn is on fire," I shouted. Being far from the house, there was nothing we could do. There was no water close by. The barn burned to the ground, along with fifty-five bails of good hay.

After the wood portion burned, the hay smoldered for days. Afterwards, we walked the debris and found a broken lantern. Someone deliberately set the fire. Considering the fact no one came from Frank's place to assist in putting out the fire, that indicated to me it was planned.

Without saying anything to Fargo or the boys, I went out the back door and rode to Frank's.

You have never visited here before," expressed Frank.

"This is not a social call Frank. Depending on your answer to my question, I'm here to kill you." Frank stiffened and said nothing. "You and your people could not have missed my hay barn burning. You offered no assistance. Did you or did you not set fire to my barn or have someone do it for you?" I had my revolver pointed at his belly.

"Either way I answer your question, you will not believe me. The boys did see your barn burning, but there was nothing we could do to assist you. There is no water nearby. The results would have been the same," replied Frank.

"We found a broken lantern in the smoldering hay. Someone set the fire."

Frank looked me straight in the eye. "It wasn't me or my boys."

"Hold on Andrea, Frank's not armed," spoke Fargo as he rode up. "You shoot him and it will be murder."

"No more than what he did to my folks," I answered.

I cannot recall in my lifetime ever being as mad as I was that day. I can't say for certain, but if not for Fargo, I would have probably shot Frank.

Days later I began thinking it was time to have a talk with Fargo. Next morning after breakfast, I poured us a cup of coffee and sat at the table.

I couldn't think how to start the conversation, so I blurted out. "Fargo, tell me about your Indian lover and your missing daughter." Fargo stared at me with a surprised look. He rose from the table to leave. I called him back. "You don't have to tell me, but if you stay, I'll need to know your story. How was it you were not killed?"

Fargo sat back at the table. "I want to stay Miss Andrea. I like it here; it feels like home." He poured himself another cup of coffee and asked, "What do you want to know about that and how do you know these things?"

I replied, "I will answer your question after you answer mine."

Fargo paused for some time before he began to talk. "I wanted my daughter, but the tribe would not allow me to take her away with me. My brother volunteered to steal her for me and bring her and my wife to Tombstone. I left for Tombstone the day before my brother took the girl. I never saw him, the wife or the little girl again. They never made it to Tombstone. Now, how do you know these things?" I searched his face and spotted a tear in one eye.

"Fargo, brace yourself. I am that missing little girl. I am your daughter."

Fargo stared at me for some time before speaking as tears ran down his cheeks. "Please, tell me about my wife; is she alive?"

For the next hour, I explained about my father finding me in the wagon after his brother and his wife were killed and how I was raised as his own.

Fargo raised himself from the table and uttered, "Miss. Andrea Hamrick, do I have permission to hug you? I've never stopped loving you and my wife all these years."

I stepped up to him, looked him in the eye and replied, "Please do Father." I never felt such joy. I was in the arms of my birth father for the first time. I knew the way he held me, he did still love me.

"Would you take me to the grave site as your Dad did for you?" I answered that I would. We prepared to leave the next morning.

We arrived midafternoon and I was surprised to see one cross still standing. Fargo slowly dismounted and stood before the cross. He began to softly sob as he went down on one knee. I walked away a few paces so Fargo could pay his respects in his own way.

I waited and watched. When he rose, he turned toward his mount and withdrew from the saddle bags a beautiful scarf. He carefully wrapped it around the cross. He said nothing as he mounted his horse and turned from the grave. We rode a while in silence. To break the silence I softly spoke. "That was a beautiful scarf you left on the grave Fargo."

We rode a little farther and he replied, "It was hers." After some time he spoke. "Where do we go from here?"

We decided it best we keep our wonderful surprise to ourselves for the time being. Arriving at the ranch, I told Fargo there was more to the story. "Come into the house." I then explained that Cloudy was my half-brother.

As weeks passed I couldn't understand the strange feeling I had inside me. I had felt this way since Fargo told me his story. It seemed as though something was missing. I pondered the situation each night as I lay in my bed.

One evening as I was preparing for bed it came to me. I wanted to meet my birth mother. To do this I would need to explain to Cloudy how it was that he was my half-brother and Fargo was my birth father.

Weeks later while in town, folks told me Frank was talking that he wouldn't stand for *some little frilly-laced female* to outdo him and he would have to do something about it. I was sure I knew what he meant by that remark. I took it as a challenge. I would show him what a *frilly-laced female* could do.

A few days later I called the boys together and told them we were going to fence a certain forty that had never had a fence before.

Felix questioned, "Are you talking about the forty that Frank drives his cattle over?"

"I mean no other," I replied. "He can drive his cattle over the hills. I'm no longer going to sit back and let Frank do as he pleases. From now on it's an eye for an eye."

Sheriff Yancy got word of what I was doing and came out to see me. He said this kind of thing could lead to a range war. I reminded him that what Frank had been doing could also lead to a range war, but up to this moment I had kept myself in check. Now it was my turn to make a move. Fargo mentioned he was keeping close to my side from now on.

Three days after the fence was in, the boys rode in and announced the fence had been cut in three places. I was so mad I strapped on my hand gun and was ready to have it out again with Frank.

Fargo uttered, "No, this time it's my turn. I'm not going to hurt him; I'll just put a good scare into him."

Fargo rode to Frank's place and told him that he knew Frank didn't do any of the things Andrea thought he did, but he also told him he knew he was having those things done. Fargo finished with Frank by saying, "The next time a fence is cut or fence posts are broken, cattle are missing or anyone is hurt I'll be back with gun in hand."

Frank went directly to the sheriff and filed a complaint that his life had been threatened by Fargo. Sheriff Yancy rode out to see me about the threat. I told him that Fargo did go to Frank's ranch, but only to put a scare in him. I explained that my new fence had been cut and I thought enough was enough and I was about to go see Frank myself when Fargo mentioned he would go.

We rode out to the fence with the sheriff so he could have a look around. "Whoever did this used mules to carry off the fence wire. There are mule shoe tracks all over the place. Who owns mules in this part of the country?" I couldn't think of anyone who owned mules and none of the boys had seen mules at any time. Yancy uttered, "Don't talk around about this; I have a few ideas to follow up on. I'll be in touch."

That very evening, I had the worst scare I ever had. I came downstairs to take my bath and as I was about to throw off my robe and step into the tub, I heard a noise and saw movement at the window. For a brief moment it looked like Frank, except for a heavy beard and messy hair. I froze for a moment and then ran back upstairs screaming as I went. I got my revolver and was about to go back downstairs when the boys came busting through the front door as they heard my screaming.

I quickly explained that we had a peeping tom on the property. Chico and Felix went outside to look around while Fargo stayed near me. They found no one, but did find foot prints under the window.

That night and for a number of nights thereafter the boys moved their blankets onto the front porch. From that night on, everywhere I went, day or night, I carried my revolver. The next time I would shoot first and ask questions later.

Cloudy was coming around and doing light chores around the ranch. I asked him if he felt up to going into town for some supplies if I gave him a list. He replied he did and began to harness the horse to the wagon as I went into the house to make the list.

Suddenly, Cloudy called out, "Miss. Andrea, you better come out here!"

Coming through the gate was a gypsy woman. She was dirty and greasy-looking with long unkempt hair. By this time I was aware of these people's method of stealing things. I told Cloudy to stay with her as I turned back toward the house. Sure enough, two other ladies were in the house and were going out the back door with my pots and pans. I ran back out front to head them off but they were out of range for my revolver. Cloudy made an attempt to chase them but he wasn't up to it.

I decided to ride to town with Cloudy and inform the sheriff about the ladies in my house. It was no surprise when sheriff told me it was the same method the gypsies used at other ranches in the county. Deputy Tom was ready to round them up and put them in jail when the sheriff uttered, "No, not yet. I'll let you know when."

Getting back to the ranch that evening, I pulled Fargo to the side and informed him of what I had been thinking for a few weeks. He said he wasn't sure he approved of my decision, but he did understand why I wanted to do such a thing and he would not talk against it.

The next day I called Cloudy into the house and had him sit at the table. I sat across from him and began telling him I discovered Fargo was my birth father and he was my half-brother. Cloudy just set and stared at me without speaking.

Finally he replied, "Oh no Miss. Andrea, Fargo is not my father."

Cloudy didn't understand. I explained that Fargo is the father of your missing sister and I was the sister. Your father is the man your mother married after I was born. The man that was killed in the wagon so many years ago was Fargo's brother. I than begin telling him I wanted to meet my birth mother, who was his mother.

I wasn't sure Cloudy was getting everything I was telling him, so I went over it again, slowly.

Suddenly Cloudy jumped from the table and shouted, "You're my sister! You're my lost half-sister." He grabbed and hugged me. "What we do now?" he asked. I repeated I wanted to meet his mother, my birth mother.

Cloudy replied his mother was still living on the reservation with his father, but he would need to see his mother first and tell her he found his half-sister and get her permission for a visit.

I told Cloudy to go ahead and prepare to leave. I told him that if Fargo consented he would be coming with me on the visit. He may wish to tell his mother that Fargo would also be with me.

Cloudy left the next morning. Chico and Felix asked where Cloudy was headed and why was he leaving? I told them he was going to the reservation to visit his mother. Nothing more was mentioned.

Since the night my Mother was killed I was sure Frank was behind all the problems I was having. I knew there had to be a connection between those people and Frank and I passed my suspicions on to the sheriff. He agreed, but we had to get positive proof before he could act. I told the boys that when they came across any of those people they were to treat them with kindness and respect and perhaps down the line someone would talk.

I was totally attached to the ranch. It was something I owned and managed and the ownership of it affected me. It was in my blood and I loved it. I knew I would never sell. The last two cattle drives gave me sufficient funds to operate and pay the boys some of what I owed them.

I was busy getting out the invites for a Christmas party when Fargo asked if I was inviting Frank.

"I have not and don't intend to" was my answer.

Fargo commented, "Frank will be offended if he is the only one in the country to not receive an invite and he could cause more trouble because of it."

I pondered that for a while and finally agreed. I would invite Frank, but I expressed, "Don't be surprised if I have to ask him to leave the party."

Fargo replied, "Daughter, if it comes to that let me handle it." I noticed he called me daughter. It sounded good and I liked it.

I wrote out the invite and instructed Felix to deliver it to Frank. He thought I was kidding him. After I assured him I wasn't kidding, he left to make the delivery.

After Frank read the invite, he said, "Tell Miss Andrea I will be there."

The evening of the party, Frank arrived and announced himself, but no one paid much attention to his antics. He went straight to the punch bowl and poured in the contents of a flask he took from his jacket.

Fargo observed him doing so and informed him, "If Miss. Andrea had wanted such a drink she would have made her own mixture. One more wrong move by you and you will go home." Frank laughed it off. The evening was going well as the three-piece orchestra was playing one tune after the other.

Suddenly a female guest screamed and came running down from upstairs. Her dress was badly torn. As Fargo ran up the stairs he found Frank just coming to the top of the stairs.

My guest pointed toward Frank and shouted, "He grabbed me, tore my dress and tried to pull me into a room."

Fargo turned to Frank and shouted, "Downstairs mister, you're going home." As Frank started down the stairs, Fargo gave him a shove and Frank went head over heels down the stairs. As he landed at the bottom Fargo kicked him on the rear end and he was up and running toward the door.

He mounted his horse and called out as he rode away, "You'll be sorry for this."

It was a great party and things went smoothly the rest of the night. The people started for their homes at about daylight. I was tired but happy about how everything went after Frank was forced to leave. Fargo came to me and commented he was sorry about talking me into inviting Frank. He thought it would help the situation. I told him not to worry. It was a pleasure to see Frank take the short way down the stairs.

It had been a while since Cloudy had left for the reservation and I was becoming concerned. I informed Fargo of the talk I had had with Cloudy and asked him if everything worked out, would he ride with me to the reservation?

"I told you I would protect you. I can't do that if I am here and you are on the trail," he answered. "Of course I will go with you."

Two more weeks passed before Cloudy rode into the yard, dismounted and came to the house. Cloudy reported that his mother was surprised to hear her daughter was still alive. She had cried for a long time.

"I told her you wanted to come and meet her and bring your birth father with you.

She suddenly stopped crying. 'He is alive?' she asked. I told her the story you told me and she again began to cry. She would love to see you, but not so sure about seeing Fargo."

Cloudy mentioned his father was dead. He had gotten into a fight with a white man in Farmington and was shot when he pulled his knife. He was buried on the reservation.

I told Cloudy I would make plans to visit my birth mother and would let him know when. "Keep this to yourself for now."

The very next day a group of Gypsies attempted to cross over my land and I headed them off and ordered them back. I wore my revolver and Fargo was by my side with his hand on the butt handle of his revolver. They turned back without comment.

Sheriff Yancy came by a couple of days later and mentioned I had them bottled up on Frank's land and they couldn't leave. Perhaps if I let them cross they would leave and not come back. He would stand by and not allow any of them to dismount or to leave their wagons while crossing.

Soon the entire clan was on the move toward my cattle gate. I stationed myself at the gate and began to search every face that passed, looking for the ladies that stole things from my house. I could not identify anyone for certain.

Towards the end of the caravan, a wagon driven by a large male approached the gate. He had large eyes, flat nose and a face of hair. He had large arms and he looked like Frank.

Suddenly rage came upon me. "Hey, you there, if I ever see you on this property again I will kill you. Do you understand?"

"What you say senorita? I do not understand."

"Oh you understand alright, you understand exactly what I mean and why I say it." He shrugged his shoulders and followed the others through the gate.

Things did settle down for a while and I decided it was time to make the visit to see my birth mother. I informed both Cloudy and Fargo and asked Fargo if he was ready to travel. He replied he was, but only as protection for me. I understood.

Two days later we left the ranch. I told Chico and Felix to keep on their toes. Don't allow any strangers on the property.

We traveled three days before reaching the reservation. I had butterflies in my stomach. Cloudy exclaimed his mother lived on the far side of the reservation. Fargo expressed he would linger back a ways.

As we neared the little house, I became a little light-headed and needed to stop for a moment. Shortly after, we rode into the yard and Cloudy went inside. I waited.

Soon Cloudy came outside followed by a very pretty middle-aged lady. She shaded her eyes as she looked at me. She then smiled and came towards me with her arms outstretched. We met in an embrace. She began to cry alone with me. We held each other for a long time.

Cloudy spoke. "You two can let go now; we will be here a while." It was then Fargo slowly dismounted from his horse and stood there.

As we were breaking from our embrace, Shirley, my mother, began looking at Fargo. She shaded her eyes again. She stepped closer to him and spoke. "It's been a while Fargo; how have you been?"

"I'm doing fine Shirley, how about you?" Shirley invited us into the house, but Fargo decided to stay outside.

Shirley turned to him, "You're part of this family; don't isolate yourself. Come inside?"

The inside of that little house was spotless with everything in its place. As we settled at the table, Shirley announced she wanted to hear our story again, as she got only part of it from Cloudy.

I went through the story, not leaving out any detail. Shirley turned to Fargo and asked, "Why didn't you come looking for your wife and daughter when they didn't arrive in Tombstone?"

"Because, I thought my brother and wife ran off to gather with my daughter," answered Fargo.

I turned to Fargo, "You never told me that."

"I know; I didn't think it made any difference. My brother was always soft toward my wife."

Shirley began putting lunch on the table as Cloudy and Fargo washed up. Sitting around that table gave me a feeling of disrespect, for I suddenly remembered I had another mother and father who were now dead.

As we ate, I noticed Shirley would often glance at Fargo. She finally asked, "Fargo, what have you been doing all these years?"

"Not much of anything Shirley, just hanging around Tombstone and taking jobs as they came along."

"You were a go-getter back in the day; what happened?" asked Shirley.

"I lost my wife, brother and daughter. That's what happened," answered Fargo.

I told Shirley we would stay only one night. We would leave about noon the next day. It was then Fargo asked a question that surprised me.

"Shirley, when we leave tomorrow there's room for one more on the trail. Why don't you fill the space?"

Shirley looked at Fargo, "You wanted to ask me that same question many years ago but you couldn't. I disliked you for that reason. I disliked you all these years, until today. My husband is dead and your wife is dead. Our child is alive and needs our love and help. Yes, I will go with you, but not as you're wife or lover. With Andrea's permission I will become her housekeeper until we have gotten used to each other. After that, we'll see what happens." Shirley turned to me and asked, "Daughter, it's your ranch. You make the decision. What do you say?"

I looked to Fargo and then to Shirley. "There's plenty of room at the ranch house. I say yes."

Cloudy asked his mother, "What happens to this house?"

"My sister can live here. She needs a place," answered Shirley.

As we departed the next day, Shirley looked back for one last look and shouted to her sister, "Take good care of the place. It's yours if I don't return."

Returning to the ranch, Cloudy and Fargo decided to remain in the bunk house until the appropriate time to tell Cisco and Felix.

I soon began thinking again about when my Mother was dying, she formed the word Frank, but who she saw was the big hulk of a man that was driving the wagon. He was also my peeping tom and perhaps the one who murdered my Father. As I lay in bed, I began thinking, why would that man commit murder?

I went to town with Cloudy the next day to see the sheriff and explain my thoughts. He listened carefully to everything I had to say.

He then replied, "There's been one thing that has bothered me from the start of all that has happened---why does Frank allow those people to camp on his land and protect them the way he has?"

"I cannot account for anything Frank does," I answered. "Perhaps the Gypsies have something on Frank and he protects them to protect himself."

"Andrea, you go on home and let me do a little snooping. There's bound to be someone who knows more than we do about that mob of thieves and why Frank protects them."

I went back to the ranch, called the boys together and informed them about my thoughts and of what the sheriff had to say. I also informed them my birthday was coming up and my mother and father were killed on my last two birthdays; perhaps I was next to die.

The boys had already set a schedule for a patrol around the house property and were taking turns while sleeping on the front porch. I felt more secure that night than I had felt for a long time, but it was short-lived.

Two days later the boys came riding in to inform me that eight of my best steers were dead about a quarter mile from the house. I saddled and rode out to find the grazing area covered with bales of hay.

Fargo began looking around. "There's crystal-like particles in this feed hay. I believe these animals have been poisoned."

I was frightened; poisoned hay could kill my entire herd. It was decided by the boys that a twenty-four hour watch was needed to protect the herd. Chico went into town to hire a couple of drovers to assist in the watch.

I remembered about reading how gypsies hang around together, never travelling as individuals. I couldn't remember if any were around when mother was killed. I did remember they were around when dad was killed.

I went to town to see Deputy Tom as he usually rode herd on the gypsies when they were around. "Yes, there were gypsies around when your mother was killed," he answered. "Matter fact, it's the same tribe of gypsies that have been giving you trouble all this time. I've wanted to bring a few in for questioning but sheriff didn't want to tip our hand that we were snooping around and suspecting them of all the trouble."

I rode back to the ranch not feeling any better about the situation. Deputy Tom had told me to be patient and wait for the sheriff to contact me. A few things were beginning to come together.

A few mornings later Sheriff Yancy rode into the yard. "Andrea, we must talk." I took him into the house and asked Fargo to follow.

The sheriff began. "A few things have happened the last two days which may have a bearing on your mother and father's deaths and explain a lot about your gypsy troubles. There have been some internal problems within the gypsy camp. A young girl of fifteen was found hiding from the elders down in the bottom lands. Seems the leader of the gypsy group wanted to take her as his wife but she was in love with another younger man and refused to marry the leader. She gave her name as Rita, no last name."

I remembered Dad telling me gypsies had no last name as juveniles but could choose a last name when they came of age.

Yancy continued, "The leader of the gypsy group is named Romano and he already has a wife. Rita was to be his second wife. She expressed she did not want to return to the clan as they would punish her severely for running away." Yancy paused a moment.

"Andrea, hold on to your seat; Romano, the clan leader, is Frank's son."

"Frank's son! Oh my heavens, that explains it all. He has been doing all of Frank's dirty work. Frank has been trying to run me off of this ranch."

Sheriff Yancy continued, "I sent Deputy Tom out to the clan to bring in Romano's wife. We have her in protective custody. Her name is Tasha and she was more than willing to talk. She is furious with Romano for wanting to take another wife. She told us plenty."

"When Frank was a young man in New Mexico, back in 1881, he fell in love with a young gypsy girl and she bore him a son. Frank deserted the clan, but they kept their sights on Frank. Frank then married the widow Jessie Youngblood and the ranch became his upon her death. The gypsy clan settled nearby and Romano soon put the bite on Frank for a place to stay whenever he wanted. Frank wanted your ranch but your folks wouldn't sell. Frank offered Romano $500 to kill your mother. When that didn't work he offered another $500 to kill your father. We think perhaps you were next and Frank could buy the ranch from the bank."

Yancy continued. "This is what we want to do. You sign a complaint against both Frank and Romano for murder. We'll ride to Frank's and arrest him and then we'll arrest Romano. Will you sign the complaint?"

"You bet your life I will," I bellowed. Both sheriff and deputy then left to arrest Frank.

After reading the arrest warrant against him Frank began to laugh. "Is this more of your tom foolery sheriff?"

"If you think this is foolishness, your crazier then I think you are," replied Yancy. "You're under arrest." Frank made a halfhearted attempt to resist, but Deputy Tom drew his revolver and Frank quickly realized it was of no use.

Sheriff and deputy rode to the gypsy camp the next morning, but Romano was gone. They tracked him to Nogales, where he crossed the border earlier that morning. Yancy was mad at himself. He realized he should have arrested Romano at the same time as Frank.

We could not put Frank on trial without Romano to testify against him. Rita and Tasha said they would not testify against Frank without Romano also being behind bars for he would find a way to get even. There was always the chance that both Rita and Tasha could get cold feet and refuse to testify. We needed Romano, to claim he was paid by Frank to kill both my mother and father. We had to get Romano back in this country, but how?

Procedures at the border these days are not like it was back then. In those days, anyone could cross the border from both sides without papers, except law officers. Law officers were never allowed to cross for any reason. We thought of many solutions but none were workable.

I began to ponder the problems that may occur if I did what I was thinking. Fargo noticed me in thought and asked if I had a plan.

"I'll go after Romano and bring him back," I answered. "I can cross the border, no one will stop me. I speak the language as well as I speak English."

Fargo uttered, "If you go alone, you'll never come back alive. A single woman in Mexico, especially an American woman, would not stand a chance. I'll go with you. I also speak the language and if a physical encounter is made, you'll need help."

I went to the kitchen and wrote letters to each of the boys and wrote their names on their envelope. I called the boys together and informed them of what we were about to do. I handed each their envelope with instructions to not open the envelopes without positive proof of my death.

Mother Shirley expressed her fear for me. She didn't want me to go. "I don't want to lose you again."

"I'll protect her with my life Shirley; she is my daughter too," voiced Fargo.

We slipped away and crossed the border at daylight. Speaking the language, we had no trouble in making the crossing.

We asked questions of everyone we encountered as we rode south and discovered that Romano had crossed the border riding a large brown mule and leading a white burro, loaded with supplies. We were told he was only a few hours ahead of us. We learned he was most likely going to join the gypsy camp at Guayas, which was a three-day ride farther south.

Every person we encountered told us he was only a few hours ahead and "Si senorita, he is riding a brown mule and leading a burro."

Fargo suggested we not make camp for the night but continue south and we would soon catch up to him. As we were getting closer to our prey my horse went lame. Fargo suggested he would try to trade for a fresh mount. I made camp for the night and waited. I didn't see Fargo that night or the next day.

I rode into the local town and found that Fargo was in their hospital. After explaining the horse was lame, he offered to pay a boot for a fresh mount. The horse trader's helper didn't know the situation and thought Fargo was sneaking in a lame horse for a good horse and pulled a knife and carved Fargo up pretty good. The knife carver was also in the hospital with bullet wounds to both legs, and under arrest. They informed me Fargo would be laid up for better than a week.

Fargo looked terrible. He had been cut from his neck to the center of his rib cage. He also had a bad cut on his cheek. Fargo mentioned the fellow that did the carving would be crippled for the remainder of his life. Fargo shot him in both knees.

I was now alone in my pursuit of Romano. I took Fargo's horse and continued the chase.

A short distance outside of Guaymas, a sentry confirmed that a man riding a brown mule and leading a white burro rode past last night, just before dark. I continued to the outskirts of town and made camp.

As darkness approached I built a small fire and was enjoying a cup of coffee when three men rode into my camp unannounced and dismounted. They began helping themselves to the coffee while going through my supplies.

I told them they were trespassing on my camp. One fellow approached toward me.

"Are you not alone senorita?"

I thought quickly, "No I'm waiting for my partner who is due here from town."

The three began to laugh. "Senorita, your partner is in the hospital." I knew then I was in trouble.

"What do you want here? I have no money to speak of, only my gear and supplies."

"We know senorita, we do not want your gear or supplies," he replied with a nasty smile.

My revolver was in my saddle bags about ten feet from me. I told them I would give them what money I had as I walked toward my saddle bags. As I opened the saddle bag I grasp the butt of the revolver and quickly turned to point it at them.

The one who seemed to be the leader began to laugh and came toward me. I told him to stop. He didn't and I shot him in the foot. He began to scream and curse me. I told him the next shot would be a killing shot. The others quickly backed off a ways. I told them to take their friend and leave.

One of the three uttered, "We will be back senorita and we will even the score."

I pondered his remarks and decided to prepare for if they returned. I know now I should have packed and left immediately.

I put a large log on the fire, moved my saddle close to the fire and spread my blanket to look like someone sleeping. I took position behind a bush about ten yards away, checked my carbine and revolver and waited.

I dozed off and on through the night. Sometime well after midnight, a faint sound alerted me. Those two fellows had returned and were creeping towards the saddle and blanket. As they reached to remove the blanket, I fired a shot in the ground next to them. As I walked from behind the bush, the younger one reached for his revolver and I shot him in the arm.

"This is my last warning," I shouted. "Leave and don't come back. If you do, I will kill you." I had no more trouble that night.

Next morning I continued the search for the gypsy camp. I was told to go past the large hacienda and make a right turn. As I approached the camp, I noticed there were very few gypsies in camp and I hoped none would recognize me.

I began inquiring about the man on the brown mule who I mentioned was an old friend. I was surprised no one had seen him arrive or leave. One gypsy said perhaps he was at the much larger main camp at Mazatian.

I rode back to the last sentry I had encountered and took directions to Mazatian. Upon arriving, I went to the chief of police and asked about Romano. He replied he knew of no such person arriving in camp, but he would find out if I would wait. He soon returned and told me no such person had passed his way nor was he in the gypsy camp.

I was tired and needed rest. I backtracked to Santa Ana and took a hotel room. While at the hotel, I met a gentleman named Mark Jeffry, an American mining engineer.

For some reason I began telling him why I was in Mexico and described who I was chasing. He was a good listener and for the first time in a long time I felt like talking.

We had dinner together and sat and talked for some time. I told him of the trouble I was having at the ranch and about how Frank was always attempting to buy the place.

Mark told me that while he was riding in from a mining property in Pitiquito he saw such a man as I described. I told Mark I would be leaving the next morning. He offered to go with me, but I declined. He replied he would be there when I returned. Pitiquito was a two day ride so I left early the next morning.

Arriving at Pitiquito I thought it best if I report to the town constable. I inquired if there were gypsies in the area. He replied, "There are many at Caborca and you should check with the chief of police there. His name is Senior Eulaida. He is a good person and will help you."

When I inquired of Senior Eulaida about gypsies, he replied, "Americans arriving here, looking for gypsies usually means trouble. Why are you looking for those people senorita?"

"It's very important," I answered. "The person I'm looking for is a large man with much hair on his face and with large arms. He is riding a large brown mule and leading a burro."

He replied, "If he is here I have not seen him, but I know who will know. Wait here."

I was about to give up waiting when he returned, leading a stocky Mexican with a large mustache.

"Senorita, this is Cisco, he knows all that goes on in this part of the country."

Cisco politely removed his hat to me and asked, "You are looking for gypsies senorita?"

I hesitated, but figured now was the time to tell why I was looking for the gypsy man. I told Cisco I was looking for a man who is a fugitive from justice. He fled from America to escape prosecution for murder. There is a warrant for his arrest. He has killed twice.

"Who did he kill, senorita?"

"He killed my mother and father," I answered.

Cisco's voice softened and his eyes narrowed as he uttered, "That is bad senorita. Are you the one who shot two of my men?"

I answered, "Yes, they were trespassing on my camp."

Cisco replied, "Then they deserved to be shot. You should have shot the third one also. Come with me senorita." I looked to Senor Eulaida for approval; he nodded and spoke to me in English.

"Go with him senorita; you will be safe with him. He will help you." That assurance set me at ease and I followed Cisco.

Riding out of town, Cisco sat the saddle with a straight back and with authority. A number of people on the street waved to him and he acknowledged each person that did so.

Cisco began to talk. "Senorita, we dislike gypsy people in this country. We do not trust them. We put them in a special place so they can rob and steal from each other. The man you are looking for is in that place. I did not like him when I saw him. I knew, because of him, there could be trouble within the camp."

As we were approaching the camp Cisco pointed, "Senorita, look! The one standing next to the big tree is your man."

I recognized Romano immediately. As we got closer Romano saw me and began to run, looking for a place to hide. He then dove for the bushes. We spurred our horses and drew up in a shelter of land.

"Look out!" yelled Cisco, "He's going to shoot." I drew my carbine and leaped from the saddle as Romano got off a shot. He then ran into higher weeds, out of my sight.

At the sound of the first shot, other gypsies came running toward us. Cisco raised his hand toward them and they stopped. They seemed to know Cisco.

Cisco then turned to me and spoke, "Be careful senorita." Cisco was well protected behind the shelter of land and I ducked down beside him just as a bullet from Romano splattered against a rock. Cisco uttered, "I am sorry senorita, but I am unarmed."

"Do you know how to use a revolver?" I asked.

"I can assure you I do," was his reply. I then caught sight of Romano's feet as he was crawling through the bushes. I got off two quick shots and Romano screamed. We waited for some time without any other shots from Romano.

Cisco soon peeked out from the land shelter and shouted, "I think you got him senorita. I will take a look."

I gave Cisco my revolver. "If he's still alive, you may need this." Cisco carefully walked toward Romano.

As he approached Romano shouted, "No mas, no mas." Romano had already dropped his pistol and Cisco stood over him a moment, before kicking him in the side.

"You shoot well senorita. One shot in the knee and one in the foot. You have crippled him for whatever remaining life he has left."

I looked upon Romano and felt as though the world had ended. I was repulsed at the sight of the man who had killed my mother and father.

Cisco grabbed Romano by the shirt and dragged him into the road; all the while Romano was complaining about pain.

"Shut up senior, or I will shoot you in the other knee," uttered Cisco.

Romano was taken to the town hospital under guard by soldiers, as directed by Cisco. I was somewhat taken back by the authority Cisco seemed to have over the soldiers and everyone else.

As we rode back to town, I thanked Cisco for being such a great help and I asked, "What is your full name?"

Cisco looked at me for a moment and answered, "Senorita, here I am called Cisco, because my real name is Francisco. Some places they call me Francisco Pancho Villa. When your man is able to travel, I will have him taken to the border and turned over to your authorities. We don't normally do this, but he is a bad one and we don't want him in our country."

Cisco's name meant nothing to me back then, but it was a name that became known by millions of Americans in 1916. I was impressed with his leadership when I first met him. I didn't know he was in hiding and had a price on his head.

I was held by the authorities for a few days until my story was verified by telegraph from Sheriff Yancy. Afterwards, I returned to the hotel in Santa Ana where Fargo was staying. While there, he met my friend Mark Jeffry. Mark traveled back to the border with us and as we were departing, Mark mentioned he would like to visit me at my ranch in the near future. I of course answered, "Yes."

Romano refused to testify against his father Frank. Romano's wife was afraid of Frank and refused to testify against her husband. All the evidence against Romano was circumstantial. Sad to say, Frank went free, but Romano received twenty-five years to life in the Yuma Prison. He was killed in an attempt to escape after serving five years. He was unable to limp fast enough to get away.

People would not do business with Frank. His reputation traveled far and wide. There were a number that said Frank probably did kill his wife Jessie to get her ranch.

Frank struggled with his ranch for almost a year before he gave up. He could not get workers for the ranch. He realized he could no longer live in this part of the country. He informed the bank his ranch was for sale.

The banker contacted me and inquired if I was interested. I bought Frank's ranch and combined the two ranches into one of the finest cattle ranches in the state.

The man Mark Jeffry, whom I had met in the hotel in Mexico, did come for a visit and he stayed. I married him.

My birth Father, Fargo, became my ranch foreman. He and Shirley became comfortable with each other and decided it was the right thing for them to marry. I had four parents whom I loved very much and they loved me. What more could I wish for?

Fargo died in 1926, and Shirley died in 1929. I wanted to make Fargo a partner in the ranch shortly after we returned from Mexico, but he refused.

He suggested, "Cloudy is your brother; make Cloudy you're partner." I still miss my birth father. I wish I had known him longer.

The boys had not opened their envelopes I left with them when going to Mexico. I told them to retrieve and open their envelopes and read what I had written.

Chico and Felix were to be crew bosses, each having their own crews. In addition, they each would have twenty-five percent ownership in the ranch and would share in all profits. They earned and deserved all they got.

I told Cloudy to open his envelope. Cloudy was my partner. After my demise he would own the remaining fifty percent of the ranch. I never before heard a gown Indian cry over anything.

The notorious Frank moved back to New Mexico where he discovered he was still known there from years ago when he lived there. He ended up working as a common laborer. Frank borrowed a friend's car in 1923, and the gas tank of the automobile exploded when Frank was refueling. He forgot he had a lighted cigar in his mouth. Frank burned to death.

The End

Runaway

Frank Blalock was a strict head-of-the-house farmer, who would never allow his children to disobey him. When he mentioned a certain job needed attending to, he expected it to happen without further discussion.

Relocating his family From Main to Central New York in 1859 was the opportunity he had long waited for. It was probably the last chance he would ever have of owning his own place. He was not about to pass it up.

Blalock was a big man. He stood six feet seven inches at two hundred seventy-two pounds. Frank was thought by many to be a violent person. He never did anything to deserve the reputation, but his towing hulk and sometimes attitude made people think him violent.

Sam, Frank's oldest son, was sixteen years old and big like his father. He stood six-two and weighed in at two hundred twenty-five pounds. Sam completed his schooling and was the wrestling champ. He had not been beaten in two years.

Sam never told his Dad what he wanted to do when he finished his book learning and he wasn't sure the time was right to do so. It wasn't easy being the son of a man that demanded absolute obedience.

Sam wanted to spread his own wings and experience what life had for him. He expressed his wishes to his mother and in her tender way she replied to Sam.

"Men your age should be thinking of such things, but you will need to convince your father. He is expecting you to help him here on the farm."

One evening after his younger brother and sister had gone to bed, Sam began telling his dad about the wonders of the West and how much he wanted to be a cowboy, work cattle and someday have his own spread.

Frank gave his son a severe tongue lashing for even thinking about going out on his own. He was needed on the farm. He would not allow him to leave.

Sam had never before disrespected his dad, but his mind was made up. "All right Dad, I'll stay and help you on the farm for two more years, and then I will leave and go out on my own." Though Sam's mother sided with her son, she would not speak against her husband.

Sam stayed as he said he would. He worked hard. The two years were almost up. Sam again mentioned he was making arrangements for travel to the West.

His father replied, "I will make you a full partner in the farm if you stay on." Sam declined his father's offer.

Frank exploded! "You will not leave this farm without my permission. You will start plowing the family garden area tomorrow morning."

Sam left home that very day in the middle of the night in 1861, and traveled to where he could hop a train going anywhere.

Pulling himself into an open car, Sam was immediately pounced upon by two men. They began punching him about his body. Sam was so taken by surprise, he took several blows before he was able to assure himself he was under attack. Sam began to fight back and he soon became the aggressor. He lifted one fellow and threw him from the boxcar. The other fellow, realizing he was along with this big guy, jumped from the boxcar, leaving Sam to nurse his sore body.

After two days travel the train came upon a crew of workers, members of the Central Pacific Railroad Company, building track toward Omaha, Nebraska.

Sam applied for work and was assigned to the rail laying crew. Sam, being big and strong and a good worker, quickly became a favorite of his fellow crew members.

Sam was singled out for no particular reason by his foreman Delbert, as being lazy and useless, not worth his wages. The man's attitude reminded Sam of his father. Sam took it without comment. He needed the job.

One day as the crew was breaking, the foreman dressed Sam down in the worst way. Sam broke. He grabbed a nearby shovel and as he raised it to swing, the foreman attempted to cover himself with his arms.

Sam suddenly realized the damage he would do if he hit the foreman. Sam stood over him with the shovel in hand. "Go to the Superintendent and return with my wages, I'm through."

The Chinese workers began to laugh and gibber among themselves, slapping Sam on the back. They didn't like the foreman either.

Shortly, the project boss came to Sam, followed by the rail foreman and inquired as to why he was leaving.

"I don't wish to dwell on the subject," replied Sam. "May I have my wages please?"

The grading foreman abruptly stepped forward and explained that Sam was a good worker, but Delbert singled Sam out for his own pleasure. The Chinese were nodding their approval of what was being said.

The boss turned to Delbert. "Don't you want this man in your crew?" Delbert looked around him. He could see the Chinese waiting to hear his answer. "No. I don't," he answered.

The boss turned to Sam and handed him his wages. As Sam began to walk, the Chinese workers dropped their tools and followed Sam.

Delbert shouted, "What's going on here? Where do you people think you're going? Get back here."

"Sam no work-ee, we no work-ee. He good man. We go with Sam."

Suddenly, every Chinese on the payroll within hearing distance laid down their tools and began following after Sam.

Sam turned about. "Fellows, it's not necessary you quit your jobs."

"You no like-ee fore-man. We no like-ee fore-man. We go," they replied.

The Big boss turned to Delbert, "You evidently made a mistake about this man. These Chinese like him enough to quit their jobs to follow him. It looks to me, you're the problem here. You're fired. Pack you're gear and get."

Sam realized what was happening would delay the railroad. Sam also knew Delbert had a family to support and he was many miles from home.

Sam turned to Delbert and put his hand out, "I'll let bygones be bygones, what about you? You had your fun, let's both go back to work and build this railroad." Delbert took Sam's outstretched hand, smiled and uttered, "Done."

The boss informed everyone there would be a layover until supplies and material were brought up from the supply center. "Perhaps two days at the most."

The Chinese began their gambling games among themselves and some of the Americans began wrestling games. Sam joined the contest. He wrestled four matches without a loss.

The Chinese were watching the matches when one of them said, "Our man better your man"

A rail worker held up two dollars and shouted, "Two to one says he's not. Where is your man?"

"He come next supply run." They answered.

Next day the largest Chinese man Sam had ever seen arrived with the supply train. He stood six feet five inches and looked to be around three hundred pounds. Those men so eager to make a bet before were now not so eager.

"What are the rules big fellow?" asked Sam as he approached the man.

"No rules, just wrestle." The men formed a circle and the big fellow stretched himself to his full height. As he slowly approached, Sam kicked him in the stomach. As he bent over, Sam brought his knee up square on his jaw. The big fellow went down. He was out. The Chinese looked on with silence, slowly turned and went back to their gambling games.

Sam continued with the railroad until they reached Omaha. Sam and Delbert continued being friendly toward each other until Sam left the railroad.

In 1866, Sam found himself in Las Vegas, New Mexico, working in the stock yards. It was a hard way to learn about cattle, but Sam figured he had to start somewhere.

Sam worked the stock yards for two years when one of the local ranchers came into town with his crew, looking to relax a little at the Wild Horse Saloon. Sam happened to be at the livery when two of the cowboys wanted their mounts rubbed down and fed.

One cowboy, a big man, told Sam to take his horse and attend to him.

"Sorry mister, I don't work here; Luther the owner is in the back. He'll be right along." replied Sam.

The big cowboy, already starting to feel his oats, said, "I didn't ask if you worked here." He reached down and pulled his duster aside, giving him access to his revolver. "I told you to care for my horse. Now get to it."

At that moment Luther came in from out back and immediately saw the trouble Sam was in. "I'll take your horse mister, Sam don't work here."

The cowboy was now perturbed, "If this half-wit don't take my horse and do as I ordered, someone is going to get hurt."

"Take your business elsewhere mister," replied Luther. "I don't want your kind in my livery." The cowboy hit Luther square on the jaw, knocking him to the ground.

It was then Sam exploded. He kicked the cowboy in the stomach. Just as his partner jumped in to help, Sam kicked the partner in the knee and heard a loud pop as he did so. The knee gave way and the cowboy went down in pain. The one kicked in the stomach was retching his guts out. He held up his arm. "Enough, I've had enough."

As Sam turned to walk away, the cowboy drew his revolver and aimed at Sam, just as his ranch boss kicked the revolver from his hand.

"You were going to shoot him in the back! I don't want your kind in my outfit. Draw your pay. Take your crippled friend and get. You're both fired."

Sam thanked Lance, the rancher, and turned to leave. Lance called after him, "You ever work as a drover?"

"No sir, can't say I have," answered Sam. "Why do you ask?"

"I'll need someone to replace the one with the broken knee. The other fellow weren't any good no how. What's your name?"

"Sam Blalock is my name and I don't know the first thing about being a drover. I'm willing to learn, but I don't own a horse or saddle"

"In that case you're hired, I'll teach you as we go. You can pick a horse from the corral and use one of my spare saddles. You'll need to get yourself a revolver though. There are times it's needed on the trail." Sam never asked what the wages were.

After two days on the trail, Lance decided to bed down the herd a little early. Everyone needed a rest, and besides, there was good grass and water.

While the chuck wagon was being brought up, three men rode into camp. One of the three was the one Sam had kicked in the stomach and attempted to shoot him in the back.

Lance stepped forward. "What do you men want here? You are trespassing on our camp."

"I'm here to settle the score with that feller there," as he pointed to Sam.

"Stand up mister."

Suddenly the two men with him drew their revolvers and told everyone, "Stay as you are."

"I'll have you arrested for this Talbot," said Lance. "If you shoot Sam, you will hang."

"I'll worry about that after I kill him," replied Talbot.

Sam stood up. "It's ok Lance, I can doctor this saddle sore."

At that very second, Sam drew his revolver and shot the two men with drawn revolvers, even before Talbot could clear leather. With his revolver aimed at Talbot Sam asked, "What's your full name Talbot?"

"None of your business, besides, what's that got to do with anything?"

"I would like to know what name to put on the headstone when I kill a man," answered Sam. Talbot slowly removed his hand from his revolver.

Sam told Talbot to unbuckle his belt and drop his holster. "Now, take your two wounded friends and leave from here. If I see you again before the end of the trail, I will kill you. By the way, I never bluff."

As the three rode from camp, Lance turned to Sam. "Why didn't you tell me you knew how to handle a revolver?"

"Didn't think it was necessary Lance. I began practicing with hand guns back when I was sixteen years old, knowing someday I would be coming west. This is the first time I had to use one."

The cattle drive ended in Denver and Sam found himself being pulled in two directions. He could return with Lance and have steady work, continuing to learn about cattle, or he could stay in Denver and do whatever came along. He was beginning to see that working cattle wasn't all he thought it to be.

Sam liked the city and the excitement of all that was going on there. Sam had saved his money since he left home and he had almost $300 after receiving his pay of sixty dollars from Lance.

Sam was twenty-four years old when he hired on at the Denver supply house. Other than the saloon, it was where the old timers gathered around the potbelly stove to talk about gold and warm themselves. Sam didn't ask many questions of the old timers, but he kept his eyes and ears open.

A little fellow wondered in one day with ore samples, looking for a partner and a grubstake. No one paid any attention to him. As he was leaving the building he announced, "I'll find someone and you fellows will be sorry."

One week later that same prospector entered the store. The little fellow purchased a new outfit with boots and hat. He then went across the street and had a bath and haircut. From there he went to the saloon and bought drinks for everyone in the place.

One miner sitting around the warm stove commented. "Old Stubby has found himself another sucker. He'll start all over again just as soon as the money runs out."

Those fellows didn't know Stubby wasn't fooling this time. He discovered one of the better mines in the area and cashed in to the tune of thirty-five thousand dollars. His buyer in that enterprise was the president of one of the largest combines working the area. He purchased Stubbs mine outright.

Sam made purchase of a piece of ground on the edge of town and set about building a small cottage, while continuing to work at the supply house. Sam was content with his situation for he didn't need much.

Sam was busy stocking shelves when a worn out middle-aged prospector wandered in looking for a hand out. The old timers knew him, but paid no attention to his wants. One fellow threated to throw him out if he didn't leave on his own. Sam remembered how the old timers treated the last prospector that came into the store.

"Hold it right there mister. No one has the right to throw anyone from this building unless they own the place and you, mister, do not own this building or the business."

Sam turned to the prospector, "How long you been out mister? You look like you could use a little food. How long since your last meal?"

"George Lancaster is the name young fellow and it's been three days since my last morsel."

"Come with me," replied Sam. Sam took George to the Denver house and told him to order anything he wanted. As George was eating, Sam sat with him and began asking questions about prospecting, learning that George had been a prospector for near twenty years.

Sam questioned George as to ever having any luck.

"Sure I have, even now I have a good prospect, but don't have supplies or equipment to work the place."

Sam studied George, "How much in supplies do you think you will need?"

"Bout $75 ought to do it, but there's the matter of equipment. Why do you ask?"

"If I were to grub stake you how much of the mine would I own if it pans out?"

"Half mine and half yours," answered George.

George continued to eat while Sam observed him. "George, are you an honest person? Can I trust you?" George stopped eating and slowly lifted his eyes to Sam.

"If you've never trusted anyone before I will change that. You can trust me on this and on any other subject we talk about. I will never lie to you or talk behind your back. The prospect I mentioned is a good one and I think it will produce somewhere around $100,000, more or less. Probably more."

"After getting your supplies, how soon would you be leaving?" questioned Sam.

"I could pack the supplies today and leave tomorrow," was George's reply.

"Don't you want to rest up a couple days George?"

"No, the sooner I get back the better. You never know who is wondering around on this land."

"OK George, I'll stake you to a fifty/fifty split. Go back to the mine and bring in ore samples and we'll have them assayed."

George stood up. "Shake partner."

Sam took George to the bank and withdrew $75 and handed the money to George, telling him he knew more about what he needed and he would see him in about two weeks.

Sam returned to the supply house and informed those fellows still there.

"The next time a prospector is mistreated in this store, that person or persons will not be welcomed to sit and warm himself at the stove."

Two weeks later, George walked into the supply house and motioned for Sam to follow him. Sam followed George to the assayer's office where he removed ore samples from the burro's pack and gave them to the assayer. Both men stood by while the samples were processed.

After some time the assayer spoke. "Where did you get this; how much is there?"

"Just tell us what we have," answered George.

The assayer held up one of the samples and replied, "This ore comes out somewhere around $300 in gold per ton. There's also a little silver in the mix at about $15 per ton." George calmly took back the ore samples while Sam paid the assayer for his work and they left the office.

As they got to the outside, Sam began to speak. George held his hand up to Sam. "Not here." Sam took George to his cottage, unloaded the remaining supplies and closed the door.

"I knew it was a good one; I just knew it was!" exclaimed George.

Sam smiled, "What do we do now George?"

George sighed a little, "We have to be very careful who we talk to and what we say. Here is my suggestion based on my experience. We cannot work the mine without proper equipment. The cost of equipment is high, taking away much of the profits of a small mine such as this. We also have the expense of getting the equipment to the mine. I suggest we consider selling the mine to one of the combines in the area. Our profit will be less but so will the headaches."

Sam thought for a moment. "Suppose we don't sell the mine, but we work it on a small scale and take out about a thousand dollars each per month. That way we have a monthly income for a very long time."

George pondered Sam's suggestion and told him what he wanted to do with his profits. "I want to go home and take care of my elderly folks and make their remaining life easier. I also have a wife who deserves an easier life then what I have given her these past years. To do these things I need at least $25,000. I figure to sell at half of the mine's worth. With the split, I should have at least that much. That will do me for what remaining time I have left."

Sam understood George's position. "I'll get back to you on that tomorrow; meanwhile you can sleep here in my place," replied Sam.

Sam contacted a friend who he knew to be honest and who owned a considerable amount of mining equipment. Sam showed him the assayers report. "Pay me $25,000 for an even split in the mine and we will share all profits until the mine no longer produces."

"I will need to see the mine to determine how much ore is there before giving you an answer," said the friend.

Sam met with George and told him he had a potential new partner and his buy in was $25,000. George was pleased and said he would take the deal. Sam wrote the contracts to be signed after his new partner, John, approved the mine. George agreed to lead them to the mine the next morning.

Two days travel brought them to the mine and everything checked out just as George said it would. The claim markers were checked for correctness and the contracts were signed. Returning to Denver, George received his money, said his goodbyes and was never seen again.

Sam and his new partner Johnathon Bowers made their plans. They located to the mine and built a small cabin and began extracting ore from the mine. The mine produced over $300,000 the first year and another $50,000 the second year before the ore ran out. Sam and Johnathon netted $175,000 each, but of course Johnathon had paid $25,000 for his share.

After closing the mine, Sam began looking around Denver for an investment as he was no longer employed at the Denver supply house.

Sam also began thinking about his mother back in New York. Though he had not written since leaving home, Sam often thought of her. She was a sweet and loving mother, yet obedient to her husband who was a tyrant.

Sam went to the express office and sent a telegram to his mother. While waiting for a return message, Sam began a tour of some of the nearby gold camps, getting a feel as to what living in such conditions was like. He wasn't pleased with what he found.

Returning to Denver, Sam called at the express office and found a return message from his mother.

"My dear son Sam, how wonderful to hear from you after so long. I have missed you so. Your Father is dead. Are you coming home? Love always, your mother."

Sam studied the message for some time as tears filled his eyes. "Yes! I am   going home." He immediately began making plans to travel to New York and, if possible, and bring his mother back with him to Denver.

Sam took the train to Chicago and then to New York. He walked the last twenty miles to the farm and as he was approaching the house Sam heard singing. Sam quietly approached the front porch and looked in the window.

There sat his mother with other ladies, singing from church hymnals. Sam could not remember ever seeing or hearing church services in the house when he was growing up. Sam opened the door and walked inside. His mother did not see him for a moment, but when she did she screamed out loud, "Praise God, my son is home." Sam hugged his mother to him as she cried tears of joy. The other ladies quietly left the house leaving Sam and his mother alone.

Sam made a tour of the house and was heartbroken. The house was in deplorable condition. Major repairs were needed. The furniture was worn or broken and needed to be replaced. Sam noticed his mother still cooked on a wood burning stove, and a nearby outhouse was taxed to its limit. Sam sat with his mother and told her where he had been and all he had done and how fortunate he was in grubstaking his friend George who had the gold mine.

Sam asked his mother if she would consider returning with him to Denver. His mother, with tender loving fingers, traced the lines of her son's face. "Sam my son, I have lived here most of my life. I raised my children here. Your father is buried here. I will be buried next to him someday. I know he was hard on you and the other kids, but he loved you very much. When you left, he cried like a little baby. He never forgave himself for the things he said to you at this dinner table that night. He often said afterwards, he wish he had the opportunity to ask for your forgiveness."

Sam was surprised at what his mother was saying, for he always thought his father disliked his children.

Composing himself, Sam spoke. "If you won't come with me, will you allow me to do the things needed around here? You need new furniture, and indoor plumbing with running water into the kitchen. You need a new roof on the house. The front porch needs replacing and you need new windows throughout. You need a new cooking stove. I also notice a church is needed in this neighborhood. I'll build one for you and your friends."

Sam's mother was overwhelmed with joy at what she was hearing. "You can do all these things my son?"

Sam smiled, "Yes mother I can, and I will be starting tomorrow."

Sam went into town the next morning and contracted with the best carpenter to do all he told his mother he would do. The local furniture maker was also contracted to make new chairs and tables and to furnish the best bed and sleeping mattress available.

After all arrangements were made Sam took count of the dollars. The total bill came to $9,250, including the new church building. Mother was going to have an almost new house.

Sam's brother and sister came for a visit, bringing their families. It was another joyous reunion. Sam gave his brother and sister $5,000 each and told them if need be, they could ask for more. Sam felt good being able to help his brother and sister. They both told Sam they planned to purchase their small farms with the money.

Sam replied, "You will need something in reserve." Sam gave each another two thousand dollars.

Sam stayed at home until all projects were completed. He made contract with local farmers to work mother's land and to pay her after harvest for use of the land. Sam further made arrangements for the farm to go to his brother and sister upon his mother's demise. After completing all arrangements Sam left home, assuring his Mother he would write often.

Sam returned to Denver. He had no job nor prospects for one. He decided to look around for a while and find something with a little excitement. There was no rush; he still had well over a hundred thousand dollars.

Sam began to think, perhaps there was a chance to accumulate even more than he already had. He had been living a soft life and a little excitement would do him good. Sam remembered the excitement in the gold camps when a miner found a good amount of gold. Though their living conditions were less than desirable, that could be improved upon with a minimum amount of labor and materials.

Sam had been hearing talk of a mining camp called Silver Plum, about 35 miles west of Denver. The camp was producing high quality granite as well as silver, gold, lead, zinc and copper. The opportunities were endless for someone with capitol and willing to take a little gamble.

In May, 1868, Sam bought a good wagon and two mules and closed down his cottage in Denver. He loaded what he thought he would need and headed out to Silver Plum. Sam was not sure what he would do there, but he decided he would dedicate himself to two years in Silver Plum, come what may.

Sam had traveled about 17 miles and pulled up to make camp for the night. He staked his mules and got a fire going with coffee brewing. Bacon and beans were soon ready. Sam filled his plate and took a seat.

"Hello in camp. Travelers here. Smelled your coffee and saw your fire. Permission to enter camp."

"Come ahead," answered Sam as he located his revolver in his waist band.

Sam stood to face the two men as they entered camp. They were both young, somewhere about Sam's age.

"Howdy, thanks for the invite. I'm Jason Wright and this here is my brother Wilber. If'n you don't mind, we could sure use some of that coffee and a plate of them beans. We'll pay you for it."

"No pay necessary. Help yourself. My name's Sam Blalock. Where you fellows headed?"

"Were headed to Denver, looking to get a few good meals and a couple nights' sleep. We're coming in from Silver Plum." Sam pulled out two more plates and handed each a fork.

"I hear tell Silver Plum is the place to be for a young fellow if he has the gumption to work," replied Sam.

"It's good all right, no doubt about it, but you have to be careful. The camp is full of dishonest speculators. Strikes are made almost every day, but you can't get an honest offer for your claim. That's why were headed to Denver."

"You fellows looking to get a grubstake or partner in Denver?"

Wilber eyed Sam, "Could be, but why do you ask?" Sam handed each a coffee cup and poured the coffee.

"I might have some interest in a new adventure myself if the prospect is a good one." Jason and Wilber looked at each other, but said nothing.

"Say, you fellows are welcome to bed down here tonight and I'll share breakfast in the morning."

"Thank you Sam, we'll take that offer." Sam crawled under his wagon and rolled himself in his blanket, shifting his revolver in his waist band. Sam slept well, as he thought Jason and Wilber were honest prospectors and would cause him no harm.

Sam woke to the smell of coffee and bacon. Jason and Wilber took upon themselves to cook breakfast.

"Hope you don't mind Sam; me and Wilber decided being as you invited us to breakfast we would do the cooking. Here's coffee." Jason handed Sam a cup.

Wilber sat down next to Sam. "Say Sam, last night you mentioned you may have some interest in an adventure. What did you mean by that? Do you invest in gold claims and grubstake?"

Sam eyed both men and began to talk. "Fellows I've asked this question one other time in my life and I'm going to ask it again. Are you two honest men; can I trust you?"

"We've never done harm to anyone that we know of and we're looking for an honest partner or grubstake," answered Jason.

"What's the cost of a partnership or grubstake and which would you prefer?" ask Sam.

"Well Sam, we would prefer a partner," said Wilber, "But the problem is, right now we need both. We're flat busted. We were hoping to sell some of our gear in Denver for food and a hotel room for a couple nights to get some needed rest and then look around for a grubstake. We been out for almost five months and darn near starved."

"Tell me what you have fellows; perhaps I can make you an offer," said Sam.

Wilber began. "We have a good prospect which runs alongside of another claim. The fellow who owns the other claim insists ours is part of his claim. It isn't, his seam runs north, ours runs southwest. We can't refute him as we don't have the money for lawyers."

"Just how close are you to his claim," ask Sam.

"Were twelve yards. After we staked our claim and in the middle of the night he moved his claim marker beyond our marker for about thirty feet and made claim it was there all the time. He paid a couple other fellows to say the same thing and he has got himself a lawyer to fight us in court."

"What do you think your claim is worth?" ask Sam.

"We don't rightly know; we don't know how far the seam goes, but we did some testing and it looks to be around a year's work."

"What do you need in a partner?" ask Sam.

"Money to hire a lawyer and fight in court. We'll make it a three way split," Answered Jason.

"That would be quite a gamble for someone, as there's no guarantee you will win in court. You and your partner would be out of any investment," commented Sam.

"That's true alright, but we have the eye witness of a young man who saw the other guy posting his marker sometime after midnight. He told us in confidence that he woke about midnight and needed to go to the outhouse and that's when he saw this fellow named Jackson tying his marker on a tree bush."

Sam reached over for another cup of coffee and asked, "Why did this young man tell you what he saw if he has no interest in your claim?"

Jason and Wilber looked to each other, "Well, we don't rightly know; he just mentioned it to us."

Sam was thinking of the last time he invested in a claim and it turned out well. This could be another good paying investment.

"Where is this young man now?" asked Sam.

"He's back in camp with his pa," answered Jason. "He and his pa have a small claim about fifty yards from us and are doing alright."

Sam eyed Jason. "How old is this fellow?"

"Bout sixteen I'd say," answered Wilber.

"Fellows, I'll pay your expense for a lawyer for a three-way split. What do you say?"

Jason and Wilber both stood, reached across to Sam and said, "Shake partner."

Sam and his new partners proceeded to Silver Plum and immediately searched out the young man who saw Jackson relocate his claim marker. Sam carefully asked questions that he thought would trip up the young man, but without success. That was a good sign.

Sam decided to employ a lawyer from outside the camp, just to be on the safe side. Clem Sawyer had a reputation for winning most of his cases in surrounding camps. Sam explained the details of the case and offered a third of his partnership as payment if he won the case.

After looking over the Jason and Wilber claim Counselor Sawyer agreed to Sam's offer. Sawyer applied for a court date and was informed the case was due to begin in three days.

As Sawyer stood facing the jury he carefully observed the faces of each member of the jury. He noticed one particular jury member occasionally glanced toward the Jackson table and slightly nodded. That was the one person he would stand between the Jackson table and himself so they could not see each other. Each time Sawyer stood to talk, he would position himself between him and Jackson.

Shortly, the judge noticed the jury member stretching his neck to see around lawyer Sawyer. The judge asked the jury person if he was a friend to Jackson and his answer startled the judge.

"I sure am your honor. Mr. Jackson is a fine person. He buys me drinks and occasionally meals as well. Same as he does for most of us on this jury. Why just yesterday he bought me a whole bottle. Now that's a good person."

The judge slammed his mallet on the pad and announced a mistrial. "This trial has cost the county untold expenses and I will not retry this case again. Jason and Wilber, you maintain your ownership of the claim in question. Case dismissed."

Sam made arrangements for Jason and Wilber to forward his share each month to him back in Denver. Lawyer Sawyer would receive from Sam each month a third of Sam's share.

Shortly after the mistrial, Jason and Wilber received an offer to sell to a combine for half a million dollars. Sam's share would be $166,666, less a third for lawyer Sawyer which came to $55,333, leaving Sam a cool $90,333. Not bad for a few weeks work. Sam now had well over $200,000 total cash on hand.

Sam decided that gold mining was a thing of the past as far as he was concerned. He would take his time for his next investment.

Walking the Denver streets one day, Sam heard his name called. He looked about him, and sitting at the Curb Restaurant was his former rail boss, Delbert. Sam was pleased to see him again. Sitting beside him was his family. Delbert introduced his family and invited Sam to join them.

Delbert commented that Sam looked prosperous and healthy. "What are you doing in Denver Sam?"

"I live here Delbert and have for some time now. What are you doing here?"

"The railroad sent me here to supervise the construction of a new terminal and repair yard for the Denver operation. They're expanding all over the west these days. What about you Sam, what are you doing for a living?"

"Nothing at the present; I'm looking around," answered Sam.

"Say, I could use you Sam; do you need a job? Lousy workers are hard to find."

Sam smiled at the tag Delbert gave him and answered, "I don't think so Delbert, bully supervisors upset me."

Delbert laughed. "I'm authorized to pay a thousand dollars a month to the right man Sam, and I know you to be that man."

"What's the job?" asked Sam. "

"Assist me in ramrodding the construction project and when it's finished you manage the entire operation with an increase in pay," answered Delbert.

"What other particulars do I need to know?"

"You sign a five-year binding contract with the railroad, but they have the option of releasing you at any time," answered Delbert.

Sam thought for a moment, "I sign a contract, binding me to the railroad for five years without recourse, but they have the option of releasing me anytime they want to?"

"Yes, it's the way they do business Sam; they want assurances in all they do," answered Delbert.

"Thank you for the offer Delbert, but I think I'll continue in the same direction I'm heading."

"You're an independent cuss Sam and that's not all bad. Sometimes I wish I was more like you."

At that moment a young lady walked past the restaurant and Sam took a second look in her direction. As she glanced in Sam's direction, he quickly tipped his hat and continued to watch her as she meandered down the walkway.

The supply house where Sam once worked had changed hands and was owned by Phillip Sampson, a former school teacher who had lost his wife a few years back and was raising his daughter as best he could. Sam also discovered Phillip was struggling a bit in the business.

Things had slowed down a little in Denver since a few of the mines had closed and business wasn't as brisk as it once was, but Denver was still a good business town and the future looked bright.

Sam stopped in at the supply house to make a purchase and Phillip inquired if he didn't once work there.

"I did," replied Sam. "It was a fine place to work." Phillip asked why he left the business. Sam explained he had a couple of offers in a different line of work that made him a little money.

Phillip inquired about where Sam was now working. "I'm looking to make an investment but hadn't yet found the right place," replied Sam.

"I could make a partnership if you're interested," expressed Phillip.

Sam knew the business was ok, but could do better. Sam inquired of Phillip as to why he would consider having a partner.

"I have raised my daughter who is now twenty-one-years old and wanting to go to college. Even now, she thinks she has waited too long. I need funds for books and living expenses while she is away. Besides, I could use the help as the business takes all my time. I'm tired and could use relief from my daily grind."

In this year of 1870, Sam was twenty-seven years old. He knew he needed to settle and build some roots. Phillip was about fifty or so and he looked it. He seemed to be an honest man and was wanting to do the right thing for his daughter. Sam told Phillip he would think on it and let him know in a few days.

As Sam was leaving, the young lady Sam saw walk past the restaurant appeared at the door of the supply house. Phillip was in the back room when she entered and Sam hollered to Phillip that he had a customer. Phillip came out from back and greeted his daughter whom he introduced to Sam.

Sam was flustered and could hardly speak. He quickly removed his hat in her presence. "I am pleased and honored to meet you Samantha," uttered Sam.

Sam turned back to Phillip; "I would like to talk some more about that partnership." Phillip looked to his daughter and back to Sam. They both seemed to be oblivious to his presence.

"We could do that over a fine meal at my place tonight, say around six?" replied Phillip.

Sam, all the time looking at Samantha, said, "I'll be there and thanks."

Sam left and hurried to his cottage where he took a bath and shaved. Then he took out his good clothes, dusted his boots and put on clean socks. He was ready to go. He checked his watch, but it was only four p.m. The next two hours were the longest in his short life.

Sam arrived at Phillip's place right at six. As Phillip answered the door, he looked past Sam. "Say mister, did you bring Sam with you? There's nothing formal here Sam, just down home cooking in our modest home. I must say, you do clean up good. Come on in and have a seat. Dinner's about ready."

Samantha came into the room and Sam jumped to his feet with hat in hand. "Good evening Samantha, it's nice to see you again so soon."

Samantha looked Sam in the eyes and smiled. "Gentlemen, dinner is served."

Sam used his best table manners and complimented Samantha on such a fine meal. Having coffee in the parlor afterwards, Phillip began explaining to Sam the particulars of the business and showed him the company books.

Sam didn't seem to be all that interested as his eyes followed Samantha doing her chores in the kitchen. Phillip finally realized the situation and set the books to the side. "Just how interested are you in getting into this business? Your mind doesn't seem to be on it."

Sam apologized for showing a lack of interest. "Just how much is a half interest in your supply house and how involved will I be in the function of the business?"

Phillip thought on that for a moment and answered, "If we work together on a daily basis the price would be $5,000 and your involvement would be the total business. If you just want to buy in as an investment without responsibilities the price is $8,000."

"It's getting late. Time I was getting along," replied Sam. "Will an answer tomorrow be soon enough?"

"It sure will," answered Phillip. Samantha came into the room to bid Sam goodnight and followed him to the door.

Sam didn't sleep much that night. He knew he was taken by Samantha, but the question of the investment was also on his mind. Did he want to settle down and work the business or just invest his money? Samantha was going away to school and he wouldn't get to see her during that time. Perhaps being in business with her dad would work in his favor. He could correspond with her while she was at college.

The next day Sam went to the supply house to meet with Phillip. I'll buy in at $5,000 and work the business daily for two years. At the end of the two years, if I still want the partnership, but no longer wish to work it, I'll pay you an additional $2,000 for a silent partnership. How does that sound?"

Phillip smiled and put his hand out. "It's a deal."

Sam began working and learning the business. He also called on Samantha a couple of times a week as she was waiting for the next college session to start before leaving for the East.

Sam enjoyed dining with Samantha at the Denver House Restaurant. It was the best place in town for a good meal and it had private tables. On occasion Sam invited Phillip to join him and Samantha. Those times when Phillip didn't go to the restaurant, Samantha always took something home for her father.

Phillip had done a fine job of raising his daughter. She was a real lady and Sam was always proud to be seen with her.

In August that year, Sam and Phillip escorted Samantha to the train station and assisted her aboard. As the train pulled away, Sam suddenly had an empty feeling. It would be two years before he would see her again.

Sam was good to his word. He worked the business every day that year, learning all that he could. Phillip taught him to do the books, maintain the inventory and re-order product. Phillip soon realized Sam was no ordinary partner for he worked diligently in every area of the business. Sam was good at public relations and the supply house became a favorite with the town's people. Sam wrote Samantha every week and always took time off to read her return letters. The letters were becoming more personal and Sam was pleased.

One day as Sam was assisting a local rancher to load his wagon, a group of cowboys came rushing into town as they were racing to the saloon. Sam immediately noticed two small girls following their mother across the street in the path of the racing cowboys.

Sam jumped from the wagon as the smallest girl stopped to watch the cowboys, not realizing her danger. Sam ran to the little girl and grabbed her from the path of the rider in the lead of the other cowboys. As he did so, horse and rider veered away in the opposite direction as did Sam. The horse fell as the rider was thrown into the horse watering trough.

The rider was soaked head to toe. The other cowboys thought the situation funny and were laughing until they discovered the horse had broken its neck and was dead.

The soaked cowboy was more concerned about the little girl and was pleased no one was hurt in his recklessness. The cowboy, with permission of the mother, took the little girls to the store and bought candy.

Sam was pleased that the cowboy showed remorse for his actions and asked him if he had another horse. He answered it was his only horse. Sam told the cowboy to follow him to the stable. Sam made purchase of the finest horse available in the stable and presented it to him.

One day the following week, Sam was in the back room of the Supply House and Phillip was up front tending the counter. Suddenly, Sam heard a commotion and as he emerged from the back he was met with a revolver pointed at his head. Two gunmen had entered and the other had Phillip on the floor.

They demanded money and as Sam reached to the hiding place, Phillip yelled, "No, don't give it to them!" The one standing over Phillip hit him over the head with his pistol and Phillip lay still. As he hit Phillip, his face mask slipped a bit and Sam thought he had seen him before.

Sam gave them $2,000, all that was in the store. As the robbers were leaving, Sam rushed to Phillip. Phillip was already rising from the floor and headed to the door to follow after the robbers. Sam grabbed Phillip and jerked him back into the store to protect him. As he did so, Phillip stumbled and hit his head on the corner of the service counter. Phillip collapsed on the floor. Sam turned him over. He had a nasty cut on the side of his head near his right temple. Sam rushed to the back to get a damp cloth. When he returned, Phillip was dead.

Sam took the revolver from behind the counter, rushed outside and fired two shots into the air. Sheriff Matthew and his deputy came running from down the street. Sam quickly explained about the robbery. The sheriff formed a posse of four men and left town in search of the bandits.

Sam was disturbed; he had never been involved in a situation such as this. He gathered his wits and had Phillip removed to the undertaker's shop.

Later that day the posse returned and Sheriff Matthew went to the supply house to see Sam. Sam was nervous and wasn't himself. "Sheriff, we need to talk."

Matthew eyed Sam, "Come down to the office, we'll have coffee."

Sam took a seat as the sheriff poured the coffee. Matthew told Sam he could find no trace of the two men out on the trail.

"That's not why I'm here sheriff; those two men did not kill Phillip. When the robbers left, Phillip ran towards the door to chase them and I grabbed him, thinking they would shoot him if he went through the door. As I jerked him back into the store he lost his balance and hit his head against the corner of the service counter. He collapsed to the floor and didn't move. I turned him over and he was dead. I was only trying to protect him sheriff, I didn't want to hurt him."

Matthew continued to stare at Sam. He then went behind his desk, took pencil and paper and began to write. Sam sat silently and waited. After some time he handed the paper to Sam.

"Does this read correctly as to what you just told me?" Sam read the paper and nodded yes. "Then sign it, that's you're confession." Sam signed the paper.

"Now," uttered the sheriff, "tell me every detail you can remember about what took place when the robbers entered the store." Sam went over everything he could remember, including the one robber that looked familiar when his mask slipped as he hit Phillip over the head. The sheriff was making notes while Sam was talking.

"Alright Sam. I'll accept your story for now, but this thing is far from over."

Sam lowered his head, looking at the floor. "I know. I've now got to go to the express and send a telegraph to Samantha."

Matthew looked to Sam with sympathy, "I don't envy your duty Sam."

Sam waited all the next day before receiving a reply from Samantha.

"Leaving tomorrow for Denver. Will arrive Friday. Samantha."

The procession to the cemetery was agonizing for Sam, for he knew Samantha would want to be present, but things as they were, Phillip was buried under a large shade tree in the corner of the cemetery. Sam sat at the grave for some time before returning to his cottage. He was not looking forward to seeing Samantha under these circumstances.

Two days after Phillip was buried, Samantha arrived on the train and Sam met her at the station. Sam took her to her home for a brief rest and then escorted her to the cemetery. Samantha was well composed for the situation but it was obvious she was not herself. Leaving the cemetery, Samantha broke. She leaned against Sam and let it all out. She began to weep uncontrollably and it hurt Sam to see her in that condition.

Sam took her home and made arrangements for a couple of ladies from town to stay with Samantha for a few days. After three days Sam went calling and Samantha seemed to be doing better. Samantha asked Sam for the details of what happened to her dad.

Sam explained about the robbery. Samantha inquired as to the robbers being caught. Sam sadly answered.

"No, they have not, but there's more to the story." Samantha sensed Sam was holding back something.

"What more are you talking about Sam?"

Sam sucked up a breath and began to tell how Phillip wanted to go after the robbers and what took place after that. Samantha sat and stared at Sam with tears in her eyes.

"Do I rightly understand, you accidentally killed my father after the robbery?"

Sam replied, "Yes Samantha. How do I apologize to his daughter for such a blunder?"

"You don't Mr. Blalock, you don't," replied Samantha.

Samantha rose from her seat, left her house and began walking toward town. She entered the Sheriff's office.

"Did Sam tell you he killed my father?"

"Yes he did," answered Matthew.

"Then why is he not in your jail?"

"Sam reported it as an accident Samantha, but the investigation is not over," answered the sheriff. It was then Samantha began to weep.

"I had plans to marry Sam, and now this."

Sheriff Matthew, as tenderly as he could, began to explain. "Accidents do happen, even to the very best of people with the best of intentions. If the final investigation proves Sam is telling the truth, and I think he is, then it must be accepted as just that, a tragic accident resulting in a person's death, unfortunately it is your father who died."

As Samantha was about to leave, Jenkins, the barkeeper from the saloon across the street, entered the office. He walked toward the sheriff and dropped a heavy sack on the desk.

"That's my share of the money we took from the supply house a few days ago. I'm turning myself in. I don't wish to be charged with something I didn't do. That man was alive when we left the store. As we were leaving, I saw him emerging from the store. His partner grabbed him and jerked him back inside."

"Jenkins, why don't you have a seat and tell me every detail of what happened when you entered the supply house."

"I'm not under arrest?" uttered Jenkins.

"Not yet. First I want to hear your side of the story and then I will do whatever duty is required," answered the sheriff.

Jenkins gave the exact same story as did Sam, in every detail.

"Which of you hit Phillip?"

"The other fellow that was with me," answered Jenkins.

"What is his name and where can I find him and where did you fellows go when you rode out of town?"

"We never left town Sheriff. I live here. My partner in the crime was a drifter who had been in town for a couple weeks. We ran around to the back of the supply house and waited until you and the posse left town and then walked back to the saloon. I don't know where he went after that for he only stayed in the saloon for a couple hours before he left."

Samantha was silent through all the talk. She then looked to Jenkins.

"If you had not done what you did, my father would still be alive. Why did you do this? Did you need money so bad that you were willing to rob for it?"

Jenkins paused for only a moment, "Yes Samantha, I needed money that bad. My wife and I have been on the run for a very long time. We can't run any more. Were tired and the kids need medical attention and nourishing food. I did what I did for them. It doesn't make any difference what happens to me, but my wife and kids should not suffer anymore."

Sheriff Matthew and Samantha spoke almost in unison, "What are you talking about? What do you mean you have been on the run? Explain yourself." Jenkins began telling an amazing story.

"Back sixteen years ago I fell in love with my wife who at the time was an inmate at the New York State Women's prison. She was only eighteen years old at the time. She had killed her own father who was attempting to rape her. She fought him with all her strength. He began to choke her. She was able to reach a knife and she stabbed him directly in the heart. The jury did not believe her and she was given forty years to life for murder. I was a guard at that prison. I fell in love with her the moment I saw her."

"I began making plans to assist her in escaping from the prison. It took me two years to make all the arrangements. Somehow the assistant warden found out my plans but made no attempt to stop me. One day she approached me and said she needed $500 to look the other way. I of course had to pay. It was all I had at the time."

"The escape was successful. We left the state and came west. We were married in Las Vegas, New Mexico and we set up house there. I was bartender at a restaurant and saloon. We soon had two children and were doing well. One day a gentleman came into the restaurant with his wife and I recognized her at once. She was the former assistant warden to whom I had paid the $500."

"As they were sitting at the table I took their order and served the food. I noticed as she was eating she began looking in my direction. Suddenly she smiled and nodded. I knew then she remembered me.

As they were leaving, she walked past the bar and said, "I'll be in touch."

"Three weeks later, early in the morning when the place was empty, she walked into the saloon and came directly toward me. "I'll need another $500, she whispered."

"I of course had to pay. Every place we went after that, she was able to find us. I have been paying her every year since the New Mexico days. She found us here in Denver and demanded another payment. I didn't have the money. You already know the rest of what happened."

Samantha and the sheriff looked to each other in disbelief. "Where is your family now?" inquired Samantha.

Jenkins explained his family was living in the rear of an old barn on the outskirts of town. "They need food, clothing and medical attention. I don't deserve it, but I thank you for anything you can do for my family.

Samantha rose from her chair. "I'll return later sheriff."

Samantha searched out the old barn and found Mrs. Jenkins with her kids in a deplorable condition. Samantha encouraged them to gather what they had and follow her. She led the Jenkins family to her home. She had each of them take a bath. She cooked up a fine meal for them and then took their clothes sizes and went to the supply house. She soon returned with a new dress for Mrs. Jenkins and new clothes for the children, including shoes and under things.

Samantha told them, "Stay in the house; do not wander outside until I tell you it's ok. I'll soon return. You may use all that you see here."

Samantha returned to the jail and inquired of Sheriff Matthew if he had any leads on the other robber.

"No I don't Samantha." He then turned to Jenkins, who was now behind bars,

"What was your partner's name?"

"I don't know for sure, I just called him Jake." answered Jenkins.

"Is there any way I could identify him if I saw him?" Jenkins described him as tall, about six feet, slender with black hair, dark eyes and missing part of the thumb on his right hand.

"Do you have any idea where he was heading?"

"The last thing he said to me, he was going to check out a few of the mining camps in the area."

Samantha looked to Matthew. "Well sheriff, what are you waiting for? The man could be getting further away every minute you stand here. Go after him."

"I plan to Samantha, just as soon as I get a little rest," replied Matthew.

"You can rest on the trail. I suggest you get cracking at once." Sheriff Matthew stared at Samantha for a moment.

"Now Samantha, that's not the way things are done. We have to be patient and do things that bring the most results."

"Yes, I can see the results from here. You have an empty jail cell," uttered Samantha.

The sheriff reached for his rifle, holstered his revolver, set his hat back on his head, walked to the door, mounted his horse and rode down the street, all without saying a word.

Samantha returned to her home to attend to the Jenkins family. As she was approaching the house, Sam was coming from the other direction. Sam attempted to talk with Samantha but she told him she was not yet ready to talk with him about anything. "Please, leave me alone." Sam was hurt by Samantha's outburst, but he also realized she had now lost both her parents and it was clogging her mind.

Next morning Sam opened the store at seven a.m. as always and was surprised when Samantha arrived a few minutes later and began working the front counter, putting things in order and waiting for the first customer. Sam told her she didn't need to be there, he could handle it.

Samantha turned on Sam and told him she was now his partner and she was there to do her part and he better get used to it. Sam was again hurt by her outburst, but he said nothing.

Later that day sheriff Matthew entered the store and as he approached Samantha she bellowed, "If you're here to tell me you have captured the other robber, well and good, I don't have time for useless talk."

Sheriff studied Samantha a moment. "Samantha, I know this is hard on you as it would be on anyone under the same circumstance, but you are being unreasonable and you're taking your feelings out on everyone you come in contact with. I feel for you and so does Sam, especially Sam. He worked every day here with your Father and they grew a friendship. I know you don't intend to hurt anyone, but the things you're saying and doing are hurting everyone around you. You should not be here in the store with that attitude. You will only hurt the business and you certainly won't be helping Sam. Now I suggest you go home."

Samantha was quiet as she listened to Matthew. Tears began to swell in her eyes. Suddenly, she fell to the floor sobbing uncontrollably. Sam knelt before her, put his arms around her and let her cry. Sheriff Matthew told Sam, "Take her home; I'll stay here in the store until you return."

Samantha took to her bed for three days.

Sam was in the store when Samantha walked in. She had a smile that Sam had not seen for some time.

"Good morning Sam, how is my partner today?"

Sam paused in his work. "Just fine Samantha, but a life time partnership would be better."

"Not now Sam, I'm not ready. This is not the time or the place. Where do you need the most help?"

"Just work the front counter and be your beautiful self; I'll be in the back moving things around."

A few ladies came into the store, made their purchases and Samantha did just fine. They expressed their sorrows to Samantha and she acknowledged with grace.

The remainder of the week went well with Samantha working the counter and Sam doing the heavy work. Saturday afternoon Sheriff Matthew entered the store, greeted Samantha and asked for Sam.

"He's in the back. Sam, the sheriff wants to see you."

Sam came from behind the partition and removed his work apron. "Hello sheriff, what's up?"

"Sam can you come down to the office, I need to talk with you?"

"Sure sheriff, I'll be back soon Samantha."

"Sam I've been asking questions all over town about those two men who entered you're place and robbed you. I have Jenkins in jail, but no one remembers seeing the other fellow around town. Are you sure there isn't something more you could tell me."

Sam suddenly realized the sheriff thought the robbery was perhaps an inside job. He was a suspect in his own store robbery.

"No sheriff, I have told you everything that took place. There's nothing more to tell. Would you please make it plain as to what you are saying?"

"I'm not saying anything yet Sam, I'm just doing my duty as sheriff. I need answers to every question."

Sam began to talk, "Sheriff, I'm not your man. Phillip was my partner. We got along well in our dealing with each other. I would have no reason to rob him or anyone else. I love his daughter and want to marry her. What could I possibly gain by robbing the store? As you know, I don't need his money. I have my own. Find a tall slender dark headed man with a short thumb on his right hand and you will have solved the case."

"I know Sam. Sometimes I don't like this job. Go back to the store. Try to forget what just took place here."

"I'll forget it when you've captured the other guy, not before," said Sam.

Returning to the store Samantha asked Sam what that was all about. Sam fluffed it off as just questions and answers, but he found he couldn't concentrate on the business at hand. Something about this whole thing didn't seem right. Something was missing.

Sam went into the back room, took pencil and paper and began writing down every single step that was taken during the robbery. Even the smallest detail was listed. Sam began reading over and over everything he had written. He carefully concentrated on every word. Suddenly it hit him.

Sam told Samantha he would be back shortly and rushed for the sheriff's office. As Sam entered, he shouted, "Sheriff, I didn't do it, I didn't do it."

"Just what is it you didn't do Sam?" replied Mathew.

"I didn't kill Phillip," answered Sam in an excited voice. "Someone else killed him."

"Why don't you tell me how you arrived at that conclusion Sam?"

Sam began telling the sheriff all that he remembered. Sam presented the paper he had written and began explaining some things he had left out in his earlier conversation.

"When Phillip hit his head on the counter after I jerked him back into the store, he fell to the right of the counter and was unconscious. I went to the back room to get cold presses and when I returned, Phillip was lying on the left side of the counter, facing the front door. Phillip regained consciousness and was hit again by someone who came into the store and left before I returned to Phillip. The next day I was taking inventory when I discovered one of my most expensive hats was missing which was on display next to the front door. Find a fellow with a brand new expensive hat and you have the killer."

Sheriff Matthew leaped from his chair, reached for his Winchester and raced to his horse. Without saying a word, he was on his way out of town.

Sam returned to the store and thought it best if he told Samantha all that took place between him and the sheriff and about the sheriff rushing out of town.

For the remainder of the day and into the next, nothing was seen of the sheriff. About one hour before sundown two riders were seen advancing toward town. In the lead was a cowboy wearing a new hat. Following behind him was the sheriff. As they were riding past the store Sam walked out on the walk way. The cowboy glanced at Sam and quickly turned back to the front as they proceeded toward the jail.

Samantha removed her work apron and was heading towards the jail when Sam called after her.

"Samantha, let Sheriff Matthew do his job before you go storming into his office." Samantha stopped, turned to face Sam and nodded.

"Yes, your right."

Nothing more occurred that evening. Next morning, the Sheriff came into the store and announced the arrest of a suspect in Phillip's murder.

"Sam, you told me about the missing expensive hat. The other day while riding a few of the gold camps, I saw this fellow in a saloon. The only good set of clothes he had on was his hat. The moment you mentioned it I remembered. I could only hope he would still be in that camp. He was. I had him remove his riding gloves and I saw his short thumb. Now he's in my jail."

"Samantha, I sent a telegraph to New York to the prison authorities informing them I had Jenkins and his wife. I'm waiting for an answer as to what happens next with those two. I also informed them the former assistant warden was in Denver and she assisted the Jenkins in their prison escape."

A trial was set to take place in two weeks against short thumb. No lawyer in town wanted to represent short thumb, especially after the Jenkins confession. The judge ordered a Public Defender to defend the man.

Two days out, a messenger from the telegraph office rushed to the sheriff's office. Sheriff Matthew read the telegraph. He slowly holstered his revolver, donned his hat and began a slow walk to the supply house.

Sam was in the front of the store.

"Where's Samantha?" asked the sheriff.

"She went to the house to check on the Jenkins," replied Sam. "She should be right back. What's up Sheriff?"

"Let's wait until Samantha gets here," replied Matthew.

Samantha shortly returned to the store and the sheriff began to read the telegraph from New York.

Sheriff Matthew, the charges against Mrs. Jenkins were dropped ten years ago as proof was presented to prove her innocence by her mother and siblings. It would cost too much to try Mr. Jenkins at this location. Under the present conditions, the States Attorney General refuses to try the case. Mr. Jenkins, though he is guilty, is a free man. As for the assistant warden, arrest her and hold her, for she assisted others in a prison break and also black mailed them over the years.

Sheriff Matthew pointed out the charges still pending against Jenkins for the robbery. Samantha looked to Matthew.

"What robbery are you talking about sheriff?"

"The one here inside your supply house," answered Matthew.

Samantha turned to Sam. "Sam, did we have a robbery in this supply house?"

"Not to my knowledge," answered Sam. Samantha and Sam looked to the sheriff.

"Well I must be mistaken. I locked someone in my jail by mistake. I should go and release him," replied Mathew.

Sam gave Samantha his arm, "We'll go with you sheriff to make sure you don't make any more mistakes."

Matthew unlocked the jail cell and told Jenkins to go home to his family. "Samantha and Sam will walk with you and explain everything. I don't want to ever see you on the back side of my jail cell again. You and your wife are free. You can come and go as you please."

The trial was brief and Short Thumb was found guilty as charged. He was given forty years to life at hard labor. During the trial, it was discovered Short Thumb went back to the store to get the hat and Phillip saw his face, as Short Thumb had removed his mask. Short Thumb hit Phillip again on the side of the head, killing him. Phillip fell on the left side of the counter facing the door.

Samantha made arrangements for the Jenkins family to move into the house next to her home. Her and Sam took the kids to the supply store and fitted them out with all additional clothes they would need. They informed Mr. and Mrs. Jenkins that they would have to earn their new clothing by helping her and Sam take inventory at the store. Arrangements were made for the local grocery store to supply food for the family, until Jenkins could find work. The bill for such was to go to the supply house.

A normal daily routine was slowly coming around and one day as Sam and Samantha were taking their lunch break, Sam mentioned how far it was to the nearest restaurant. Someone needs to establish an eating place at this end of town. Samantha looked at Sam in surprise.

"That's the answer Sam. Jenkins has experience in food service and he could be the manager of such an enterprise. We could lease one of the empty houses at this end of town and convert it into a restaurant."

Sam agreed. "Let's talk with Jenkins."

Jenkins was excited with the idea. Sam and Samantha leased the empty house two doors down from the supply house and put Jenkins in charge of the conversion and setting up the restaurant.

As opening day was arriving, Samantha asked Jenkins if he was going to install a sign on the outside and he said he ordered a sign but it had not arrived yet. The day before the opening, the sign arrived and was installed above the door entrance. The sign read, "Phillip's Restaurant. A Supply House Enterprise."

Most stories would be nearing their end about here, but not this story. Sam and Samantha were married and had three kids. The oldest, a boy, was named Phillip. The second was also a boy, named Samuel. The third child was a girl, named Sue Samantha.

The Denver Supply House became the largest of its kind west of the Mississippi, becoming a distributing center for the Western States. Phillip's Restaurant enlarged three times to become a Western tradition, famous throughout the West.

Sheriff Matthew left his position and became Denver's Police Chief and served with distinction for ten more years.

The assistant warden was extradited to New York and served 20 years at the same prison where she once helped inmates to escape.

One day a reporter from a Denver newspaper came into the restaurant and wanted to interview Jenkins on his success as the proprietor of the famous restaurant. Jenkins informed him that he was not the owner of the restaurant, he was the manager. The owners were Sam and Samantha Blalock of the famous Supply House. The reporter convinced Sam and Samantha to submit to the interview with Jenkins.

Sam and Samantha began telling the reporter all they were aware of from the time Jenkin's wife escaped from prison with

Jenkins's help and with the knowledge of the assistant warden, including her bribery of Jenkins.

Jenkins then began to talk. He explained how his wife and family had lived all those years in nothing but shacks, mostly not fit for humans and how he at times stole food for his kids. All the money he made went to the former assistant warden for she threatened to notify the State of New York of their whereabouts.

The story went on to explain the incidents that took place at the Supply House where Phillip was killed and how Samantha felt compassion for the Jenkins family.

The story appeared in local papers and was soon repeated all over the country in other papers. A famous writer contacted the Denver paper to inquire if an exclusive was issued to them. It was not. The writer contacted all parties involved and contracted to write a book about "Sam, The Runaway."

My fellow book readers, you just read the book. I hope you enjoyed it.

End

My Name is Jack Larson

October 3, 1930

My dear Son Jimmy,

I've been in this old folks' home for two months now and I'm disappointed. It's not near what folks told me it would be. Half the people here don't even remember their name and the other half think they are somebody other than they are. I tried talking with a few of them and it was like talking to a horse. They just look at me and say nothing. The only folks I can talk with are the people working here, those that wear them white outfits.

Most of the time I take walks around the grounds, feed the pigeons and take in the sunshine. I stay out of the building as much as I can. I'm one of the few that can come and go as we please.

A small group of people were wondering around the grounds the other day, talking with us few that were outside. Seems they were with the local newspaper and were looking to find a story they could run as a series in the community section of the paper.

They finally caught up with me and asked some unimportant questions before getting to the point. They wanted to know if I had a story I would share with them for the local paper.

I told them, "Everyone has a story and I'm keeping mine to myself." I don't expect they will bother me anymore. Later Son. Don't forget to write.

"Mr. Larson, it's lunch time sir. Would you like for me to bring you a tray, or do you prefer eating in the cafeteria?" asked Nurse Mary.

"Say, that would be a nice change; I'll eat out here and thank you," I answered. "Would you mind dropping my letter in the box on your way back?"

"I'll be happy to sir, and you're welcome. Would you mind a little company while you eat?" she asked.

"That would be nice; not many people here I can talk to."

"I'll be right back with your food tray," she replied.

Mary was the favorite of those who spend time outdoors. She always seemed to get pleasure out of helping.

"Here you are Mr. Larson; we have a fine meatloaf today, with mashed potatoes and peas. I brought you coffee, is that ok?"

"Thank you Mary, that's just fine," I answered.

"Mr. Larson, I see you had a visitor today from the newspaper people. Do you have a story for them?"

"Please Mary, Call me Jack. I have a story alright, but I'm not telling them anything. They always build the stories into something that never happened."

"What is your story about Jack?" inquired Mary.

"I had an unstable life when as a young boy and it didn't get much better as I got older. In fact it got worse when war broke out. I reckon I was 15 or 16 years old back then."

"Would you tell me your story Jack?" Mary asked.

"You're a nice lady Mary and I like you," I answered, "but I don't care to talk about those things; too many people still mad about certain happenings back in them days."

Mary eyed me. "Jack, that was sixty- five years ago. You need to get it off your chest. Tell those newspaper people your story. If it's about the war era, the world needs to hear it. If it will help, I'll be here with you as you tell your story."

"Okay Mary, you can tell those people I have a story to tell, but it will be on my terms."

Mary made all the arrangements and the next day a young lady and a staff writer arrived shortly after breakfast. We took seats under the large oak tree as Mary served iced tea.

"Tell us your story Mr. Larson, and if it's worthy well pay you for the story," said the young lady.

"I don't need your money young lady," I answered. "Besides, some things are not for sale."

"How old are you Jack?" she asked.

"I was 88 on my birthday and haven't had one since," I answered as Mary took her seat next to me.

Here is my Story.

My name is John Jack Larson. I answer to the name Jack. My family---me, Mom and Dad, moved to Tennessee in 1852. Dad needed to start over after failing while in Illinois. Times were hard for folks back in them days. Dad worked hard to support Mom and me. Farming on shares for a living wasn't easy. Never has been.

Things weren't good between the Feds and the Southern States back then. Dad's folks were from Alabama and he took sides with the South when it came to choosing sides. It looked as though a conflict was going to happen and Dad was invited to join the Union Forces, which he refused to do. More and more pressure was put on Dad until one day Mom and Dad decided it was time to move again to escape from the possible conflict.

We moved to San Antonio, Texas where Dad found a farmer looking for help on his large farm. The gentleman had two houses on the farm and told my Dad he could move his family into the spare house as part of his pay. Dad took the job.

Dad was a hard worker. He could do and build almost anything. The owner was pleased to have Dad. He even gave Dad extra pay on occasions. We were doing real well and things were looking up for the family.

Dad talked to the owner about becoming a partner on forty acres in the wooded area, after he would grub out the tree stumps. The owner agreed to the proposition and dad began clearing the forty acres.

One day, Dad was hitching the plow to the two mules when they began to run for no reason. Dad had the reins around his wrist and the mules drug Dad into a tree stump, breaking his neck. My Dad died two hours later.

I attempted to take my Dad's place on the farm but the farmer wasn't pleased with my work. He told my mom he was going to look for another family to live in the house.

Mother had an uncle living in El Paso and wrote him, asking for help. He answered, telling her to come to El Paso and he would do what he could to help. So we moved to El Paso.

The trip from San Antonio to El Paso in those days was a hard ride for anyone. The trip was especially hard on Mom.

We didn't have much money or food, so we lived off of wild rabbit during the trip. Catching those rabbits wasn't easy. My mom came down sick during the trip and didn't recover sufficiently to do much. She spent most days in bed. Instead of getting better, she kept getting worse.

I worked for Mom's uncle and he only paid me enough to just get by. We never had any extra. One day I asked Uncle Ralph for a little extra pay so I could get a doctor for my Ma.

He replied, "She'll be alright in time. Don't worry yourself over it." He was a terrible person to work for. He didn't really want to help us; he just wanted us there for cheap labor. On occasion I would leave the field for a few minutes to check on Mom and Uncle Ralph would reduce that time from my pay.

One evening stands out in my mind, for it was my nineteenth birthday and it was the turning point in our lives. Mom was very sick and needed medicine, but we had no money. Matter fact we were out of food and fire wood. I knew I had to do something. It had been raining all day and it was dark and cold outside as well as inside.

I got myself dressed to go out into the weather. I told my ma I was going after something for us to eat and I would look for something from the barn to burn in the fireplace to warm up the house.

I was about to leave when I suddenly heard a voice. "Hello in the house." I had never had anyone come to the house before and I was somewhat afraid to open the door.

As I cracked the door open, a gentleman was sitting his horse at the yard gate. In a loud voice he bellowed.

"I'll not harm you. I need shelter for the night. May I use your barn?"

I walked out on the porch. "I guess it will be alright mister, but the barn is cold and damp. We're out of fire wood, but the house is better than the barn. You're welcome to come inside and sleep on the floor after you take care of your horse. There's some hay in the loft for the horse." After he took care of his horse the gentleman came into the house. He paused and looked around.

"I can pay for any food you can spare."

"I'm sorry mister, we don't have any food neither."

"I'll be right back." That gentleman returned to the barn and gathered all the wood material he could find. He also dismantled three water barrels and brought the load into the house and started a fire. A warmth filled the room at once.

He then walked over to my mom. "Is this your mother?"

"Yes sir, it is and she's been sick for a long time. We don't have money to pay a doctor." He bent over my mom and carefully looked her over. He looked into her eyes and checked her hair. He looked at her hands and feet.

"Where's the nearest doctor?" he asked.

"About three miles in town," I answered.

"I noticed another horse in your barn. May I borrow it for a trip into town?"

"Well sure mister, but what are you going to do?" I asked.

"Trust me on this young man. I'll not steal your horse. I'll return." The man left immediately.

Very early the next morning a gentleman arrived from town with food supplies for the day. He said they were paid for and other supplies were forthcoming. Later that day, the gentleman with my horse came to the house driving a buckboard wagon loaded with firewood. Trailing the wagon was my horse and a burro with more food then I had ever seen at one time.

The man came into the house and told me to unload the wagon and burro. He then went directly to my mom. I watched him as he lifted my mother's head and told her, "Take this; it will soon make you feel better."

I went outside to do as he asked, first bringing in firewood to warm the house. I got the fire going again and brought in the food. By this time the man had my mother in clean warm clothes and under warm blankets. He had her propped up in bed and was combing her hair.

I was surprised to see my mother sitting up. The man said she was suffering from what he called Rabbit Fever. "Taking it easy and with good care, she should be much better in a few days." He then gave me the medicine and told me how to give it to her and for how often.

He then began cooking up a broth for my mom and he fed her with crackers crushed in the broth. It seemed that mom got better almost at once.

He then asked, "What's you name young man?"

"My name is Jack Larson sir," I answered.

"I may be back this way someday. Watch for me," he replied.

He then went to the barn and saddled his horse. As he was riding out he mentioned, "Someone from town will be coming for the wagon and burro tomorrow."

I hollered, "Say mister, what's your name?"

"Call me Andy Andrews." He then rode away.

Mom got better, just like Mr. Andrews said she would. Folks near town knew we were looking for a place to live and work, and they hired mom and me to work for them. Mom did the cooking and light house cleaning. I took care of the family garden, milked the cows and everything else that needed to be done around the yard and barn.

It was three years later when my mom died from old age. I was about 21 or 22 years old then. I didn't want to leave El Paso. I remembered Mr. Andrews said he would be back someday. I owed that man and wanted to be there if and when he returned, but I met a young lady who caught my fancy and I asked her to marry me. She had relatives in Santa Fe, New Mexico and she wanted to live near them. I let everyone near me know I was moving to New Mexico, just in case Mr. Andrews did return.

I told my wife about Mr. Andrews and how he helped me and Ma. After hearing the story, she commented, "He would be welcome in my house anytime. Such a man is soft-hearted and can be trusted. His kind are always looking to help others."

One day some years later, my two kids were playing in the yard when they yelled, "Pa, someone is coming to the house." I walked outside and a white-haired gentleman was dismounting his horse at the gate.

"My names Andy Andrews, is this the Jack Larson residence?"

I recognized him at once. He looked older of course and looked as though he could use some rest. I held out my hand to him and answered,

"Yes it is and your welcome here Mr. Andrews. I have been waiting for you a long time. Come in and meet my family. It's wonderful to see you again."

I introduced him to my wife Christine and my kids, Bertha and Jimmy. As we sat at the table, Christine began putting together a meal while we talked about that time eighteen years ago. I told him how my mother got well and lived three more years before she died.

I was about to ask what he had been doing all the years when Christine served up the food. Andy devoured the meal and afterwards we had coffee in the front room. I asked Andy if he would stay with us. He was welcome to stay as long as he wanted to.

Andy said he had no particular place to go so he would. "I'll have the kids bunk in together. You take their room until I finish building a spare room on the back of the house, which I have started. When it's finished, it's yours." I told him.

Andy went to bed early that night and slept until almost daylight. I mentioned I was going into town for more building supplies and asked Andy if he wanted to go along.

"No, I don't think so," he answered. "I need to take care of my horse and attend to a few other things."

I returned from town late that afternoon and Andy had cleaned up the barn area and made some repairs on the chicken coup. He was hoeing weeds in the garden area when I returned. We had an early supper and sat out on the front porch with our coffee. I then asked Andy what he had been doing all the years.

"Not much Jack, just going from place to place. Staying a while and moving on." I could tell Andy didn't want to talk about it so I dropped the subject.

Andy, "We would love to have you stay with us as long as you want," I blurted out. Andy took a long look in my direction.

"Thank you Jack. Are you sure your wife feels the same?"

"She does," I answered.

"Then I will. I'm tired and I'm not getting any younger."

"How old are you Andy?" I asked. "Well I've kind of lost track, but I think I'm somewhere around 75 or 76."

"I didn't think you were that old Andy."

"I've tried to take care of myself over the years," he answered. "Not too long between meals and no alcohol or tobacco. So far it seems to be working."

We finished the extra room and Andy moved right in. He sure was handy around the place, always looking to help out. I was concerned though. Each time I went into town for supplies and asked Andy if he wanted to go along, he always refused. I figured someday, if he had a mind to, he would tell me why.

Five years went by and Andy was 80 years old, but still spry as he was the day he came. Andy began taking walks with the family dog. Sometimes he would leave shortly after sunrise and not return until late afternoon. I knew something was bothering Andy, but I didn't want to pry.

One afternoon, after he returned from his walk, Andy announced he was going away for a while.

"When will you be back Andy?" I asked.

"I don't know; I may never come back, but then again I could be gone only a short time. It depends."

"I'm not going to ask why Andy. I've noticed lately you have something on your mind. When you get it settled, please come back to us. We'll miss you." I felt I would never see Andy again. I noticed he was slowing down a little, even though it was a healthy slow-down.

Fourteen months later, while the family was taking dinner, the dog began to bark and someone yelled out.

"Hello in the house." The kids jumped from the table; it's Mr. Andrews! We all rushed outside.

"No, not Mr. Andrews, Doctor Andy Barth at your service." Andy removed a large sack from his saddle as we went into the house. He had gifts for everyone. "Say, something smells mighty good from where I'm sitting." Christine added another plate to the table and we had an old fashioned homecoming.

After dinner, we took coffee on the porch while the kids did the dishes. Andy said it was time to tell his story.

"I attended Harvard University and got my degree in medicine. I set up my practice in South Carolina. War had commenced about two years before and I was approached by elements of the Southern cause and asked to join as regiment doctor with the rank of major. I refused. I was then conscripted against my wishes and under the direction of another doctor.

"It was soon evident the other doctor didn't know what he was doing and I did double duty to make up for his lack of knowledge. It was discovered he had a phony degree and had never studied the practice of medicine. I was assigned to a Company of Raiders as company doctor.

"Those men were of the worst element in the army. They rode through the countryside stealing food and valuables from everyone they met. Those that had sympathy for the North were sometimes killed. A number of their women were raped and on occasion their husbands were forced to watch. I tried to interfere with what they were doing. I was told to mind my own business and take care of the wounded and sick. My rank carried no authority with them. They were nothing more than criminals.

"The atrocities those men committed were of the worst kind and if the war had not ended when it did I would have deserted the unit. The Northern forces declared the Raiders war criminals and they would be tried as such upon their capture. Though I was a doctor and did not participate in their crimes, I was nonetheless one of them and was classified a criminal. A few of them were captured, tried and hung. I went in hiding.

"I was on the run when I first came to your house in El Paso Jack. I have been hiding ever since. After all these years I decided to turn myself in to the authorities. I knew it was a gamble, but I never had harmed anyone. I wanted to visit town and come and go as I please.

"I went into Albuquerque and told the authorities who I was and they sent a telegraph to Washington, asking what they were to do with me. I was confined to a jail cell for eight months while telegraphs went back and forth. I was questioned at length every time a new telegraph was received from Washington. Finally I was allowed to leave my cell and roam the building, but not allowed outside. After a total of twelve months word came from Washington. They could find no one that would testify against me. I was free to go.

"I'm sorry for deceiving you and your family Jack."

I told Andy I was sorry he had to live without total freedom all those years.

It then came to me to ask. "Andy, how was it you seemed to always have money when needed?" Andy paused for a brief moment before beginning the rest of his story.

"As soon as the war was declared over, I knew they would be looking for me and others of the Raiders. I was in Tennessee inside a bank in Nashville, changing a bill into smaller money, when suddenly a group of men entered the bank and announced it was a holdup.

"After getting the money and as they were leaving, the sheriff arrived and began a shoot-out with the robbers inside the bank. One of the robbers was badly shot in his side and the others grabbed me as hostage and led me outside to my horse, forcing me to ride with them. Reaching their hideout in the low hills country, they carried the one that was shot into the cabin.

"It was obvious he needed a doctor. They discussed the possibility of kidnapping a doctor from town and bringing him with a blindfold to the cabin.

"I decided to gamble. I told them I was a doctor and the man would not live much longer without immediate attention. I told them I would help the man if they promised to release me when I was finished. They said they would kill me if I didn't help him. I told them killing me would not help their man. They then agreed. I told them to get my instruments from my saddlebags and heat up some water.

"I began probing for the bullet. As I finished doing so a shot rang out from outside. A posse had tracked the robbers to the cabin and had us surrounded. With rifles, revolvers and shotguns they began shooting up the cabin. It was horrible. The posse never gave the robbers a chance to surrender. I lifted the basement trap door and was able to get myself and patient under the cabin, into the dirt floor basement.

"After what seemed hours, the shooting stopped. I could hear the posse enter the cabin. All the robbers were dead. They drug the corpses outside and fastened them to their saddles and rode away, never checking the basement trap door. I watched all that happened from a crack in the wall of the basement. As I turned back to my patient, I noticed the bag of money from the bank was on the dirt floor. I thought perhaps the robbers had thrown the bag inside as I was crawling down.

"I checked my patient and found he had been shot again and he was dead. I was alone. I was about to bury the bandit in the cellar when suddenly the posse returned to the cabin. I just knew I would to be captured. I began looking around and saw a small opening in a dark corner. I rushed to it and pulled some fire wood around me. The posse opened the trap door and saw the dead bandit. They pulled him out and searched around the cabin for the money, never looking back inside the basement. I waited for some time to be sure they were gone before moving. My horse was not about so I gave my special whistle and he came from the wooded area. I took the sack of money and my instruments and left as quickly as I could.

"I rode to Memphis and rented a room for the night. I tied my horse at the hitching rail and fell asleep at once. Along about midnight I woke and remembered my horse and the money in the saddlebags. I went outside and led my horse to the livery to be rubbed down and fed. I removed my saddlebags and returned to my room. I began counting the money and was surprised when the count reached $4,000. Even as a doctor I had never had that much money at one time in my life. I continued to count and finished with $5,450.

"I was on the run and needed money to live. I knew it was wrong, but I kept the money. Next morning, when passing the saloon on my way to the livery, I noticed a poster on the wall, listing the names of Raiders still wanted. My name was the third one on the list. I claimed my horse and headed west. After about two months I found myself in El Paso, where I met you Jack.

"When I left you that day back then, I traveled to Phoenix, Arizona. I rented a small house and hung out my shingle. I was flooded with patients and was doing very well until one day a gentleman entered my office. As I was talking to him about his sickness, he blurted out, 'Say, I remember you from the war years. You were a doctor with the Raiders who came to my farm and took all my available food. My fourteen-year-old son tried to stop you and he was shot and crippled for the rest of his life.'

"He stormed out of my office. I knew then I was again on the run. I should have left immediately, but I didn't. I don't know why. After dark that night, I removed my shingle and led my horse into the wooded area behind the house. I was certain that man would return with the sheriff.

"I packed my saddle bags and secreted myself inside the small barn. I loosened a couple wall boards for escape on the back side of the barn and waited. Along about midnight, three riders approached the house with drawn revolvers. One was wearing a badge. I went out the back into the woods for my horse and left Phoenix.

"About one hour later I heard riders coming, and I knew it was them. I spurred my horse and headed for the mountains. Not knowing where I was, I began looking for a place to hide me and my horse. I suddenly came upon a meadow with a waterfall coming down on the other side of the meadow. I rode forward and found a cave-like opening behind the fall. I dismounted and waited.

"Shortly, the three rode into the meadow and stopped to look around. They were there for about an hour before they rode away. I thought perhaps they were in hiding, just waiting for me to appear again. I stayed in that cave for two days without food for me or my horse.

"I traveled to Tombstone but didn't hang out my single. I found work in a mercantile store and rented a room in the hotel next door. I was content with my situation and was beginning to enjoy myself. One day the Earp brothers got into a scrap with some cowboys and I found myself doctoring one of the Earp boys without thinking what I was doing until it was too late to stop. That very night I left Tombstone. I knew there would be inquiries next day. I wandered over to Los Angeles where I hung out my single for the last time. I did well in that town. I met a young lady and fell in love. We were married two years when her horse spooked and ran away with the buggy. She was killed when the buggy turned over. I continued to practice my trade until I thought it time to retire. I then came looking for you jack. That brings you up to date."

"I still have $3,000 of the money. The question now is, where do we go from here?"

I quickly answered, "Andy, you are still welcome in my house and will always be. I can never repay you for what you did for my mother and me and besides, you did nothing wrong during the war and you're not a criminal."

Andy then asked, "What do we do with the money?" I told Andy I had a thought, but needed to sleep on it. Nothing was said the next day, but two days later I told Andy I was going into town and make some inquiries. I should be back in a couple days.

I went to a law office and asked about monies that were taken in a bank robbery and discovered to be left behind after the robbers were killed. I was informed the money would still belong to the bank if the bank was still in business.

I sent a telegraph to Nashville asking if the bank was still in business. The next morning the answer to my telegraph arrived. The bank folded five years ago. There were no outstanding bills owed by the bank. All monies were properly distributed to the depositors. All loans and collateral were accounted for.

I returned home and informed Andy of my findings. He still felt uneasy about the money, especially after spending $2,450 of the total. A couple of days later, Andy announced he was sending the balance of the money to the Nashville Children's Orphanage. No name and no return address. Andy did just that and I could see a worry was off his mind.

A few days later while we were sitting on the front porch enjoying coffee two men rode up. One wore a badge. He was a U.S. Marshall. "Doctor Andy Barth, you are under arrest for war crimes. It has taken a long time, but we finally trailed you here. We have been searching for you ever since you left Phoenix. We almost got you in Tombstone. We just missed you in Los Angeles."

Andy said nothing. I began telling them he had been found not guilty and all charges were dropped. You can check with Sheriff Jackson in Albuquerque. "And you sir are also under arrest for harboring a fugitive," replied the Marshall.

They bound both of us and took us to town. The sheriff was not in when we arrived, so the Marshall locked us in a cell. He then went to the telegraph office and sent a message to the Albuquerque sheriff.

Later that afternoon the sheriff arrived and asked, "Jack, why are you and Andy in my jail; who put you here?" About that time the Marshall arrived from the telegraph office and told him Andy was under arrest for war crimes and I was arrested for harboring a fugitive.

The sheriff went to his desk and withdrew a telegram he received from the Albuquerque sheriff some weeks back, confirming that Andy was cleared of any crimes during the war. No one ever came forward to testify against him. He was a free man.

The Marshall replied, I'll need to confirm that with Washington before releasing these two," which of course he did.

Andy stayed on with us for five more years before he died. I credit Andy with saving the life of my little girl Bertha. Bertha was bitten by some kind of bug while visiting the outhouse. She came running to the house and her arm began to swell. She became feverish and began to vomit. Andy doctored Bertha for over a week, both day and night. I'm sure he saved her life.

When my nearest neighbor accidently shot himself in the hip, Andy probed for the bullet. The neighbor was laid up for some time and Andy went by every day to assist his wife and young daughter in taking care of things around the house. Andy never asked for anything in return. Andy soon became the most loved person in the county. Whenever Andy heard of a sickness he would take the buckboard and ride to the residence. He always refused payment.

One day, Andy was out cutting firewood when he suddenly fell over, clutching his heart. I rushed him to town, but it was too late. Andy died.

Andy was never a bother. He carried his own weight and did all he could to help around the place. He was a kind and gentle man and he was true to his profession.

A few days after Andy died I was going through his belongings and came upon a letter addressed to me.

Dear Jack, this letter, I am sure will be a surprise to you. Three years ago I decided to inquire about my family estate back east.

My mother was from a wealthy family and had left everything to me as her only son. The bank tried to locate me without success.

Jack, my mother's estate came to $44,000, which was forwarded to my bank in a draft, which I left deposited in my account. Last year I withdrew the money and deposited it in the ground inside the barn. Go to the northeastern corner of the barn where you will find an old water barrel. Remove the barrel and dig. It's yours to keep. Enjoy it. Take good care of your family. I love you all. Your friend, Andy.

I was almost afraid to believe the letter. I called my wife Christine and had her read the letter. We went to the barn and removed the barrel. I began to dig and sure enough a tin box containing the money was there. I began to deposit a little at a time into my bank account. Within two years I had deposited it all.

I bought the farm we were living on and fixed the house up, adding indoor plumbing and lighting. I paid for my kids going to college and still had a few thousand dollars left for our old age.

My wife Christine died two years ago and I gave the farm to my kids to do with as they pleased and moved myself into this here retirement home. That was a mistake, I hate this place. People are always trying to take advantage of me. Now, that's my story. Go away and leave me alone.

"But sir, we need you to sign a release form, allowing us to print your story," said Helen.

"I'm not signing anything. If you want to print the story, do so."

The editor would not print the story without my signature. So I guess my story will never be told. But that's okay, I didn't want to tell it anyway.

End

Luke Summerset
Lucky Luke

Luke didn't have much of a childhood. Often times he had only one meal a day. Anything extra was far and between. He had little schooling. As soon as he learned to read and write at a third grade level, his schooling was over. Luke had only one change of clothes and both needed repairs.

George and Wilma Summerset, Luke's mom and dad, did the best they could with what they had. The only thing they could call their own was a horse and buggy.

Being born in a shack on the outer edge of Wonder, Arizona was not a good start in life for Luke. The town was known in the territory as the place to go after you ran out of places to go.

Wonder had one store, in a 10' X 10' shack. The restaurant was a tent with one table and three chairs. There were twenty places called houses. Only six of them were actually houses with a solid roof.

The next nearest town was twenty two miles away. That was the nearest anyone wanted to be to the town of Wonder.

In 1872, just two weeks after Luke's parents were killed in a horse and buggy accident, the town burned to the ground. According to Luke, "It took all of one hour for the whole town to burn."

Other than what he had on his back, Luke had nothing. Digging through what was left of the store, he found two left shoes. One could not walk in that part of the country barefooted. Luke put on the shoes.

Luke was fourteen years old at the time and had no working skills. His future seemed dismal, but he was willing to learn.

Luke began walking north. He had no idea where he was going. He had nothing but a little water and the clothes on his back. Three days walking and sleeping on bare ground, without a blanket and with no food, took its toll on Luke. He was near about ready to give up when he came upon some cowboys working cattle.

Luke was ragged and dirty and on his last legs. He asked for food and water. The cowboys took him to their bunk house. They fed him and had him take a bath. Luke then explained how he got himself in such a condition.

After good food and two days' rest, Luke asked for work. The cowboys replied that they had work, but without pay. It was two squares a day and a place to sleep.

Luke had no experience for the work and didn't even sit a horse very well. The cowboys loaned Luke a saddle and horse.

Luke learned to ride and soon could work a rope during steer branding. The cowboys liked Luke. He was a fast learner and he never complained about hard work. Luke was rather large for his age. He stood 5' 11" and weighed out at 180 pounds, when properly fed.

Luke learned to play cards with the cowboys. Actually, he was better at the game than most of them. Of course, match sticks as chips allowed Luke to make wild bets. Luke learned to read body language and facial expressions. He learned when to bet and when to fold.

Luke wasn't afraid of work. He often asked questions on how to become a cowboy and his new found friends always took time in teaching him the ropes.

One day, when mending fences, Luke ask his partner how it was him and the other cowboys never went to town and why he never saw any of them take a drink or smoke as he always thought cowboys did.

Lester, his partner that day, replied. "Life ain't always holding a good hand; life is playing a bad hand well." Luke wasn't sure he understood, but he never forgot the words.

When Luke turned fifteen, the cowboys gave him a used colt 45. Luke began to practice the quick draw as he had seen the others do. Luke had a single bullet the boys had given him just in case it was needed, when out on the range.

Luke didn't have money to make purchases in the distant town of Cacti, which was twenty miles east, so he had to do with what the cowboys gave him.

When Luke turned sixteen the cowboys informed him he would be a drover in the next cattle drive to market. Luke was pleased. He knew he was now a real cowboy, accepted by the others as being one of them.

The drive lasted just over a month and Luke was surprised to learn he was to be paid for his work, just like the others. Luke received $50 after the herd was sold at the Denver Stock Yards.

A few of the boys wanted to celebrate a little and meandered over to the saloon. Luke tagged along.

Luke had never tasted beer before and he found he didn't much care for it. After two small swallows, he left the remainder on the bar.

As Luke was observing a card game, he was confronted by one of the locals as to why he didn't finish his beer.

"I don't much care for the taste mister." Luke's remark was taken as not good enough for cowpunchers.

"You just step back to the bar and finish that beer," bellowed one of the locals.

"I told you, I don't like the taste," replied Luke.

We don't much cotton to you cowpunchers coming into our town acting all high and mighty. Now finish that beer or get ready to clear leather.

Luke suddenly remembered he had one round in the revolver and it was not chambered. "Listen mister, I'm not looking for trouble here. That was my first time tasting beer. Fact is, this is my first time in a saloon."

Hard Case opened his duster to better reach his hog leg. "You're no different than the others. You think you can come in here and take over. Not this time," he said as he reached for his revolver.

Luke, quick as a cat, drew his revolver and pointed it at hard case. "Mister, if you clear leather with that thing, I'll kill you."

The room was silent. Hard Case slowly removed his hand from his holster. "I was only kidding young fellow."

Luke stood firm with his revolver still in hand. "Mr. you have a crazy way of kidding. You almost got yourself killed."

Hard Case slowly backed toward the door. Just as Luke holstered his revolver and turned his back, Hard Case reached for his revolver. A shot rang out and hard case fell to the floor, grasping his shoulder.

The barkeep walked over to where the man lay with his pistol in hand. "You were going to shoot him in the back. You're never to come into my place again." As he turned to the crowd, he said, "Will some of you fellows get this piece of trash out of my saloon."

The cowboys told Luke it was time to return to camp. Arriving back in camp, Luke removed his holster and hung it over the saddle horn. Lester, his cowboy friend, checked the revolver and discovered the one round was not chambered. Lester asked Luke if he knew the round was not chambered.

Luke smiled, "Sure I did, but life ain't holding a good hand, its playing a bad hand well." Lester bellowed.

When Luke turned seventeen, he announced he was thinking of moving on. He had learned much from his cowboy friends and had become a regular hand. He received the same pay as the others and had saved all of it. Luke thanked them and shook hands all around.

Luke looked towards Lester. "Feel like taking a ride with a friend?" Nothing was said for a moment. Lester stepped up to Luke, put his hand forward and replied, "I reckon I'll stay here and play this hand." Nothing else was said as Luke rode from the ranch.

Luke felt good about his prospects. He had a little over one hundred dollars in his pocket and he figured to add to that somewhere along the trail.

Luke held a number of odd jobs along the way, mostly for grub and a place to sleep in the barn with his horse. Occasionally he was paid a little money.

Eight months went by when one day Luke came to the well-known "fork in the road." Luke took the trail farther west.

One month later Luke found himself in Reno, Nevada. The town was a busy place, and it was growing. Luke entered the first restaurant he saw and ordered a fine meal. Luke didn't look to be very prosperous and the proprietor questioned his ability to pay.

"I can pay alright. I'll never walk on a debt." Luke was served his meal and he ate every morsel.

As Luke was paying his bill he inquired, "Any place here 'bouts a fellow can get a little work?"

"Why sure, I can use a hand here in the restaurant."

Luke eyed the man and commented, "I'm a cattle man mister. I'll do most anything but swamping. I'll look around and see what's available." Luke went down the walkway and found himself outside the sheriff's office. He entered, introduced himself and asked. "Anyplace a fellow can get a job in this town, Sheriff?"

The sheriff looked Luke up and down. "You passing through or staying?"

"Well, I don't rightly know yet. Depends on what work I find."

"You look to be very young; how much experience do you have? Do you find it necessary to carry that hog leg?"

"Well, it saved my life once. It was necessary then," answered Luke. "I've worked cattle for the last few years. I'll turn eighteen next month. I can assure you I've lived beyond my years since I was fourteen years old."

"I'll ask around and let you know before the day is out. What's your name and where you staying?" asked the sheriff.

"I'll be camped on the west end of town Sheriff and my name's Luke Summerset. Don't bother to ride out to me. I'll come in tomorrow morning to see you. By the way Sheriff, what's your handle?"

"Most call me John, but a few call me Speedy."

"Which do you prefer?" asked Luke.

"My name's John Smart; John will do."

"Will now Sheriff, you got me to wondering. Why not Speedy?"

"You don't want to find out son. Just call me Sheriff John."

Luke rode to the edge of town where a creek crossed the dirt road leading into town. A few boulders were scattered up around a clump of trees. Luke set his camp and leaned his rifle against a small tree. He drew his revolver and checked to be sure a round was chambered. He hadn't forgotten a learned lesson. He soon had a coffee fire going. Luke sat on a boulder with his coffee in hand, pulled his hat down a ways and relaxed.

Luke was suddenly alert. He didn't know how long he had been asleep. He listened. He thought he heard footsteps.

"Don't move mister. I've got you covered," came a voice. "Throw that hog leg to the side. Careful now! I have an itchy finger."

Luke hadn't yet focused his eyes to the darkness. "Who are you? Why are you trespassing my camp?"

"Shut up. I'll be asking the questions. Where's your saddle bags?"

"Under the saddle," answered Luke. "Nothing much in them though. Just some food snacks."

"Throw the bags toward my voice and step back." Luke did as he was told. It was then the person stepped into the light of the fire to retrieve the saddle bags and Luke could see his face.

The man looked to be around fifty years old. He was heavy set, and dark hair covered most of his face. He was brandishing a rifle, pointed at Luke. Luke noticed the man only had three fingers on his gun hand and none were on the trigger. As the man reached down to get the saddle bags, Luke, quick as a cat, grabbed his rifle leaning against the tree and pointed it at the man.

"Drop the rifle mister, or I'll kill you." The man hadn't quite straightened up from retrieving the saddle bags. As he stretched himself to his full height, Luke saw him move his finger to the trigger. Luke fired. The bullet entered the man's right shoulder and made a large hole as it exited the back of the shoulder. He dropped to the ground.

The man never gained consciousness and he soon died. Luke found the man's horse about fifty yards away and brought it to his camp. He lifted the man onto his horse and secured him to the saddle. Then he mounted his horse and rode to town.

As Luke rode down the street, he saw Sheriff John making his evening rounds and called to him. Luke explained what took place. The sheriff lifted the man's head to get a look and made a chuckle.

"Young fellow, you just got yourself a very nice reward. This fellow is Short Hand Johnson. He's wanted by every lawman in this part of the country. He killed his wife and three kids when on a drunken spree back about six months ago over in Gold Camp. Since then he has killed three other men when he invaded their camp and took their valuables. There's a three-hundred-dollar reward for him, dead or alive. I'll take charge of the body. You come by tomorrow and collect your money. I'll send a telegraph out announcing the capture."

Luke was startled to find out just how close he had come to being killed. Even though it was justified, Luke felt terrible about taking another man's life. He wasn't so sure he wanted the reward.

Luke rode back to his camp, but he didn't sleep that night. Next morning Luke broke camp and rode into town. He stopped at the restaurant for breakfast and found Sheriff Smart just finishing up his meal. Luke asked the sheriff to join him for another coffee.

"Sheriff John, I don't think I want that reward. It just don't seem right to take a man's life and then collect money for doing so. I'm no bounty hunter."

Sheriff listened to what Luke had to say and then spoke. "Young fellow, this is a cruel world we live in. I don't like parts of my job because it requires doing what you did, but someone has to do it. Why should I not be paid to do what others don't want do. You didn't know who this fellow was. You were only defending yourself. There is no doubt he would have killed you. Take the reward. It will give you a head start. You're young and you will soon forget what took place here. Now, come on down to the office. We'll do the paperwork and I'll take you to the bank for your money." Luke followed the sheriff to his office.

While in the bank, waiting for the cashier and sheriff to return with the money, Luke was seated near the bank manager's office and overheard a conversation between the manager and a lady who evidently was having trouble making her ranch payments. The manager told her that if she didn't catch up by the end of the month, the bank would foreclose on her property and she would lose the ranch. She needed to come up with $350 in twenty days.

It suddenly occurred to Luke what he was going to do with the reward money. As the lady was leaving the bank, Luke was surprised to see she was young, perhaps not much older than he.

Luke rushed over to open the door for her. He removed his hat and introduced himself.

"Pardon ma'am, "My name's Luke Summerset. I would like to offer my assistance. I couldn't help overhearing your conversation with the banker. I have $350 that I don't need and don't want. You can do me a great favor by taking it and using it to catch up on your payments. If you have any doubts about the money, you can check with Sheriff Smart. He'll vouch for me."

The young lady asked, "Why would you do this? You don't even know me."

Luke replied, "You have a problem and I have a solution. It's just that simple Miss. No strings attached."

At that moment the sheriff and the cashier appeared and handed Luke $300. Luke reached in his pocket, withdrew $50 and added it to the $300, then handed it to the young lady. "There you are Miss. Go pay the bank their money and good luck to you."

Luke departed the bank and made his way to the restaurant. As he was entering, he glanced back to the bank and saw the young lady talking with Sheriff Smart.

Luke took a table and gave his order. As he was waiting for his meal, Sheriff Smart entered the restaurant and walked directly to him.

"That was a fine thing you just did Luke. That young lady lost her husband four months ago and she's having a rough time out on her ranch. All of the hands have left because she is unable to pay them and she was getting further behind. She also has a young son, about two years old I reckon. She needs help and don't know how to do much in the way of running a ranch."

"In that case sheriff, I reckon I can be a little more help to the lady. Tell me where her ranch is and I'll ride out and offer my help. All I need is a place to sleep and two squares a day. I know what it is to need help."

Luke rode by the livery and filled both canteens with fresh water and filled his saddle bags with oats for his horse. Two hours' ride brought him to the ranch. As he rode to the front of the house, the young lady appeared on the front porch, brandishing a double-barrel 12-guage shotgun.

"Hold on mister, this is private property." Luke eyed the shotgun and noticed the lady could hardly hold it upright because of the weight.

"Yes ma'am, I'm sure it is, just like all ranches in these parts. I didn't come here to create trouble or to cause you harm." Luke removed his hat. As soon as he did so, the lady recognized him.

"Mister, what are you doing here? I appreciate what you did, God knows how much I needed that help, but that don't give you any privileges." Luke started to dismount.

"Stay in the saddle mister. I know how to use this thing."

Luke put his hat back on. "I'm sure you do ma'am. The sheriff told me about your troubles. I know what it means to need a helping hand. I see you have a bunk house. I could sleep there and give you a hand in taking care of this place for two squares a day. I noticed when riding in, your cattle need care. I have experience in doing that. No strings attached ma'am. I'm sincere in my offer."

"I remember you said your name was Mr. Summerset. Is that correct?"

"Luke Summerset ma'am. My I ask your name?"

"My name's Sara Rodgers. Get down and come in the house."

Luke dismounted and followed Sara into the house. "You drink coffee Luke?"

"I sure do Sara, straight from the pot if you please."

Luke watched Sara as she poured the coffee. She was a striking figure of a woman and Luke could see that she was still on her guard. "How old are you Luke, and where did you get this experience you talk about?"

"Well Sara, I'm all of eighteen and for the last two years I worked cattle down in Arizona. I know I'm young, but that don't mean I don't know what I'm doing. You need help Sara and I need a place to stay and a little food. I can take my meals in the bunkhouse and I can take a bath in the creek. Take a chance with me Sara. You won't be sorry. I can help you."

"Alright Luke. I already know you have a soft heart. I'll take your offer. Go ahead and move into the bunk house." As Luke stood to leave, a small youngster in diapers came waddling into the room and eyed Luke.

"This is my son. Sam, meet Mr. Summerset." Sam smiled and Luke gave him a rub on the head.

"Good to meet you Sam. We'll be seeing a lot of each other, I'm sure."

Luke looked things over in the bunkhouse and was pleased to see it was clean and comfortable. He walked over to the barn and found the place needed some repairs; also the two horses and one mule needed attention. He quickly took care of that. He then mounted his horse and rode out to look over the spread. He estimated about five hundred head on a thousand acres. More work than one man could handle. Luke noticed fence work was needed in a number of places.

It was getting late and Luke rode back to the bunkhouse to wash up. As he was tending to his horse, Sara came into the barn and announced she would bring his supper to the bunkhouse.

Luke replied, "Don't bother Sara, you can hand it to me on the porch and I'll take it from there."

Sara served up a fine meal. Potatoes, beef, corn on the cob, a well buttered biscuit and coffee. As he returned the platter to the porch, Sara was rocking her son Sam in the chair and Luke thanked her for the fine meal.

Sara said nothing, as she eyed Luke and pointed to her sleeping son. Luke understood and returned to the bunkhouse.

Luke didn't sleep well that night. He was mostly thinking about what needed to be done on the ranch, but he also thought of Sara. She was the finest looking woman he had ever seen. Of course, he had never been close to any woman before and didn't rightly know how or what to say to them.

Come morning, Luke was up at the crack of dawn and did some needed work in the garden. He gathered up corn, string beans and cabbage and deposited them on the porch for Sara. He returned to the bunkhouse to wash up for breakfast. As he waited, Sara came outside and deposited the platter on a table on the porch and collected the vegetables. "Good morning Sara, I hope you rested well last night."

"I rested well Mr. Summerset."

"Oh, were back to being formal again. Very well Mrs. Rogers. I'll be in the barn taking care of the animals and then I'll be riding out to tend to the stock and make some fence repairs. You stay here and tend to your son. I'm sure he will enjoy the attention." Luke turned and walked to the barn, thinking to himself, "I sure have a lot to learn about women."

Luke put in a long day and it was well after suppertime when he returned to the bunkhouse. He washed up, thinking he would walk down to the creek after supper and take himself a bath. He walked to the porch of the house and found his meal on the table. The food was cold and so was the coffee.

Luke knew he had worked a little long in the day, but serving cold food after a hard day's work was uncalled for. Luke called out,

"Mrs. Rogers, could you please warm up my food?" He received no answer. "Mrs. Rogers, are you there?" Still no answer. Luke opened the screen door and called out. "Mrs. Rogers, where are you?" Again no answer. Luke suddenly became alarmed. He wandered through the house. Sara and the baby were gone. He rushed to the barn. One horse and the buckboard were gone.

Luke realized Sara was not the kind of woman to just up and leave without an emergency. Luke re-saddled his horse and headed for town.

Entering from south of town, Luke saw Sara's buckboard in front of the doctor's place. He rushed inside to find the doctor standing over little Sam. Sam wasn't moving.

Sara looked up and saw Luke standing there. Sara cried out, "He fell off the porch and hit his head on a rock. He hasn't opened his eyes since." Luke removed his hat and looked down to Sam. The doctor glanced at Luke with a slight nod of his head and spoke softly. "He has a broken neck, I can't help him."

Suddenly, Sam stopped breathing. Sara stood transfixed, looking at her son. She began to sob and fell to the floor. The doctor put his arms around Sara to comfort her as she continued to cry.

It was a very uncomfortable situation for Luke. He felt terrible, remembering what he had said to Sara early that morning before departing the house. He knew Sara would now need help more than ever. She had lost both her husband and son, and if she stayed on the ranch she would need someone with experience on running such a spread. Sara knew little about cattle and how or why things were done a certain way. Also Sara had no money to run the place and Luke remembered he had only $50 left in his pocket.

The doctor consoled Sara the best he could. He took her to another room and had his wife stay with Sara, while he took charge of little Sam. It was times like this when being a doctor was at its worst, for it was now necessary to ask Sara if she wanted her baby buried in the city cemetery of did she wish to take little Sam home to the ranch for burial.

Doctor Jack asked Luke who he was and why he was there. Luke explained his reason for being there and how he had been helping Sara at the ranch. Luke told the doctor how it was a delicate situation for Sara, as it was only the two of them at the ranch and Sara attempted to keep things as formal as possible. Doctor Jack understood.

Doctor Jack went into the room where Sara had somewhat consoled herself. Being as delicate as he could, he asked Sara, "I need to know what your intentions are in regards to your son. Should I make the arrangements for you here in town?"

Sara faced the doctor with swollen eyes, "No thank you doctor, I'll take my son home to be buried next to his father there on the ranch."

"Very well Sara, I'll prepare him and do the paperwork. You stay here with my wife."

The service at the ranch was a small affair. The doctor and his wife were there, along with the sheriff and Luke. The minister mentioned that the good Lord had himself another angel to work with. He then expressed his condolences to Sara, boarded his wagon and rode away.

The doctor's wife took Sara to the house while Luke and the sheriff lowered the small box and covered the grave. There was nothing more to do but continue as before.

After the others had left, Luke went to the bunkhouse. He felt terrible. He knew Sara was in the big house with no one to talk with or to attend to and she would be lonely and confused.

Luke got little sleep that night. As daylight approached, Luke went to the well to wash up and saw Sara sitting among the two graves. He decided it best if he did nothing. He went to the barn and attended to the horses and mule. He would forgo breakfast that morning and work around the barn and house, just to be close to Sara. At the least, she would know someone was around and she wasn't alone.

Luke kept himself busy all day. About supper time, he saw Sara bring the food tray to the table on the porch and turned to go back into the house. Luke called to Sara.

"Mrs. Rogers, would you care to talk with me while I eat here on the porch?"

"No thank you Mr. Summerset, I have things to do in the house," answered Sara.

"I have things to do also, but I can take time for supper and a little talk. Don't isolate yourself Sara. You won't gain anything by doing so."

Sara stopped and turned to Luke. "Mr. Summerset, I have no intention of isolating myself. I understand I now must run this ranch and I intend to learn all that I can to make it a paying ranch. If you wish to stay, you may do so and I thank you for it. If you wish to leave, please do so as soon as possible. I have no time for idle talk. That's all I have to say at this time."

Luke was surprised. "Well now Miss Rogers, there's no way you can run this spread by yourself. Fact is, the two of us can't run this place very long without another hand. I think I'll ride into town and make inquiries. What do you think of that?"

"Suit yourself Mr. Summerset. I'm busy in the house." Luke took Sara's comment as an approval of his remark about another hand.

"I'll be riding to town in the morning. Good night Miss Rogers. Have a good night's rest."

Luke was up early. He did his chores, then saddled his horse and rode out. Arriving in town he went directly to the sheriff's office.

"Sheriff, I'm looking for another hand at the ranch. Someone with a little experience with cattle and who needs a place to relax after a day's work. The job pays two squares a day and a comfortable place to live and sleep. Do you know of anyone with those qualifications?"

The sheriff chuckled, "Luke, were all looking for someone like that. If I find him I'll keep him for myself, but I'll ask around anyway and let you know. Where are you going to be?" he said as he offered Luke a cup of coffee.

"I'll be around. I'll check back this afternoon before returning to the ranch. See you, and thanks."

Luke had left the ranch way before breakfast that morning and he was hungry. When leaving the restaurant, Luke was passing one of the town's many saloons and heard loud talking and laughing. He stopped and looked over the bat-wing doors and observed a game of poker in progress, with a small crowd around the table.

Luke had always enjoyed the game of poker with the boys back on the ranch where he had gained his cattle experience. But of course, they always played with match sticks for money. He had never actually played for real money before.

Luke decided it was time to acquaint himself with real poker. He entered the Wild Horse Saloon and discovered the ante was only ten cents a hand.

"Say, is this an open game?" ask Luke.

"Well it is If'n you got any money," answered one player.

"I got a little," replied Luke as he pulled up a chair to the open spot at the table.

Luke entered his ante for the next hand, received his five cards and waited. One fellow bet twenty-five cents. The next two follows dropped. Luke took a look at his cards and raised $.50. The next two fellows dropped, leaving Luke and the original better in the hand. The fellow smiled at Luke, "Think you got yourself a hand there young fellow?"

"It's the best hand I've had all year," replied Luke.

"Well, before I raise you young fellow, let's have a drink. Barkeep, two whiskeys here."

"Sorry mister, I don't drink," replied Luke.

"Just how old are you young fellow?"

"I'm eighteen and we need to get along in this poker hand if you don't mind," answered Luke.

"Sure thing kid, I raise you a dollar." Luke called.

"How many cards you want kid?"

"I think I'll just play these if you don't mind," replied Luke. Everyone at the table turned toward Luke.

"The first hand being a pat hand is a bit unusual kid. You sure you know how to play this game?" asked his opponent.

"We'll soon find out," answered Luke. "I'll take one card," said the opponent.

"It's your bet mister," said Luke.

"Well kid, you don't drink and I see you don't smoke. I like you, so I'm going to take it easy on you and bet only ten dollars."

Luke took another peek at his hand. "I don't have much money mister, but I can call that bet and raise you ten dollars. Luke put twenty dollars on the table. Patrons began to gather around the table.

"That's good kid, I call your raise and raise you twenty dollars."

Luke took another peek at his hand. "I don't have any more money mister."

"What are you going to do kid? You're out of money," replied the opponent.

Luke thought for a moment. "Any of you gentlemen in this here saloon care to share in this hand for a split?" There were no takers. There was no doubt in Luke's mind, he had the winning hand.

"Tell you what mister, I'll stay in the hand and work for you for as long as it takes to pay you back. For every dollar I lose, I'll put in a day's labor." The crowd around the table began to murmur. Some thought the kid was bluffing.

"You're on kid." Luke called the twenty dollars and raised twenty five dollars.

"That's a hefty bet kid. I can use the extra help at my ranch, so I'll call that twenty five and raise you fifty."

Luke began to think. This thing is getting out of hand. I've got a good hand, but obviously he does too.

"No use dragging this thing any further. I'll just call your fifty mister." The gentleman smiled and turned over five red hearts.

"That's a nice hand Mister, but I don't think I'll be working for you any time soon." Luke turned over three fours and two sevens---a full house.

The crowed in the saloon went a little wild. Luke's opponent stood up and reached across the table.

"I want to shake your hand kid. That was the most exciting poker hand I've been in for quite a spell. What's your name?"

Luke extended his hand. "Luke Summerset is my name, what's yours?"

"My name is John Middleman. I own this here saloon and a thousand-acre ranch and farm down in the Carson Valley area. Are you looking for work?"

"No Mr. Middleman, I've got myself a job. It don't pay much, but it's a nice place to work."

At that instant one of the patrons commented, "It should be a good place to work with that Sara Rogers gal there and just the two of you."

Luke turned and hit the man square on the chin. As the man was lifting himself from the floor he was also drawing his revolver. Luke drew his hog leg and had it pointed at the man's midsection before he could even clear leather.

"Mister, that kind of talk could get you killed where I come from. Mr. Middleman, do you know this man?" Middleman looked at Luke.

"Why yes, I do, and please call me John."

"OK, John, what should I do with him?"

"Just let him go Luke. He's a good man and he's had a little too much to drink. If he was sober he would never say such a thing."

"All right John, I'm taking your word for it. Go home and sober up mister."

"Where you from Luke?" asked John.

Luke began putting the money in his pocket. "I'm from down Arizona way. A Place called Wonder, or did. It burned to the ground the day I left."

"Where you headed when you leave here?" asked John.

"Well, I don't rightly know, but I'll know it when I get there. Meanwhile, I'm going back to the Rogers Ranch. Sara needs help out there.

John studied Luke. "The way I see it, you just won yourself a smart amount of money. I'll draw cards against you for that amount."

Luke studied John and asked, "Did you ever go three or four days without anything to eat John?"

"Why no, can't say I have, but what's that got to do with anything?"

"I have John, more times than I care to count. Sorry John, but I need the money," answered Luke.

"I'm not one to go lightly when losing at the poker table Luke. I want a chance to get my money back. Tell you what. I'll put up this here saloon against your winnings. We draw one card each from the deck. High card wins the bet."

"Are meals included in ownership of this saloon John?"

"Why yes they are. I eat two squares a day here."

"Then I can't hardly pass a bet like that. Which one of us draws first?" asked Luke as he put his money back on the table, while John wrote out a bill of sale on the saloon.

"We draw twice, first for who draws first, second for the bet. Fair enough?"

"Sounds fair to me John." Luke turned toward the bar. "Barkeep, you mix the cards please. By the way, if I win do you stay on as barkeep or leave with John?"

"I'll stay with the saloon," answered the barkeep.

Luke drew a jack. "If that's high card I want to draw second." John stepped up to the table and drew an eight.

"My jack's high, you draw first John. Tell you what, if I win you work for me here in the saloon for the next three months, no pay, just found. You win; I'll work the same for you here in the saloon, just found."

"That's a deal Luke, shake."

Luke turned to the keep, "What's your name barkeep? I'd like to know who all will be working for me."

"My name's Luke, just like yours. You can call me Big Luke," he said as he finished mixing the cards. Everyone backed away from the table. John turned toward the bar, downed a shot and approached the card table, drew one card and turned over a queen, as a wide smile creased his face.

"That's a right smart draw John. Don't give me much room does it?" commented Luke. Luke stepped to the table and started to reach when John interrupted.

"Hold on Luke. I need help at the ranch. I'll sweeten the pot. I'll put up the ranch with the saloon, your choice if you win. If I win, you work for me for five years, regular pay."

"What all you got on that ranch John?" asked Luke.

"Not much, just a ranch house, bunk house, barn, a few mules and horses and two hundred head of cattle on one thousand acres. Cattle not part of the bet though."

"I'll take your bet; shake," replied Luke. "By the way John, where is your ranch located in that Carson Valley?"

"My ranch borders the Rogers Ranch, Luke. You can continue to help Miss Rogers while taking care of your place. That is if you win."

Luke stepped to the table, drew his card and turned it over. Queen of spades. The crowd in the saloon went wild. "Never seen nothing like this before," one bystander shouted; you fellows will have to draw again.

John began to sweat. "Big Luke, pour one for me."

Luke, sitting at the table, was deep in thought. "John, I'll add another five years to the bet, if you throw in the cattle."

"You've got yourself a bet Luke," uttered John.

Big Luke mixed the cards and stepped from the table.

"Your cards, Mr. Middleman." John reached over and took one card---the ten of hearts.

"That gives me a little more room," said Luke, as he took his card. Before turning it over Luke asked John,

"Is the bet over or do we continue?"

"Bet's over," said John. Luke turned over a king of diamonds.

"Drinks on the house," shouted Big Luke.

"Hold on Big Luke, you don't own this place. It's me or John that owns it. John, which of the two places gives you the most income?"

"Well the saloon gives a steady income, I get paid every day. The ranch pays as it goes as I sell cattle or rent out my horses and mules."

Luke thought for a moment. "I'll take the ranch."

"Done," shouted John. "Ok Big Luke, serve those drinks," said John.

"What amount of capital will I need to run the ranch?" asked Luke.

"Won't take much," answered John. "You'll need money to pay the drovers to do the branding and to drive the cattle to market, unless they're willing to wait until you sell the cattle."

"Big Luke, bring me a coffee while I think this over." Luke sat quietly by himself enjoying his coffee. Suddenly he sprang to his feet and shouted, "John, how would you like a chance to get part your ranch back?"

"I'm listening Luke; which part and what's the deal?"

"One hand of draw poker. If I win, I get the saloon. If you win, you get your ranch back, but less the cattle."

"What good will the ranch be to me without cattle?"

"Not much," answered Luke, but if I win, I'll trade you the cattle for the saloon."

"That's about a no win situation for me Luke. Not much of a loss for you either way."

"That's the deal John. What do you say?"

"Did you say you were only nineteen years old kid?"

"Yes, I'm nineteen," answered Luke. "You in or out John?"

"I'll need to sweeten the pot a little, sort of soften the odds," answered John. "If I win and after we trade Cattle for the saloon, you work for me for five years on the ranch. Regular pay."

"Done," answered Luke. "Big Luke, shuffle the cards."

Luke and John took their seats at the table as a crowd gathered around. Luke and John had suddenly become the most popular men in Reno.

"Whatever happens John, let's be friends. You're a good winner and you're a good loser. If I end up working for you I'll be a regular hand during work hours. Big Luke will be my manager in the saloon. Ok with you Big Luke?"

"Ok Little Luke."

Luke smiled, "Call me lucky, if you please."

Big Luke dealt the cards. John peeked at his cards first as Luke studied him.

"Got yourself a hand eh John?" Luke took a look at his hand. He had nothing but an Ace and a King. No pairs.

Big Luke turned to John, "Cards John?"

"I'll take two," answered John.

"Three of a kind. Want to win this hand John? You'll need to sweeten that hand."

"How many cards do you want Luke?" asked Big Luke.

"I think I'll just play these," answered Luke. John took a glance at Luke,

"I got my hand Luke, what you got?"

"You were dealt first John, you show first," answered Luke.

"Luke, you sure you want our friendship to start or end this way?"

"What you getting at John?" asked Luke.

"Let's make a final bet. Throw these hands away. Play three hands of poker, first to win two hands takes all. You win everything I own or I win everything you own. No other side bets. Very last hands. What do you say?"

"I came in here with nothing; the worse I can leave with is the same. You got yourself a bet Mr. Middleman." "Please Luke, call me John!"

"Big Luke, get a new deck of cards, shuffle them good. We're about to play some poker, the likes neither of us fellows have played before. That right Luke?"

"That's right John."

Bystanders began betting among themselves as to who would be the winner.

"Hold on fellows, no betting among yourselves. We don't want any hard feelings after the hand. No other betting until this hand is over, that right Luke?"

"I'll agree to that John."

Big Luke finished shuffling the cards and dealt five cards each to the players.

"How many cards you want John?"

"I'll take three cards, thank you."

"How about you Luke?"

"I'll take a like amount."

Both men turned over their hands. John had a pair of sevens. Luke had a pair of threes.

Big Luke dealt the next hand. "How many Luke?'

"I'll take two cards." You, John?

"I'll take one card."

Both men turned over their hands. John had a pair of fours and a pair of nines. Luke had a pair of jacks and a pair of two's. One hand a peace. Now for the final hand.

"Gentlemen, any last words before this hand is dealt?" asked Big Luke.

John stood up, reached across the table, "Always friends Luke?"

"Always," answered Luke.

The cards were dealt.

"How many John?" asked Big Luke.

"I'll take three," answered John.

"Likewise," said Luke.

Both players turned over their hands. John had a pair of fours, a King, Ten and Three. Lucky Luke had a pair of fours, a King, Ten and Three. Both men stared at the cards. No one had ever seen such a hand of cards. Nothing was said for a few moments.

John slowly rose from his chair, looked over to Luke, extended his hand and asked, "Partners or one more hand?"

Luke took the hand and answered, "Partners John!"

Word soon spread over town about the most unusual poker game and about the outcome. No one had ever seen or heard of anything like it. It had to be a first in the west.

There was one more hand to be played. High card draw for who does what. High card gets the choice of running the ranch or bossing the saloon. Luke drew first. King of diamonds was his card. John drew a three of hearts.

"Well Lucky Luke, I'll guess you want the saloon?"

Luke studied John, "Not necessarily John. I hope to make this a three way deal."

"You got something you want to talk about Luke?" asked John.

"Yes I do John. Let's take the table in the corner and talk."

The two men took a seat and Luke turned to John. "You said the Rogers ranch borders your ranch. You have one thousand acres. The Rogers ranch is also one thousand acres. She has five hundred head and you have two hundred head. Seven hundred head roaming on two thousand acres would be a good thing. We would have two barns, two houses, two bunkhouses. In other words we would have double of everything we now have as partners. I of course have not talked to Sara about this, but I can't think of any reason she would turn us down. It would save her ranch and give her a secure place to live. She's all alone. To tell you the truth John, I think I have gone soft for the lady."

John studied Luke. "I figured that when you hit that fellow on the chin. I think it's a grand idea. If she's for it, then I'm for it."

It was then the sheriff entered the saloon. "Well Luke, I've talk around town. No takers. You'll have to come up with another idea for help at the ranch."

Luke smiled. "I think I just did. Thanks anyway sheriff. I'm heading for the ranch. Wish me luck."

"You couldn't have any more than you already have," replied John.

Sara wasn't on the porch when Luke arrived and the front door was closed. That usually meant she was retiring for the day. Luke went to the bunkhouse and there found Sara cleaning the place. Sara looked to Luke. "You need to do a better job of keeping the place clean Mr. Summerset."

Luke bit his tongue before speaking. "Sara, I've had just about enough of this formal situation between us. I'm going to call you Sara and I expect you to call me Luke. I not here to do you harm, I'm here to help. I understand the position you're in and why you need to act the way you do toward me. Some people may not understand what is really going on here. Actually, I don't care one iota what they think of me, but I do care about what they think you. Now, if you don't want me here, please say so. I can be gone within the hour."

Sara just stared at Luke. She then started toward the house. Suddenly she started to run and tripped and fell. Luke rushed to her. He knelt next to her and asked if she was ok.

"I'm ok Luke. Just leave me alone for a while. I have some thinking to do."

"Ok Sara. I'll be in the bunkhouse if you need anything."

Night soon fell on the ranch. Luke had a few pieces of hardtack and water. He was not going to disturb Sara now.

Daylight came much too early for Luke. He was tired and hungry. He went to the barn and took care of the animals and then washed up. He didn't know if Sara would be serving breakfast. If she didn't, he would take it as meaning he was to leave the ranch.

Luke was looking out the bunkhouse window when he saw Sara come out on the porch with a tray of food and put it on the table. He felt relieved that she wanted him to stay.

Luke retrieved the tray and was walking toward the bunkhouse when Sara called after him. "You're welcome to eat here on the porch if you please Luke. We can talk."

"Good morning Sara. Thanks for the invite. I will." Luke began to eat, for he was very hungry. The coffee was hot and the biscuits were well buttered. Luke devoured the meal. Sara watched him as he ate. Finally she spoke.

"What do we do now Luke?"

Luke looked up from his food. "I've been waiting for you to ask that question Sara." Luke set his plate aside. "I want you to listen to what I have to say and I want you to think hard when I'm through talking before giving me an answer.

I spent all day in town yesterday. I got lucky in a poker game with a fellow named John Middleman. He has the thousand acres joining your thousand. He lost a poker hand to me and we became partners in his ranch and the Wild Horse Saloon in town. You have a chance to become the third partner, if you're willing to join the ranches to gather and make one large spread. It's an answer to your problems Sara, and I'll get to see you every day. Now, think hard before answering."

Sara looked to Luke with a slight smile. "I like the part where you get to see me every day and having a larger spread with 700 head is much better than the 500 we now have. I like the idea Luke. I can't keep living this way. I need female companionship, someone of my gender to talk with."

Suddenly Luke looked over Sara's shoulder and saw riders approaching the house. They looked to be riding fast.

"Sara don't ask questions, just do as I say. Go into the house. Barricade yourself in a bedroom. Take your shotgun with you. Don't let anyone in." Sara immediately ran inside the house. Luke ran to the bunkhouse for his rifle and revolver and ran back to the house and posted himself just inside the front room.

As the riders entered the yard, they slowed their mounts. One fellow dismounted and called out. "Anyone here?"

"Just me mister, what do you want," answered Luke.

"We need water for our horses and a little grub if you please. Come on out so's we can see you."

"Water's in the well. I don't have any grub," answered Luke.

"Sure would like to see who we're talking to. Come on out." Luke saw the other two riders dismount and creep towards the house.

"You tell those other two to get back on their horses and ride out with you. This is private property. You're not welcome here."

"That's not very hospitable mister. We just need something to eat and a place to rest our horses. Do you have any feed in the barn?"

"There's feed in the barn alright, but it's for my stock. I don't have any extra," answered Luke. "You fellows will have to ride on."

Luke noticed that one fellow took rifle in hand and chambered a round.

"If that fellow points that rifle at the house, I will kill him and then you mister. Now, ride out before someone makes a big mistake," shouted Luke.

"We'll leave mister. I don't much like your hospitality. We'll be back. You watch for us."

"If you come back, there won't be any talking. I'll kill the first of you that comes into the yard." The three left and Luke watched until he could no longer see them in the distance. He called out to Sara. "Come on out, there gone for now." Sara came out with shotgun in hand.

"Stay here in the house. I'll harness the horse to the buckboard. I want you to ride into town and inform the sheriff what just took place here. Take the backroad to town. It's a little longer around, but it's safer. Don't come back with the sheriff. Stay in town until I come for you. Do you understand?" Sara was now crying. She was scared for Luke.

"What are you going to do Luke? Those men will kill you if they get the chance."

"We don't have time to talk about it Sara. Stay here. I'll get the buckboard." Luke harnessed the horse and drove to the front of the house. Sara came out and mounted the wagon. Luke handed her the shotgun and slapped the horse. Sara quickly rode out.

Luke went into the house and closed and locked the window shutters. Each shutter had a gun slot, so Luke could see anyone approach the house. He moved furniture against the front entrance and put a brace across the rear entrance. He went to the attic and made himself comfortable. He could see far in the distance. He would see anyone approaching long before they expected him to do so. Luke began the long wait.

Luke awoke with a start. It was just turning daylight. He rushed down to check his fortifications. Nothing had been changed. He rushed back to the attic and scanned the horizon. Nothing was moving. He sure could use some of Sara's breakfast cooking. He continued to wait.

The sun was high in the sky when Luke saw a movement out near the old corn crib, about 75 yards away. Suddenly, there were three of them---one behind the corn crib, one behind a rock and the third behind a large tree. Luke cocked his rifle and checked his revolver. He knew they wouldn't expect him to be in the attic. Luke took position and pointed his rifle, waiting for one to show himself. The one behind the crib came out in a crouch and moved toward the house. Luke fired his rifle. One down, two to go. The others opened fire at the house, never firing at the attic. Luke didn't want to return fire and give away his position. He waited.

When Luke didn't return fire, the two remaining thought they got him on their first volley. They cautiously approached the house. When about 25 yards from the house Luke fired. Two down. The last of the bunch began to retreat.

In the far distance, Luke saw riders approaching and a buckboard trailing the riders. The robber's horse was too far away for him to get to in time. He dashed to the corn crib in an attempt to hide.

Sheriff Smart rode into the yard and yelled out for Luke. "Luke, you there? You ok Luke?"

"I'm as ok as I can get sheriff. The last of the bunch is hiding in the old corncrib. Careful sheriff, he's armed."

The five-man posse all pointed their rifles at the corncrib. "You better come out from there mister, we've got five rifles pointed at you. You don't have a chance. If you fire on us we'll kill you," shouted Sheriff Smart.

Slowly the crib door opened and a rifle was thrown out, followed by a revolver.

The robber appeared with his hands in the air. He was soon tied to his saddle and sheriff Smart told the posse to take him to town and put him in jail.

"There will be an inquest on this situation Luke. You come into town tomorrow morning," ordered the sheriff.

"I'll be there sheriff and thanks for the helping hand."

"From what I see here, you didn't need any help," answered the sheriff.

Sara was in sitting the buckboard waiting for the conclusion of everything. Luke went to her. "I told you to stay in town. Are you okay Sara?"

"I'm as okay as I'm going to get Mr. Summerset." Sara smiled at Luke and began to laugh. Luke began to laugh also.

"I'm Glad to see that you're okay Mrs. Rogers."

Sara looked to the house. "Looks like someone tried to shoot the place apart. Can you explain that Mr. Summerset?"

"I sure can Mrs. Rogers. Some fellows wanted to steal my girl from me and I put up a fight." Sara stared at Luke. She started to smile.

"Seems this Mrs. Rogers owes someone a thank you." Sara went to Luke and kissed him on the cheek.

"Seems this Mr. Summerset liked that thank you, and now he has one of his own." Luke took Sara in his arms and kissed her. "How is that for a thank-you Mrs. Rogers?"

Sara looked deep into Luke's eyes and replied, "I would like another thank you Mr. Summerset.

Luke again took Sara in his arms, and as she closed her eyes he whispered, "Will you be my saddle mate?"

Sara answered, "I will."

End

Buster Johnson

Introduction

Sitting around the campfire after the day's activities, old Buster Johnson loved to tell stories about his adventures. Buster had a different story to tell each night we stayed at his dude ranch.

One of Buster's stories really impressed me and I asked for permission to write the story and have it printed into book form. Buster consented, but insisted, "Don't embellish the story or leave anything out."

Buster is a little bent over these days and his get-along is a little slow, but his eyes are as bright as his mind is sharp. Buster's been around these parts since 1865, and everyone who knows him highly respects him.

One particular evening after the beans and hardtack were consumed, Buster scraped loose pebbles away from a spot in front of the fire and took a seat. He fired up his pipe, took a deep drag and for a while studied the stars, letting his pipe grow cold after a final draw. Buster took a sip of his coffee and began his story.

******

The northern fork of the north fork of the Yuba River flowed down from somewhere above Sierra City, California. Our camp was somewhat southwest of the town, about 50 yards in from the river. The ground was so rich one feller once collected $500 from one shovel full. That's why they named the place, "One-Shovel."

I was 25 years old in 1865, and was one of the earlier arrivals. I had already staked my claim and was busy in laying out the foundation for my shack when I looked up to see this feller leaning on his shovel and giving me the eye. He was tall and slim. His clothes loosely hung on him like they were two sizes large. He looked lost standing there leaning on his shovel. I thought he was the most unusual looking feller I ever did see.

Not knowing his name I says, "Hello Slim." Not knowing my name he says, "Hello Shorty." From that time on everyone that knew us in One-Shovel referred to us as Slim and Shorty. I inquired where he was staking his claim.

He leaned a little harder on his shovel and replied, "Right here's my corner if you don't mind."

There was something about the man that I took to right off. I suddenly felt I'd found my partner. "That's alright with me Slim; why don't we double up on the deal and make our claims so nobody can wedge between us?"

Slim leaned on his shovel, bobbed his head up and down, "That sounds like a good one to me. My Name's Gus Ferro." Slim continued to lean on his shovel and asked, "What'll we do now?" I suddenly thought I had a greenhorn on my hands.

"My Name's Buster Johnson; you have any mining experience Slim?"

"Well, I got a little, but not much."

I told him, "I would never have guessed it, but that's ok, you can learn as we go." Slim almost let a smile cross his face.

Slim staked his claim next to mine and we each built a shack about twenty feet apart, but under one roof, making a shed between us for storage.

I told Slim, "I earlier tested the ground and there was about eight feet of gravel down to bedrock. We'll need to sink a draft to get at pay dirt."

"That sounds like a good one to me," replied Slim.

I mentioned, "The best colors will probably be along the draw that runs through both our claims. We'll need a hoist to bring dirt to the surface. If you help me hoist one day, I'll help you hoist the next."

Slim nodded, "I reckon that's a good one."

Well, that's the way we set things between us. Each working for his self and yet helping the other.

After completing our shacks and setting the grounds the way we wanted them, we built the hoist and went to work. Slim surprised me. He would work the hoist, dump the bucket on the dirt pile and send the bucket back down faster than I was ready for it. He worked like a beaver and never complained about being tired. Slim also insisted on doing the cooking for both of us. Course, bacon, beans and coffee weren't all that complicated.

At the end of each week we would clean up and wash our dirt pile. I could never figure why I always had more gold in my pile then Slim. One week I had over fourteen ounces while slim said he had only nine ounces.

Slim had his usual way of explaining things. "You're a better washer then I am and don't spill as much as I do." I let that pass.

It was getting along in the year and Slim was doing better in saving gold from his pile, but he was still short of what I was saving.

One morning in early October it was, I went to the river for a bucket of water and felt a chill in the air. Getting back to the claim I mentioned to Slim, "We should be thinking about getting supplies in for the winter."

With Slim's usual lost look, he asked, "How do we get supplies in here and how much will it cost?"

"Bout $300 apiece should do it," I answered. "We'll need beans, sowbelly, flour, candles, tobacco and a few other things."

Slim took another lean on his shovel, "I can't spare that much. Maybe $200 is the best I can do."

I told Slim, "You can pay me back next year." I then went looking for Pack Mule Joe and gave him our order.

Joe arrived back in camp with our supplies just before the first snows came. Good thing too, for after being snowed in, the only way to get anything into camp was by snowshoes and backpack.

Those fellers who didn't do well in their cleanup went packing just before the first snow. Some went into Downieville and some to Grass Valley and a few to Nevada City. They couldn't afford the price of winter supplies. As it were, we paid as high as $.20 a pound for our supplies to be hauled into camp. Pack Mule Joe also brought in newspapers from the outside and sold them for a dollar apiece. Me and Slim read them papers till there weren't enough left to start a fire.

Slim was always thinking about how to save. He suggested we bunk together in the same shack for the winter to save firewood. We could do all our cooking and keep warm with one fire. Slim weren't leaning on his shovel when he made that suggestion neither. We worked our claims almost every day that first winter, building our dirt piles for the coming spring.

One morning as I was in the hole, Slim called out, "You better come up here Shorty." I could tell by his voice something was up. As I crawled out of the hole, just about twenty-five yards away were four timber wolves.

Slim had his shovel in hand and shouted, "Go fetch the rifle and shotgun from the cabin." Slim stood his ground as I returned.

He took the shotgun, "Which ever one takes the first step forward was to be the first one shot for that will most likely be the leader." Slim raised his shotgun and waited. Suddenly the largest of the pack stepped out front and Slim let loose with his twelve-gauge, followed by the second barrel shot. That left only two of the four and they took off to the unknown. Slim suggested we drag the two dead ones further into the timber so the other two would find them for their next meal, keeping them away from our camp.

I must have had a certain look on my face. I was about to ask Slim how he knew so much about wolves.

"Don't bother, it's not much of a story."

On occasion someone in camp would ask Slim how we were doing with our claim. Slim always had an answer. "Well, were putting beans on the table with a little coffee and that's about it. Nothing bigger than sand. If things don't get better we may have to move on."

Pack Mule Joe, out of ear shot of the others, said, "Who you fellers kidding?" Slim would just lean on his shovel and smile.

As spring arrived we commenced to panning and sluicing our collected gravel piles. It was richer than we thought it would be. We were averaging around $300 a day, working from sunup to sundown. Afterwards we would take our meal and go right to bed as we were too tuckered to sit and talk.

We worked our claims right through the summer until late September. We then began putting our camp in winter shape again when Slim suggested we think on getting supplies into camp for the winter.

I told Slim, "I agree, but we should also be thinking about getting our gold to the San Francisco Mint for coining. We could ship our gold by express or carry it ourselves and enjoy a couple days in San Francisco."

Slim mentioned, "I would like to see San Francisco again, and while we're there I can check for any mail at general delivery."

Slim gave me an extra hundred for what he owed from last winter. We gave our order to Pack Mule Joe and told him we would be leaving for a couple weeks as we were traveling to San Francisco. "Just put the order inside either shack."

Preparing to leave, I double-bagged my gold into four gold pouches and then pocketed a few ounces on my person. I told Slim what I was doing and he commented, "I don't have that much to hide. I only have a few hundred dollars." That just didn't make any since to me, but Slim was an honest person, so I didn't comment.

We followed the trail to Downieville where we caught the stage to Grass Valley. From Grass Valley we were en route to Sacramento, when about halfway we were stopped by three highwaymen. Shots were fired but no one was hurt. We were ordered out of the stage and slim fell to the ground and began to cough and spit, clutching his heart.

In a weak and deathly sounding voice he said, "Take me first, I'm dying. My gold is under the seat in the stage." I was beside myself and didn't know what to do to help Slim.

The bandit replied, "We don't care about people who are dying; besides, you already look dead." The bandit then reached inside the stage and withdrew from under the seat a gold pouch of dust. He then took from each of us what gold he could find. He didn't find all that I had and I saved $600. All this time Slim was rolling around on the ground, spitting and coughing and making all kinds of strange sounds. We helped Slim into the stage and continued to Sacramento. As soon as Slim was back inside the stage, he came around and we all began talking about how much we had lost to the bandits.

One feller said he was taken for $800, while another said he lost $600. I told them I lost $1,200 and a gold watch. Slim said they got all that he had from under the seat.

We arrived in Sacramento and the stage driver reported to the sheriff about the robbery. Slim all this time was tugging at my coat. Finally I asked what he wanted.

"Come with me he replied." We walked around the corner of the building where we were alone and slim began pulling from every pocket of his clothing, bags of gold. He even had some nuggets inside his pipe with un-smoked tobacco on top. He took off his boots which were two sizes too large and in the toe of each boot was a sock of gold dust. Slim had secreted over $7,000 in gold on his person and had fooled the bandits into thinking the pouch under the seat was all he had. Slim leaned against the building and smiled a little, "Those fellers were sure dumb to think I was sick and dying."

We hung around Sacramento a couple days before going on to San Francisco. Arriving there we went directly to the Mint and turned in our gold and gave them the information needed to ship the coined gold to us at the Downieville Wells Fargo Express office. Slim held out a couple hundred dollars for us to have a good time. For two nights we stayed in the best hotel in town and ate the best of foods.

The first night we strolled over to Portsmouth Square and saw a sign left over from the earlier days of the city which read: "This Street is impassable, not even Jackassable!" Slim got a big laugh on that one for he remembered the last time he was there the street was nothing but mud.

We weren't drinkers or gamblers, but we were interested in what went on in those places. As we entered the Bella Union Saloon and Gambling Hall, a fellow attempted to make us a part of the wicked hurly-burly goings on there. From all that we saw, it looked as though gambling, drinking and wicked women was the life and soul of the place. Over at the El Dorado Saloon they had a game in progress where the center of the table was stacked with gold nuggets and small gold pouches with dust. One fellow won a portion of the stack and bought drinks for everyone in the place, using near abouts all he won.

San Francisco was an exciting place, but a fellow could get himself in real trouble if he weren't careful. Me and Slim were just relaxing in the lobby of our hotel our second night in town.

Shortly, a couple gents sat across from us. They began talking about a poker game they were part of last evening. One fellow said he lost $6 and the other fellow mentioned he lost $8. They didn't think that was bad considering that was their first time playing cards.

One gent turned to Slim. "Say, did either of you fellows ever play poker?"

Slim, being polite, answered, "I played a little when back east for very small stakes. Nothing to brag about."

"Well say, would you fellows like to play, just to pass the time of course. Nothing big, just small stakes. This here fellow is Jason and my name is Jack. We're new to the game. Perhaps we could learn from you two fellows."

Slim reached over and shook the hand extended toward him. "My name is Gus Ferro and this is Buster Johnson." He pointed toward me. "We don't normally gamble, but a little friendly game of poker will be no harm. We would be pleased to join you fellows. How about $.10 anti and two bits max bet?"

We followed the two fellows to their room and took seats around a card table. The whole place looked like a setting in a gambling house. I smelled a rat and so did slim.

Slim, when out of ear shot, whispered, "Follow my lead." Slim picked up the deck of cards and began to shuffle. Suddenly he began doing tricks with the cards. I had never seen such dexterity with cards. Both those fellows were surprised at what Slim was doing. Slim began to speak.

"Shorty, you remember the last time we played cards? I had a full house and that one fellow had only two pair. How about the time I had four of a kind and the other fellow only had a pair of fours? They never could figure out how I was able to win almost every pot."

"Yea, I remember," I answered. "Those fellows lost every cent they had. That was a fun night."

Suddenly Slim stopped playing with the cards. "Say fellows, did you notice a small mark on the back of some of these cards? How about getting a fresh deck for this game."

Jason suddenly said he didn't feel so good. "Perhaps we should play another time, if you fellows don't mind."

"No, we don't mind," answered Slim. "We should probably go to bed early anyway. I have to meet my brother, the police chief, early in the morning and assist him in investigating a card cheating scam in the city. You fellows should be careful you don't get caught up in any card games with those cheaters. They would take you for every cent you have; but don't worry, we'll catch them. Say, how about us getting together tomorrow night?"

Jason replied, "Gee fellows we won't be able to do that, were leaving town in the morning. Going up north to Oregon to visit friends. It was good meeting you fellows though." We shook hands all around and left the room.

Next morning at breakfast, we saw those two fellows checking out at the front desk. They seemed to be in a real hurry. Slim laughed. "They act like the devil is after them."

I couldn't hold it any longer. I was waiting for Slim to tell me where he learned to handle cards the way he did. He didn't offer, so I asked.

"Where did you learn those card tricks?"

Slim grinned, "My dad was a dealer of legal card games back in New Orleans and he taught me all his tricks. Last night was the first time I ever used them."

Arriving back at Sacramento we laid over one day and then boarded the stage for Grass Valley. Two hours out of town we were stopped by the same fellers that had robbed us while coming in. We of course had no money on us this time.

One bandit recognized Slim and asked, "Say, ain't you the fellow that was dying last week?"

Slim smiled as he leaned against the stage and replied, "Yeah, I was carrying a heavy load then, but as soon as we got to San Francisco I went to see Doctor Mint and he cured me right away. It's amazing what that Doctor Mint can do for a follow."

The bandits cleaned out the Wells Fargo treasure box and told the driver to move on. Slim still had the smile on his face when we got to Grass Valley.

We arrived back at One-Shovel just as the winter's first heavy snow arrived. Pack Mule Joe had delivered our supplies in Slim's shack so I bunked in with Slim for that winter.

The first work day we had, Slim was leaning on his shovel with his usual smile.

"What's up Slim?" I asked.

Slim leaned a little harder on his shovel. "Well Shorty, I guess I should tell you, I'm thinking of returning back home after this winter. I've got 'bout all I'll need, including what I left here in camp."

Slim caught me unawares with that answer. "What do you mean, with what you left in camp?"

Slim let another smile crease his face. "See that first pile of gravel over yonder? There's two bags of gold nuggets about one foot down. Half of it is mine and the other half is yours. When you were about camp and not looking, I took a portion of your dirt to wash and secreted the two bags for safe keeping for both of us. I think there's about $3000 to $3500 in each bag. That'll give me around $10,000 or better. That's enough to buy forty acres of land, build a house for my wife and kids and live well for the rest of my time on this old earth."

I stared at Slim for some time. I would have sworn I heard him say something about a wife and kids. I was so surprised I was speechless. Slim never mentioned he had a wife and kids and I never thought to ask.

I asked Slim, "How old are your kids?"

He replied, "They were eight years and five years when I left home to make my pile.

He then really surprised me by saying, "I left home six years ago and have never received a letter from home, even though I wrote every week for almost a year before giving up hearing from my wife."

For the next few days Slim wasn't his normal self. I guessed talking about his family life changed his attitude. We continued to work the mine and got through the winter without any problems. As the snow began to melt, Slim began daydreaming again.

About the middle of March, Slim up and announced what he had decided. "I don't want to leave One-Shovel; were doing very well with our claim. I'm going into Downieville at the Wells Fargo Express office and send a telegraph back home and ask my family to come to California to be with me. I'll send them whatever amount of money they'll need for the trip."

Slim did just that and afterwards waited for an answer. Mail would come into camp about once a week from Downieville. In early

April, Slim received the telegraph he was waiting for, but not with the answer he was looking for.

Slims wife mentioned she answered every letter he sent. Slim never received any of the letters where he was at the time. After a year Slim's letters stopped and she thought him dead. Without any word from him for four years, she remarried.

Slim read and reread the telegraph as he sat staring at the dirt floor. I did not have words to express my sorrow for Slim.

Finally, Slim rose slowly to his feet with tears in his eyes and turned to me, "Shorty, we're burning daylight. We need to mine some gold before the next winter sets in."

I felt for Slim, for I could see the news had changed him. He was quiet and was becoming introverted.

For the remainder of the summer, Slim worked like a man possessed. He refused to take a rest break. He ate only one meal each day. As slim as he was he was losing weight. Slim was six feet, two inches tall and was down to a hundred and forty-five pounds. I was worried.

Suddenly one morning, Slim announced he was going home to visit his kids. He got dressed and told me, "If I don't return in one year the claim and shack is yours." He wrote out those instructions on paper and handed it to me. We embraced each other and Slim was gone.

I got through the winter without any trouble, except for the loneliness. I sure did miss Slim and his smile. His shovel was standing in the corner and each time I looked at it I was reminded of Slim.

As the month of May was coming around I was thinking more and more about Slim, for a year was almost up since I last saw him. I was determined to wait for Slim. I didn't want to file the paper for ownership of his claim.

One morning in June, just as big as life, Slim walked into camp. He looked good. He had gained weight and he had that smile back. I handed him his shovel and as he leaned on it he said, "I've brought my wife and kids back with me. I left them in Sacramento until I can make arrangements for them in Downieville."

I was caught without anything to say, so Slim did the talking. Shortly after he had received the telegram from his wife last year, the man she remarried was shot and killed in a saloon brawl. Slim reconciled with his family and they were now waiting for him in Sacramento to be brought to Downieville.

I was happy for Slim but I knew our times together in our cabins were over as Slim would now spend all the time he could with his family. I mentioned this to Slim. He had already talked over the arrangements with his wife. He would stay at the mine Monday through Friday and spend Friday night through Sunday night in Downieville with the family as long as the mine continued to produce.

The next morning Slim had breakfast with me and he then headed to Downieville. After making accommodations in town he would continue on to Sacramento to fetch his family. I didn't see Slim again for three weeks and I was beginning to worry when he walked into camp. We went right to work on the mine and on Friday afternoon Slim invited me to go with him to Downieville to meet his family and spend the weekend with them.

Slim's oldest was fifteen years and the youngest was now eleven years. What surprised me the most was Slim's wife; she was a beautiful woman. She was a dark blond with blue eyes and about five feet five inches tall. Right off you could tell she was a refined lady. She made me feel welcome as we sat at the table for dinner that night. What a meal it was. After dinner the kids did the dishes while me, Slim and his wife Jenna had a nice visit on the back porch of their rental house, overlooking the Yuba River. It was the finest weekend I had had in a very long time.

Come Monday morning me and Slim headed back to the mine. As soon as we walked into camp it was obvious we'd had a visit with bears while we were away. Most of what we had stored outside was all over the place. Flour, whole beans and even some of our tobacco were missing or destroyed. As we walked around the shacks we noticed one of the windows in Slim's shack was ripped out of its frame. As we looked through the open window, one of the bears was still inside the cabin.

I told Slim, "Go around to the front and when you hear my pistol shot, open the door and stand back."

Slim looked at me with a smile. "Gotcha."

127

I gave Slim about one minute and fired my pistol inside the cabin. As Slim opened the door the bear came running out like the devil was after him. I bet that bear is still running. That of course was the only fun part of that incident. We had to clean up the mess, repair the shack and order supplies to replace what the bear ate or destroyed.

We soon settled into our new routine and began mining our gold. As winter was coming on again, Slim invited me to spend the winter with him and the family in town. I thanked Slim but declined. I said, "Someone needs to be present so no other miner sneaks in and drifts our claim." Slim didn't think that arrangement was fair to me, so he suggested all gold mined by me during the times he was out of camp was to be all mine. I didn't think that was fair to Slim. We settled the matter with every fourth bucket of gravel being Slim's. We shook on it.

Slim didn't spend all his time at home. He would on occasion come to the mine on snowshoes and work for a couple days before going back home. The mine was still paying like it did when we first started working it. Fact it was probably the best claim around.

We finished the winter and in the spring, I reckon March it was, Slim announced to me that at the end of the coming summer, he was moving to San Francisco with the family and the mine would be mine. I didn't like it, but Slim was a happy man when he was with his family, so I thanked him and let it lay.

One morning Slim mentioned he was going into Downieville with his gold and deposit it with Wells Fargo Express for delivery to their office in San Francisco where he would call for it upon his arrival there.

"How much do you figure you have Slim?" I asked.

"Best I can figure, bout $8,000. With that and what I have left over from my trip back east, I've got about $15,000.

Come September, Slim bid me goodbye and he and his family boarded the stage for Grass Valley. As they were pulling away, I shouted to Slim. "Hide it under the seat." Slim bent over laughing.

I didn't hear from Slim during that whole winter, but come spring when the snows melted, I received ten letters from Slim. He was settled in the city and had formed a partnership with two friends in the mercantile business. He mentioned they could use a forth partner as business was brisk. The last dated letter read, "Come and see me, let's talk partnership."

I went to Pack Mule Joe and explained I was leaving for a few weeks and asked if he would look after things while I was gone.

As usual he said "How much you pay?" I said, "No pay, just free food until I return."

Joe smiled, "Sounds like a good one to me," mocking Slim.

I carried my gold to Downieville and deposited it with Wells Fargo to hold until my return. The charge to me for that service was $55.

The trip to San Francisco was uneventful and Slim met me at the stage coach stop with his two partners. After introductions we went directly to the hotel restaurant and ordered lunch.

Slim offered me a full partnership in the business, but not in San Francisco. Their plans were to have four separate locations, each managed by a partner. I was offered the San Jose location. I asked where the other locations were planned.

Slim's partner Jack Anderson answered, "Sacramento and Monterey."

Before going any further in the conversation I asked the price of a full partnership.

Slim answered, "We each put in $10,000, you're share will be the same."

"I accept if I can have the Sacramento location," I replied. The three put their heads together and answered, "Deal."

I spent a couple days in San Francisco acquainting myself with the business in that store. Slim and Jack explained what I needed to know about certain functions of the business and how to maintain inventory.

I returned to One-Shovel and gathered all that I wished to keep. I searched out Pack Mule Joe and explained what Slim and our other two partners were doing. I then told him I was signing our claim over to him and he could work it or sell it. Joe knew it was a good producer. IIe said he would work it along with his Pack Mule business. I left for Downieville to catch the stage for Grass Valley and Sacramento. Before doing so, I forwarded $10,000 in gold to Wells Fargo in Sacramento to start the business.

As owner-manager of the Sacramento location, I had the responsibility of searching out suitable land for the new building. That done, construction began almost immediately. Within two months the building was complete and merchandise was put in place for sale.

Opening day was set for the following Monday. As I walked outside to admire the building, I focused on the sign which I had not seen before it was installed. In the lower right had corner in small letters was painted, "Slim and Shorty, partners."

Sacramento was growing so rapidly in those days and business was so brisk it was almost impossible to get time away from the business. My receipts for the first year came to $132,000. The corporation netted a little over $45,000 from the Sacramento store. With this profit we expanded the two other locations within the year.

One Sunday afternoon, I was walking the plaza when I heard a female voice asking for help. She was having trouble with her horse as it refused to pull the carriage. I offered my assistance and as I walked to the front of the carriage, I rubbed the flanks of the horse, patted his nose and checked the bridle bit. The bit had come loose in the mouth. I reset the bit and offered to drive the carriage to her location, wherever that was.

To my surprise, she said she was going to the mercantile store two blocks over. I informed her the store was closed for the day.

"How do you know, do you work there?"

"Yes I do. My names Buster Johnson and I manage the store.

"Oh! Then you can open the store."

"No, I'm sorry," I replied, "The policy is the store is closed on Sunday. Perhaps I can be of service tomorrow, we open at seven a.m."

She rode off without giving me her name. There was something about her that attracted me. I was looking forward to Monday with the chance of seeing her again.

All the next day as I was working in the store, every time someone came in I looked toward the front of the store, but it was never her. Along about three o'clock in the afternoon a buggy pulled up in front of the store being pulled by matching horses, handled by a young man about my age. Sitting alongside him was the lady I had been looking for all day. They seemed to know each other quiet well. She put her arm in his as they came into the store. I went forward and was surprised to see the gentleman was Jack Anderson, one of my partners from San Francisco.

I greeted Jack and he in turn introduced me to his sister, Yolanda.

"Oh! Mr. Johnson and I have already met. He's the store manager here."

Jack turned to his sister. "Buster Johnson is the manager alright, but he is also my partner in this business and three others just like it."

"Oh! What a wonderful surprise," replied Yolanda.

I inquired of Jack what he was doing in town. His sister Yolanda had come in on the train three days ago and he was there to greet her and escort her to San Francisco.

"By the way Buster, we're giving her a reception in the City on Saturday and if you can tear yourself away from here we would like for you to attend."

I looked at Yolanda and replied, "I'll be there; count on it."

Friday was slow coming. I left my assistant in charge and boarded the stage for San Francisco at 5am, arriving about ten that night. Hotel arrangements had been made for me at the Palace and I got a good night's sleep. The next day, Saturday, I was surprised to see how much the city had grown in the past two years.

As the evening approached I made my way to the Mark Hopkins and joined the reception line, as a member of the Mercantile Corporation. Many of the cities dignitaries were arriving. As I was greeting each one, a person who looked familiar stepped in front of me and spoke.

"Hi Buster, how you doing?" He was immaculately dressed in a tux and if not for the voice I would not have recognized him. "Pack Mule Joe, you rascal, it's great to see you, and I'm doing just fine as you can see."

"Slim invited me to this here fancy party and I'm sure glad I could make it; do you folks live like this all the time?"

"No Joe, we actually work most of the time," I answered.

Joe began telling me how well he did on the claim me and Slim gave him. He mined a little over $15,000 and was now living in Downieville full time and managing his freight business from there.

He had four lines of freight mules and twelve employees. I congratulated him on his success.

Suddenly the orchestra played an overture and at the top of the stairs was Yolanda. What a site she was. My heart skipped three beats as she came down the massive stairs. Arriving at the bottom, she walked directly toward me, put her arm in mine and asked if I would escort her to the banquet table. All eyes were on the two of us as we led the guests to the table. I was so excited I almost walked right past the table without realizing what I was doing. Yolanda gave my arm a small tug and I pulled out her chair. As she sat down, she looked at me with a big smile.

"Thank you Buster Johnson." It was then I knew---I was in love with the lady.

Jack came over. "I see you too are getting acquainted. Yolanda has informed me she intends to stay in California, perhaps live in Sacramento. Would you look after her for me Buster if she does move to Sacramento?"

Being a little flustered, I answered, "That would be a pleasure I would insist upon."

The remainder of the evening went so fast I didn't realize it was 2 am. Yolanda asked me to escort her to her quarters, which I did and bid her good night.

As I returned down stairs, Pack Mule Joe said he was leaving on the next boat going across the bay and wanted to say once again "Thanks." We shook hands and as Joe was leaving I noticed a tear in the eye.

I called out, "Joe, just a minute." Joe came back, "My part of the partnership is in Sacramento and if you ever have trouble obtaining supplies, contact me. The price to you will be wholesale less ten."

Joe smiled from ear to ear. "I don't think that will be necessary. I'm thinking of selling out to one of my employees and moving to Sacramento."

Joe surprised me with that statement and I asked, "What are you going to do in Sacramento?" Joe didn't know yet for he had not completely made up his mind about selling out. I told him, "Be sure you let me know when you decide."

Joe again smiled and answered, "I will."

I only got about three hours sleep the remainder of that night and I was quiet tired throughout the day. I walked to the offices of the corporation on south Market Street for a business meeting. Slim took charge of the meeting as we partners went over the books. For laughs, Slim began talking.

"Well fellers, it looks like we had a grand time of it this past year. This here corporation took in over a million dollars and after getting all the bills paid, we should net somewhere around $400,000 for the year. What'cha think of that?"

Jack broke in with, "That's a right smart amount of money."

I responded with, "Sounds like a good one to me."

The next day as I was preparing to leave the hotel I was expecting to see Yolanda in the hotel restaurant but she didn't show. Slim came in and we had a brief conversation. He mentioned there may be a change in the Monterey location sometime in the near future as Frank was having health problems and was thinking about retiring from the corporation. "I'll keep you posted."

Just as I was leaving, Yolanda walked into the restaurant and I found I needed another coffee. I invited her to join me at the table. She asked if I would assist her in finding a proper place to live if she moved to Sacramento as she was thinking of doing. I assured her my time was her time and I would be happy to look out for her interest in finding a proper place.

As I boarded the Bay Flier that would take me across the bay waters, I saw Yolanda wave to me. I was surprised to see her at the dock. I assumed that was a good sign.

By keeping myself busy, I kept my mind off of Yolanda. I hesitated to write for I thought it to be presumptuous of me to do such a thing. I finally couldn't control myself and penned a letter to Jack asking for his permission to correspond with Yolanda. Jack answered that he would have thought I already did that. Of course it was okay for me to write her; he encouraged it.

I waited three weeks for Yolanda to answer my letter to her and when it came I was so excited I had to sit down with a cup of coffee to calm myself.

As I read the letter nothing was said about her moving to Sacramento until on the last page of ten pages, she mentioned she was making the move in August. I spilled my coffee all over the letter and had to wait until it dried until I could read it again.

I began immediately to look for a proper place for her to live and found a beautiful apartment just across from the State Capitol building. It had a twenty-four-hour entrance guard and a fine restaurant just next door.

I explained to management about the lady who would be occupying the apartment and gave them a sizable deposit to hold the apartment through August.

It seemed like the month of July would never end. Finally a letter from Yolanda informing me she would arrive August fifteenth.

I met her at the depot with horse and carriage and a trailing wagon for luggage. I wanted to hug her to me, but of course that would not be the proper thing to do.

As we drove through the city, many of my customers bid me good morning and the men tipped their hats to Yolanda with a knowing smile toward me. I felt proud that so many people would acknowledge our presence on the streets.

Arriving at the apartment, the doorman helped Yolanda from the carriage and assisted the luggage wagon driver in unloading the baggage. Yolanda was pleased with the apartment and she settled right in. I gave her a couple days before asking her to join me for dinner at the Downtown Men's Club.

As we walked into the entrance of the club someone called out, "Yolanda, what are you doing in a fine place such as this?"

Yolanda was embarrassed and turned crimson. Standing before us was a young man I had never seen at the club before. I pulled Yolanda behind me.

"What do you mean by that statement? This lady is my guest and I will expect you to respect her at all times or I will punch you square in the nose."

"Say mister, I don't care who you date. I know this lady from way back and as far as I'm concerned she's no lady." At that very moment I landed a punch right on his nose as blood splattered over my coat. Yolanda turned and ran from the room in tears. I ran after her and caught up to her just as she was approaching the river. I pulled her back to safety and asked her what this was all about.

Yolanda was sobbing and could hardly talk. "Take me home please,"

I got her into her apartment and she said she would tell me all I wanted to know the next day. I was concerned she would leave in the middle of the night, so I met with the doorman, gave him a sizeable tip and informed him he was to come for me if the lady attempted to leave.

I didn't sleep any that night. So many things were going through my mind. I could not imagine what that person meant by making such a statement about Yolanda. I was determined to get to the bottom of it. Early in the morning I went back to the club to inquire about who that person was and where he was living.

He was a new member and was living two buildings south of the building Yolanda was living in. I tipped the doorman for allowing me into his building after explaining I wanted to apologize for my actions last evening. I knocked on the apartment door and was greeted by a very handsome lady who said her husband was suffering from a broken nose and could not see me.

I told her I was the one who gave him the broken nose and needed to urgently talk to him. She invited me in and I waited a few moments until he appeared in the room. His face was discolored and his nose was bandaged. He stood a distance from me.

"You wanted to apologize?"

"No I don't. You deserved what you got because of the statement you made last night. You didn't need to say anything. I'm only here to find out why you said such a thing." Surprisingly he invited me to sit.

As I did so, he began to talk. "Miss Yolanda was a former saloon girl some years back. She played the piano in the Young Blood Saloon in Waco, Texas and was involved in the robbing of drunken cowboys after they left the saloon. She wasn't the average saloon girl but she did rob a number of cowboys of their hard-earned money."

"One of those fellows was found dead outside the saloon building with his head bashed in. The sheriff rounded up the saloon keeper who owned the place and Miss Yolanda. Seems those two were cousins and anything the keeper was involved in, Yolanda was always in the middle."

"The keeper was charged with murder and Yolanda was charged with accessory. At the trial, the barkeep was found guilty as charged and Yolanda was given five-year probation and ordered to never work again in a saloon in that city."

I thanked him for the information, put a hundred-dollar bill on the table to pay his doctor bill and left the building. I went straight to Yolanda's building and knocked on her apartment door.

In a muffled voice she answered, "Go away, I don't want to talk now."

I answered her, "I'll break down the door if you don't open it." She slowly opened the door and turned her back to me as I walked inside.

I went into the kitchen area and made a pot of coffee while she was fixing herself. She came out and sat across from me. I handed her a cup of coffee.

"Now Yolanda, Tell me the story." She sobbed a little and began to talk.

"After finishing college I needed a job, any job to sustain myself until something better came along. My cousin offered me the job of playing the piano in his saloon. I made the mistake of taking the job and was immediately sorry for doing so. The place was filthy and the customers were even worse. Seems like every time there was trouble I was caught in the middle. My cousin always seemed to implicate me in some way or other. My reputation was not the best as you can imagine. There was a murder and I was arrested along with my cousin. He was sentenced to thirty years in prison and I was given a five-year probation period. I had nothing to do with any of his troubles and never participated in any of his crimes. I skipped out on my probation, came to California and that's when I met you here in Sacramento."

I sat, dumbfounded. "Where did you get the money for travel and other expenses?"

"I sent a telegraph to my brother Jack, telling him I wanted to come to California and he sent me $2,000 and told me he would meet me here in the city. He did and that's when you met us both at the store."

I guess I smiled a little when I shouldn't have.

"There is nothing funny about any of this Mr. Buster Johnson and I'll not be laughed at."

I apologized for the laugh and mentioned I was thinking about the fellow with the broken nose.

"I wasn't laughing at you. I'll have a talk with him and make sure this is never mentioned again. We'll give this a couple of weeks to cool down before being seen again in public."

"Well now Mr. Buster Johnson, what makes you think I wish to be seen again in your company?"

Yolanda caught me off guard with that question and I apologized for my presumptuous attitude. I noticed a small smile at the corner of her beautiful mouth and responded.

"Now you're laughing at me." She rose from her seat, crossed the room and gave me a kiss on the cheek.

"Thank you Mr. Buster Johnson, do I have your permission to remain in Sacramento or are you going to report me to the authorities?"

I replied, "I'm going to report you to the authorities, in about forty years, so you better just watch yourself until then."

The remainder of that year was the happiest of times for me. Yolanda joined the local lady's club and was very active in their pursuits. The next year her name came up for nomination as an officer in the club and she gladly accepted. The nominations list was posted in the local paper.

That April, just two weeks before taking her responsibilities as an officer, an article appeared in the Sacramento Union about a fugitive from justice out of Waco, Texas who was living in Sacramento. The story went on to describe the charge and the court's findings. Even though the fugitive was only on probation, skipping out was against the law and now if captured, the lady would serve the remainder of her probation time in jail. The article didn't give the name of the lady fugitive, but if captured all other information about the person would be published.

I rushed right over to Yolanda's apartment, but she was gone. I inquired of the doorman if he saw Miss Yolanda leave the building. He did and she was carrying a large valise. I rushed down to the train station but Yolanda was not there. I went by the stables and the stable boy said he hadn't seen any single ladies that day. I went back to Yolanda's apartment and left a note on the table to please contact me as soon as possible. I gave the doorman a similar note to give to her in case she missed the one on the table.

I went back to my apartment and Yolanda was waiting for me in the lobby. We talked briefly about the situation and I then went to the building manager and rented a small apartment for Yolanda. She gave me a list of items she would need from her other apartment and I retrieved them for her.

I went to the telegraph office and sent a telegram to my corporate office in San Francisco informing them I would be taking an emergency leave of absence and the assistant manager was in charge until my return. I briefly explained to Yolanda what I planned to do and left for the train station.

I made a reservation for the next train leaving the city. I had two hours to pack and return for my trip east. After making a few train connections I arrived in Waco, Texas five days later and went directly to the judge's office that presided over Yolanda's trial. The judge was out until the following Monday morning at 9 am. I spent the weekend walking the streets of Waco.

Monday morning I was at the judge's office at 8:30. As the judge entered, the secretary informed him I was waiting to see him on an important matter. She escorted me into his office and served us both coffee. The judge asked what could be so urgent this early in the morning. Without much detail I began asking questions.

"Is the breaking of probation by a person convicted of a crime cause for a warrant for arrest?"

The judge answered, "Most likely yes; it could depend on the nature of the crime. If it was a capital crime, most certainly."

"What would constitute a capital crime?" The judge eyed me for a moment.

"Are you harboring a fugitive sir?"

"That's what I'm trying to find out your honor," I answered.

The judge thought for a moment and replied, "Why don't you tell me the story, off the record of course, and perhaps then I can properly answer your questions."

I began telling him of the meeting with Jack and his sister Yolanda, and the friendship we had developed. I explained about the altercation at the City Men's Club and the explanation about the incident by Yolanda.

The judge studied me for some time as I waited.

"Young man, I remember the case very well. After the barkeeper was sentenced and taken off to jail and after about three weeks, he told the warden he had a confession to make. He confessed to the murder of his patron and how he went about it. He further confessed that his cousin Yolanda had absolutely nothing to do with the crime nor did she ever have any connection with him in any of his crimes. She was an innocent person. Attempts were made to locate and notify her that her probation was no longer in effect and the records were cleared in her favor. We of course were not able to locate her to convey the information."

I left Waco that afternoon with copies of the legal papers to clear Yolanda of all charges, showing she was a free and innocent person. What a joy it was to board the train that day. Before departing, I sent a telegraph to Yolanda. "You are a free person, charges dropped. Will explain all."

Arriving back in Sacramento I went directly to broken nose and knocked on his door. The wife answered the door. I rushed past her and confronted him with the information I received from the judge. He claimed he knew nothing of what I was talking about.

I replied, "I know, but here is what you are going to do anyway. You are going to have an article printed in the paper tomorrow morning, retracting all that was mentioned earlier about the lady in hiding. If the item does not appear, I will be back and you sir are going to be in a lot of trouble, not to mention the abrasions in addition to another broken nose. I further recommend you resign from the City Men's Club at its next meeting."

"You cannot force me to resign from the club," he replied.

"That is true," I answered, "But in the interest of good health, the resignation is advisable."

I then went directly to my apartment building and found Yolanda sitting in the lobby. She was as pleased to see me as I was to see her. I showed her the papers and explained everything to her and she was ecstatic.

"Mr. Buster Johnson, how can I ever repay you for what you have done for me?"

"You can have dinner have with me tomorrow night at the club," I replied.

At the club that night, after dinner was served, the monthly meeting began. At that moment Mr. Broken Nose rose from his seat and announced he was resigning from the membership for reasons of his health. He then turned and walked out. Problem solved.

Yolanda and I continued to visit and date and I knew I was deeply in love with the lady. I sent a telegram to her brother Jack informing him of our situation and told him I was going to propose to his sister, and would he have any objections?

I received an answer the next day from Jack. "I would insist you do so at once. Signed, your future brother-in-law Jack."

The following day I received a telegram from Slim. "I'm going to pull the bag from under the seat and throw one fine engagement party for my friend. Congrats." I was receiving all of these responses and I hadn't even asked Yolanda yet.

The next day I invited Yolanda to accompany me to San Francisco to have dinner with her brother jack and the other members of the corporation. We would leave on Friday and return the following Monday.

Saturday night, greetings all around were completed and as Slim was talking with the other partners, when he suddenly paused.

"Partner Buster Johnson, you have been quiet this evening. Don't you have anything to say?"

I rose to my feet and answered, "President Gus Farro, I do." I turned to Yolanda and went down on one knee,

"Yolanda, when I first met you I knew you would be something special in my life. I didn't know then what that would be. I do know now. I love you and I want to spend the remainder of my life loving you and caring for you. Will you marry me?"

There was silence in the room. Yolanda just sat there with her eyes closed. Her brother Jack suddenly shouted, "Yolanda, answer the man."

Yolanda continued to sit with her eyes closed. She then opened her eyes. "I was saying a silent prayer, thanking my God for such a man coming into my life. Yes Mr. Buster Johnson, I will marry you, for I also love you." The room erupted in applause.

Slim shouted, "Sounds like a good one to me."

Slim was as good as his word. He gave us the finest engagement party ever given up to that time in San Francisco. Everybody that was anybody was there, even one person no one remembered inviting was there.

Sitting over in one corner was a small man whom Jack had been watching. He was well dressed and refined looking with a neatly trimmed mustache. He had been participating in the proceedings. It was obvious he was no ordinary citizen. After asking around Jack could find no one who knew who he was. Suddenly Jack rose from his seat, clapped his hands and said, "That's him!"

Jack approached the gentleman, "Sir, are you not Charles E. Bolton?" The gentleman was startled as he rose from his seat and answered in a low and melodious voice.

"Yes I am and who am I addressing sir?"

"I am Jack, brother of the bride to be." They shook hands.

"My compliments to the couple soon to be married and to the person who arranged this party. It's the finest engagement party I have ever attended." He surprisingly then uttered, "By your leave sir." He then turned and left the building. It was February 22, 1888, the year, month and day C.E. Boles, alias C.E. Bolton, alias Black Bart disappeared from San Francisco.

Buster paused in telling his story to relight his pipe. He then looked around him and saw questionable expressions on our faces, "C.E. Bolton is another story for another time."

It was decided to have the wedding in Sacramento as that was the place we were to reside and work. It was a fine wedding and everyone was there. During the festivities me and Yolanda slipped out the back door and headed to the train station. We bought tickets to San Francisco as a decoy and then rented a horse and carriage for Auburn. We of course went to none of those places as we had rented the finest room available at the Sacramento Plaza Hotel and Restaurant. We stayed there for four days before then taking the train to New York City where we honeymooned for six weeks.

Years went by and the business grew into ten separate locations, but only the original four were owners of the business. The company acquired property in the financial section of the city and built a fine two-story office building to house the growing business. We employed a hundred and twenty-five people within the business.

At that time large companies from outside America were in the process of purchasing successful businesses. Our corporation was approached by a company from England and we were offered forty million dollars to sale to them. We partners held a meeting and decided we would make the sale if all outstanding accounts were assumed by the purchasers. That was agreed upon and lawyers drew up the papers. It was further agreed all employees would retain their positions within the company. Each partner pocketed ten million dollars. I don't need to tell you what ten million dollars was in the days when seven dollars a day was top wage.

Jack moved to Los Angeles and purchased a track of land called "The Hills." He liked the area for it was away from the city and that was the way he wanted it. The land later became known as "Beverly Hills."

Slim stayed on in San Francisco and built one of the finer homes on Knob Hill. He began dabbling in politics and was nominated to run for state governor which he turned down. He said, "All I want is the simple life."

Yolanda wanted to visit New Orleans so we boarded the train and enjoyed ourselves in that city. One morning we awoke and Yolanda complained about having a sore throat. She began to gargle with salt and water but it only got worse. I took her to a doctor and he did test and informed us Yolanda was suffering from a virus of some kind. He admitted her to the hospital.

Yolanda was in the hospital for two weeks and she seemed to be getting better. I spent my days at the hospital with her, reading to her and holding her hand. I was at a nearby café having lunch when a nurse from the hospital came to the café and informed me I was immediately needed at the hospital. I departed at once, but I was too late---Yolanda had died.

Buster paused in his story and sat for some time before continuing.

To this day I do not know what I did the weeks and months that followed. My heart was broken. The woman I loved with all my being was gone. Jack took care of the arrangements. He had the body shipped back here to Sacramento where she is buried in the City Cemetery.

I began to wonder about and I disappeared for some weeks. I don't know where I went or what I did. Jack had me declared unfit to handle my own affairs and was given control of my finances by the court. Good thing to, for it was found I had been giving money away to persons I didn't even know. All they had to do was ask for it and I gave it to them. It was found I had given away over a million dollars.

As I began to come around and get control of myself, Jack came to me and suggested I look for another place to settle for a couple years to gather myself and to get away from those people who thought they were helping me, but were only making matters worse.

I thought Jack was right and began making plans. There were from time to time articles in the newspapers about certain towns in the western states becoming important centers of trade with many possibilities.

I boarded the coastal runner "Far Western" for Los Angeles. It was my first time seeing the California coast. Arriving in Los Angeles, I rented a small villa while continuing my search for where I was to live.

One day while out walking I spied a group of people milling around. They were making one of those new moving picture shows. I got as close as I could when one of those fellows came towards me. He was dressed in the most outlandish outfit I ever did see. Fancy cowboy boots, big white ten gallon hat and a six-shooter strapped to his hip on an engraved cowhide holster.

He approached me and asked, "Sir, could you please step back a ways so you don't get caught in the picture?"

I asked the name of the picture they were making and he answered, "Tom Mix Rides Again."

"Which one is Tom Mix?" I asked.

"I am," he answered, then shook my hand as I backed off a ways.

Standing off to one side was a rather interesting gentleman, distinguished looking with a nicely trimmed mustache and wearing a traditional western hat and outfit. He seemed to have some kind of influence on what was going on. First chance I got I asked Tom Mix who the gentleman was.

"Tom answered, "That's the advisor on the picture to make sure everything is authentic. His name is Wyatt Earp, a former law man." I had heard the name before but couldn't then put my finger on it.

I left the area and continued my walk. It was about suppertime so I meandered over to a restaurant for my evening meal. While I sat there studying the menu the waitress asked if I was ready to order. I looked up at her and was somewhat surprised to see such a fine looking woman serving food. Without thinking, I said, "Young lady, you should be in that picture show there making over on the next street. You're beautiful."

She thanked me for the compliment and as she took my order, I glanced at her name tag. Her name was Carol Lombard.

I left the restaurant and went to my villa to continue my search for where I was to live. I finally settled on San Antonio, Texas.

I arrived in San Antonio in August and settled in a room at the David Crockett Hotel and immediately penned a letter to Jack and Slim of my whereabouts. The next day I began a walk around the city. There was much to see and do in San Antonio, even in those days.

I searched out the best place to eat my meals and made reservations to have my breakfast and dinner there each day. They always had a table for me when I arrived.

I decided to take in all the historical sights first in the old city.

I visited the military post, Fort Sam Houston, and watched a polo match between two companies of cavalry.

I was impressed with the Alamo and read all the literature available. I took a walk to the river where the Mexican army crossed over in their charge toward the Alamo and immediately saw the possibilities available there. There was talk of commercializing the area and I made inquiries as to what they were.

The plans were to completely control the river by building brick walls for an extended distance and build sidewalk restaurants on the banks of the river. Gift shops and small retail stores would follow. I thought the plan was a folly and I turned down an offer to invest in the project.

I languished in that city for five years, doing absolutely nothing that I can now brag on. It was years wasted in my life span that I now regret, for I could have been doing things to help my fellow man as I am sure my wife Yolanda would have been doing had she been in my place.

As I arrived back here in Sacramento, I began looking around me and I was amazed at the vast improvements that occurred during my absence. Sacramento is no longer the small town it once was. The horse and buggies have disappeared and automobiles have taken their place. Thinking on it, I'm not so sure that's an improvement.

Since I returned, I visited that wonderful little mining town of Downieville which has settled into a slow and steady existence and is now the county seat of Sierra County. The old mining camp One-Shovel, no longer exists.

Pack Mule Joe did sell out his freight business and located to Sacramento. He purchased three large apartment buildings along with the finest restaurant in the city and settled into a life of luxury. He got himself married and had three kids, one of which went to college and became a big star in Hollywood. Joe joined the Downtown Men's Club and after six years became its president.

My old partner Slim got out of politics and got himself involved in education. He provided scholarships for more students than anyone else in his time. Slim passed away in 1914, leaving his two children to continue his legacy. His name will never be lost to history.

Jack, my wife's brother, immigrated to Australia. Don't ask me why. I never did find out. He was involved in one of the biggest gold strikes ever made in that country and enriched himself an additional ten million dollars, then became a philanthropist. Through his connections in America he increased trade between the two countries which added to his wealth.

Jack returned to California in 1916, and when the crash came in 1929, Jack created the Lunch Box Retreat here in Sacramento for those in need. You only had to go there and ask for something to eat, with no questions asked.

When Jack died he left two million dollars to his Lunch Box Retreat. The retreat fed people right up to World War II.

One of the last things Jack said to his family as they surrounded his death bed was, "All that has happened in the last fifty years of my life is credited to Old Slim." He then told his family, "Search the whereabouts of old Buster Johnson and if need be, give him a helping hand."

I sit here today to say, "I don't need a helping hand, just someone to say hello to each morning and to share a cup of coffee." I have missed my wife Yolanda, for she was the light of my life. Wherever broken nose is or if he is still alive, I would forgive him for I now realize what he did was the cause of me helping to clear my wife's name, but the broken nose, he deserved.

This here dude ranch is all I have to show for my life, but that's okay, for the ranch is now known far and wide. I saw an article the other day in the local newspaper about a couple who enjoyed themselves at this here Yolanda Dude Ranch and they were planning to return next year. I hope I'm still here.

Well my friends, it's getting late, and time to turn in. Be sure you douse the fire before crawling into your sleeping bags. See you in the morning. First one up makes the coffee.

Good night.

BOOK TWO

Bacon, Beans and Coffee
A Sierra Gold Adventure

Introduction

A portion of this story is based on an actual event the author experienced in his younger years while camping and mining in the mountains around Downieville, California.

Times were hard for many during the depression years. Being on the streets looking for a job, any job, was a frustrating experience. The most humble of jobs were taken by persons who once held management positions.

Standing in line for a meal was also embarrassing, but there was plenty of company. A few of the more prosperous companies set up their own soup lines.

The sudden appearance of small vegetable gardens all over the city indicated the times. Those who had space created large gardens and sold what they themselves could not use to those who could pay. Oftentimes those vegetables were given away.

In certain parts of the country, a number of men and women attempted to make their living in unusual ways. Those with the knowledge and the tools headed for the mountains. The mining of one to two dollars a day in gold was enough to keep one from starving.

Jack and Sara Dunn figured they could improve on that if they found the right location. Five dollars a day would be their target minimum. Besides mining gold, they would be having fun.

Flour, beans, canned milk, bacon, potatoes and coffee constituted the normal fare for those living in the mountains. Those who had a weapon could on occasion add a little meat to the plate. More often than not, they ate what was the fastest to prepare.

Chapter 1
Reliving the Sierra Gold Adventure

As a young boy, I learned to pan and snipe for gold from my dad while camping in and around the mountains near the old gold-mining town of Downieville, California. My name is Jack Dunn.

It's not often one has the opportunity to tell the story of their most exciting life experience.

Though I'm a much older man now, I remember the heartache in my family with the stock market crash. Dad rushed to the bank to withdraw his money, but the bank was closed with a sign in the window---*Closed Until Further Notice.*

Dad had been investing in certain stocks and all the money he had on hand was his coin collection, which was a few gold coins and a number of silver dollars. Dad was naturally upset over the bank closing, but not as bad as some folks. One fellow Dad knew did away with himself.

I was eighteen at the time of the crash in 29, and was more or less taking care of myself. I had a job at the local merchandise store as a janitor and had been saving my money. I was making plans to attend college, but those plans were put on the shelf.

My girl, Sara Henshaw, was also eighteen and we had talked about marriage, but nothing concrete. She was working part-time at the drug store.

I knew Mom and Dad would make it alright, but they would be worried about me. I told Dad I had $500 in savings and if need be, he was welcome to any portion he may need. Dad said he and Mom would be ok.

I had my model-T Ford Dad had given me, but fuel cost money, so I got my old bike out of the garage and peddled to Sara's.

Her dad, Jake, greeted me at the door. As I walked inside, Jake busied himself in stacking boxes in one corner of the room. "What's going on Mr. Henshaw?"

"I'm fifteen days late on the rent Jack. I know my landlord well enough to know he will evict us. I don't have the money to pay."

"Mr. Henshaw, where will you go without money?" was my question.

"I'm sorry Jack, I don't have an answer," he replied.

"How much is the rent Mr. Henshaw?"

"Its $20, but it might as well be $200."

I reached into my pocket and withdrew $50 and handed it to him. "This will take care of what's due and a month in advance. The extra will buy some groceries."

"I can't take this Jack. If you kids do what I think you're going to do you're going to need it. Besides, it don't seem right for me to take money from my daughter's boyfriend."

"Perhaps, but right now that's not the point Mr. Henshaw. I need to talk to Sara. Where is Sara?"

Sara came out from one of the rooms and gave me a hug.

"What is it you can't take Dad?" Jake was about to answer when I interrupted him.

"Your dad said he couldn't take the birthday gift I have for him."

"Why not Dad?" asked Sara.

Jake suddenly went a little limp. "Thank you Jack, it's a wonderful gift, I won't forget it."

The next couple of years were hard for everyone. Those of us that had jobs did extra hours at work without pay. If we didn't, someone would come along that would.

One day while visiting Sara, she took me by the hand and led me to the front porch swing. I began telling her about when I was a kid and Dad took me gold mining up in the mountains.

Sara suddenly stopped me. "Jack Dunn, you're not making any sense; what are you talking about?"

"Sara, let's get married." She looked surprised for a moment.

"Now you're starting to make sense," she replied.

We talked the rest of the day and the more we talked the more sense it made to both of us. We decided to let things lay for the rest of the week, giving me time to spring the surprise on my folks. We knew her folks would be all for it as they had asked Sara a number of times when us kids were getting married.

The next morning when I arrived at work, my boss informed me my hours were being cut back to every other day and for only six hours per day. I would work Monday, Wednesday and Friday for a total of only eighteen hours per week. It was disappointing.

That afternoon I peddled to Sara's to inform her of my loss of income. She listened and then told me her disappointing news. The drugstore where she worked was closing.

I had not yet told my folks about our decision to marry and about other plans we were in the process of making. Sara told her folks immediately and they were delighted. We talked about it and decided to marry as soon as we could get the license and make the arrangements. I rushed home to inform my parents of our decision.

I was taken aback by Dad's remarks. "You kids are too young to marry and besides, how are you going to support yourselves? It's out of the question."

I thought of Dad's remarks for a brief moment. "Is your remark out of concern about our lack of a job, or are you referring to us as too young to make such a decision?"

Dad hesitated before answering. "I mean both Jack."

"Dad, I know you just said all of that out of love for your son, but I'm not a kid anymore and Sara is the same as me. It's been a while now since the crash and times are no better. This is 1931, and we're both twenty years old. It's about time we began life on our own. I love Sara and I know we can make it in this world just as you and Mom did when you both were our age. Don't forget, you told me the story how you and Mom met and married after only six weeks of courtship. I have known Sara since we were little tykes."

"Jack, I should have known you would say something like that, but I didn't know you would be so emphatic. You have my blessing." Mom gave me a hug and Dad, being serious as usual, shook my hand, so I gave him a hug.

We each had a list of eight people we invited, not including our parents. Sara was just beautiful in her new white dress which her parents really could not afford.

We were married with a small ceremony. We had a small reception at my folks' house and Mom went out of her way to decorate the place.

We moved into a small one-room apartment in downtown San Jose. It was small, but it was our first home away from home. Our honeymoon was delayed. It would be included in the goal we set for ourselves.

We would live in the mountains in a tent and mine gold for a living until jobs were once again plentiful. Everyone thought us crazy, but in an envious sort of way. Thinking back now, we would have made the same decision for any reason. Dad mentioned my room was always available if it were needed.

One day Dad came by the apartment and told me my manager at the store was looking for me. I walked the three blocks to his office and he informed me they could use me every day through the coming holidays and into the middle of January if I was interested. That was four and a half months of steady work which would be perfect for the plans me and Sara had made. I thanked him.

"You start tomorrow," he replied.

I rushed to the apartment to tell Sara the news and we sat up until midnight finalizing our plans. We decided I would ride my bicycle to work and save the price of fuel. Sara was offered a job babysitting children in the building at $1.00 per day per child which was another $2. An additional $10 per week would really help out. We would save every cent we could toward our goal.

After the holidays and in January, my boss informed me the store was closing on the fifteenth of the month. Friday would be my last day. That was okay, since I knew the layoff was coming.

That night Sara brought out the old sock and we counted out our stash. We had $575. It would be April before we could begin our run to the mountains. In the meantime we had to figure out how not to spend what we had saved. Sara could continue to babysit until March and I would look for work and take anything that came along.

I went by to see Dad the next day and he told me about a fellow who went into the woods to cut firewood and seemed to be doing okay. The gentleman let it be known he could use some help.

Dad told me where the fellow lived and I went right over to see him. He was just leaving his house when I walked up. I asked if he was that guy who needed help. I told him who I was and why I was there.

He looked me over. "You look like you could handle the job; any experience?"

I told him, "I don't know the first thing about cutting wood, but I'm a good worker and a fast learner."

"Does $5 a day for the first two weeks sound okay? By then you should know what you're doing and I'll raise you to $7.50 a day. I work from 9 a.m. until 5 p.m. and from 8 a.m. to 1 p.m. on Saturday. What do you say?"

"I'll take it, and thanks."

"No thanks necessary, you'll earn it. You start tomorrow. Be here at 8:30 sharp; you can ride with me."

I told Sara about the job. "Goodness Jack, you'll wear yourself out before we get to the mountains," She replied.

"I'll be in good shape for the trip by that time," I answered.

After the first day on the job I told my boss, Gus, "You're right, I'll earn it."

He let a smile appear at the corner of his mouth and asked, "Are you game for tomorrow?"

"You bet. I'll be here," I answered.

Gus was good to his word. After two weeks, without fanfare, he raised me to $7.50 per day.

He sold most of the timber to three local jobbers in the area and they sold year-round to those who could afford to buy. They always sold out just before the next season set in.

Meanwhile, we continued to make our plans for the mountains. We accumulated camping items we thought would be needed and we were careful to buy the bargains. Our tent was a heavy duty canvas one room model that cost us $7. We had two gas lanterns that a friend had given us and folding chairs and a folding table. We had to purchase mountain clothes and mining equipment. We were also given three heavy duty canvas tarps.

On the first of April, while standing in his yard, I informed Gus we would be leaving the last of the month. He knew by then of course what my plans were and said he would miss me but he understood.

Suddenly a large truck passed the house, loaded with freshly cut timber. As Gus looked up he recognized the logs were from his cut timber which we had stacked for the last three days. He quickly ran into his house and called the sheriff, informing him of the situation. He gave directions the truck was headed to the sheriff told him we were going to our timber site.

Gus grabbed his rifle and we sped out of the yard. As we approached the site, two men were busy loading another truck with his stacked wood. Gus pointed the rifle at them and told them they were loading his wood and he was holding them for the sheriff.

We stationed ourselves about thirty feet from them as Gus continued to point the rifle at them. Finally, one fellow said he wasn't staying and started to move away. Gus told him to stop where he was. The fellow looked at his partner and motioned for him to move in the other direction, separating them by about ten yards.

The more aggressive of the two said "You can't get both of us before one of us gets you."

"Maybe so, answered Gus, but you won't know about it. I'll make sure you're the one I get," as he pointed the rifle at the man's chest.

Gus told me to take his truck and go down the trail to meet the sheriff and guide them in. Just as I was getting into the truck the sheriff arrived with two deputies following, who took custody of the two men.

The sheriff told us, "The other truck is still loaded with your timber and it's now parked behind my office. The two men from that truck are in jail. Same place these fellows are going."

As the deputies took the men away, the sheriff told Gus, "These four fellows have been stealing firewood throughout the county for the last three months and disposing of it in and around Bakersfield."

I got home that night and after I told Sara about the day's excitement, she informed me a fellow came by and noticed my model-

T never seemed to be moved. He wondered if it was broken down and wondered if I would like to sell it. Sara had told him it wasn't broken and it ran just fine, but that I was looking to replace it with a truck. The fellow told Sara he had a 1929 Ford pickup he could use as trade. Sara had his name and address.

Saturday afternoon after work I drove my model-T to the fellow's place and we haggled. I traded my car for his truck and $20 to boot.

We now had the vehicle we needed for our mountain adventure. Actually, the truck ran better than my model-T did, but the fellow mentioned he was good at working on cars and would have it in top shape in no time.

The last week of April I thanked Gus for the job and told him we would be leaving in a few days.

Gus replied, "If things don't work out, you can have the job back." I thanked him again and he paid me off.

Sara was already in the process of packing the clothes we would need. I took inventory of all we had accumulated and determined we had everything. That night after supper, Sara pulled out the old sock again and we began to count. We had $654.

We figured the trip from San Jose to Downieville would take two days. We planned to spend the night in Auburn and continue the trip into Downieville the next day.

The day before we were to leave, we took the entire day to spend with our families. A few tears were shed and everyone wished us good luck. Actually, both dads said they wish they could go with us as it sounded as if we were going to have fun.

Chapter 2
It was Downieville or Bust

The next morning we carefully packed everything in the truck and tied a tarp over it. Without a word between us, we got into the cab and drove away. We didn't say a word until we were almost to Fremont, which was about eighteen miles up the road.

"Jack, were doing the right thing aren't we?" asked Sara.

I quickly answered, "Yes Sara, were doing the right thing. We're doing it together and it's what we want to do. That makes it right."

Sara smiled and took my arm. "Good, I knew we were."

We arrived at Auburn around 4 p.m. and had a meal at the corner café on Main Street. We discussed our options of getting a room or camping out for the night. Sara was for camping out to save the money, so I drove to the edge of town and picked a spot for the night. I spread the tarp out from the bed of the truck for shelter. We were set for the night.

Next morning bright and early we repacked and drove back to the café for our breakfast. Bacon, beans and coffee with hot biscuits and a little egg never tasted so good. The coffee was hot and really hit the spot. We were soon off and running.

A short way north of Nevada City, we had a flat tire and it took me over three hours to repair the tire, inflate it and remount it. By the time we got back on the road it was late afternoon. The going was slow as the road was unpaved and rough. We made it to Downieville just as the sun was setting. We stopped in front of a place called Forks Bar and Grill.

I was twelve years old the last time I was here and didn't remember anything that I was seeing. As we entered the Grill, someone shouted, "Flat Landers!" The barkeep came around to welcome us.

"My name is Sam. how can I help you?"

I asked, "What is the day's special?"

156

"We don't have specials, just good food. We got mashed potatoes, corn on the cob and a little venison with coffee."

"How much?" I asked.

He smiled, "That's the special, $1.25 each."

While we were waiting for our meal a fellow came over, pulled up a chair and without asking, sat down. "Say, where you folks from?"

I was somewhat taken back, but answered, "San Jose; why do you ask?"

"Well, we don't get many folks in here this time of the evening as they're mostly all in their camps cooking their meals; besides I'm curious."

The barkeep brought our meal and as we began to eat, the fellow just sat there. "Say, do you folks have a place to stay tonight?"

"No, not yet," I answered.

"Well, if you don't you can stay here inside the Grill in the back room. We have an extra bed for emergencies. You never know what will come up in these mountains. It has clean sheets and a bathroom."

"Does the owner let you choose who stays in the room?"

"He sure does, I can let to whoever I want to."

I took a bite of the corn and it was good. "I would need to see the room first if you don't mind."

"Sure, as soon as you finish your meal. Sam, bring these folks some more coffee."

Sara stayed near the truck while I went for a look at the room. The room was as clean as any hotel room I had ever seen and the sheets were as crisp as he said they were. "How much for the night?"

"Well, I'm feeling very generous this evening, so I'll let you stay the night on the house."

"I think perhaps I should talk with your boss first, just to make sure it's okay."

He then did a funny thing. He turned his back to me and shouted, "Boss, is it okay?" He then turned back to me. "Boss says it's okay."

I began to laugh, "You're the boss."

"Yep. I own the place and you're welcome."

He pointed out a place to park the truck so it would be safe and assisted us in bringing in whatever was needed through the back door. We then went into the bar where our benefactor was seated. "I'm sorry but I haven't introduced myself. My name is Jack Dunn and this is my wife Sara." We shook hands.

"Call me Zack if you please; what'll you drink?"

"Coke for both of us will do."

Zack began to laugh, "I knew it the moment I saw you two---Mr. and Mrs. Goody Two-shoes."

"No," not really. "We have a drink on occasion."

"Well this is an occasion. Sam, bring my new friends a beer." We sat up talking with Zack until almost midnight. The place was empty. We told Zack our story and he said he would do what he could to help us.

"Tomorrow I want to introduce you to John. He is the expert around this area of the county and can help you to pick the best spot for your camp. I'm headed home to the wife; see you in the morning."

About seven the next morning I heard someone knock on the door and shout, "Get up you no lazy bums, what do you think this is, some kind of a resort? You got work to do."

We got dressed as quick as we could, brushed our teeth and walked into the dining area. Zack had the coffee ready with eggs and bacon cooking on the Grill.

"Now listen you two, John will be in shortly for his coffee and I want to introduce you. You'll like John. He's the nicest guy you'll ever meet. He is always looking to help someone."

A few minutes later a nice looking fellow walked in, nicely dressed but casual with short haircut and shined boots. I guessed him to be about my age. He glanced over at us, nodded and sat at the counter. Zack came out from in back and greeted him with a cup of coffee. They talked for a moment then came to our table.

"John, I want you to meet my new friends, Jack and Sara Dunn. They're from San Jose. They're here to join those other no good river snipers that infest the river every year at this time. Jack and

Sara, Meet John Spalding." We shook hands. John had a firm grip and looked me straight in the eye.

"If you're a friend of Zack's then you're a friend of mine. I'm glad to meet you. Don't let what Zack said upset you. He talks like that to everyone, especially if he likes you.

Zack tells me you're looking for a good place to mine and camp. I know a place that's good in the summer but terrible in the winter months. People have stayed there during the winter, but they did it only once."

It was about 10 in the morning when John mentioned he would lead us to the site, but it was too late to start today. "If you can be ready tomorrow morning about six we'll make a day of it. Zack, ok if these folks stay one more night in your room?"

"Sure it's ok, but the price is doubled from what it was last night."

I told John, "If it's the right place we won't be coming back with you, we will stay."

The next morning John was at the café at 6 a.m. as he said he would be, and he had two other fellows with him. John introduced them as Bob Mathews and Dominic Noble, two trusted friends.

"You said if this was the right place you would stay. You will need help getting your gear to the campsite so I brought along my two friends to help carry the load and to assist in setting up your camp."

John continued to talk. "The roads will be slippery this time of year so transfer part of your load into my truck for traction."

Bob and Dominic had ten bags of sand loaded in their truck and put two over the wheels in John's truck and two more into my truck.

Chapter 3
A Home in the Mountains

We headed out with John in the lead, me and Sara second and Bob and Dominic following. I told Sara to keep a sharp eye for land marks and turns.

She took a pad and began to make notes as we traveled. We traveled about five miles west on the old road to a northwest turn. A sign read Cal-Ida Lumber Company, two miles.

The road uphill was slippery as John said it would be. I could tell the bags of sand were doing their job. We came to the lumber company property where the road forked to the left to Brandy City, an old mining town, and north to who knows where. We went north. We traveled about twenty miles an hour for what seemed forever, when we suddenly came to the end of the road.

John parked his truck and we followed his lead. "Take a few items with you in case you stay and you won't have to carry them later." Bob and Dominic took a few items and so did John. Sara took two folding chairs and I took the ax, shovel and pinch bar. We began walking toward the creek. After about a hundred yards I could hear water flowing over rocks.

Suddenly John announced, "Welcome to Poker Flat, your new home." We took a look around and I knew instantly he was right. The campsite was about twenty yards from the water's edge with plenty of trees for shade and a nice large, flat area for the tent. To make a joke I said, "Well take it, how much for the night?"

John replied, "You can't afford it."

We headed back to the trucks for another load and after a third trip we had all that we had brought. Bob and Dominic began setting up the tent while John scouted out a place for a temporary outhouse. It turned out to be the final place. Sara unfolded the old army cots and placed them inside the tent. She also placed our collection of clothes alone side the cots.

John took a survey and announced, "This won't do for the long run; you'll need better cover and security as summer comes on, but don't worry, will take care of that." I didn't ask and he didn't say.

John announced it was time for them to be heading back. We thanked them for all they did and mentioned that some way we would like to repay them.

John replied, "You already have by being our new friends. Take care. We'll see you soon." They were off up the trail.

I took the shovel and began clearing an area for the camp fir, then dug a depression in the ground of about six inches deep and four feet wide. I piled stones around the edge of the depression and drove stout iron stakes, which we had brought with us to hang pots and pans.

Sara took out the lanterns and prepared them for lighting. She soon had them glowing as it was rapidly turning dark. We had brought snacks from town and that was going to be our first meal in camp. A good hot cup of coffee topped off the meal.

We sat beside the fire and talked well into the night. I told Sara the next morning I would be getting in a supply of firewood and scouting out crevices on the creek.

"Are you going to make us rich Jack?" she asked.

"Well, if I don't, it won't be from lack of trying," I answered.

The next morning, as a safety precaution, I strapped on my hand gun as I was going out for firewood. I loaded the rifle and told Sara it would always be beside our cots, just in case. She understood.

I rustled up firewood for three solid hours. I then took my gold pan, crevice tool, pinch bar and shovel to the creek to try my luck. I walked the water's edge looking for a crevice that ran into the water. They were all over the place. John mentioned he didn't think the area had been mined for twenty years, so it could be a good place with light gold. I was hoping he was right; I wanted it to be a good year for me and Sara.

Chapter 4
First Gold!

I selected a good looking crack in the bed rock and began to fill my gold pan with its gravel. I soon came to a lot of black sand and very small pea gravel which was a good sign. I filled the pan and began to wash out the lighter gravel and was soon near the bottom of the pan when I spotted what looked like the sun in the bottom of the pan. I must have had at least a quarter ounce of gold covering the bottom of the pan. I yelled for Sara and she came running.

"Are we rich yet?"

"Well not yet, but look at this." Sara was like a kid in a candy store as she looked into the pan.

"How much is that?" she asked.

"Somewhere around a quarter ounce I think."

"Well, how much is that?" she wanted to know.

"About six or seven dollars, gold is a little over $26 an ounce. Stick around while I dig another pan full."

I was down about a foot into the crack of the rock and started to wash. As I did so I thought I saw a glitter but kept washing and throwing out the larger pieces of gravel.

As I was near the bottom, there it was. The largest gold nugget I had ever seen. Sara yelped and so did I. We started to dance and laugh about our prize. It looked to be about 1-½ ounces of pure gold. We were really excited. I had forgotten about what was left to wash in the pan. I finished washing and on the bottom were gold particles and black sand. I asked Sara to fetch the glass jar we brought to put our gold in. When Sera returned, I poured the black sand and gold into the jar and made the cap tight.

Sara wanted to know why I saved the black sand. I explained. "Where you find black sand in these mountains you will most times fine gold. After we fill the jar half full we will purchase a little mercury in town and add that to the jar. Gold particles and dust will form a ball of gold and mercury. We then can burn off the mercury and have just gold left."

I could tell Sara didn't really understand, so I told her I would be sure to show her when the time came. Sara went back to her chores and I continued to clean out the crevice, collecting a few more small nuggets and dust. While doing this I had eyed a crevice on the opposite side of the creek that looked promising.

As I was crossing over, a small black bear came out of the timber about thirty yards from me and halted while eyeing me. I froze in my tracks, right in the middle of the creek. I made no movement. The bear started sniffing the air and I could tell he was smelling something different then he was used to. I slowly reached for my pistol, just in case. The bear turned and walked back towards the timber and again stopped. It turned back toward me and began sniffing the air again. By then I had my pistol in my hand. The bear slowly turned back towards the woods and disappeared. I stayed where I was for a couple of minutes and decided to return to my camp side of the creek. I would try that crevice at another time.

I didn't tell Sara about the bear; no use upsetting her this early in our adventure. I would tell her later after she felt more secure in our surroundings.

I needed a sluice box to work higher up on the bank for the light gold. It was one way Sara could mine with me if she wanted to, which she did. Once she knew what she was doing, she was very good. I would dig a crevice while Sara was doing the washing, I would fill the other pan with gravel. We would switch pans and keep ourselves busy for a couple of hours until one of us called for a break.

Sometimes we would find very little and other times we got a big surprise. Only occasionally did we find nothing. After three days we had the jar about half full. I told Sara the next time to town we needed to purchase mercury.

That's when Sara mentioned she would like to attend church on Sunday if we could manage it.

Sunday morning we dressed for church, walked up the hill to the truck and drove into town just as service was beginning. As we walked inside we were surprised. Dominic whispered, "Over here."

The organ player announced the number of the song we were to sing. The organ player was Bob. This little town sure had surprises. It was a wonderful service with the preacher acting out his sermon.

When the plate was passed around, there was very little in it when it got to me. I reached into my pocket and pulled out the large gold nugget and showed it to Sara, she nodded yes. I dropped it in the plate and passed it forward.

As the service was winding down, Bob stood up and announced, "Seems someone put a gold nugget in the plate by mistake. If you would like to retrieve it, see me after the service."

We hung around outside after the service talking with Dominic until Bob came outside. He said that John went to church up on the hill on the other side of town at the Catholic Church and always took lunch at the Forks Grill on Sunday. The four of us meandered over to the Grill and John was already seated with a young lady he introduced as his bride-to-be. Her name was Patty Armstrong, and she sure was pretty. Patty and Sara hit it off right away.

John said he was coming out to see us next Saturday and he was bringing lumber material.

"What are you going to build, John?" inquired Sara.

"A tent house, large enough for two people to be comfortable."

"Say, going back this afternoon you can take a few of the boards with you, make less of a load on Saturday," chimed in Bob.

Before leaving for camp, we drove by Bob and Dominic's place and loaded up as many of the boards as we could carry. I had mentioned earlier that I needed to build a sluice box and John called out as we were driving away, "Use whatever you need to build your sluice box."

Monday morning I gathered what I needed for the box, pulled out my hand saw, gathered some nails, put my hammer in the canvas bag with everything else and walked over to a tree stump that made a good sawhorse. Then I built my box.

For you that don't know, a sniper's sluice box is nothing more than three boards six to eight feet long, nailed together to form a U-shaped trough. The sides are six or eight inches high and its flat bottom is from ten to twelve inches wide. It has detachable riffles of wood which catch and hold particles of gold which wash from the gravel shoveled into the box. It must be light enough to carry, as a sniper will only work for a short time in one place and will continue to do so until gold is found.

I finished the box and Sara asked, "How in the world do you get gold with that thing?"

"Let's have lunch; then I'll take you to the creek and show you how this thing works." We had our lunch break and I told Sara, "Fetch the rifle and follow me."

We walked upstream a little ways to a spot I had spied out earlier. About three feet in from the water's edge I leveled out a spot by removing the overburden. I set the box in the creek so water could continue to run through the box. I placed rocks around the sides to keep it in place.

Sara was watching all this time and I could tell she wanted to ask questions, but she didn't. I began to shovel dirt from the place I had leveled. I dug deep into the dirt and loaded the box a shovel at a time. Sara just sat there. After about an hour I decided to see if I had picked the right spot. I lifted the box from the river, careful to keep it level as not to spill any gold. I removed the riffles and poured everything that had been caught by the riffles into my gold pan.

I sat down on a nice flat rock and began to wash. Sara came up behind me to look over my shoulders. As I neared the bottom, gold began to show. Sara let out a yelp that I thought broke my ear drum. I had never seen Sara that excited before.

She jumped up and began running toward our tent. I didn't know what to think of her actions. A few moments later she came running back with something in her arms that looked like a bottle. It was a bottle of champagne she had secreted in her clothes for just this occasion. She was so excited she forgot to bring glasses. She said she would be right back.

As she started back I shouted, "Bring a cork screw if you have one."

She stopped, turned around and shouted, "You party stopper." She had forgotten to pack a cork screw.

I started to laugh and so did she. We hugged each other and decided to save it until we could get a corkscrew in town.

Chapter 5
Building the Campsite

Saturday morning around 7 a.m. we heard John's voice announcing his arrival, followed by Bob and Dominic. We had just put the coffee pot on and Bob said he would take his black.

Sara gazed at the tools they were carrying. "What are you planning to build with all those tools?" she asked.

"Just a tent house," answered John.

John started laying out the foundation while Bob and Dominic went back to the trucks for the remainder of materials. By the time they returned John had started the frame of the floor and had it setting on four well anchored stones. Bob and Dominic started building the wall frames. Before long we had a solid floor and four walls six feet high with a window and a solid hinged door on one side.

We emptied the tent of belongings and we each took a corner of the tent, lifted it to the top of the walls and secured it to two-by-fours with rope. We stood back to admire our work.

Sara sighed. "If we had a cork screw we could christen it."

Dominic raised his hand, "I'll be right back." He took off up the hill like a scared rabbit and in about ten minutes he was back with a cork screw.

"I think we will christen our new home by drinking a toast to three of the finest people we know. You guys are terrific and we thank you," said Sara as she raised her glass.

John mentioned that perhaps one more toast was due. "Here is to John and Patty who will be married to each other August first. You know of course you're not invited and neither are you two guys," pointing to Bob and Dominic.

"Don't worry, we won't be there," they answered.

It was a little late to be starting back to town so we invited them to stay the night and enjoy some home cooking.

"That's a great idea, and tomorrow we can all go to town together and attend church," replied Dominic.

We sat up until about 11 that night and really enjoyed each other's company. Next morning we were up and running by 7 a.m. We were dressed for church but the boys had to go home to dress.

Arriving in town, we strolled to the Grill to see Zack and shared a coffee with him. He wanted to know if the boys were treating us right.

"They are," I answered. "I don't know how we will pay them back."

After church we met at the Grill for lunch. John brought Patty to lunch and we congratulated her on the wedding.

Before leaving for camp that morning, I took John to the side and asked him what I owed for the lumber they used to build the tent house. John replied, "We got the material free for getting it off the property of a neighbor who had built a new cabin down on the Yuba, about one mile from town. It was in his way and he thanked us for removing it."

We left for home about two that afternoon and Sara mentioned she would like to see what the old town of Brandy City looked like as it was only a short distance from the lumber company; that is, if we had time.

As we approached the lumber company we took the road leading to Brandy City, and within a short time we were in the middle of what was at one time a wonderful old mining town. We were surprised to find six people still living there. Almost all the buildings were in the process of falling down. Those living there were of two families and they were still mining for their living. We shared our snacks with them and began to visit when Sara reminded me it was getting late and we'd better get home before dark. We asked if we could visit another time and they answered, "Please do."

We arrived at our parking place with about thirty minutes of daylight left, which was just enough to see our way to the tent house. We made a note to always take a lantern with us in the future, just in case.

As the sun was coming up the next morning, I smelled fresh coffee and bacon cooking. Sara was already busy. After breakfast, we took inventory of what needed to be done next. I mentioned that taking a bath in the cold water of the creek was horrible and she agreed.

A couple of days back I had seen an old fifty-gallon drum. It was a good thing Sara reminded me of the time, for it had looked to be useable. "I'm going after that old drum and make us a shower."

Sara wanted to know how I could possibly make a shower out of an old drum. I told her it would be easier to show than explain. I told her to stay alert while I was gone. I would be only an hour or so.

I got the drum loaded in the truck and returned to my parking spot; from there I rolled the drum downhill to the camp. It took me quite some time to cut off the top with a hammer and chisel. I then punched small holes in the bottom as drain holes. I flattened out the top so it would fit into the drum. I fastened a handle on the top lid, tied a ten foot section of small rope to the handle and mounted the whole thing in a tree branch about seven feet high. I nailed boards on the tree so we could climb to the top of the drum.

I told Sara, "Heat a couple buckets of water from the creek." I climbed to the top and poured the warm water into the drum, got undressed, stood under the drum and pulled the rope. Warm water cascaded down on me, I released the rope, soaped myself and pulled the rope again rinsing myself off.

Sara was delighted. She shouted, "Next."

The next day I built a canvas cover around the shower for modesty, as if I needed it.

On Wednesday I took my sluice box and gold pan to the creek for some serious mining. I had seen a spot downstream that I wanted to try. I cleaned out the crack in the rock and sat on a rock to pan when I heard a familiar sound. I slowly turned around and looked all around me but saw nothing. As I started again to wash, I again heard the sound. This time I knew it was near. I froze. I held the position for some time, trying not to move a muscle. Shortly, from the corner of my eye, a rattlesnake that had been sunning itself on a rock about three feet from me began to move away. I continued to hold my position for a few moments before jumping to my feet. I began looking around me for any other snakes. I found none.

It suddenly occurred to me that this was snake country, and as the summer got warmer the snakes would be coming out. I left my tools and walked back to camp. Without saying anything to Sara, I began to dig a trench around our tent house.

By now Sara knew what I was doing and she asked, "Did you see a snake?"

"I sure did," I answered.

"A rattler?" she asked.

"Yep," I told Sara to cut strips of canvas about ten inches wide and as long as she could.

After finishing the trench, I lined it with the canvas strips and sealed the joints as best as I could. I carried a couple of buckets of water from the creek and poured it into the trench. The water held. I told Sara we needed to keep water in the trench as best as we could, and she understood. Every time either of us went to the creek, we were to bring back another bucket of water. Nothing more was said about the snake and Sara didn't ask. We knew we were not to sit anywhere without looking the place over very carefully.

I did a lot of thinking the rest of the afternoon and decided we needed to establish some safety rules for both of us to follow. I told Sara I would always wear my handgun in camp and the rifle was to be loaded at all times and leaning in the corner of the tent house.

I had an old whistle in my locker and I got it out and told Sara to tie it around her neck and if she needed me and she couldn't get to the rifle, she was to blow the whistle as loud as she could and I would come running. She was only to use the rifle in an emergency situation. That way, if I heard the rifle I would know it was an emergency.

I told Sara I was going back to get my tools, for I would work that crevice some other time. I also told her that in the future when I was away mining we should set a time limit for my return and if within a ten minute span I wasn't back she was to come looking for me, bringing the rifle.

Just as a precaution, I wrote the regulations on a paper and hung it in the tent house so we could refer to them from time to time. I didn't want either of us forgetting what we were to do in a situation.

Sara got into a habit each morning of reading the paper, which was good.

Chapter 6
Trouble in the Mountains

The next few days were warm and beautiful and my mining was not as good as it had been. I needed a new spot and I began looking around. I told Sara I was going a little further upstream the next day to scout out a new crevice. I would return at 1 p.m.

After breakfast the next morning I put my tools in the sack, grabbed my pinch bar and shovel and took off up creek. I went about a hundred and fifty yards and saw a crevice with promise. I began working the gravel out and putting it in the pan. I searched around to make sure no snakes were about and took a seat to wash the dirt.

As I was working the pan I thought I saw movement to the right of me. I paused and looked around but saw nothing. I went back to work.

Suddenly a voice said, "What are you doing here? This is my claim, pick up your stuff and get out of here." He was pointing a rifle in my direction.

"Now hold on mister, I mean no harm. I didn't know this area was a claim."

"Well you know it now."

"Where are your claim markers? I haven't seen any."

"My claim marker is right here in my hand." He waved the rifle at me again. "Where did you come from?"

"I'm camped downstream a ways." I answered.

"Then get going," he ordered.

He began following me with the rifle and I was concerned. Getting closer to camp, I began talking louder so Sara would hear me. "You don't need to point that rifle at me mister."

As we walked into camp Sara was not in sight. I was thankful for that. "Ok, now take off that holster and drop it on the ground," he demanded.

At that very moment, Sara stepped out from behind a large tree. "Don't move mister. If you do I'm going to shoot you. Don't even turn around. Drop the rifle and walk away five steps." He dropped the rifle and I grabbed it. I went to Sara as she had our rifle pointed straight at the man.

I drew my pistol and told him to turn around. I wanted him to see that we meant business. I told him to walk to the tree nearest to him and sit on the ground and wrap his legs around it. I told Sara to keep the rifle pointed at him. I went in the tent house for rope and tied each ankle separately and then tied the ankles about six inches apart. I then tied to the cross rope between ankles and tied that end to another tree five feet away. There was no way he could get lose from that.

I told Sara to take the handgun, go to the truck and drive to the lumber company and have them contact the sheriff. Explain the situation and come back here with the sheriff.

I sat with the man's back to me, holding my rifle all the while. After looking over his rifle I was surprised to find it was not loaded. I tried to get him to talk, but he just sat there saying nothing.

It was about 4:30 p.m. before Sara and the sheriff with three deputies came into camp. The sheriff took charge of the man by cuffing him to a waist chain. The sheriff recognized the man immediately. He was an escapee from Folsom prison, serving forty years for murdering his wife.

It was completely dark before the sheriff and his men started up the hill to their vehicles. I led the way with two lanterns as the path was hard to see in the dark. Sara came following after me.

"You're not leaving me there alone." We thanked the sheriff and started back to camp. Neither of us was able to sleep that night.

The next day was Saturday and we were exhausted from the day before so made a lazy day of it by doing nothing. I could tell Sara was uneasy about the happenings. Later in the day Sara spoke of the situation.

"Jack, I'm concerned about staying here. You had a close call by the snake and now the encounter with the escaped convict. I love the place, but I'm afraid."

"I understand how you feel honey; let's make it for two more weeks. If nothing happens in that time, we'll talk. If we have another encounter during that time, we'll leave." Sara agreed, but I could tell she was uneasy.

Sunday morning we dressed to go to church. It seemed like everyone in Downieville knew about what happened to us on Friday. Bob and Dominic greeted us at the Grill as we were having a cup of coffee. John came in, but he didn't know anything about what happened as he was in Reno and had gotten back late Saturday evening.

A couple from church came into the Grill and spotted Sara. They came over to us.

"Good morning Miss Anne Oakley, how are you this morning?"

Sara smiled and replied, "I'm just fine thank you."

I decided to change the subject, so I asked John if he knew where I could purchase a small gold scale. John said he had one he would loan me and I could pick it up after church.

We went by John's place for the gold scale and then we headed home. I noticed Sara was thinking about something, so I just waited for her to speak.

"Jack, did you notice anything different about John today?"

"No, not really, why?"

"He seemed to have his mind somewhere else today. He was not looking at everyone as he normally does when he speaks to them."

"If there's a problem I'm sure John will tell us," I replied.

We arrived back at camp and I started a fire while Sara whipped up a snack with coffee. We talked into the night about the wonderful people we had met and the exciting things that happened. It's as if all things were planned for us---they just fell into place. I ask Sara about her stepping out from behind the tree with the rifle. "How did you decide to do that?"

"I was getting ready to take some dirty clothes to the creek to wash. As I was approaching the creek, I saw you coming down the bank with someone behind you carrying a rifle. I knew you were in trouble. I ran back to the tent cabin, got the rifle and went over behind the tree. I heard you talking to the man about pointing the rifle. As you came into the camp, I heard him tell you to drop your holster. That's when I stepped from behind the tree. I shudder to think what he might have done if he'd had ammo in his rifle."

It was Monday and the beginning of another week for us. I told Sara that perhaps she should accompany me whenever I left camp. Sara thought it would be safer if we were split up. That way we cover each other like before. I agreed, but we needed another signal.

"From now on, I'll tell you the time I'll return to camp. You take the rifle and go down toward the outhouse about ten minutes before I'm due and wait there until you see me coming. That way, if there is a problem, well, you have the rifle."

For the remainder of that summer, we never saw another bear, nor did we encounter any other animals that were harmful. I promised Sara we would talk if we had any other problems. As I started to do so Sara stopped me.

"Not necessary, I've gotten used to our routine and I feel comfortable in all that we do. Our signals work well for us."

The month of July was uneventful. I found a good crevice down river and worked it for five days. I started out about two feet up the bank and ran about three feet into the creek. The more I dug the wider it got until I had a crevice that was about a foot and half wide and about two feet deep.

I took five ounces of gold from that crevice the first three days. I then took a one day break, and after returning to the crevice, I took another ounce and a half. It was the best find yet.

Sara informed she wanted to try her luck. "Who knows, we may have to do this longer than we think." She was right, so off we went together. She carried the rifle and I had the hand gun. As we walked along, I explained how to identify a good crevice and how gold was trapped by the cracks in the bedrock.

Sara pointed, "Like that one there?" I had been by that crevice a number of times but never paid much attention, as it didn't look that good to me.

"Well maybe; you want to try that one?"

"Sure, why not."

I said, "Okay, scrape off the loose gravel on top until you get to hard gravel. Then load the pan with all that you dig out. When you finally get to the bottom, scrape real hard with the spoon end of the crevice tool. Sometimes you don't reach bottom because the crevice may go much deeper than you can reach. That's when we take the pinch bar and pry open the crevice, but sometimes the crevice won't pry open. In that case, your finish with the crevice and you move on.

Sara dug until she had a pan full. I found a good rock where she could sit with both feet in the water and the pan in front of her. As she got to the bottom of the pan I could already see small particles of gold with black sand. She yelped with joy.

"Well my darling, you're now a seasoned miner."

We poured the contents in the jar and Sara turned back to the crevice and began digging again. She worked that crevice for about two hours until she couldn't reach the bottom. I took over as my arms were longer than hers, but the bottom was as hard as concrete and I was able to get very little. She washed the remainder of the pan and had about the same amount in gold as the first two pan loads.

We dug another crevice that day and weighed the gold that night. We had one and three quarter ounces for the day. Sara was excited about learning how to mine. She wanted to know how much gold we had.

After weighing all that we mined, we had eighteen and one half ounces of gold. At twenty seven dollars per ounce we had almost $500. With $300 from our original stash, we were $800 rich. If we had stayed in San Jose, after paying rent and all that goes with living in the city, I am sure we would not have had near what we had, and we had given away an ounce and a half. Sara was happy and so was I.

Chapter 7
The Wedding

We went to town the next day for provisions and stopped at Zack's for refreshments. Zack and John were deep in conversation about something. Sam brought us a coke each and while enjoying the taste, John came over and broke the news.

"I have been offered a job in Reno, but I don't know if I should take it. It's for four months of steady work. But I would have to live there. It's a night job. Patty thinks I should take it, but it would result in us postponing our wedding. It pays more money than I have ever made before, but with rent, food, fuel and other incidentals, I would only be able to save a little each month. Being away from Patty that long and postponing our wedding makes me think I would be making a mistake. Jack, if you were in my shoes, what would you do?"

I thought for a moment. "John, being the old hand that I am in this married business, I would marry Patty right away and take her with me and make a honeymoon out of it. These are hard times, and who knows, somewhere down the road this same outfit may want to hire you again, but by turning down this opportunity they would be hesitant in their decision to hire you."

John pondered that a while. "I'm going to marry Patty right away, but I won't take the job. I'm young enough to overcome any problem my decision may cause. Patty's folks are getting up in years and she wants to stay close to them. Staying in Downieville with my friends and being close to Patty's parents seems the best decision I can make for both of us."

Sara had been listening to all John said. "John, you're a good man. You're thinking about Patty first. Each spouse should always come first to the other and that's what you are doing. You two will do just fine in this old world."

John said he was going to tell Patty his decision right away and he would let us know about the wedding date. We headed for the truck and drove home. As we were riding, I said to Sara, "That was a nice thing you said to John about the spouse coming first. Just don't forget it." Sara laughed, put her arm in mine and we sang all the way to camp.

August was fast approaching and I mentioned we hadn't heard anything about John and Patty's wedding. As we were taking our lunch break, low and behold, John came walking into camp with Patty hanging on his arm.

"Just wanted you folks to know were tying the knot this Saturday afternoon at the church on the hill. Be there at 2 pm if you want to see two scared kids get married. Zack says you can bunk in the spare room Saturday night if you want to."

Sara replied, "We'd rather drive home in the dark."

"Sure you would," laughed John.

Sara whipped up a little grub for John and Patty and we visited for about an hour. Patty mentioned she had to get home and take care of a few things.

John replied, "Just like a woman, when everything is going good, she wants to go home." As they left John called out, "See you Saturday. It'll be a short ceremony."

Bob began playing the wedding march and Patty began her walk, holding on to her father's arm. She sure was pretty in her all white dress. John was dressed in white slacks and jacket with black shoes and a black bowtie. We had never seen him that dressed up before.

Sara whispered, "John sure looks nice doesn't he?"

After the ceremony a few people whipped out their box cameras and took pictures and then we went to the Grill for an informal reception. Everyone toasted Patty and John. Zack had a little speech to make.

"Here's to John and Patty. May your blessings be many, may your troubles be less and may your children be as nice as you both are." Everyone toasted to that. Patty thanked everyone and turned her back to throw the flowers until she realized there were no single females to throw to.

John shouted, "All you single men form behind Patty." Patty threw the flowers.

Dominic caught it, saying, "I'm never getting married." *Yeah, sure.*

We took Zack's spare room that night and attended church the next morning. Driving home we talked about how the people in Downieville really loved each other and were always looking to help each other out, never asking for anything in return.

I spent every day the next week working with the sluice box in an area that had a lot of black sand. I worked all day before cleaning up the sluice box. At the end of the week I had collected 2-¼ ounces of very fine gold.

I mentioned to Sara we would need to cash in before too long as I didn't want to accumulate too much gold in camp. She agreed without asking any questions.

Chapter 8
Pay Day

At the end of the week, we rode into town for supplies and I ask Zack if he knew of any honest gold buyers in town. He did, but he said they would not pay as much as the jewelry buyers would over in Reno. That was the place to cash in small nuggets and pieces. Any gold dust should be shipped to the mint in San Francisco. They would charge for the purification and would pay in gold coin or greenbacks. I told him that on our next trip I would bring all the dust we had collected. He said we could take it to the express and they would take it from there.

Before leaving town, we drove by to see John and Patty. They had moved into a small two-bedroom cottage on the road that paralleled the Downie River. Each bedroom had a bath and shower. John said he was working for a gentleman in Serra City for the next two weeks in setting up his business as a broker in investments of gold, silver and platinum. He established his office in the old Wells Fargo building at the east end of town. He was buying, selling and investing in small mining claims and doing very well.

I didn't say anything to John about the conversation I'd had with Zack about selling our gold. I had been thinking it over and decided I would go to the bank in town and rent a safety deposit box to store the gold. That way I could cash in anytime I wanted without worrying about the gold being in camp and the wrong person finding out about it.

September arrived and I could see the weather starting to change. We had received a few rain showers and the days were mostly overcast. I gathered all the gold we had accumulated and we drove into town. I went directly to the Bank and opened an account and got a free safety box as a new customer. I deposited $250 in a savings account and made sure Sara was on all account numbers so she could always get to the money and gold if needed.

John finished his assignment in Serra City and was at home when we went by. He said he was coming out to see us the next day as he had something to discuss with us.

John mentioned an early winter was coming on and we were going to need a place to stay as we couldn't stay in the mountains in a tent house.

He then surprised us. "We have a spare bedroom with bath. We could split the cost of everything and make it an easy living expense for everyone. It would really help us if you and Sara would consider bunking in with us for the winter. Besides, we think we like you."

Sara and I talked over the offer for about five seconds and told them we would be delighted to share the cottage with them for the winter. John invited us to stay the night and have dinner with them. As Sara and Patty were in the kitchen, I asked John how the job in Serra City turned out. He answered, "Everything ended just as the boss had planned and I received a fifty-dollar bonus when the job ended."

Everyone that knew John had nothing but good things to say about him, and the more I talked with him the more I was convinced, John would always be my friend.

John mentioned that we would need to shelter the tent house for the winter to keep the snows from destroying it by erecting a pole type barn. I didn't know what that was and he said instead of explaining it he would show me next week as he had the lumber lined up and ready to go.

"How much for the lumber?" I asked.

His answer surprised me. "You have already paid for it. You remember the nugget you dropped into the collection plate in church?"

"Well yes, but I didn't know anyone knew."

"Well Dominic and Bob knew. Bob took the nugget to Reno and sold it to a jewelry maker and got $75 for it, as it was a 2-½ ounce nugget and would make a beautiful pendant. The congregation knew about you and Sara camping at Poker Flat and knew you would need shelter for the winter. They authorized Bob and Dominic to purchase the materials for the pole barn and were coming to your place next week to build it. We'll stay overnight and I'll bring Patty as company for Sara."

I was without words to answer John. The friendship these people had shown kept getting better each day. I had never known people like these---they were a special breed. I didn't tell Sara about Patty coming to camp with John. I would let it be a surprise.

The next morning as we were preparing to leave, John said he would see us on Tuesday.

Sara turned to John. "You're coming to see us on Tuesday?"

"Didn't Jack tell you?" replied John.

Sara looked to me, then back to John. "Tell me what?"

"Never mind, you will find out Tuesday," answered John.

Chapter 9
Winter Preparation

All the way home Sara kept after me to tell her why John was coming to see us on Tuesday. I told her she was being nosey. That didn't settle with her and she almost demanded to know. I insisted she wait and see.

Sara smiled, "You're a sneaky husband Jack Dunn and I'm not going to stand for it." I returned the smile. After being bugged all day Monday by Sara, Tuesday at around 9am, John, Patty, Bob and Dominic all came walking into camp carrying lumber materials and pulling a load on a ground sled. Sara was delighted to see them and especially Patty. We unloaded the sled and all went back up the hill to fetch another load.

Sara kept after us on what we were going to build and finally Dominic spoke up. "If you really need to know, were going to build an office building. You guys are going to need it to house the office staff that's needed to keep track of all the gold you're finding."

Sara smiled. "You're as bad as my husband, neither of you are any good."

I soon learned what a pole barn was. The boys lined out a square surrounding the tent house and dug holes about two feet deep at each corner. The corners were sixteen feet apart. They then dug a hole between each corner at the same depth. They placed eight foot poles in the holes and as Bob used the level to plumb the post the others began to back-fill and tamp the gravel into place inside the holes around the post. They then nailed a 2 x 6 board about two inches from the top all the way around. Then they cut the top of the poles even with the 2 x 6 creating a rafter anchor. Using a 2 x 8 as a ridge board, they fixed the ridge board at five feet above the level part of the post. Upon attaching the rafters to the ridge board, it created a very steep roof, which would help in shedding the snow. They added bracing where needed and began sheeting the roof.

By this time it was getting late and John announced we could finish tomorrow within a couple of hours. Sara and Patty had been preparing dinner of hamburgers and onions and potatoes with catsup. The real surprise was the apple pie Sara brought out, which she had purchased while in town on Sunday. I never saw six people devour a whole pie in such a short time.

The next morning everyone was up early and ready to go after we had our breakfast. The only thing left to do was complete the roof sheeting, which took about two hours. We all stood back to admire our work and it sure did look nice with a solid roof over the tent house. John said it should hold through the winter, protecting the tent house.

The boys prepared to leave and they left before John and Patty. They said they were going sniping upstream on the river at a place they checked out as having a lot of loose slate rock with millions of cracks where gold could catch.

We visited with John and Patty for about an hour and set a date to move in with them. There were certain items we would leave here at the camp as John and Patty didn't have much storage space. The folded cots, cooking stove and mining equipment we could leave in camp.

As they were leaving, John waved. "We'll see you a week from Monday."

It was noticeable that the creek wasn't running as much water the last few days as it had been. Because of that, a number of crevices I hadn't noticed before were showing. I found one crevice that ran clear across the creek to the other bank and decided I would work it.

I started about one foot above the water line and began working downward. There was a lot of small gravel and sand, even on the top. I just knew this was going to be a good one. After filling the first pan I began to wash and before I was half way to the bottom of the pan I could see gold. The pan bottom was just covered with small pea size nuggets. It was the best pan I'd had to date. I poured the contents into the jar, filled another pan and began to wash. Almost instantly I spotted a large nugget and grabbed it. I stopped washing and examined the nugget. It was a beautiful heart shape that would make a nice piece of jewelry. I put it into my pocket and continued to wash. Again the bottom of the pan was covered with small nuggets.

I worked that crevice for three full days without weighing any of the gold. On the third day I pulled out the scale. I had over nine ounces of gold from that crevice. When Sara wasn't looking, I checked the large nugget and found it too heavy for the scale. I then put the large nugget on the basket and poured small nuggets on the opposite basket until I had a balance. I then weighed the smaller nuggets and found I had a 4-¾ ounce nugget. This gave me a total of 13-¾ ounces from that one crevice. At $27 an ounce I had mined $360 from that crevice.

It was Thursday and we had four days before we would vacate the camp. We decided we wouldn't go to church Sunday as it would be our last day in camp and we needed the time to pack and prepare. I already decided I would pack some of the items to the truck on Saturday and tarp it to protect it from the weather. Doing so would make it easier for both of us on Sunday and Monday morning.

That Thursday night Sara mentioned she would like to go with me the next day and do some mining herself as it would be the last time for her for a few months. We could work together by using the sluice box.

Next morning we gathered the few items we would need and I shouldered the sluice box. Down river we went. I found a spot I had eyed before and set the box in place. I began by removing overburden and as I hit dirt we began to shovel into the box. We worked for about an hour and Sara wanted to see how we were doing. I didn't like removing the riffles from the sluice box, but so what, Sara deserved to have some fun too.

I carefully lifted the riffles from the box. Even before I began washing the sand from the box I could see several specks of gold. To my surprise the specks became flakers, and then tiny nuggets. This all multiplied as the water flushed the sand from the box into the gold pan. I was almost as excited as Sara was as she was looking over my shoulder.

"Oh, Jack, we've hit it, just look at that gold, look at those nuggets."

I never expected us to find anything like that. It was no great strike and I knew it, but to be sure it was a lot better than I expected it to be. We worked that area for about three more hours and decided to call it a day. I lifted the riffles from the box and poured everything into the pan and washed to the bottom and then poured that into our jar. We picked up our gear and headed back to camp.

That night as Sara was preparing our nightly snack, I took down the scales and began weighing our day's catch. We had over 5 ounces that day alone. If someone had told me we were going to find this amount of gold our first few months, I would have thought it was a joke.

While eating our snacks, Sara asked, "Jack, are we this good or are we just plain lucky?" I thought on that a moment.

"Luck has nothing to do with it. We have the right tools and knowledge, and the blessing of the good Lord. Sara looked at me with love in her eyes, smiled, bowed her head and said, "Amen."

Saturday we slept later than usual. I was normally up by six and here it was almost eight. That was ok, as the only thing we had to do was carry a few things to the truck and tarp them down. We lay around all day and I did a little reading while Sara slept on and off.

Sunday we did more of the same, except we carried everything else to the truck that needed to go except for what would be needed our last night in camp.

Monday morning I had a strange feeling about leaving, but I knew John was right; winter in these mountains could be fatal.

As we headed uphill to the truck, I turned for a last look. Sara took me by the arm, leaned her head on my shoulder and cried. "Jack, I have fallen in love with this place. I love it here and I hate to leave. I'm afraid we might not get back."

"We'll be back, I promise."

Chapter 10
A Hospital Stay

We drove into the yard at John and Patty's just as Bob was rushing from the house in a panic.

"What's up Bob?" I shouted.

"Can't talk, ask John." He kept running. I went inside and John was getting some gear from a closet.

"What's going on John?"

"Dominic has fallen down a cliff and broken his leg and he has a nasty cut on the leg. We've got to get him out and to a hospital."

I told Sara, "Stay with Patty and store the equipment as soon as I throw it out of the truck."

John's truck was smaller than mine so he jumped in with me and we were off. Bob was right behind us in his truck. John filled me in while I drove. Dominic and Bob were sniping upstream on the Yuba when Dominic slipped and fell about twenty feet. Bob was on his way to notify the ranger station when he ran past me. The ranger would contact the hospital in Grass Valley to inform them we would be bringing Dominic there.

We were about a mile upstream when Bob blew his horn and waved us over. Bob passed us to lead the rest of the way. Another half mile and we were there.

Dominic was in a lot of pain. The first thing we had to do was figure how to get him up to the road. Bob lowered a cot down to Dominic and climbed down to help him into the cot. It was slow going but Bob was able to get him onto the cot. Bob attached the rope to all four handles of the cot. I told John I didn't think the two of us could pull him up.

John shouted, "We got to try." As a little luck would have it, two forest rangers arrived and between the four of us and with Bob guiding the cot, we got Dominic to the top.

As we were loading him in my truck the town doctor arrived and took a look at Dominic. Doc gave him something for pain and then got in back with Dominic. He said he would ride back to town from there.

We dropped Doc off and Bob jumped in back with Dominic as we continued on through town to Grass Valley. It was 45 miles on rough dirt roads. I drove as best I could. We didn't get to the hospital until three o'clock in the afternoon, but they were waiting for us and took Dominic immediately. They gave him a quick exam and rushed him into surgery. It was too late to start back. We decided to get a place to stay. The hospital informed us they had extra rooms for just such an occasion and we could stay there on cots.

John asked if there was a way to get a message to our wives in Downieville. The nurse said she could call the sheriff and have them notify the ranger in Downieville and they in turn could deliver the message. We thanked her. Just tell them we are staying for the night and everything is okay.

Next morning we went to Dominic's room to see how he was doing and he informed us he was ready to go home. The nurse told him his mind was ready but his body was far from it. We left him with the promise we would see him again before he was released. The doctor said he would be in the hospital at least a week for he also had a mild concussion.

We got the truck and were headed home when John said, "Dominic has no money to pay the hospital or the doctor. We may need to pass the hat in town to get him released from the hospital."

That night I mentioned to Sara what John said about Dominic's situation on finances. I suggested we do our part and she agreed. On Wednesday the two of us took a ride to Grass Valley to visit Dominic and he was doing fine. I went to the office and inquired about the hospital and doctor's bill. The lady didn't have all the information at that time but it probably would run around $700 for both bills. She told me Dominic was scheduled to be discharged on Saturday. I thanked her and we left.

Sara and I talked about the bill on the way home and we decided, although it would be a big chunk of our funds, we would pay it. Dominic, Bob and John had done so much to help us we could not just sit back and let others have the burden.

The next day I went to the Bank and withdrew $600. We let it be known that Dominic was to be released on Saturday. Zack said folks had been dropping off their donations toward Dominic's release from the hospital and he had his own donation to offer. Zack put in a $100, bringing the total amount to $256.

Zack mentioned, "In order for Dominic to have a comfortable ride home he should have a car instead of that beat up old rusty rattle trap that Jack drives." Zack donated his car for the trip there and back. He himself couldn't make the trip for he had to stay at the Grill to watch the no-good lousy workers he had working for him. Of course Zack was smiling all the while.

Saturday morning at about 8 a.m. the three of us headed to Grass Valley to get Dominic. I was driving so I took it nice and easy on the slippery roads. We had no trouble and we arrived at 11a.m. Dominic was already sitting up on the edge of the bed and waiting for us. I excused myself for a few minutes and went to the office. I asked for the bill and was presented an invoice for $675. I paid the bill and told the lady she was not to reveal who paid the bill. As we were gathering Dominic's things the administrator came in and presented Dominic a bill marked paid.

"Who paid this bill?" asked John.

"An anonymous person," was her reply.

"You can't tell us who paid it?"

"I'm sorry, but no I cannot."

"But who do we thank for this generosity?"

The lady smiled, "Well, it is obvious they do not want to be recognized."

Bob spoke up, "What will we do with the money the town folks gave towards Dominic's release?"

"We can figure that out when we get back," John answered. "Let's go."

We left the hospital with Dominic sitting in the back by himself. The three of us jammed into the front.

After a couple of miles, Dominic replied, "It sure is comfortable back here, how are you fellows doing?"

John told him, "One more crack like that and you'll be walking on two bad legs."

"Until Dominic is able to care for himself I'll take responsibility for his care for $50 a week plus all I can eat," Bob said.

Dominic shot back, "I'll not pay someone who doesn't know head from tails, and besides, I don't like you."

Bob came back with, "Well I don't like you either, but for fifty dollars I'll make an exception."

"Why do you two even hang around together?" John asked.

I then had my say. "It's caused by that empty space between the ears." We made fun of each other all the way home.

Sunday was a day at church, but Dominic wasn't up to it after the ride home. He was sore and tired, so he took the day off. We followed our regular Sunday routine and enjoyed each other's company. Monday morning I took a walk around town with Sara, doing a little window shopping as Patty and John took a ride into Sierra City. Later that afternoon they returned and while at the Grill, John took me to the side.

"That was a nice thing you did for Dominic."

"I don't know what you're talking about," I answered.

"I know, but thank you anyway," answered John. We dropped the subject.

We still had the matter of the money donated towards the hospital bill. Zack said he didn't want his donation back. We had a notice printed in the town newspaper, explaining how the bill was paid by others and we would in one week, donate the money in equal amounts to each church. Those who wished to do so could call at Zack's and get their donation back. No one came for their money.

Chapter 11
Happy Holidays

October passed without incident and we were into November. With Thanksgiving coming up John announced that we should plan what our meal would be. Sara suggested a little venison and Patty said we should include some ham.

"Are we going to have dinner for just the four of us or are we going to invite some of our sniper friends?" asked John.

Patty, "I don't like your friends, but to fill the table we should invite someone, especially those two bums who live down on the river." Sara suggested we should make room for Zack and his wife. John thought that was a great idea.

John would contact the two bums on the river and I could make the invite to Zack.

When John went to see Bob and Dominic they didn't think they should attend, but because it was a special day, they would make an exception, just to be sociable.

I approached Zack on the invite and was informed he and the wife were booked for the remainder of the year, but they would see what they could do to squeeze us in for that day. "I sure hope it's not going to be another of those occasions where we have too much food and people pretend they like each other when we know they don't."

Of course, anything Zack said was always tongue in cheek.

It was one of the finest Thanksgiving dinners we ever attended. John gave the thanksgiving prayer and did a fine job of it. Bob and Dominic took a little venison back with them and Zack and his wife Betty took a little desert. Patty's Mom and Dad thought we were all crazy, but in a nice way. They enjoyed themselves.

Now that Thanksgiving was over we started to plan for Christmas. I went to the post office for our mail. We had three letters. One was from my folks and two were from Sara's folks. Both our parents talked about getting together for Christmas. We weren't sure how we could handle that situation.

We talked to John, Bob, Dominic and Zack to get their ideas. Zack came up with the best idea. He had a friend in Grass Valley that owned a nice but small motel that was always empty during the winter months. He would contact him and explain that we need a place for a gathering of fourteen people and could he accommodate us in his motel.

Zack received an answer within the week. Yes, he could accommodate us on Christmas Eve, Christmas day and the day after.

Sara wrote her folks and I wrote my mine, explaining to them our accommodations in Grass Valley and could they meet us there for those three days. To our delight, they answered, "Yes, we will be there." In addition, Zack made arrangements for our meals at the restaurant around the corner from the motel.

On Christmas Eve at 4pm Sara's parents and my parents arrived together. We settled them in their rooms and then we all walked to the restaurant around the corner for dinner.

After the food was served, John spoke about how wonderful it was to celebrate Christmas with such good friends. "Let's not forget the reason for the season." John then gave thanks for the food.

Christmas morning, as a group, we went to church in town and then back to our rooms to exchange presents. Dominic got a broken pocket knife. He joked that he would use it to cut off the leg cast when the time came. Bob got a used crevice tool and a sniffer bottle. I got a used leather wallet and John got the best looking present. It had large ribbon with a bow and beautiful paper. John opened the box and had a half roll of toilet paper.

John made a funny over that. "Each of you may share, but only a little bit at a time." Zack and his wife Betty received a container of used coffee grounds.

"That's what I'm going to serve to the lot of you until it's gone. It's the best I can do for you freeloaders who continually take advantage of my generosity,"

Sara got a bag of clothes pins and Patty received little booties for the future. Patties parents each received a pair of worn foot slippers. The last to open their presents was my mom and dad and Sara's parents. Dad and Mom received from me and Sara a bright 1-½ ounce gold nugget. They were delighted. Sara's mom and dad received 1-½ ounces of gold dust in a small bottle. All in all, it was a wonderful three days, and our best Christmas ever.

We said our goodbyes and shed a few tears. Mom and Dad said now that they knew Sara's folks better, they would be getting together often.

Downieville, being a small town, became even smaller as some of the folks went to the flatlands to ride out the winter. Those that stayed and were able worked around their places making minor repairs, cutting fire wood, feeding the potbelly stoves and a few of us even visited the Forks Bar and Grill. Zack made it clear that those few were the freeloaders some people called friends.

Zack had a soft heart for anyone needing help, and often he gave breakfast to them on early cold mornings. Even though his meals were free to them, he always invited them to return. He was one of the most respected people in town.

We became very attached to John and Patty. They were the nicest couple we had ever met. John was always thinking about the other fellow and of ways that he could help them. One thing I noticed about John was his habit of waking very early in the mornings and sitting before the fire and reading while sipping coffee. I never inquired about what he was reading and he never told me.

One particular morning I was wide awake, and after tossing and turning I got dressed and fetched a cup of John's coffee and sat down across from him. It was then I noticed what he was reading--- The Holy Bible. I waited until John looked up at me before say anything.

"John, I didn't know you read the Bible every morning before starting your day's activity."

"It's the best way to start the day Jack. I have read it through four times. I am now on my fifth reading. Every time I read it I get something new and good. Have you ever read the Bible, Jack?"

I was embarrassed to say "No, I haven't, but I do go to church as you know."

"Yes," he answered, and "I am glad to see that you do. I knew when we first met we were going to be friends."

About that time Patty and Sara began to make it known they were up and around. I told John I would like to talk again about the Bible.

"My time is your time Jack," replied John.

Chapter 12
A Celebration

As January passed into February our routine of four people sharing a small cottage never became a problem for us. Our friendship became stronger each day. One morning after reading, John mentioned he received a letter from his former boss in Sierra City about another job that was coming up. He of course couldn't drive his truck there because of the road conditions and he wanted to know if I would like to ride in a small buggy with him and make a day of it.

I discussed it with Sara and she thought it was a good idea. We two guys could spend a little time together without two nagging women. I agreed, but with a smile.

John made the arrangements for the horse and buggy and we left at six o'clock the next morning. Those were the longest twelve miles me and John had ever been over. The snows had softened the road so much we at one time considered turning back. "When times get tough the tough get going," replied John, as he urged the horse onward. We arrived without any other problems.

I spent time just wandering around town, having a cup of coffee here and a little there before wandering back to the café where John said he would meet me. When John showed up he immediately said, "Let's go." I didn't question him on why the hurry. We went to the stable for the horse and buggy and left town at three o'clock. John didn't say anything for some time. He finally told me that he was sorry but he was so mad he just couldn't talk right now. When he cooled down he would tell me all about it.

John said nothing more about the job offer the rest of the way home. I told John to go on home and I would take the horse and buggy to the stable and be right along.

As I approached the cottage I knew something was wrong, as there were no lights coming through the window. I cautiously approached and carefully opened the door.

Suddenly, lights came on and the room was full of people. They began singing happy birthday. I was completely speechless as I had forgotten it was my birthday. I was twenty-two years old and didn't know it.

As it turned out, the whole day was all planned and the trip to Sierra City was just to get me out of the house and away from town for the day.

John's former boss wasn't even in the picture. It was all made up. I later told John how bad I felt for him not being able to take the job. I also told him I would never believe him again, but I said it with a smile.

What a party. Zack gave back the used coffee grounds that were given to him at Christmas. Of course mine and Sara's folks were not there, but Sara read a nice letter from them congratulating me on getting over the twenty-one hump. Bob and Dominic presented me with a fine store-bought sluice box and announced that all gold found with this contraption was half theirs.

March was uneventful and as we approached April, Sara mentioned we should be thinking about getting back to our camp. John overheard Sara's comment and said he and Patty wanted to talk with us and could we sit for a spell.

"We always have time for you John, I answered."

195

Chapter 13
New Partners

Up until this time I didn't know Patty had a sister living in Los Angeles. She was planning a return to Downieville to take care of hers and Pattie's folks by living in the bedroom Patty vacated when she got married. It would free up Patty so that her and John, after much discussion, could do something they had been thinking of doing for some time. Before they did, they wanted to talk with us first.

"We want to come with you and Sara and mine for gold." Sara became excited and so did I. What a wonderful surprise. We could not think of a better situation for the four of us. John had already talked to Bob and Dominic about building another tent house and a pole barn for them, but only if me and Sara agreed to the plan.

I looked John in the eye and said, "We will not allow anyone to camp anywhere near us and that includes you two snipers, unless you want to be partners."

John stuck out his hand, "Howdy partner."

We started to assemble the building material we would need for their tent house and pole barn. John made arrangements to store Pattie's and his extra clothing and other items not needed at camp. We enjoyed the month of April as we completed our plans and we were ready to move to camp on May first.

Everyone in town by this time new of our plans and offered their help if and when needed. The morning of the first, we had three pickup trucks lined up with our gear, building materials and mining equipment. We were off and running.

We were somewhat surprised to find our camp in excellent condition. The weight of snow didn't do any damage to our pole barn or tent house. John and Patty began a search for the best location for their camp and chose a spot about fifty-five yards from our camp.

The boys began immediately to lay out and build the tent house. After building the floor and sides it dawned on them that John had never purchased a tent for the top. Everyone had a gut laugh over that one. All that we did and all the plans we made, never included buying a tent for the house.

Dominic, not yet in the best of health, volunteered to leave immediately for town, purchase the right size tent and return tomorrow morning. We all agreed and off Dominic went. We completed the assembly of the tent house, lined up the cots inside and had everything in place, but without a roof. We spread a canvas over the top for the night as we gathered around the camp fire and had our dinner.

Bob, just to make conversation, said we had forgotten to make a place for him to sleep so he was going back to town immediately. We of course began to rustle up a nice comfortable spot next to our tent house with blankets and pillow. He said he would try it out for one hour and if he didn't like it he was going to ask for his money back. Bob was snoring in just a few minutes.

About 7:30 next morning Dominic came into camp carrying a big gray canvas tent and announced he was there for breakfast and would like ham and eggs with toast, a side order of tomatoes and a bucket of coffee.

Sara replied, "Sure just as soon as you find enough gold to pay for it."

We did have a nice breakfast that morning. We finished the tent house for John and Patty and cleared a path between their campsite and ours. We even gave them permission to use our outhouse at the cost of one dollar per visit, payable in advance.

Bob and Dominic prepared to leave and wished us best of luck and they would see us on Sunday. Off they went up the hill. The place suddenly seemed quiet and remote. Patty and Sara began their chores in their respective places and John and partner went in search of a good crevice.

We searched out three good-looking crevices and decided we would tackle them tomorrow. We returned to camp for an afternoon break and I suggested we needed to set a few regulations to follow in case of trouble. I explained those that Sara and I had set last summer, but now we need to improve them. We needed a signal that would identify who was in need of help so we would know where to go in case we were needed.

I explained that one whistle was *come home*, one shot meant *emergency; come running!*

John mentioned, "Those are good signals," said John. "I'll have to get Patty a whistle, but how will we know if it's Patty or Sara calling us?"

"How about two blasts on the whistle for Patty and if we need to come running, three blasts," I replied. Patty agreed. We also explained about our time schedule for return to camp and where they were to hide near the outhouse.

John thought that an excellent idea so we wrote it out and posted a copy in both tent houses to be reviewed each day so we didn't forget.

The next early morning John came to our site. "Say partner, how about you and me doing a little gold mining."

I answered, "Sure and I'll try to take it a little easy on you as mining is hard work."

John smiled, "Just you try to keep up."

I hoisted the new sluice box and John put two gold pans and the crevice tools in the bag and grabbed the pinch bar while I also carried the shovel.

We told the girls we would return at 2 p.m. "Don't forget what you're supposed to do."

Walking toward the creek we discussed our destination and I suggested we go upstream as there seemed to be more crevices to work and I remembered one good spot for the sluice box, the one I was working when I was stopped by the escapee. We decided to try it first.

I began removing the overburden and filling the gold pan. John took the pan to wash while I continued to clean the crevice.

Suddenly John shouted, "Wow! Take a look at this." John had at least a half ounce of gold in the bottom of the pan.

We worked that crevice for two hours before we reached the bottom and we scraped it clean. All the gold went into the jar.

We then set the sluice box in the water and secured it as usual and began shoveling dirt from the close edge of the creek. In another two hours we knew we were getting close to 2 p.m., when we were due to return to camp. We left the box in the water and hid the tools behind a large rock and returned to camp.

The girls were hiding near the outhouse as they were supposed to do with Sara carrying the rifle. Security plans were working. John added a little mercury to the jar and waited for the gold to form a ball of gold. We then burned it off, weighed the gold and discovered we had 3 and ¼ ounces on our first day as partners. That of course did not include what we left in the sluice box. We would include it with the next day's find.

Sara told us that the need for both of them cooking each night was eliminated. They would alternate nights while the other helped. Tonight was Sara's turn to cook. They both set in to doing what girls do when they cook while John and I enjoyed a good cup of coffee and discussed the next day's schedule.

I asked John if he or Patty owned a pistol or rifle and he said, "No." I told him that it might be something for him to think about, as anything could happen that would require such protection. John was silent for a while, so I asked, "John do you know how to handle a pistol or rifle?"

John answered, "Jack I do, but I don't know about Patty."

"Would you consider purchasing those weapons John?"

"No Jack, I would not consider it," he answered.

It was then the girls interrupted with a call to supper.

As we began to eat John said, "Say, putting two good cooks together sure makes for a mighty fine meal.

Patty responded, "Yeah, and tomorrow night we eat at our camp."

With tongue in cheek I replied, "Then it will be my turn to make a compliment."

Next day we returned to our mining spot and began to shovel dirt into the sluice box. We kept at it for about three hours and decided to clean up. We lifted the riffles and let the water run everything into the gold pans. What a wonderful surprise we received. The bottom of both pans was covered with fine gold. We poured everything into our jar and went back to shoveling dirt. We continued until about 30 minutes before we were due back in camp. Again, we left everything at the site and returned. The girls were again hiding near the outhouse.

While John and I were mining the girls had taken showers in our drum shower and were freshly dressed for the evening. Sara and Patty went to John's camp to start dinner while we took our showers.

As we were dressing we suddenly heard two whistle blasts. We took off running toward the camp. I drew my pistol, ready for whatever the problem was. A black bear had walked right into camp and was about twenty feet from the girls before they saw it. The bear took off for the woods when he heard the whistle. John looked at me. "I'll make that purchase now."

Chapter 14
Competition

Saturday rolled around and finally we cleaned up our area where we had been mining. We returned to camp, added mercury to our jar and let it set. We spent the rest of the day gathering firewood for both camps until we had enough to last a couple of weeks.

We burned off the mercury and weighed our gold. We had six and three-quarters ounces. For the week we had mined 12 ounces of gold. John was clearly surprised at how well we were doing.

That night while sitting around the fire I mentioned to John that we would probably need to take one day in town to sell or store our gold. John said, "I already have an account at the bank," and he knew that I did also. "Why don't we weigh out and make a split?" I thought that was a better plan and said so. We got the scale out and weighed all that we had collected. We had a total of fifteen and a quarter ounces. We made the split, shook hands, had a good laugh with the girls and called it a day.

Sunday morning as we headed to the trucks, John asked me to remind him about his needed purchase after church.

We met up with Bob and Dominic as John and Patty went to their church. After the service we gathered at Zack's Grill for lunch and I reminded John about his purchase.

We told the girls to stay with Zack while we did a little business. We went to the trading post and John said he thought a rifle would be the best for him as he had talked with Patty and she said she had fired a rifle before and didn't like pistols. John picked up a good used Winchester for $50 and spent an additional $5 for a box of ammo. We walked to the trucks and John secured the rifle inside under the seat. We then returned to Zack's to pick up the girls.

From that day on, neither John nor Patty were ever without their rifle. When John was mining, Patty had the rifle. When he was in camp, he carried the rifle. John had also purchased a whistle for Patty and she always had it around her neck.

One day as we returned to camp we were surprised to find two men and two women talking to Patty and Sara. They had arrived with camping equipment and had the same plans we had. They were from Santa Barbara and one of the men had mined this area about twenty years ago and knew it to be a good area. They didn't think there would be anyone here, but of course they saw our trucks up the hill. They asked if we had claims here.

John answered, "No we don't. The area is open."

"Good we can set up anywhere we want," was their reply.

We didn't say anything as we watched them wander off down toward the creek and go upstream. They set up camp about a hundred yards from us, meaning they would be mining the same area as we were.

They would also be our competition for firewood. It was of course a free area and they had the same right to be there as we did. John decided it was time to gather more firewood now, as it would soon be necessary to go further from camp for it.

John was thoughtful. "They didn't tell us their names even after I told them ours; perhaps they will later." Bob and Dominic were due in camp the next day to start the pole barn for John and Patty. For some reason I felt it would be a good thing for our newcomers to see that we had friends from town that visited often.

Next morning as Bob and Dominic arrived the newcomers were traveling through our camp toward the path to their vehicle up the hill. Bob and Dominic had seen the vehicle upon their arrival and were cautious as they came into camp. I told the newcomers that we would introduce them if we had their names. One fellow said, "I'm Frank and that's Jim, that's my wife Sal and that's his wife Sherry." They shook hands with Bob and Dominic and went on up the path.

We already had most of the material in camp to build the pole barn so the four of us began the project. We worked for about four hours and called for a break. It was about then the newcomers returned and asked what we were building.

Bob, with tongue in cheek, said, "A two story office building."

Frank replied, "What are you, some kind of bad comedian? You think we're stupid?"

Bob countered, "I was attempting to make a funny. Perhaps you are the stupid one."

John stepped in. "Hold on fellows, let's don't get off on the wrong foot. We may all be here for a while. We need to get along."

Frank countered with, "Well, we got one smart fellow in the group."

Nothing more was said as they went toward their own camp. We settled for the night as Bob and Dominic slept under the pole barn and John and Patty went to their camp.

It was decided that breakfast would be served at John and Pattie's the next morning and Dominic started the morning by giving Patty his order. "Two eggs over well with slices of bacon and a little ham, with biscuits with gravy and hot coffee."

Patty answered, "Coming right up sir, anything else?"

"Yeah, make it snappy," he replied. Patty served Dominic last with the same thing we all had---pancakes with coffee.

"Just for that I'm withholding your tip," Dominic said with a smile.

We spent the remainder of the day finishing up the pole barn. We had a little lumber left over so Bob and Dominic built a small porch cover on the entrance side of the barn, giving John and Patty extra cover.

It was 4 o'clock in the afternoon and Bob and Dominic figured they had enough time to get to town before dark if they left right away. They said their goodbyes and up the hill they went. "Well see you Sunday."

That evening John and me sat and talked about where we should mine the next day. He suggested we go further upstream where a lot of bedrock was exposed at the water's edge. He figured when the water was running heavy it would throw light gold into the creek edge bedrock crevices and it was just waiting there for John and Jack.

Next morning after breakfast we hefted our equipment and told the girls we would return at 3:30. Patty was to spend the day with Sara. The girls had both rifles and as usual I strapped on the pistol. We started up stream and as we were passing the newcomers, Frank yelled out, "Where do you fellows think you're going?"

"Upstream a ways to try our luck," answered John.

"Upstream a ways is our territory," replied Frank.

"I'm sure there's room for everybody on this creek," answered John.

"Not anymore," answered Frank. "We claimed this section of the creek one hundred yards upstream and one hundred yards downstream. While we were in town yesterday, each of us claimed fifty yards each in each direction from our camp. We will be setting our markers today."

John requested to see the claim papers. Frank went into his tent and returned with forest service claim papers for the area he said he had claimed.

We were stunned for we knew the area he claimed was one of the better prospects, as we had mined it a little earlier and did quite well. There was nothing we could do. Just to show his authority, Frank commented, "Don't let me catch you fellows mining in our area; it could go hard on you." John and I looked at each other.

I asked, "Just what do you mean by that?"

"If I catch you in our area you'll soon find out." replied Frank.

"As soon as you set your markers we'll go beyond them to do our mining; we'll not trespass on your claim," replied John. Then we returned to camp.

We explained to the girls why we returned early and decided we would do our mining downstream from our camp until we could talk with the rangers in town. We didn't like it but there was nothing we could do if their claim was legal.

It was Friday morning and John took me to the side and said, "Jack, I want to go into town and check on their claim. I feel something is wrong about it. I know the rangers and they know me. I'll get to the bottom of it. I need you to stay here with the girls and I'll return as soon as I can."

I told John I was thinking about all of us going to town. He didn't think we should vacate the camp with those people around. John kissed Patty and up the hill he went.

I spent the day gathering more firewood. I also did a little repair on our outhouse and improved the shower. It was four in the afternoon before John returned. We gathered in the tent house and John began telling us that the claim was bogus. No claim was recorded and none was issued. What the rangers thought happened was a break-in at the ranger station. Someone entered but they could find nothing missing or broken.

They checked their supply of claim papers but could not determine if any were missing. They suggested we continue to honor the claim markers, and they would take matters from there.

Next morning John and I went to take a look and sure enough, claim markers were posted just as Frank said they would be.

We were gathering our equipment to go downstream just as six rangers came into camp. They knew John and asked where the people were camped. They left and told us to stay where we were until they returned. An hour had passed before we saw the rangers returning. The two men were in handcuffs and the four of them were walking in front of the rangers. The rangers took them up the hill and the ranger who knew John explained what had taken place.

The claim forms were stolen from his office and forged. No such claim was issued nor was any claim requested. The four were determined to run us off and take over the improvements we had made for themselves. They were being charged with breaking and entering a federal government office and taking unauthorized material. They could receive up to two years and probation. The last thing he said as he started up the hill was, "You can remove the claim markers."

The four of us sat around our fire and talked about all that had happened during the months we had been there and decided to put it behind us for all that we were doing was within the law. We had ourselves a better than average place to mine, good shelter, plenty to eat and the friendship of four happy people. During those times, what more could we ask for. Later, we found out the two men who broke into the rangers office received eighteen months of probation.

Chapter 15
Another Setback

John grabbed up our tools and said, "Were wasting time in these mountains, let's go mining." We decided to try the area we were heading for when we were stopped by Frank and his crowd.

We set the sluice box and began shoveling dirt. John would use the shovel for an hour and I would take over his end of the shovel for the next hour.

Suddenly John yelled, "Hold it!" He reached into the box and lifted a piece of quartz about the size of a baseball. It was laced with gold. It looked to be about evenly quartz and gold. I had never seen anything like it. We decided to call it a day and clean up the box.

We poured all we had in the box into a pan and washed to the bottom. The bottom of the pan was covered with small pea-sized nuggets. We poured everything into our jar, gathered our tools and headed to camp. Sara and Patty were surprised to see us so early. We bragged and showed them the quartz nugget and the pea-sized nuggets.

John got the gold scale and we began to weigh our day's work. All gold we mined that day excluding the quartz nugget weighed 8 ¾ ounces. I reached for my hammer and John asked.

"What are you going to do?"

I answered, "I'm going to crush the quartz nugget for the gold."

John replied, "It will be worth much more as it is to a specimen collector." I hadn't thought of that, but John was right, so we kept the quartz nugget as it was.

John said, "If Frank and his group had been honest miners they would have eventually found the crevice we worked and they would own the quartz nugget."

As we were relaxing and enjoying a cup of coffee and a sandwich, John thought we should perhaps be thinking about staking claims of our own.

As I turned to face John, the largest buck I had ever seen walked into our camp, not more than fifty feet from us, and just stood there looking at us. As I spoke to Sara, the buck turned and began walking away. Suddenly it stopped and turned back. Patty took a piece of her sandwich and held it out toward the buck.

"Careful Patty, that's a wild animal," I replied. After a short moment, the buck took a couple steps toward Patty, stopped, turned back around and slowly walked into the timber.

"That was some mighty fine looking venison we let get away," Sara said.

"I hope we never get that hungry, replied John."

The rest of the week we worked in the same area but didn't do as well as we did earlier in the week. Our average after that first day dwindled to less than an ounce per day, but as John said, we were probably doing as well or better than the old pioneers did in the 1850s.

Saturday afternoon we went downstream a little ways with our fishing poles and caught a mess of 10 and 12 inch rainbow trout. We cleaned them and I turned them over to the two chefs with orders to be quick about it. "This is no resort you know."

Patty eyed the two of us. "I don't know about the rest of you folks, but as of now, count me as being on vacation. I refuse to lift a finger to help in preparing these fish for the dinner table."

John responded, "You sure are going to get hungry with that attitude."

"Oh, well In that case I'll help a little," she responded. After enjoying trout with potatoes and fried onions we visited until about 10 p.m.

John stretched and yawned. "I sure am tired for some reason. Think I'll hit the sack."

Next morning as John and Patty were getting ready for our Sunday routine, John said he was feeling feverish and nauseous. By the time we hiked up the hill to the trucks John was sweating and he didn't look so good. We continued on to town and as we arrived John was not himself. Patty said she was going for the doctor.

Zack got John into the spare room as the doctor arrived. He looked him over carefully but could not determine what was wrong with him. The doc had the girls leave the room and had John strip down. He immediately noticed a small bite mark on John's lower leg. John said he didn't remember getting bit by anything.

Of course the doctor didn't know what the bite was from so he began a series of tests and the best he could determine, it was a small snake bite. The doctor went to his office and returned with a bottle. He had John take a spoonful, but it came right back up with his supper. He was getting very weak. Doc gave him some water and John threw up again. After the third glass John held it down.

Doc examined the bite closely and determined it was not a serious deep bite but enough to inject a small amount of venom. Doc scraped the bite wound and took a sample to forward to Grass Valley to determine the type of venom.

John was weak and feverish for two days as he lay in Zack's room. The report from Grass Valley confirmed John was bitten by a small rattle snake, perhaps only a foot long, and the venom wasn't very potent but potent enough to make him sick.

That was a close call for John and for all of us. We took him back to camp with instructions from the doctor for John to take it easy and not to overdo himself for a while.

Dominic smiled and said, "That won't be a problem for John; he never overdid himself on anything."

Bob responded with, "Yeah, just like Dominic."

Thursday, Friday and Saturday we did very little in the way of mining. I gathered up more firewood and did a few things around the camp that needed to be improved. I went fishing one morning and caught eight trout for breakfast. They sure were good with eggs, potatoes and coffee.

John was beginning to feel his oats and we did some light mining with me doing most of the labor, but that was okay. I told John when he felt up to it, I would relax in his place. "Have the girls do the labor while we both relax," he replied.

Getting back to camp we informed the girls, we are no longer responsible for the hard labor required in this camp. We're through. It's about time you girls start earning your keep.

Sara and Patty laughed it off, "Okay, we'll change sides. You guys are in charge of doing the laundry and the cooking, washing the dishes and cleaning the tent houses."

John elbowed me, "We should have known there would be a catch."

Sunday we decided not to go into town for Church. We would wait one more week for John to feel normal again.

Sara laughed. "He's never been normal before; what makes you think one more week will do it?"

John favored us with one of his famous laughs and smiled ear to ear. "One for Sara."

John took out his Bible and read aloud a few verses. We had prayer and Sara asked John if he ever thought of being a minister.

"Yes, but it was when I was a young teenager.

"What about your family, where do they live?" I asked.

John got a sad look on his face. "Both parents are dead and have been since I was twelve years old."

John was silent for some time before continuing about his parents. "They both were killed in a steamboat explosion while traveling from Sacramento to San Francisco. They never found their bodies. I lived with four different families until I was sixteen and then went on my own. I moved to San Francisco and attended junior college for two years before returning to Downieville. This little town gets in your blood and it's hard to stay away."

Sara chuckled. "I know, I have the same feelings."

"People in town want to know where you folks are," shouted Dominic as he walked into camp. "This is Sunday and you're supposed to be in church. When they saw that none of you were in church they dispatched me to check on you. Now that I'm here and I see you're alright I'll leave, unless of course I'm asked to share a cup of coffee with you bunch of no good river snipers."

Patty replied, "It's about lunch time. I guess one more free-loading river rat want make that much difference."

Dominic took a seat, "A lot of thanks I get for wasting my precious time and fuel on a bunch of river snipers that don't know the first thing about hospitality, or about mining for that matter." We had a good laugh on that one.

We enjoyed a nice sandwich of venison and tomato, washed down by a small glass of wine. As we were sitting at the table, it amazed me that we had found such wonderful people. I began to get the feeling I didn't ever want to leave the place.

Dominic spent the better part of the day with us and as he was preparing to leave he mentioned that him and Bob may leave the area for a while. They had an offer to mine over in Allegheny, as that mine was still going full blast and it looked like the price of gold was going to be raised by the new president. He suggested we should hold on to any gold we had and wait for the price to rise before selling. They would see us again before they left, if they took the job.

About the middle of the week, John was feeling himself again and we decided to do some real mining. John remembered seeing a large boulder about two or three feet below the waterline on the opposite side of the creek and thought perhaps we should give it a look, as light gold would be caught when the creek was running high water.

John suggested we take the come-a-long with us in case we needed to move the boulder. We crossed the creek and discovered the boulder was sitting right on top of a large crevice and from what we could determine, it had been there for a very long time.

We attached the come-a-long to a large tree and wrapped the boulder with the harness straps then began ratcheting the boulder out of the way. We moved it about three feet from our working area and took a sample of gravel from under where the boulder had been. We filled our gold pans from about a foot down and began to wash. What a surprise!

John had about an ounce and a half in the bottom of his pan and as I continued to wash I saw gold filling the bottom of my pan. We deposited the gold in our jar and kept digging. That crevice was about three feet deep and a foot wide when we finished for the day. We had told the girls we would return at three, so we had to get started.

We decided to surprise the girls and tell them we had a bad day. While waiting for dinner that night John took down the scale and we weighed out a little over seven ounces of small nugget gold. We called over the girls. "This is all we found today."

Sara and Patty yelped with joy as they looked into the pan. We told them we were not through with the crevice where this came from and we would go at it again tomorrow. The girls were so excited they wanted to go with us the next day.

The next morning we had our breakfast and the four of us started down-creek to our little gold mine. While crossing the creek, Patty fell and got completely soaked. Sara reached down to help her and she also slipped and fell. Both girls were soaked to the skin. We laughed all the way across the creek. The girls were put out until they realized how funny they looked and they began to laugh with us.

For safety, we decided to move the boulder a little further away from our work area and we soon were back to digging the crevice. Patty wanted to learn how to wash and Sara said she would teach her. "The last time you offered your help we ended up taking a bath together," laughed Patty.

John filled a pan with gravel and handed it to Patty. With Sara's help, Patty was about to the bottom of the pan when gold began to show. Patty was so excited she asked for another pan. I handed her mine and she began washing. As she neared the bottom of the pan, she forgot to keep the pan level and everything in the pan went back into the creek.

She just sat there and stared into the water. No one said anything. Finally, John handed her his pan and Sara sat down next to Patty and replied "Let's do it again." Patty began to cry.

John put his arm around her. "Where that came from there is more. Don't worry about it; we'll deduct it from your pay." That broke the ice and we went back to work. We dug in that crevice for the remainder of the day and Patty became a real pro with the gold pan.

That night in camp John fetched the gold scale and we weighed out five and three quarters ounces of gold. John was surprised we were finding so much gold. Somewhere up creek the source was still throwing out gold and it would be nice to fine that source.

Chapter 16
A New Friend

We were in camp one day when a young man approached our camp after walking the creek. He made himself known by calling out his name before entering our camp. He had walked all the way from the main road at Brandy City and he was told by the folks living there that somewhere along the creek he would fine us in camp. He had neither equipment nor supplies.

John asked what his intentions were. He answered, "I want to learn to do what you folks are doing. People mentioned you were mining for a living and I thought perhaps you would teach me. John asked what folks he was talking about and he said the folks at the church.

John was sure it wasn't Bob or Dominic that talked, but some of the church members didn't know we would rather not advertise what we were doing.

"Where are your supplies and equipment?" asked Sara.

"I have none," he answered.

"How do you plan to work and live without proper tools and supplies?" asked John. That question resulted in an answer none of us expected.

"I was hoping you folks would assist me in acquiring those necessary items until I could pay you back."

It was then John became concerned. "Just how do you propose to pay us back for those items?"

"I'll work for you for as long as you say I need to or until whatever it takes to compensate you for any expense I impose upon you," was his reply.

"How old are you?" asked Patty.

"I'm seventeen tomorrow."

"Well, happy birthday, but what makes you think we can afford to do these things?" John asked.

"I don't know one way or the other. I'm only hoping you can help me."

John then told the young man to take a walk down the creek while we talked over his request.

"We don't know anything about this person. We don't know where he came from or why he is here without his parents," commented Patty.

"He needs a bath and he looks like he hasn't eaten in a while," said Sara. "We can't just turn him away without feeding him."

"Were not going to turn him away, at least I'm not," continued John. "I will find a way to assist him. Hopefully we will all find a way. I'll invite him to have dinner with us and we'll see where it takes us." We agreed.

John went down the creek and found him sitting on a rock. John told him that he must be careful of rattlesnakes in the area, and be sure to look before sitting.

"Come back to camp with me; we want you to have dinner with us."

As they entered camp the boy spoke up. "My full name is Tom S. Sanders. Who do I have the pleasure of addressing?"

We introduced ourselves, then John told the girls to take a walk to the other tent cabin and prepare dinner while Tom took a bath. Tom was surprised but grateful. Later as we were sitting around the table, the girls served the meal and Tom bowed his head and began to pray.

"Dear Lord, bless these people for their grace toward me. We thank you for this table of food we are about to eat and for the energy it will provide. I ask that your will be done in all that takes place here. Amen."

John turned to Tom. "Do you always pray before a meal Tom or are you attempting to impress us?"

Tom paused for a short moment and replied, "I never attempt to impress anyone by praying. Praying must come from the heart; no one knows my heart but the one I pray to."

Patty said, "Okay, let's eat before it gets cold." Everyone was watching Tom, for he was eating like a man on his last meal.

"When was the last time you had a real meal Tom?" inquired Sara.

Tom thought for a moment. "Best I can remember, about a month ago."

John asked, "Where are your folks Tom?"

Tom suddenly stopped eating, "I don't know. I was raised in an orphanage and I left on my own accord, about six months ago or thereabouts."

"What have you been doing all this time?" asked Sara.

"Working my way north from San Diego. I worked mostly for food, but every so often someone would give me a couple of dollars for my work."

"What kind of work were you doing Tom?"

"I worked mostly around churches, cleaning and a little yard work or whatever they needed."

"Why did you choose to work around churches?" asked Sara.

"Can you tell me a better place to find a helping hand," was Tom's reply.

I noticed John studying Tom quite closely. "Tom, I think you are an honest person and we would like to help you, but how do you propose to go about obtaining the things you need?"

Tom thought for some time before answering. "I'll do whatever work you ask me to do and I'll assist you in any way I can in your gold mining for one month without any pay. Two meals a day will do me just fine. After one month, I'll be on my own and will begin to pay you back as quick as I can from whatever gold I find."

John thought over Tom's answer and said, "I speak for myself in this matter Tom. I'll take you up on your proposition, but it's up to the others what they want to do."

We answered almost in unison, "We agree."

"In that case my new friends, I should be looking for a place to sleep and store my vast supply of equipment," answered Tom as he turned his pockets out. He had one pocket knife, a can of sardines and a comb. We decided that tomorrow we would go into town and make purchase of items that Tom would need to live in the mountains and mine for gold.

The following day John and Tom left for town while I stayed in camp with the girls. I picked out a spot about twenty-five yards from mine and Sara's tent house and erected a canvas cover over the best looking spot for a sleeping bag.

Sara came over and said, "That won't do; he needs a cot to sleep on. He can have the extra cot we brought with us which is stored in town at Zack's place. If John doesn't remember it, we'll pick it up on Sunday."

Later that afternoon John and Tom came back to camp with arms of supplies and equipment, and they had the sleeping cot from Zack's place. They also had a nice tent which Patty's folks loaned Tom. That evening as we sat around the fire, John handed Tom the receipts from the day's purchases and told him, "You keep track; we trust you."

Tom was true to his word. He worked like a little beaver, doing all that he could while learning how to pan and dig a crevice. When he panned his first gold he got a smile on his face that would outshine the sun.

Saturday afternoon everyone took turns in the shower area, for Sunday was approaching and we were all going to church. Tom rode with Patty and John into town while Sara and I followed.

We introduced Tom around and a few said they had already met Tom. Now we knew who informed Tom of our whereabouts. Tom and Dominic hit it off right from the start and sat together in the pew. Bob began playing the organ. It was an old song that everyone knew and we began to sing.

Suddenly Tom stood up as the music was ending and started singing Amazing Grace. Bob caught up on the organ and what a wonderful sound those two made. Tom had a beautiful singing voice and it was obvious he had voice training.

As Tom finished, the preacher came forward, paused for a moment and replied, "My friends, this is a special Sunday, for we have in our midst along with the spirit of God a young man of tremendous talent. His name is Tom S. Sanders and I have known of him for a number of years. My sister is the charge of an orphanage in San Diego where Tom was residing until about six months ago. Today he is among us and I am going to ask him if he will give today's special message. "Tom, will you come forward please?"

Without any notes Tom began to speak and to this day, I have never heard a Sunday morning message that was better or even matched Tom's special message that morning. When Tom finished his message, he had an alter call, the first one we had witnessed in that church.

After service that morning, we took Tom to the side and asked him why he didn't tell us he was a preacher.

"I'm not a preacher. I'm a layman just like you. I was in charge of services at the orphanage." We ask him how he learned to sing like that. "I can only tell you it's a gift from God," was Tom's answer.

That morning at Zack's, everyone from church was there. John and Patty asked about the occasion. We then told them about what occurred in church that morning and who Tom S. Sanders really was.

John was overjoyed to hear about Tom and he announced that next Sunday he was going to attend our church to hear Tom sing. It was then the preacher entered the café and walked straight to Tom. He stuck out his hand and replied, "Tom, it's good to see you; my sister has sure been worried about you. I can now tell her you're doing just fine."

Tom replied, "With the grace of God and these fine people, I am."

The preacher then dropped his surprise. "Tom, I'm going on vacation after next Sunday and I would like for you to take charge of the Sunday service until I return. Will you do it?"

"I'll do it sir, even if I have to walk all the way here."

Sara spoke up and said, "That's just what you will have to do, we're not going to carry you anymore." Tom laughed and everyone joined in the fun as we knew we had found a new and trustworthy friend.

During the following week, we three guys worked every day with our gold pans and sluice box and on Saturday before showers, we weighed our weeks take. We had mined almost nine ounces. We did our split as Tom announced he was going to hit the sack early as he was a little tired.

After Tom left the camp, John asked, "Jack, do you think we could set a little aside for Tom? He sure is a hard worker and I don't think he will ask for anything he can't pay back. We could make it a gift at the end of the month when he goes his own way."

I eyed John for a moment. "Are you sure you're not a mind reader of sorts John?"

John smiled, "I knew you would."

Sunday morning we drove to town and went straight to the church. The place was already crowded as everyone in town had heard the story about Tom and wanted to meet him. Bob began playing the organ and everyone began to sing. The pastor approached Tom and led him to the front of the church and asked him to lead the singing.

I was beginning to think Tom was a miracle worker as I had never heard such wonderful church singing. The pastor thanked Tom and began to explain that Tom would be taking the service after today until he returned from his vacation.

After service that morning, John asked Tom for a moment of his time. The two of them walked a few paces away from the crowd and I was unable to hear their conversation. Shortly, they both began to laugh and shake hands. They had made a deal of some kind and I was curious as to what was to transpire.

We all went to the café and I was waiting for John or Tom to fill me in, but neither said anything. The rest of the day and during the ride to camp, nothing was said. Monday morning as we were preparing for breakfast, Tom appeared and announced he felt like a good day's work was ahead of us. Nothing more was said.

We three worked hard all week and took almost five ounces of gold. Saturday we did our showers, gathered firewood and made repairs as needed. Sunday we drove to town and Bob and Dominic met us outside the church. We did our good mornings and John and Tom went inside, leaving the rest of us outside until service was to start. Soon Bob went inside to arrange the music for the organ as Dominic, Sara, Patty and myself took our seats.

Bob sat at the organ as Tom and John appeared in the center isle at the rear of the church. At their sudden appearance, Bob began playing "How Great Thou Art." Both John and Tom began to sing as they walked to the front of the church.

What a wonderful surprise it was. As they reached the front they signaled for everyone to rise and join in the singing. John's singing voice was a perfect blend with Tom's and they sounded like they had been singing together for a long time.

The sermon was wonderful as Tom spoke about the wonders of Jesus and his mercy. As the service was ending and as we were leaving, low and behold, sitting in the last pew was Zack and his wife. Later conversation revealed that it was the third time Zack had attended church. The first was his marriage and the second was last Christmas in Grass valley.

In camp on Monday, Tom was up and moving around by six am, gathering our equipment for the day, as he had picked out a spot downstream about a quarter mile from camp. Being that far away from camp we told the girls to forego the whistle and use only the rifle if we were needed.

We began setting up the equipment along with Bob and Dominic's store-bought sluice box. Tom said he was going to set the wood sluice box also, for with three of us we could move twice the gravel that one sluice box would carry. We dug and shoveled all day long up to an hour and a half before we told the girls we would return. We cleaned up the boxes and panned out the day's catch. Over half of all we had was small nuggets, about the size of a match head. We started toward camp to weigh our gold.

The girls were in their hiding place as we arrived. John went directly to the gold scales and we began to weigh the nuggets. We had just over nine ounces of small nuggets. John could hardly believe we were so fortunate. John weighed out four ounces for each of us and gave the balance to Tom.

I noticed every time any of us gave Tom something, he made a note in a small booklet which he always carried in his pocket.

For the remainder of the week we worked the area until the labor was much more than the returns in gold. On Saturday afternoon we weighed all we had mined except for Monday which we had already divided. Tuesday through Saturday we had gathered another seven ounces from that one place. Me and John divided six ounces and gave Tom one ounce. Again Tom pulled out his booklet and made notes.

Chapter 17
More Trouble

Sunday morning after church, Bob and Dominic announced they were going to take the mining job over in Allegheny and would be staying in that town as long as the job lasted.

John asked Bob who was going to fill in at the organ while he was gone. Bob said to not worry, it was covered.

The group of us meandered over to the Grill where Zack was busy talking with a small group of first-time visitors. We took a booth and ordered coffee all around while we studied the menu. Zack then came over to greet us and announced that those people he was talking with wanted to buy the place. Everyone looked to Zack with questions and he soon realized we were waiting for an answer.

"I told them the place wasn't for sale. It's the only place in town where lazy good-for-nothing river snipers can get a good meal at a cheap price. Where would they go if I were to sell?"

It suddenly occurred to me something was different among the group. We didn't seem to have the joy we normally had when gathered together. I looked around me and the only recent change was Tom who was now one of us. Everyone seemed to be more subdued than usual. Maybe it was just me, but that feeling stayed with me for the remainder of the week.

Wednesday of the week while digging a crevice with John I asked, "John, have you noticed any change in our group of friends?"

"What kind of change do you mean Jack?"

"Well, we seem to be more subdued than usual and a little more serious about everything."

John chuckled, "I did notice everyone was a little more serious last Sunday and I think I know why. Tom has come among us as a very surprising person. He's very religious and has a great talent. We are more subdued because of his presence. When he's around we wish not to offend him as he is more like a pastor to us than just another person in the group. It's the only thing I can put my finger on."

Sunday rolled around and as we arrived at church, Tom immediately went inside while we stood around outside greeting everyone. We went inside and took our usual seats.

Tom came from behind the partition and seated himself at the organ and announced we were going to sing hymn number 34. Then he began to play. For a short moment we forgot to start singing. Tom paused the music and started again. We began to sing. We sang through four of our favorites before Tom walked to the front of the platform to speak. "I didn't mean to startle you by my organ playing. I only learned to play in the last two years. I hope you will forgive me." I thought if Tom could play the organ after just two years like he played that Sunday, we should all take lessons from whoever taught him. He was magnificent.

After church that Sunday, we did our usual lunch at the Grill and headed home to camp. That evening after Tom excused himself to an early bedtime, I proposed to John that we cancel the verbal contract with Tom and make him a full partner as he worked as hard or harder than we did at times and I felt as if we were taking advantage of him.

John pondered my proposal and replied, "I agree, but Tom won't agree. He made a contract with us and will insist on completing that contract before becoming a full partner."

"We can tell him the contract is completed as far as we are concerned," was my response.

The next morning as we were preparing to go upstream, John told Tom he was now a full-fledged partner with us and the split would be three ways.

Tom was surprised. "I will be happy to be partners with you fellows just as soon as I complete the contract."

"As far as we're concerned, the contract is completed," I replied.

"I thank you for that thought but you see, I will know it isn't completed, and that would make the difference. I still have two weeks to complete the contract; after that if you fellows feel the same, then we can talk again. In the meantime, we continue as we have been and I thank you for your offer."

We had no choice but to accept Tom's decision, so up the creek we went.

We had a good day as we mined two full ounces, with Tom doing most of the work, as usual. We gave Tom a half ounce of what we mined. Again Tom took out his little booklet and made notes.

At the end of the two weeks, we again approached Tom about the partnership. Tom said he was hoping we would still feel the same and he would be proud to be partners with us, but under one condition. "I must be allowed to repay you for the clothes, food and other good things you gave me."

"Tom, if we do that it's like another contract," John replied.

Tom pondered a moment and said, "How about this, I'll divide the amount I owe and donate half to each of the two churches in town under your names."

"That's a great idea, but no names, just the donation will do," we answered.

Tom smiled, "Done."

We could tell that a burden had been lifted from Tom as his attitude was different. He began taking more interest in the doings of the camp. No longer was he going off to his campsite early each night, he was now sitting around the campfire and talking about the day's activities. We were partners and all of us felt better about it.

One evening as we were sitting around the fire, Tom was busy working in his little book. I ask what he was doing.

"Just putting together the amounts to each church. I figure another seventy-five dollars will be about right and then we'll make the donation."

Tom then said something none of us expected. "With the gold you fellows gave me over the last few weeks and with the salary the church paid me for leading the services, I figure another seventy-five dollars will balance the book of what I owe. Being partners with a three way split, and with the way we have been finding gold, I figure another couple of weeks or so will give me the amount I need."

John spoke up, "Tom, we didn't expect you to use all that you had to make the donation; you can make a little at a time until you feel the amount is payed. Besides, you need funds to live on."

Tom thought about John's comment for a few moments and replied, "John, is that why they call you the smartest fellow in these parts? When push comes to shove, you always come up with the right answer and you're right. I will need funds to live and to pay my fair share. I'll make a donation this coming Sunday and every Sunday thereafter until the amount is paid."

Sara had been listening all this time and asked Tom. "What is the total amount Tom?"

"Well, if I haven't made a mistake in my calculations, the amount is three hundred and twenty six dollars and since I came here the grocery bill being split five ways comes on my part another forty-three dollars. I hope that's right."

Patty, who had been quiet this whole time, replied, "Tom that's more than just right, according to my calculations you own me nothing. I can't speak for the others, but for me, it's another donation to the church. You're bill is paid." Almost in unison we all said "Amen."

For the rest of the week we worked like little beavers. We cleaned up three crevices and took almost five ounces. On Sunday we went into town for church services and to do a little shopping. After service we gathered at Zack's place and was informed by him that the new president had raised the price of gold to $35 per ounce and word was that a few of the old closed mines in the area might reopen.

John asked, "Zack, when did you hear about this?"

"The information came on the radio last Monday."

"Folks it's time we were headed to camp. I'll explain later; let's go," exclaimed John.

On the ride back to camp, Sara wondered about John's sudden decision to leave town; she knew John would never make such a decision as that without an important reason.

After walking the trail to camp, John called us together and began to speak. "With gold at $35 per ounce, these mountains will be crawling with prospectors in a very short time. We need to prepare to protect what we have. I suggest we each stake a claim on a portion of the creek and mark that portion with a claim marker. There are five of us. We can have a sizeable claim up and down the creek. We'll do this tomorrow and on Tuesday we'll go into town and file our claims, making everything legal. Are you with me?"

Sara spoke up, "John, why did you think it so important we leave town so quickly?"

John answered, "Sara, the news about gold being increased in value was almost a week old when Zack told us about it. That's plenty of time for someone to come to these mountains, find our camp, destroy or take over all that we have here. Besides, we need to protect our hidden gold. Tomorrow we should rent safe deposit boxes at the bank to store our shares of gold." I mentioned that I already had a box at the bank.

None of us had even thought of such a thing. Again John was right. Monday we began setting our claim markers until we had five separate claims which covered about 200 yards up and down the creek from our camp.

Tuesday morning we drove into town and had breakfast at Zack's. When the bank opened John and Tom rented boxes and deposited their gold. We then went to the Ranger Station and filed our claims. The ranger in charge said he already knew of the improvements on our claims and we were doing the right thing in filing. We each now had a legal gold claim at Poker Flat.

We spent the remainder of the day in town as everyone was talking about mines in the area coming back to life. It was exciting to hear some of the old-timers talk about what they said were the good old days of mining. Some of those tales would make good book reading. Around three that afternoon, we headed to camp.

Wednesday morning John had another suggestion. "We need to talk about security for the camp. I hope I'm wrong, but I've seen things happen before in these mountains. There's always someone looking to get what they want without working for it. They'll often destroy what they can't have. We should have rules to protect what is now ours."

I spoke up. "John is right; our present rules won't protect us in case someone invades our camp. One of us three men should to be in camp at all times to protect the girls and our equipment. The person in camp will need to carry the revolver while the rifle is loaded and in its regular place. We'll need to purchase an additional revolver the next time in town for the two mining crews to carry when they're away from camp."

My short speech caught everyone off guard for they stared at each other for some time without making comment.

Tom spoke first. "I am against carrying a firearm, but that doesn't mean I won't. I agree with everything that has been said here and as a third partner I will do what the others agree upon. With the grace of God I will never have to use it, but be assured, I will if need be."

To hear Tom say such a thing I knew he was one that we could count upon to carry his part. John agreed as well. All other rules we had been using were still in effect.

We continued our daily routine but the mining was done with only two of us. We took turns by rotating each day and just as John had predicted, we had a problem.

On Saturday a group of four young men came into camp unannounced and began making themselves at home right next to our camp.

John was on duty and informed them the campsite was taken and they should search a better place to set up camp. The larger one of the four told John they would set camp wherever they chose and it would be best if he minded his own business.

John told them the camp was part of five mining claims on the creek and they were trespassing. They asked to see the papers. John showed them the papers and the larger one took the papers and tore them up. It was then John fired off a shot.

Tom and I heard the shot and dropped everything. I grabbed the rifle and we began running to camp. Just as we arrived one of the four had a large knife in his hand and had told John he was going to cut him up. John had the revolver pointed at him.

I shouted, "Everyone freeze." as I pointed the rifle at them. They were startled to see two more men in camp.

John quickly told me what had taken place and about the claim papers. I told them, "This is a legal gold claim for about 200 yards up and down the creek which includes this camp. You need to find another place to camp or we will send for the authorities and have you removed."

The so called tough guy said he wasn't going anywhere and took another step toward John. I took a step closer to him and aimed the rifle at his knee.

"If you advance any closer I'm going to shoot you in the knee and you will be crippled for the remainder of your life."

All the while his three friends were trying to talk him into leaving the area. He dropped the knife and backed off a few steps. "We'll leave for now, but we'll be back. You watch for us."

They started up the path toward the trucks and I suddenly thought they would take it out on our trucks. I told John and Tom to stay in camp for I was going to follow them and make sure they left the area without doing any damage to our equipment.

When I reached the top their truck was parked next to mine, but they departed without comment. I was relieved but thought perhaps they would return later and do damage to our trucks for revenge.

I returned to camp and told the others of my concerns and that I would return to the trucks with a sleeping bag and sleep in the bed of the truck that night just in case.

It was a good thing I did, for just about midnight the four drove up beside the truck I was sleeping in and as they were getting out of their truck I rose up and pointed the rifle at them.

"I told you people you're not welcome here. Leave immediately. If you come back, I will shoot first and ask questions later. By the way, I never bluff."

They left without saying anything. I was unable to sleep so I took my sleeping bag under a large tree and sat in it for the remainder of the night. I thought perhaps they would try returning, but they didn't and I was relieved as I had determined I would use the rifle if they returned.

Next morning I returned to camp and told everyone what had taken place during the night. John suggested we report to the rangers and have them contact the County Sheriff. Though it was Sunday we had to forego church service, except for Tom as he was giving the message that morning.

The rest of us went to the ranger station, explained about the situation and were informed the four men had been arrested for attacking two campers at the Rams Horn Campsite at daybreak that morning. The sheriff had them in custody and they were in jail. One of the campers they attacked was in the hospital with a bad knife cut to the chest. It had taken twenty-five stitches to sew him up. Other campers at the sight heard the commotion and went to the aid of the two campers being attacked. They had held the attackers for the sheriff.

We were relieved to know we were now fairly safe and didn't have to actually use the rifle to protect ourselves and our equipment.

We hurried to the church just as the service was ending and everyone wanted to know why we were late. I told them, "It's a longer story than you have time for---maybe later."

We gathered at Zack's for lunch and everyone was talking about the attack at the Rams Horn Campsite. We made no comment.

Returning to camp that afternoon we decided to go over all that happened and to make sure we did the right things for our protection. We decided that being together in one group in camp while others were mining was not a good thing. If we were surprised again we could all be harmed at once, unable to help each other.

Tom came up with the best answer. The ladies should stay in their own camps while others were mining. If either needed help they were to blow their whistle. Upon hearing the whistle, the other would get off a shot alerting the miners to return to camp at once. By following this procedure both camps would not be surprised at the same time. On days when the ladies were mining with us, one male would stay in camp to protect both camps.

We talked over the good and bad of Tom's suggestion and decided it was a good plan to follow. One male could keep himself busy doing chores for both camps while keeping an eye out for any trouble.

The following week was a little slower than usual in the finding of gold and we decided it was a good time to locate a better place to hide our gold.

Tom again came up with the better suggestion.

We could dig a second fire pit and encircle it with stones. We would put our jar of gold in a metal container and bury it in the center of the fire pit. Each morning we would put our burned wood in the second pit, making it look like it had been used. We could add to the container every other day. Only a few inches of dirt would actually cover the gold container.

It was a great idea and we put Tom in charge of the gold pit. Every other week we would take our gold to town and make a deposit in our safe deposit boxes.

Sara and I lay in bed one night talking about how much gold we had accumulated. As we had not weighed our gold for the last week, I told Sara we had about thirty ounces, counting the gold in our safe deposit box. With gold now worth $35 per ounce we were rich to the tune of $1,050. We still had some funds left over from when we first arrived here, giving us a grand total of about $1,275. After expenses, we were doing very well.

Sara said she never wanted to leave this place. Not just for the gold, but the mountains had grown on her and she loved living in the outdoors. I agreed, but told her every good thing must come to an end someday. When things got better with the economy, we would need to return to San Jose and go back to work like other folks.

Sara questioned, "Why can't other folks do what we do and come to the mountains?"

"If they did," I answered, "You would soon want to go to the city to get away from them."

Sara laughed. "You're right about that."

The next day was a Wednesday and as we walked to the creek, we noticed the water was running a little slower than usual. John said, "Since the snows melted early this year, most of the water has run the course. It will get even slower in about a month and some of those crevices in the deeper water will be workable. We may find some large nuggets in those crevices."

Back in camp for lunch, I suggested we take the next day in town for a little relaxation and just visit friends. I got a unanimous "yes" on that suggestion.

Thursday morning early we loaded up and drove to town and had breakfast at Zack's. Zack wanted to know why five free-loading no-good snipers were bothering him on a work day.

"I have customers to take care of. Sam, bring these loafers some coffee; maybe then they will leave."

Sam came around with five coffees. "That will be two dollars each please."

Tom was surprised and asked, "For what?"

Sam smiled and answered, "It's the fastest way to get rid of loafers and dirt poor snipers.

Tom laughed out loud and commented, "Oh, for a moment there I thought you were referring to me.

Sam answered back "If you're not dirt poor, then the price to you is three dollars for a cup of coffee."

"Put it on my tab," was Tom's answer.

"You don't have a tab," said Sam.

"Start one," answered Tom.

"Ok," answered Sam.

While we were enjoying out coffee, a fellow limped in with a walking cane. He went over to Zack and had a short conversation. Zack nodded and brought him over to our table. "Ladies and gentlemen, I want you to meet Albert Ellender, a friend of mine and one of the most informed gold miners in these parts." We shook hands all around as we introduced ourselves and invited Albert to sit with us.

"Thank you for asking; I was hoping you would. I'm not one to beat around the bush so I'll get to the point."

Chapter 18
Gold Mine, Anyone?

"I have a gold mine a little ways up north and I'm going to lose it if I don't do my accessory work pretty soon. I also would like to sell my mine if I can interest you fellows." We were caught off guard and just listened to what Albert had to say.

"Here is my pitch. I'll take you to the mine so you can test it to make sure in your own minds it's a good producer. If you decide it's good, you work it for a month and give me a fourth. If after that time you decide you want to purchase the mine, I'll sell for $5,000. You pay me by working the mine and giving me back my own gold until the $5,000 is paid. The mine is then yours."

We were speechless. John was first with a question.

"Albert, why have you come to us with this proposition?"

"I've been inquiring around and your names kept coming up from almost everyone I talked to, especially your name John. Jack and Tom, I know you're newcomers here, but if you hang around the likes of this fellow, you're okay in my book, and I trust you same as I trust him."

Sara and Patty were silent, but I could see the question in their eyes. Finally Patty spoke. "Is there room for two ladies at this mine?"

"If need be, you can make room," answered Albert. "What do you say fellows, do you want to talk it over? You have one hour before I leave."

"You're also a man of few words Albert?" replied Tom.

Albert left the booth and went to the bar and ordered a beer. The five of us just looked at each other for a few moments without talk.

Sara spoke first. "He sure seems to be an honest man, what do you think John?"

"I know of this man and he is the best miner in these parts. If he says he has a good paying mine you can take it to be true. We're well invested in where we are now. We need to determine how mining his claim will affect our situation where we are."

Everyone agreed to that. We motioned Albert back to the table and told him we were interested, but we needed to talk about adjustments we would need to make in order to work the mine.

"Can we continue to live where we are now and work the mine?" asked Patty.

"Where is the mine and can we drive to it by truck?" asked Tom.

"To continue living at Poker Flat may be difficult. The mine is between the old Monte Cristo and Excelsior mines. There are no roads from your campsite to the mine. The only road is from Downieville. The last mile is a very rough dirt road. You can get to within a hundred yards with a truck."

"Are there any buildings on the site?" asked Sara.

"There are two buildings. One is for sleeping and the other is for cooking and eating. The sleeping building has two cots and the cooking building has a wood-burning cooking stove, four chairs and a table," answered Albert.

"How soon can we see this mine?" asked John.

"Tomorrow would do just fine," he said.

It was decided Tom would stay in camp with the girls the next day and John and I would accompany Albert to the mine. Any other decisions would be based upon what we found there.

Monday morning we met Albert at Zack's for breakfast and then departed for the mine. Albert wasn't kidding about the condition of the road. It was like a washboard with holes. We parked the trucks and began our walk, taking pinch bar, gold pan, shovel, snacks and water.

About a hundred yards in we found two shacks damaged by snow, but the buildings were standing and habitable. Albert didn't hesitate, "Don't waste any time boys; it takes a while to get out of here."

We took samples from five different places and walked to the creek which was about 25 yards and began washing. Every pan full had small nuggets. Of those five sample areas, we washed an ounce and a half of gold and we had been at it only two hours.

John wanted to sample five more areas. After washing, we again had about the same as the first samples. John was convinced and so was I.

Albert began checking his claim markers to make sure everything was still in place. He mentioned he hadn't been here for two years and it looked like no one else had either. That was good. It was hard traveling.

John asked Albert for permission to return tomorrow and bring Tom and the girls for a look-see.

"You sure can," said Albert, "But we better leave now as it gets dark real early in these mountains as you well know."

That night around the campfire, John explained everything about the mine. It was just as Albert said it was. Every pan full we washed had nugget gold.

Daylight next morning was slow coming as everyone was up long before the sun made its first appearance. We reached Zack's café just as he was putting on the coffee. I asked him why he was so late getting started this morning.

"I was up late last night babysitting a couple of your no-good sniper friends that returned to town. Those two loafers named Bob and Dominic showed up here about nine last night and we sat up talking until midnight."

We had our breakfast and headed out for the mine. The girls didn't like the road and when they saw the mine buildings they disliked them even more.

"With the amount of gold here, we could repair the buildings and add other rooms to the house," commented John.

Sara wanted to wash a pan so I dug a pan full and followed her to the creek. It was just as it was the day before. Small nuggets in the bottom of the pan. Sara was thrilled.

The five of us put our heads together and figured, based on the samples taken, we should be able to mine a minimum of four, maybe five ounces per day. If we three guys did the digging and the girls did the washing, we could increase the take perhaps to six or seven ounces. To be conservative, five ounces would do it. At $35 an ounce, that's a $175 day. Anything over that would be a bonus.

Our investment of approximately a thousand dollars would be enough to improve and add to the buildings. We couldn't afford to spend a lot of time working on the buildings when there was so much gold to be mined.

"Zack told us this morning that Bob and Dominic were back in town; we could hire them to make the building improvements while we do the mining. Let's head back to town for a talk with Bob and Dominic," suggested John.

Sara suddenly spoke up, "Does this mean were going to move here? Are we going to vacate Poker Flat?" She had tears in her eyes.

I put my arms around her and said, "Yes dear, we would need to leave Poker Flat to mine this area. From our present camp to this location is a two-hour drive. We couldn't afford to drive that distance every day. That would be four hours each day out of our mining time. Actually, we would be closer to town in case of need, so that's an advantage in itself."

Patty spoke up, "I feel the same way Sara does about Poker Flat, but I can understand the benefits of being at this location. Besides, there's a lot of gold here and that's what we're after. Let's do it."

Sara smiled and hugged Patty. "Thanks, I just didn't know how to say it."

We loaded up and headed for town. Our first stop was Zack's Café. Lucky for us Bob and Dominic were there. As we entered, Zack replied, "Here comes the rest of your loafer friends. When are you people going to get real jobs?"

Tom answered, "Real jobs require work; we're not ready for that."

We pulled two tables together and ordered lunch. Bob and Dominic told us their job with Allegheny was over. When gold went to $35 an ounce, the mine owner hired back their regular crews.

Bob grinned. "Were going to do just as we did before, Snipe for gold and become rich."

John spoke up, "Say, would you fellows be interested in doing a little construction work for a bunch of snipers?"

Dominic spoke up, "Sure, why not? Who would they be?"

Zack chimed in, "It can't be you loafers; why you can't even afford free coffee."

We explained the situation. "Sounds as though you need a pole barn with underneath improvements," replied Bob.

As we were eating our lunch, Albert entered and came right over to our table. "Well fellows, what do you think? Is it a deal, or what?"

We invited him to sit. Tom asked, "Albert, what are your terms on the $5000?" That was a question none of us had thought to ask. We were thinking of one lump payment.

"Well, it's like I told you before, the first month of mining you pay me one fourth of the take. You keep the record. I trust you. After that, you pay me $250 a month until the $5000 is paid and the mine is yours. I'm not able to do anything with these legs of mine and all I need is the monthly payment from you to get along. I already have a little put away so I should be okay until that certain time comes. How does that sound?"

The terms were better than a lump payment. We nodded to each other. "It's a deal, but it's already the middle of August and the weather starts setting in pretty quick in September and snow can be expected any time after that. We won't get much mining done before snow. How do you want to handle that?" asked John.

"I thought of that," answered Albert. "You fellows go ahead with your planned improvements and everything will be ready come next spring. When you move to the site, our verbal contract begins."

Bob and Dominic said they would do the work now and wait until mining started to get paid as they had enough set aside to get through the winter.

Albert rose to leave, "I'll be seeing you folks. I'm going up the grade to see my brother. He lives up in Old Morristown. Been there all alone since '29. He likes a little company once in a while. He also likes beer and cigarettes. Zack, sell me a couple six-packs and some smokes."

We shook hands all around. The next day Tom and I went into town and made purchase of the building materials needed. Bob and Dominic loaded all they could and we loaded my truck with the remainder.

Just as we were getting into our trucks, a worker asked if we had heard about Mr. Ellender up in Old Morristown. "His brother Albert found him dead; he had been tortured to death. Albert knew where his brother's gold stash was and he went there, but the gold was gone. Albert struggled to get his brother into his vehicle and drove to the ranger station. An investigation is underway."

Albert was crushed. His brother was a gentle person and never harmed anyone. Albert reported he thought his brothers gold stash was around 80-90 ounces.

We were heartbroken for Albert. He himself was a gentle person, like his brother. We asked the worker where he got the information. He said his brother was the ranger on duty when Albert brought his brother to town.

Bob and Dominic followed us to our new mining site. Upon arriving, Dominic let out a whistle, "Wow, paradise. You sure there's gold here?"

"There's gold here alright and were going to get every bit of it come the next couple of years," I answered.

We quickly unloaded and returned to town to console Albert with our support. He thanked everyone. "I loved my brother. He taught me everything I know about mining and how to be nice to people. He didn't deserve what happened to him. He's in good hands now."

We returned to our camp and Tom and I went over what improvements we needed, then left it up to Bob and Dominic to decide the best way to go about the construction. They had their sleeping bags with them and enough grub for a week. I told them we would set up an account with the lumber yard for any additional material they may need. Meantime we would stay where we were and start looking for accommodations for the coming winter.

We did our business at the lumber yard and stopped at Zack's for lunch. Albert wandered in, saw us and came right over to our table. "You fellows get everything up to the mine?"

"We sure did. Bob and Dominic are staying up there while they do the improvements," I answered. "Why don't you join us for lunch?"

"Say, I meant to mention this yesterday, but we were so caught up in our deal I plumb forgot," replied Albert. "Do you and you're partners have a place to stay for the coming winter?"

"That's our next bit of business Albert," replied John. "We plan to get right on it."

"In that case I have another deal for you, if I may. You know I live in that big house up on the hill north of the Catholic Church. I have five bedrooms, three baths and a sleeping attic. I have a hard time occupying them by myself. I need help. Would you fellows consider helping me out for the winter?"

"That's quite an offer Albert; what are the terms?" asked John.

"No terms, just move in and make yourself at home. That big house is the loneliest place in the world during the winter months and I would love to have the company."

Tom asked, "What will your wife say about that Albert?"

"My wife died four years ago. The house is paid for without other expense. Just supply firewood and make yourself at home. You can come and go as you please."

"We'll talk with the others and let you know tomorrow. Will that be ok?" I asked.

"Sure, but don't take too long, I have a waiting list you know," replied Albert.

That night around the campfire we brought everyone up to date on the improvements and told them about Albert's offer for the winter. Everyone was excited about the offer.

Suddenly Patty brought up a subject none of us had thought about. We still had the mining claims on Poker Flat. She asked, "What becomes of them when we move away?"

John informed us the claims would continue to be ours as long we do the accessory work each year. It was then Tom came up with an idea that could solve the problem.

"Why not offer the camp site to Bob and Dominic while we're mining the other site. All the gold they find is theirs."

John spoke, "Those no-good loafers will let the place go to pieces. I'm against it, but I do make exceptions on occasion." All agreed. The deal was set, that is if Bob and Dominic would agree.

Two days passed and I was selected to take a run to the new site to check on Bob and Dominic and to make the offer on the campsite. Sara went with me and what a surprise we received when we arrived. A pole barn was stretched over the bedroom building and a pass-through to the cooking building was constructed. Both buildings were repaired and look as good as they ever did. The guys explained the other improvements they planned as we sat to eat our lunch.

"We have an offer you guys may be interested in," I told them. We went over the plan.

Dominic said, "I would never live in such a dumpy place."

Bob agreed with Dominic. "But because we dislike you we'll take the deal and you can be sorry later." It was settled. Every place was accounted for and everyone had a place to stay and a place to work with the opportunity to make money.

We decided to stay put until the first rains came, announcing the coming of winter. Bob and Dominic finished the improvements on our future home, but none of us saw the final results. We would wait until spring.

Albert's place was roomy and well kept. We made purchase of three cords of firewood, hauled it to the cabin and stacked it under the steps.

Sitting around the dinner table at night was a pleasure for all of us. Albert was well pleased as we fellowshipped and talked about our future. The snows came in early October, not heavy, but cold.

We told Albert about our last Thanksgiving dinner and would he have any objections if we repeated it this year.

"Are you going to invite those two fellows down on the river and Zack and his wife?" asked Albert.

"We were certainly hoping to," answered Patty.

Albert laughed, "Good, let's do it."

We got the invitations out and everyone said they would be here.

Zack as usual had a remark to make about the invitation. "I sure don't like attending shindigs of people I dislike, but because it's that time of year, I'll make another exception. I sure wish you people would stop inviting me to these things, I have a business to run."

John got off a response to Zack. "You call this run down shack a business? I can get better service at the cemetery and a lot cheaper."

Zack looked at John, almost smiled and said, "Now that hurts. The price of coffee to you just doubled."

It was a better thanksgiving than last year. Patty's sister Joyce attended with Patty's folks and she said a better time she'd never had. Zack stuffed himself and claimed it was the only way he was ever to get anything from us no-good sniping loafers.

Albert was glad to see friends gathered at his home for the holiday and he was looking forward to the next gathering.

Chapter 19
Family sickness

The next gathering would be Christmas, but Sara received a letter from my folks informing her that both her mother and father were sick and if a get-together was in the plans we should not include them or my folks.

No information about the sickness was included. Sara was worried, and thought perhaps we should visit them for Christmas. Her folks were up in years. Any sickness at their age could be fatal. We began plans to go home for Christmas.

We left Downieville on December 14 and arrived at San Jose on the sixteenth. Mom and Dad put us up in my old room and Sara and I went directly to her folks.

Her dad had gotten sick from an insect bite of some kind and her mother got herself sick by taking care of him both day and night with very little sleep.

She was just plan tired and worn out. I left Sara with her folks for a couple of days so she could give her mother some relief, while I went back to my folks.

Mom and Dad were doing fine. Their question to me was, "How are you kids making it as miners?" We sat around the table that night and I told them all that had taken place since last Christmas and about plans for spring and summer. I told them about Tom as the fifth person in the partnership. Mom said it was good that we had such a fine Christian as a partner.

I went to see Sara the next day, and she looked tired. Her dad had a high fever though the night and she hadn't had any sleep. I told Sara, "You're dad would be better off in the hospital."

"Mom and Dad can't afford the cost," she answered.

"I know, but we can."

We talked to Sara's Mom and she agreed that he needed hospital care. I made contact with the local hospital, explained the situation and they agreed to take him. My dad agreed to transport him in the family car so he would be more comfortable. We got him checked in and the doctors examined him immediately. After a look at the bite injury, they determined he was bit by a black widow spider and the venom was potent. They did some tests and sure enough, a black widow spider it was. In those days, a bite by that insect could be fatal without proper medicines.

The doctors began treatment immediately. In three days we were told we could take him home. He was going to be alright. I went to the hospital office and paid the bill. The doctors and hospital bill amounted to $622. A rather large sum in those days, but Sara and her Mom were pleased that Dad was going home. I don't regret one single penny.

It did cut me and Sara a little short on funds as we had a little over a thousand dollars before our share for the building material at the mine, which was $150. After the hospital we had almost $400 left in our account.

That was ok, as we still had gold in our safe deposit box at the bank.

We remained with the folks through Christmas and New Year's. Sara's dad was back to good health, so we decided to return to Downieville on January tenth.

As we were about to get in the truck, Sara's dad came to me, took me in his arms, and gave me a hug I'll never forget. "Son-in-law Jack, I thank you with all my heart. I don't know if I'll ever be able to repay you. Somehow, someday I hopefully will."

I told him, "I don't expect payment; through the grace of God, we had the funds. What we have, we have as a family. Ours is yours. The bill is paid."

As we pulled away, tears were shed, not only for the sadness of leaving, but they were also tears of joy. We stopped at Auburn for the night and drove into Downieville the next day. The last few miles into town was slow going as snow was on the ground and I had to be very careful on certain wet and icy spots in the road, but we made it without incident.

Wiley Joiner

Chapter 20
Back Home

As we pulled into town and entered Zack's place, Sam said in a loud voice, "Strangers in town; flat landers I believe." The gang was all there as we had sent a letter informing Zack when we would arrive. We had lots of news to tell and so did they.

"Dinner is on the house for the newcomers," announced Zack. "The rest of you no-good penny-pinching river-sniping loafers can pay." I knew then we were back home.

With spring coming on fast, we began our plans for moving to the mine. John and Tom brought in two more cords of wood so Albert would be warm through April and we began taking inventory. Tom had by this time accumulated his own clothes and personal items. All other items were part of the partnership, to be shared by all.

Bob and Dominic came by and said they would be going with us the first day as they wanted to be sure everything we wanted at the mine was completed as we requested. Besides, we would need help in setting up.

April third was to be the day. Bob and Dominic came over early that morning, helped load our gear and supplies and followed us to our new home for the next few months.

As we arrived, we each took all that we could from the trucks. What a surprise we had. Bob and Dominic had done a wonderful job. The sleep building was enlarged to two sleeping areas with a covered walkway to the cooking house. Both buildings were covered with a pole barn. They had built a separate tent house for Tom which was also covered with a smaller pole barn. The place was as it was when Bob and Dominic left it, with no damage from the snow. After two more loads from the trucks, we guys took a look around while the girls began putting things away.

As we walked around the far side of the mine area, we noticed a portion of the hill had slid down from the weight of the snow.

"Good thing the rest of the hill didn't move; it would have done damage to the campsite," commented John.

Bob and Dominic said their goodbyes and went up the hill to their truck. Poker Flat would be their new home. Except for Sundays, we wouldn't see each other for five months.

We took all the next day to gather firewood, build a portable shower and build two outhouses---one for us guys and one for the ladies. It didn't take long before each of those wonderful inventions were in use.

That night around the campfire we set the security rules. We had two revolvers and two rifles. We each had a whistle which we were to carry on a string around our necks at all times. The way the mine working area was situated we would very seldom be out of eye contact of each other, but on occasion it could happen. We felt very secure in our surroundings.

The next morning we began our quest to become rich. We went to the place we had taken samples, back when we had first come. Tom said he would take first duty on the shovel as John and I did the washing. It suddenly occurred to us the creek water was about twenty yards from our work area and the gravel would have to be carried to the creek for washing. That being the case, we would only be able to carry one pan each at a time. We needed two wheel barrows so we could carry one to the creek and return with the empty to refill.

Sara and Patty said they would go into town and make the purchase, but we guys were not about to let them go alone. We told them we didn't want to lose out cooks. We drew straws and Tom won. He would go with the girls for the purchase. We had already established a credit account at the lumber supply house and the girls could charge the wheel barrows.

Chapter 21
Independence for All

John noticed the snow had melted overnight at the place where the hill slid down, so he went to investigate. Suddenly, John blew his whistle and I went running with my revolver out of the holster.

John was pointing at the quartz ledge. "Look at that." There was gold and gold matrix all over the ground and in the exposed ledge. We were speechless. We could not believe our good fortune. One piece of gold attached to matrix was about the size of a small frying pan. We began gathering all that we could see, until we had two gold pans full. We then got Sara's cooking pot and began to fill it.

We used the shovels to clean the ground of the smaller nuggets and as we finished, we sat back and laughed and laughed. We were so excited we had to calm ourselves. We decided to surprise Tom and the girls upon their return.

We built a fire, took from storage a bottle of wine, set up the glasses and waited, all the time making plans for the use of the gold.

As Tom and the girls arrived, we were sitting around the fire. Right away they knew something was up for we were acting like a couple of young school boys. We poured each a small cup of wine and said, "This is to us, may we always be as rich as we are now."

The three looked at us, "Just how much of this drink have you two had?"

"This is our first glass."

"Ok, so what's up?" asked Patty as she folded her arms.

"Should we tell them now or wait until after dinner?"

Sara answered back with, "If you want any dinner, you better tell us now."

John took one of the new wheel barrows and we went to the cook house and loaded the two gold pans and the cooking pot and brought them outside for all to see. They were dumbfounded. They just stood and looked, speechless.

Suddenly Patty spoke. "It's gold! Look at that gold! Where did you get it? How much is there?" We began hugging each other and laughing and crying.

It took a while for us to settle down and talk. I explained how John blew his whistle and what took place after that. We all walked around to the exposed hill and were surprised to notice what we didn't see before. The slide had exposed a quartz ledge that was loaded with finger gold running all through the quartz. We again were like little kids in a candy store.

Tom spoke. "We need to settle down and make some important decisions about how we are going to handle this wonderful situation."

We returned to the campfire and took seats, and John began to speak. "I think what we need to do first is make sure we all understand the danger that now exists. We will have exposed ourselves to great danger if word gets out about this. Secondly, we need to establish a way to transport the gold into town without arousing anyone's curiosity. Does anyone have suggestions?"

I spoke. "We should weigh the gold before transporting it. Gold that has quartz attached will have to be crushed to remove the gold. We will also need to protect ourselves and the gold while it's in camp. I know Albert has a gold scale that can handle a full twelve-troy-ounce pound of gold. We can weigh out small rocks to equal twelve ounces. We can continue to do this until we have ten equal twelve ounce piles of rock. That of course is 120 ounces of rock. We build a balance bar of wood with an equal weight container at each end. We load one end with the rocks and continue doing the same at the other end with gold. When we have a balance we have 120 ounces of gold. Does anyone have a suggestion on how to hide the gold in camp? We had a pretty good system at Poker Flat that should work here as well. What do you say?"

Everyone agreed. The next problem to solve was the crushing of the quartz and matrix gold. Tom said he couldn't help with any of the suggestions as he was still new to the game but he would do his part in any solution we agree on.

I noticed John was rubbing his chin and I could see the wheels turning. "What are you thinking John?"

"We need help in whatever we do as this is no small decision. We need to hide the gold in two separate locations, just in case one location is compromised. There are people in this town I trust without question and we could use their help in hiding the gold. We could offer to pay them for their security. We also need help in the labor end of the business. I trust Bob and Dominic with my life. We could use their help. Besides, they both have extensive experience in mining gold and would know how to go about crushing the quartz."

Everyone agreed with John. It was settled. John would go to Poker Flat and talk with Bob and Dominic. I would have a talk with Albert and with Zack about the hiding places. Meantime, Tom was to create the in-camp hiding place, just as he did at Poker Flat.

The following morning as John left to see Bob and Dominic, I went to see Zack and Albert. I knew I would have to be careful with Albert as he would have a hard time believing me as to what had happened.

Zack was busy in the kitchen and I had to sip coffee until Sam came to work at eight a.m. Zack then came over and asked, "Ok, what's up? I can tell it's something important by your attitude."

"Is it that noticeable?" I asked.

"Yep, it sure is."

I began. "Zack I'm here as the representative of our group. We trust you with all we have or ever will have and that's why I'm here. We need your help."

"How can I help a bunch of lousy river snipers?" ask Zack.

I then told him the whole story. He just sat there with opened mouth. "This is not April first, so what's the joke?"

"No joke Zack, I'm telling it the way it is. It's the truth."

"Ok, I believe you; what do you need from me?"

"We need you to help us hide a portion of the gold in the best secure place you have on the property. We also need to establish a way of transporting the gold and transferring it to your hiding place without arousing curiosity. We will pay you for your security and the chance you take by having the gold on your property."

Zack was silent. He then let out a low whistle. "Tell me Jack, just how much gold are we talking about?"

I answered, "It's many thousands, but at the present time we don't know the amount as we have to crush and weigh it. Right now we have a certain amount we need to hide. Can you show me your secure hiding place?"

"You bet. Sam!" he called. "I'm taking Jack down to show him our new boiler; take over."

"Am I getting extra pay for being the boss?" asked Sam.

Zack answered, "No."

Sam replied, "Ok, I'll do it anyway."

We went down the stairs to the new boiler and Zack reached over and pulled a knob attached to the wall behind the flue. A closet-sized door opened and inside was enough room to store almost anything.

Zack asked, "Do you think this will do?"

"It's impossible to tell there's a room back there." I replied.

"That's the idea isn't it?" commented Zack.

We went over a few minor details and I told him I would be in touch as soon as we were ready to move the product.

I then went to see Albert. He was surprised to see me so soon. I knew there was no one in the house so I began to tell him the story. He was even more dumbfounded then Zack.

"You mean to tell me that gold was there all the time I worked that mine? If I bend over, will you kick me?"

I informed him, "The contract we have with you is void as it would not be fair to inforce the contract as things are."

Albert thought for a moment and replied, "Jack, the contract is still in force; you guys made the contract with me in good faith and I must honor it as it is. When you have paid me the $5000, the mine is yours."

"Alright Albert, but for your help, extra pay will be forthcoming and it won't be a small amount. We'll figure that out later. What do you say?"

Albert replied, "Done."

Albert took me to his pump house and showed me his hiding place. I was surprised to see some of the most beautiful gold specimens I had ever seen. Albert told me they were worth somewhere around twenty thousand in gold dollars, but much more to a specimen collector.

Now I knew why Albert wanted such a small amount for his mine. He didn't need the money. I asked to borrow his large gold scale, thanked him and told him I would be in touch soon.

I headed back to camp and Tom and the girls were waiting with questions. "I'll explain everything as soon as John gets here," I answered.

About an hour later John came into camp to tell us that Bob and Dominic would be here tomorrow and they would be bringing mining equipment.

I explained everything that took place with Zack and Albert and the terms we settled on. Everyone was satisfied that we were now set to mine some big-time gold.

John immediately began weighing small pebbles and making piles of twelve-ounce rocks. Tom began making the balance board. Sara and Patty brought identical cooking pots and we attached one to each end of the balance board. John put three piles of twelve-ounce rock in one pot and we put gold in the other pot until we had the board balanced. We then knew we had thirty-six ounces of gold. We continued the same procedure until we had weighed $12,600 in gold and we hadn't even scratched the surface.

Tom took the weighed gold and placed it in the new hiding place. Patty made notes in her record book and we finished for the night.

Dinner that night never tasted so good. None of us could sleep and we sat talking until around midnight before Sara and Patty gave up and said their good-nights. I followed Sara and before long it was daylight.

As we were having our breakfast, Bob and Dominic came into camp with the most outlandish contraption I had ever seen. It was the bottom quarter of an oil drum with drain holes in the bottom and legs attached with another bottom attached to the legs.

Sara immediately said, "Now I suppose you're going to tell me that thing is going to help us crush the quartz."

"Build the fire and heat about two gallons of water and I'll show you," answered Dominic. Bob located a level place and set the drum in place. We put a number of quartz rocks with finger gold in the bottom and poured in the hot water and waited. Dominic took a sledge and Bob did the same and began beating the quartz rock. The hot water expanded the quartz which made it easy to break open. The bottom of the drum was covered with loose gold. All we had to do was remove the loose quartz rock from the drum.

Everyone received backslaps and Tom as usual said, "Let's get to work."

"Before breakfast?" asked Bob. We were so excited we completely forgot about hospitality.

John got in his two cents worth, "You two bums come in here from Poker Flat and suddenly think you can push us around?"

"We'll take our quartz crusher and go home," answered Dominic.

Patty spoke up, "In that case, what would you fellows like for breakfast? You name it, I'll cook it." Bob answered, "Eggs over easy, with bacon and ham, toast with jelly and a pot of coffee."

"Coming right up," said Patty, as she served them pancakes.

"Best ham and eggs I ever tasted," replied Dominic.

We gave Bob and Dominic a look at the quartz ledge and both agreed, there was more work here than anyone thought. If the ledge held out, we could be working there for two or three years.

Dominic was the first to speak up. "Working here for a few years will require even better accommodations then what you already have. I suggest we return to Poker Flat and disassemble what we built there, transport it here and reassemble it."

"Why don't we just purchase new materials and build?" asked Tom.

"If we do that, someone is going to start asking questions about what we're building, where and why," was Bob's answer.

"Bob is right. We need a meeting of the group here and now," replied John. Everyone gathered around as Bob and Dominic walked away a short distance.

John turned to them. "Where are you fellows going? This is your party as well as ours." John then looked at each of us and we knew the question he had in mind. We all nodded, "Yes."

"Bob, you and Dominic are hence forth full partners in this enterprise. There's enough gold here for all of us. Get yourselves to the meeting."

I have never seen two people with larger smiles then what Bob and Dominic displayed at that moment. "Are you sure that's what you fellows want?"

Sara spoke up, "There's not one lazy good-for-nothing, no-good river sniper here that deserves it more than you two guys."

Dominic said with tongue in cheek, "Yeah, I know; you guys have never done anything to help us."

That settled, John being a good organizer took charge and appointed Patty as our secretary. "Jack, you have already established contact with Zack and Albert about security of the gold. You're in charge of security and transporting of the gold to the hiding places. Sara, Tom and Patty are in charge of sanitary conditions in camp. I will be a regular hand in camp and available for all tasks. What do you say?" Everyone agreed.

Bob and Dominic were waiting for their assignment and when John left them out, Bob spoke up. "What are we, two bumps on a log? What are we in charge of?"

John let a smile appear at the corner of his mouth and replied, "If you two snipers knew anything about construction you could be in charge of all building and repairs, and the set-up of gold mining methods. I guess we'll need to look around for someone to cover that responsibility. Do either of you know anyone like that?"

Dominic replied, "I understand two good looking fellows living down on the river have a little experience in those areas, but their hourly rate is extremely high. We'll go ask them if they want the job."

John's come-back was, "I suggest you get started right away." John continued, "I'm sure there are other important projects that will rise from time to time and we can address them as they come up. Let's all get cranking."

Bob and Dominic left immediately for Poker Flat and planned to be gone a couple of days. I left for town to inform Zack I would be delivering supplies tomorrow. He understood. Zack gave me a couple of wood boxes and exclaimed, "Put the catsup and pickles in these boxes; it'll be easier to store."

When I returned to camp, everyone was busy getting their respective jobs in order. I told Patty I was transporting gold tomorrow so she should make an entry in the books as to the amount. I knew we had over $12,000 in the camp hiding place, but we now had more to add to the pile. I began using the balance scale and found we had an additional $14,000, giving us a total of $26,000 in gold to be transported.

I told Sara she should plan to go into town with me tomorrow, making it look like a shopping trip.

Sara replied, "Let's do make it a shopping trip. I'll make a list of food items and other needs and we can make those purchases while we're there, and let's not forget to pick up our mail."

There was no mining done that day as everyone was busy with their respective chores. John spoke up. "Perhaps everyone should make it a practice of getting his own mail in the future. If one person gets the mail for everyone, someone is going to figure out how many people are here and began to wonder why." It was an excellent suggestion and everyone agreed.

That night around the dinner table, Tom gave thanks for the food with a prayer which brought tears to everyone. As we were eating, Patty asked Tom, "Do you have any special plans for your portion of the gold?" Tom was hesitant to answer, but he did.

"I want to go to seminary and become an ordained minister. I want to build a church on the grounds of the orphanage and make it a ward of the church. With God's grace, I will then be satisfied."

"Can I come to your church Tom?" Ask Sara.

"Sure you can, just as long as you don't bring any of these no-good loafers with you." We had a good laugh with that one.

"How about you John? Ask Tom. "What are your plans?"

John thought for a moment. "I'm still forming my plans and when I think I have them in order I'll discuss them with Patty for her approval. If she agrees, I'll then let all of you in on the plan."

It was then everyone looked in my direction. I told them that everything had happened so fast that I hadn't even thought about it, and it was a subject that needed some thought. I'm like John---when I know and Sara agrees, I'll let everyone know. We sat up that night talking about anything but the gold. We had decided the less we talked about it the better.

The next morning before breakfast I took a little walk to the quartz ledge and found John already there, looking concerned. "What's up John?" I asked. "

"There's got to be a way to get water up here from the creek. There's a lot of wasted time in transporting gravel to the creek to wash. Even though we're dealing with hard-rock mining, there's much gravel to be washed as well," answered John.

"How about Bob and Dominic; have they ever come across a situation like ours? They may know a way to solve the problem."

"I wouldn't be surprised if they do. We'll wait for them."

That morning after breakfast Tom announced that a second shower was needed in camp and he was going to search out the location. It would need a wooden stall around with a wooden platform to stand on. When Bob and Dominic arrived with everything from the old camp, the shower barrel would be used for the ladies to have their own shower.

Sara and I prepared to deliver the supplies to Zack and do some shopping. We arrived at 1 p.m. and Zack had been waiting for us. He said it was best if I parked around back as it was closer to the grocery storage area. I understood. Zack took one box and I took the other.

"This catsup is heaver that I thought." commented Zack.

"I'll inform the people at Grass Valley to put less in each box in the future," I replied.

Sara went to do her shopping while I took care of business with Zack.

Finishing, I drove to pick up Sara and we got our mail. We headed back to camp and arrived just before Bob and Dominic. When I mentioned that hand-carrying everything from the trucks to the camp was a chore, Bob said he would take care of that. I told them both that we had made our first delivery of groceries to a secure site in town.

Dominic asked, "How much?"

I answered, "About 26 jars of catsup and pickles." Bob whistled.

Dominic said they had about three more truckloads to transport and would like to do it all at once. We decided John and I would use our trucks and make one final trip, but we would not travel as a caravan. We would space ourselves one hour apart. We would also cover the loads with tarp, for loads of lumber always created questions.

Next morning Bob and Dominic left first, followed by John and me at intervals. Everything went as planned with no problems. Bob had stopped by their place on the river and loaded his small trailer with large wheels so in the future we could haul heavy supplies to and from the trucks on the hill. They began erecting the tent house while the rest of us helped out wherever we were needed. The new pole barn was up and completed by late afternoon and the three single guys were comfortable with the accommodations. Now it was time to do some mining.

It was a long day and everyone was tired. For the first time in a long time everyone was ready for bed by nine o'clock. That night I slept better than I had in a long time. I felt secure and happy. I'm sure the others felt the same way.

The following day John had a meeting with Bob and Dominic about bringing water to the mining site. Dominic had a two-horse gas water pump down on the river that could be used to pump the water to a long tom, but we would need to purchase a four or six inch hose to carry the water.

Tom spoke up. "Don't make the purchase in town, for that would cause questions. I'm sure we can get the hose in Grass Valley."
It was decided I would follow them both to town and withdraw money from my account to purchase the hose. That done, Bob and Dominic left for Grass Valley.

Patty was kept busy keeping notes in the book. She commented, "If we get any busier than this I'll need an assistant just to turn the pages on this book."

John began building the long tom that we would use when we got the water running. It was about twenty feet long and had to be set in place so it would not move. We had to move a bit of rock to make it secure.

Everything was coming together. We took inventory and decided we had everything covered for now. We knew things would crop up from time to time, and we could handle them as they came. We were pleased with what we had accomplished.

Chapter 22
Another New Friend

We began removing quartz from the ledge and stacking it for crushing. It was slow work but we were removing gold with every piece of quartz we cut from the ledge. "Crushing this quartz by hand with sledge hammers is going to wear some people out real soon," exclaimed John. We need to think on this problem and come up with something better."

As John began to walk away, he suddenly stopped and turned back. "I've got it! Jack, you remember that fellow I worked for in Sierra City a while back. He is a gold buyer, speculator and processor and very successful. Most important, he is honest and that is one of the reasons he's so successful."

"What are you getting at John?" I asked.

"Well we could, after a talk with him, have him take a look at our operation and possibly make an offer to purchase and process the quartz gold. That way the physical part of the operation would be in other hands and the responsibility theirs."

"Do you think he can afford that amount of purchase?" I asked.

"I don't know. It could work this way. He puts up a deposit, amount to be determined. He processes the product, takes his profit and we receive the balance. The transportation logistics would need to be established and I'm sure between us and him we could handle that."

I suggested that as soon as Bob and Dominic returned we should have a meeting to discuss this. It sounded like a winner for us. We could continue mining the gravel gold, using the gas pump and all the profits from that would be ours.

It was late the next afternoon when Bob and Dominic returned from grass valley. They had made a purchase of seventy-five feet of six and four inch hose. After dinner, John called for a meeting.

John outlined the problem in crushing the quartz and his idea on having others handle that situation at a cost. He mentioned everything was predicated on the other party for we had not yet contacted that person.

John and I would meet with his man in Sierra City and outline the plan. First we had to make sure he was still in Sierra City.

Next morning John went to the ranger station and asked them to send a message to Sierra City to confirm the man was in town and would be available to talk business. Within the hour the message was answered. Yes he was there and would be available any time for the remainder of the week.

Early next morning John and I were off to Sierra City. We arrived at nine a.m. and had breakfast at a local café. We walked to the old Wells Fargo building, which was the largest building in town. As we entered, a gentleman of about forty years, well dressed and distinguished looking, came forward to greet us with his hand extended toward John. "John, it's great to see you." John took the hand and introduced me as his business partner.

"Matthew, we need to discuss important business with you this morning, in private."

"Private is my favorite kind of business. Follow me gentlemen." He led us upstairs to his living quarters, motioned toward chairs, closed the door and took a seat next to us, not behind his desk. That told me he was showing us respect as equals in business.

"Now gentlemen, we're alone. May I offer you a refreshment?" We both declined. "How may I be of service?"

"Matthew, we have a processing problem at our gold mine and we're hoping you can reduce or eliminate the problem for us." As John continued to speak, Matthew quickly digested what he was saying.

"Gentlemen, it has been a long time since anyone came to me with a mining problem, especially a processing problem. I'm all ears. Continue please."

John looked to me and I said, "It's your part of the plan John, you go ahead."

John began by explaining what we had in partnership and the number of partners. He told about the gold we put into storage. He explained about the quartz ridge and the gravel gold. He then explained about the problem of crushing the quartz and that was why we had come to see him. "For an honest profit for yourself, we need your help."

Matthew was speechless for some time. "Do I understand you gentlemen correctly? You have a gold mine that could amount to many months or years of work to remove all the gold?"

"Yes Matthew that is correct," I said.

"Do you have an estimate of the tonnage of rock to be removed and processed?" Matthew asked.

"No we don't" answered John.

"In that case gentlemen I would need to see your mine before we can continue these talks; would you agree to that? Before you answer, I will insist on a contract of silence and secrecy between me and all your partners about the location and any value that I may see while at your location. If we cannot come to an agreement, the contract becomes even more important for all persons involved. It's for your protection and mine."

John nodded towards me and I said, "We will need a vote of partners before giving you a tour of the mine."

"I would expect so gentlemen," answered Mathew. "Here is my suggestion---if it is agreed after your vote, go to the ranger station. Send a message that reads the time of day that you wish to meet again. I will assume the day after receiving the message we will meet at Zack's at the time you list on the message."

As there was nothing further to discuss, we returned to camp with the secrecy form and called for a meeting to explain all that transpired between us and Mathew. Everyone took a look at the form and we then decided to take a vote. Patty was busy taking notes.

As we were counting the votes we heard a noise. We rushed to the mine area to find another portion of the hill had collapsed, exposing even more of the quartz ledge and spreading large pieces of float all over the ground, along with more rattle snakes than any of us had ever seen. They were moving all over the place. We grabbed shovels and began swatting the snakes.

A few made it toward rocks to hide and we had to remove the rocks to get them. Even those we killed kept wiggling for some time. After about an hour of searching out the snakes, we had killed eighteen of them. When the ledge collapsed it had exposed a snake den and we had concerns that perhaps we didn't get all of them. From that moment on and for a few days every step we took around the ledge we would carefully search the ground around us.

After disposing of the dead snakes we all stood back to admire our gold ledge. None of us had ever seen such a sight before. Finger gold was exposed throughout the quartz ledge. Bob let out a whistle. Dominic began to laugh. Sara and Patty began to cry. The rest of us were in shock. None of us had ever seen that much gold at one time in one place. I think all of us realized the enormous responsibility and secrecy of the situation. Our meeting with Matthew was now more important than ever. Our vote count was unanimous.

Next morning John went to the ranger station and sent a message that read, 10:30 a.m. Before leaving town, he went by Zack's and made a reservation for a booth with privacy for 10:30 the next day.

Ten a.m. next morning found me and John sipping coffee and waiting. Thirty minutes later Mathew entered the café. He was dressed in working clothes and boots with a large sloppy hat. He reminded me of an old-time mining prospector. He came over, greeted us and took a seat.

Matthew ordered coffee and an order of toast. Zack came around and greeted Mathew with his usual comment. "Matt, why are you hanging around with these no-good loafers?"

Matthew responded, "They'll do 'til another like you comes along. Good to see you Zack."

As Matthew was finishing his toast, John presented the signed secrecy form. Matthew looked it over and replied, "Gentlemen, let's go take a look. I'll follow you."

After parking the vehicles, Matthew looked around and commented, "This is rough country; how far to the camp?"

"About a hundred yards," answered John.

Everyone was busy as we entered camp and all came forward to meet Matthew.

As he was introduced to Tom he said, "I've heard about you young man and I'm pleased to meet you." Matthew took a look around and commented, "You have quite a set up here. I'm impressed."

"Allow me to lead the way," said Tom. Matthew fell in behind Tom and the rest of us followed. Matthew was so surprised he just stood and stared. No one said anything. It was sometime before Matthew spoke.

"Ladies and gentlemen, I have never seen anything like this. This is astonishing and hard to believe. I agree, you do need help and if I didn't help you I would be a bigger fool then some people think I am. As I understand it, you need the quartz crushed after you remove it and have the gold processed into shipping bars, then to be forwarded to the mint. Is that correct?" Of course the answer was "yes."

"Then we need to work out the logistics in all that we do here, including the transfer of the quartz to my location. We need contracts of profit for my company. We will need security during the transfer of the quartz which you should supply. It must be understood, my responsibility does not start until I accept the truckload of quartz which is upon my driver getting behind the wheel of the loaded truck. Once the quartz is transferred to me your responsibility ends. Not before."

We listened to Matthew outline the procedures we needed to follow. "I don't know how long you can keep this operation a secret. This much material to be moved will eventually cause someone to ask questions. Do you have a security plan?"

"We do." answered Tom.

"Good, stay on top and don't hesitate to make changes when things change within the camp. Now ladies and gentlemen, this is a subject I hate to bring up, but my experience in the past tells me each of you men should at all times carry a loaded firearm. It is not only protection for yourself but for your fellow partners. Tom, I know about you and your beliefs. Are you willing to carry a revolver?" Tom answered, "I am, but I will never shoot to kill; I will attempt to only wound the aggressor."

Matthew said he had one more suggestion. "From this moment on, no one should leave the camp alone. You should always travel in pairs or more. It makes no difference why or where you are traveling. It's important; you will find out how important it is as this operation goes forward."

"Now my new friends and associates, this meeting is over, except for setting the next meeting day, time and location. What say you?"

John spoke, "We need to move as fast as possible, the sooner the better."

"I'll get my end of things rolling and tie any lose ends. Give me at least three days of working time before the next meeting," replied Matthew.

Bob had a say. "This is Friday, how about next Wednesday at 10 a.m.?"

All agreed. Matthew asked, "Should we meet elsewhere before coming to camp? "Just coming to camp would be okay," said Dominic. "Settled; meeting adjourned," replied Matthew.

John, Tom and I walked Matthew to his truck and thanked him for his expertise. Just before Matthew drove away he said, "Keep on your toes and a keep sharp lookout. You never know."

As we walked back to camp, I told John, "From what I see and what I've heard, I think you have chosen the right man."

All day Saturday we shoveled gravel into the long tom while Bob and Dominic worked the pump and hose. About three o'clock we decided to take a look at how well we had done. Bob brought the drum bottom to the end of the long tom as we removed the riffles and let what gold we had fall into the drum. We were absolutely amazed. We had nuggets and pieces covering almost the entire bottom of the drum. That night after dinner we brought out the scale and began to weigh. We had collected over 90 ounces of gold for the day's work.

Tom took control of the gold and secreted it into the camp hiding place. We relaxed for the remainder of the evening, talking about the future of our mine

Sunday morning Dominic and John stayed in camp while the rest of us went to church. We gathered at Zack's for lunch and as he greeted us he said, "Don't forget to pick up your catsup and pickle boxes before you leave. You may need them for your next shopping spree." We thanked him and said we wouldn't forget.

As we were finishing up our lunch, Albert limped into the café, spied us in the corner and came right over.

"My friends, this is just a social visit, no business. Nothing is changed between us, but I am a curious person and would like to see for myself all that you have told me. Do I have your permission to do that?" Sara quickly spoke, "Albert, you don't need permission, you are welcome anytime to our summer home. Just be sure when you come, you show up hungry."

"I thank you for that. How about tomorrow morning?"

"About 10 a.m. would be good for us," Bob answered.

"I'll be there" said Albert as he headed for the door.

Monday morning found us going over everything that happened the previous week when Albert announced himself as he came into camp. Patty offered him a coffee with breakfast. He took just the coffee with thanks.

Albert looked around him and was amazed about the improvements we had made.

"Is this the same mine I contracted with you folks?"

Sara answered, "It sure is Albert and we thank you for your generosity and your friendship. You're a wonderful person."

Albert answered, "Careful now young lady, talk like that will cause me to purchase a larger hat. Say, do I have to drink coffee all day? I came here to see a gold mine."

We fell in behind John and Albert as we walked to the ledge. As we approached Albert stopped some distance from the ledge, saying nothing. He began walking from one end to the other. Then he turned to face us. "From past experience I would say you have enough work here for the next five years, more or less." He then let out a yell, threw his walking stick in the air and danced a little jig, all the time laughing with the rest of us.

Albert went to each of us and gave a hug. When he got to Tom he asked him to pray for guidance and wisdom in all that would be done here and that we would be good stewards in the use of the gold.

Tom bowed his head and began to pray. "Dear God, we're here today humbled before you, giving thanks for your generosity. This is your gold mine Father and you have chosen us, your servants, for stewardship so that we may go forward and do good things for our fellow man. Father, you have chosen Albert to be our benefactor and we thank you. Bless him Father for his deep belief in you and your wonderful plan. We ask Father for your blessing and protection in this venture and that we would each do your will in the use of this vast fortune. Give us wisdom and compassion as you would have it. Amen." There wasn't a dry eye in camp.

Albert then said, "I'm going home, this is more than an old man should have to endure. I'm glad I chose you folks to take over the mine. You're good people and I know you will each do the right thing with your new found wealth. I've had my day in the sun, now it's your turn.

Sara spoke up. "Albert, you haven't had anything to eat. Stay and have lunch with us."

"Can't eat, I'm too worked up inside. See you at Zack's." Albert was off up the hill.

We took seriously everything Matthew suggested. We began setting additional rules to be followed by everyone. Those that didn't own a revolver were to make a purchase for themselves, but not in Downieville. The purchase could be made in Sierra City or Grass Valley. A minimum of two people were to be in camp at all times. Everyone traveled in groups of two or more. We were never to discuss the mine outside of our partnership. Actually, everyone was waiting and looking forward to Wednesday with Matthew.

Chapter 23
Processing the Gold

Wednesday morning at 10 a.m. Matthew walked into camp. We had a table and chair under the pole barn for him and we gathered around. "My fellow associates, the ball is rolling. I'll bring you to date from my end."

"I have made contact with the people that handle my rock crushing problems. It is a two hammer crusher, small but adequate for this operation. The less the better. My most trusted employee will assist in the transfer of the gold ore. Unless you have a better solution, here is my suggestion."

"We will have three separate transfer locations. Each truck is to be covered with a tarp when it leaves your location. For the first transfer load, you will need two trucks, one loaded with quartz and one empty. Upon arriving at the transfer point, my driver will then take your loaded truck and you can return to camp in your empty truck. My driver will deliver the loaded truck to the crusher. Said truck will then be returned to you the next delivery time in exchange for another loaded truck."

Matthew continued to speak. "You will need to purchase another truck to make it easier for everyone as you only have three at the present time. I suggest you make that purchase in Grass Valley. Now, as for the transfer points. We will use a different transfer point each day. I have three locations set and ready to go. They are Union Flat, Loganville and Wild Plum. John knows these locations and can point them out to you on a map. Each location will have a set time for the loaded truck to arrive. Union Flat at 10 a.m., Loganville at 1 p.m. and Wild Plum at 3 p.m. Patty, are you making notes my dear?" Patty was so spellbound she had stopped writing. She quickly caught up.

"Are there any questions about the transfer procedures? No questions? Good, let's proceed."

"I do not have the funds to post a bond for my end of the operation. If we are to do business, we will do it on a hand shake. All other elements of the operation will be by contract. What say you?"

John looked to each of us. "Matthew, I have done business with you in the past and I know of others who have also. They have all said the same thing about you. You are an honest man. I am willing to do business with a hand shake, but I don't speak for the others." Without a ballot, we all agreed with John. We each shook hands with Matthew. With a broad smile Matthew said, "With your kind permission, let's eat, while we continue."

"Procedures for the gold shipments to the Mint are most important. After the gold has been separated from the ore, it will be melted and formed into shipping bricks. Each brick will be weighed and stamped with a number. Each brick will be recorded and accounted for. Upon arrival at the mint, each brick will be checked against the recorded list for accountability. It will then be weighed as per the mint's procedures. After the mint purifies the gold a check will be cut, paying the shipper or the owners. You can request payment in gold coin or greenbacks, but I suggest you form a company and incorporate, so all payments from the mint go directly to your bank and into the corporate account."

Matthew paused. "I see questions in your eyes my friends and I know what they are. My cost to you for these services will be $5,000 per month. What say you?"

John quickly spoke, "The contract must allow the corporation to cancel all procedures at any time."

Matthew answered, "Yes, I agree, but the contract must also be renegotiable at the end of each fiscal year."

It was decided the first transfer of quartz to be crushed was to take place on Friday, until John spoke up and mentioned we had to work out the problem of getting the quartz uphill to the trucks. It was a problem none of us had thought of. John told Matthew we would send a message to him as soon as we resolved the problem. The message would read, "Problem solved." Which would indicate the first loaded truck would be the day after he received the message.

Matthew then mentioned a situation that had nothing to do with the contract, and which none of us had even thought about---the security and protection of the mine and facilities during the coming winter months. Someone was surely going to get curious about all the activity taking place in the area. They would also wonder why river snipers would have a credit account at the lumber yard. Even though winter was months away, we had to consider and settle on a plan as soon as possible to insure the security of the mine during the winter months.

Shortly after Matthew left to return to Sierra City, we called a meeting of all hands and began a discussion on protecting our mine. It was already settled that myself, Sara, John and Patty, along with Tom would be staying at Albert's during the winter. Bob and Dominic would stay at their place down on the river. That of course left no one at the mine. Everyone was asked to think on the matter and at another meeting in three days we would discuss all suggestions. Meanwhile we had to settle the truck loading problem.

Bob and Dominic had already been thinking on the problem and had a suggestion. There's a gasoline truck engine for sale in Grass Valley that could be our mule power. We mount the engine at the top of the rise with a pulley and cable attached to a cart with large wheels. A cable would run through the pulley at both ends and as we put the engine in gear, it would pull the cart up the hill to the flat area where the trucks are parked.

Not everyone knew what Bob and Dominic were talking about, but we knew they had the experience to do the job. We voted and allotted Bob and Dominic one thousand dollars to make whatever purchases were necessary and to build the contraption. Bob and Dominic left the next morning for Grass Valley. John, Tom and I continued to remove quartz from the ledge and stack it in piles until ready to load.

The next day, Thursday, as we were sitting at the table for lunch we heard loud voices coming from the direction of our parked trucks. John quickly told the girls to go to the kitchen, lock the doors and stay there until we returned. The three of us took off up the hill.

As we approached the trucks a model T was parked beside my truck and two men and two girls were heavy into drinking from the bottle.

When they observed us approaching, they started yelling and cursing us in filthy language. It was then Tom stepped forward to make a plea for calm.

The smaller of the two men pulled a large knife strapped to his leg and lunged at Tom. Tom quickly sidestepped the knife and grabbed the arm and twisted it up and behind his back, forcing him to drop the knife. The other man and two girls retreated to the car and got inside.

Tom told the man he didn't want to hurt him and asked if he let him go would he behave in a manly manner. The fellow began cursing Tom. It was then Tom reached around and grabbed the other arm and brought it around his body as if to cuff him. Tom produced a length of rope and tied the wrists together. He then had the man sit on the ground. Tom took the knife and drove it into a nearby tree. He then twisted the knife until it broke loose from the handle.

We were so surprised at the events and the quickness of Tom's movements we just stood there and stared. Tom walked over to the others in the car and began talking to them. We couldn't hear everything Tom said but we could see the three in the car become calm and attentive to Tom. They then opened the car door and stepped outside. Tom stepped forward and put his arm around the shoulder of the man as he led him to the shade of a tree. They both sat on the ground as Tom talked to him. We stood off a distance and waited for Tom. Soon Tom left the man and walked to the girls and told them everything was going to be alright.

Tom then walked to the bound one and sat on the ground with him and began to talk. Tom talked for some time. Suddenly, Tom put his arm around his shoulder and began to pray. Tom prayed like I never heard him pray before. Upon finishing the prayer, Tom untied the man and helped him to his feet. The man then put his arms around Tom and began to weep, asking Tom for forgiveness. Tom accepted his apology and both men shook hands.

A few words were exchanged as the four got into their car and drove away. We approached Tom and as we were about to make comment, Tom raised his hand, "The less said the better. This incident is never to be talked about." Tom then turned and began walking back to camp. None of us ever mentioned the incident again.

It was three days before we again saw Bob and Dominic. They came into camp and asked me to follow them to their cabin on the river. They unloaded what gear they brought with them and I followed in my truck. They pulled their truck under a shed and hoisted the engine onto their truck. They then loaded my truck with large tires, a wheel axle and heavy six-foot long one-inch thick lumber. We covered everything with a tarp and headed for camp. Bob and Dominic began immediately assembling their contraption. After a day and a half, they were ready to give it a try. They connected the cable to the new cart, started the engine and put it into gear. The cart rolled up the grade with ease. We were in business.

John went to the ranger station and sent Matthew the message, "Problem solved." The next day we started the transfer of quartz rock.

For the first trip, Tom and Bob drew short straws and were designated drivers. Bob drove the loaded truck while Tom followed in the empty truck. The first transfer point was Wild Plum at 3p.m., which was approximately 15 miles from Downieville, just east of Sierra City.

Bob's transfer truck was well loaded for this first trip. As Tom was following he noticed Bob's truck fishtailed a couple of times and each time it did, Bob would slow down a bit before continuing. The trail from camp to Downieville was the worst. Once past Downieville the road was considerably better to Sierra City. Just east of Sierra City, the road turned southeast to Wild Plum. Just as Bob reached the transfer point, loose gravel caused the truck to fishtail again and Bob lost control. Over went the truck. Quartz rock went in all directions.

Bob was stunned, but otherwise unhurt. Matthew was at Wild Plum for the first transfer and immediately ran to Bob and assisted him out of the badly damaged truck. Mathew had Tom bring his truck forward and immediately began gathering up the loose quartz and loading it into the truck.

Matthew's transfer man took the truck to the crusher as Matthew transported Tom and Bob back to our camp. Needless to say, Tom and Bob didn't sleep well that night.

After discussing the situation the next day, it was decided we would never load the trucks over the side rails again. We salvaged the engine, tires and transmission from the wrecked truck for future use around the camp.

John mentioned we still needed to discuss our winter security problem. As we gathered around, those that had something to say had their turn to suggest or to comment about the matter. No one seemed to have an answer about our dilemma until Bob and Dominic made their suggestion. They said they were tired of their little cabin on the river and could use the change if we all agreed. They suggested that the two of them live at the mine during the coming winter as security. With the proper amount of firewood and supplies they could be comfortable for a few months.

Dominic then said the only problem we have with this suggestion is the vacancy of our little shack down on the river. If someone isn't there during the winter, little varmints will move into the place and destroy it. No one had an answer to settle that problem until Tom spoke up.

"I could live there and prepare myself for the seminary through study. It would only be for a few short months and I could use the time wisely. I could still visit at Albert's place or you could visit me. What do you say?"

John asked Tom if that was what he really wanted to do or was he just trying to help the group by his suggestion?

"I need the time to study and to reflect on my situation. I figure the gold will hold out for a couple of years and after that I'm going to the seminary. This is not only my choice but God's chosen way for me," was Tom's reply.

"It's settled then," commented Bob. "Us two river snipers will live at the mine while Tom hermits himself at our shack while the rest of you no-good lazy snipers enjoy a comfortable few months in Albert's house."

As it turned out, this arrangement stood for the remainder of the time the mine was in operation. Many improvements were made at the mine to include better shower conditions and a modern cooking stove was purchased.

During the second year of operations, Patty's Mother and Father died, only a couple weeks apart. Patty's sister Joyce needed work and the group hired her to be the chief cook and bottle washer at $600 a month. For the work she did and the meals she put out, she was under paid. At the end of all operations, the group awarded her a bonus of $100,000. She was worth every penny.

During the time of operations, Bob and Dominic's shack on the river was upgraded during the summer months to the conditions of a modern vacation cabin. As it turned out, Bob and Dominic did make it their vacation home for themselves and family. Unfortunately, the cabin was destroyed in a river flood in 1955.

The Friends and Partners Mine operated for a full year before word filtered into the community as to what those no-good river snipers were doing. We suddenly had friends we didn't know. Many times as we were on the streets of Downieville, we would be approached by people that wanted a job at the mine, but to continue the security as we had it, we could not hire outsiders to work inside the mine property. We therefore hired nine men to work eight hour shifts, three men per shift, to patrol the perimeter of the property with whistles. Those men never had to use their whistles.

We felt bad that so many wanted work, for we knew all about hard times. Our group held a meeting about the problem and it was decided that a community meeting place was to be established where the Friends and Partners Mine Corporation would sponsor two meals each day for those in need. We hired two cooks to oversee the operation and to keep the corporation informed of its needs. Once a month Sara and I would grocery-shop in Downieville for supplies for the community center. Items not carried in Downieville were purchased at Grass Valley. We would load our truck to the side walls with powdered milk, can beans, can vegetables, can tomatoes, bread, smoked hams, eggs, bacon, coffee beans and any other items the cooks requested.

We soon realized our trips to Grass Valley took much of our mining time, so the corporation purchased a pick-up truck for the center. They could then do their own shopping.

The people at the store in Grass Valley always knew when the shoppers were due to arrive and would stock up their shelves. Those meals at the community center continued until the outbreak of World War II.

At the end of the first fiscal year the corporation account was balanced at $2,255,356.

We renegotiated Matthew's contract and increased his monthly cost to the corporation at $8,000 per month with a bonus of $10,000, payable the first work day of each year.

After the end of the second year as a corporation we added Matthew as a partner for we could not have done any of the things we did without his expertise. You could say Matthew was the leader of all that followed. Matthew also became our legal counsel.

After we closed the mine and dismantled the corporation, Matthew's reputation became known throughout the state. Matthew established the largest and most profitable investment house in California.

Albert passed away during our second year as a corporation. Though it was a sad time for all of us, Albert wasn't through with his surprises. Albert left his large home to Tom, me, Sara, John and Patty. Albert also left instructions that his gold specimens be sold and the proceeds to be given to the San Diego orphanage where Tom had lived. Those proceeds came to $75,000.

John and Patty purchased the house shares from the three of us, as they made plans to stay and live in Downieville. Later John and Patty purchased Zack's Forks Bar and Grill. They made barkeep Sam a partner and manager of the restaurant. After extensive alterations the business was renamed the "Gold Pan." The place became so popular with its specialty, John and Patty started a franchise and within ten years had restaurants in twelve western states. The menu special was a hamburger patty on an open face golden brown bun smothered with beans, bacon chips and chopped onions, served with coffee. The "Snipers Sandwich" was priced at $1.75. Sam became CEO of the franchise with the head office located in Grass Valley.

Bob and Dominic moved to Grass Valley. They each got married and between them had seven kids. They bought the motel where we stayed our first Christmas. They remodeled and enlarged it, making it Grass Valley's finest motel and restaurant. They also purchased nine hundred acres and turned it into a summer camp for boys and girls to age fourteen. One of their specialties was teaching kids how to mine for gold.

Zack and his wife moved to San Francisco after selling out to John and Patty. Zack built one of the finest restaurants San Francisco had ever seen. He named the restaurant, "Zack's," and he let it be known that certain free-loading no-good river snipers were always welcome at Zack's without charge.

Zack and his wife were awarded a million dollars by the partnership for their help and friendship. Zack's was awarded the Chamber of Commerce Restaurant of the year award for five straight years. As usual Zack made comment. "I had a lot of lousy help to get this award."

Tom went on to seminary and became an ordained minister. He located to San Diego where he purchased one hundred seventy five acres on the eastern edge of the city. He built a large church and also built a new orphanage for children to the age of sixteen. He made the orphanage a ward of the church. Those orphanage students who applied to attend a seminary were sponsored by the church for all costs.

Tom named his church, "Sniper's Cove." He notified all of his old friends and partners about the first day of service at the new church. We got together and chartered a plane, arriving in San Diego Saturday night, where Tom had made reservations for all of us at the Hilton.

Sunday morning we found a section roped off, down front, with a sign reading, "Pastor Tom's no-good sniper friends." Zack smiled and commented. "Tom finally got it right."

Tom hired a full orchestra for that Sunday morning service. The city mayor was present along with other dignitaries. Tom gave his sermon on the goodness of people and the grace of God. He gave the finest prayer I ever heard at the end of service. The entire congregation was invited to lunch, sponsored by the church. Tom introduced the children and their teachers from the orphanage. It was a Sunday none of us will ever forget. It reminded us of that Sunday at Downieville when Tom gave his first sermon there.

Chapter 24
Conclusion

I started this story by telling you I was a much older man now. I have seen eighty-four summers and I've seen most of them with my wife Sara.

How wonderful the years have been. We reside in San Jose, where we first started. We have a fine home where we raised our three kids who have now all graduated from college. Our oldest lives in Downieville, for he fell in love with the town and its people. He's the town mayor and the Sierra County Museum Director. He reestablished the meals program for the elderly and set up a senior center for all those who tabbed themselves *over the hill*.

I know you have questions about how we did with our mine. We operated that mine for almost five years just as Albert said we would, before the ore gave out. Even then there was gold to be mined on a small scale. We donated the mine to the food program so proceeds from the mine went to the program.

We deposited in the corporation accounts $142,000,000 after all expenses and taxes were paid. When we broke up the corporation Zack said, "I never thought I would be thanking a bunch of no-good filthy river snipers for anything. It just happens, they are the best lousy river snipers I have ever known." Zack made that statement with tears in his eyes and a smile that spread from one ear to the other.

Without knowledge of any of the members, Tom made arrangements with the grave stone cutters to have two beautiful head stones cut and erected on the graves of Albert and his wife, for Albert was laid to rest next to his wife.

On the wife's stone is engraved: "Though we did not know her, she is known by God. He has taken her to him and she will live forever."

On Albert's stone is engraved: "A man of generosity, kindness and love of his fellow man. Also known by God, for he has been rejoined to his wife by the grace of God. Thank you Albert. Your friends."

When I reached my fifty-fifth birthday, the former partners organized the "Partners for Life Foundation." Those students throughout California who displayed honesty, compassion, sportsmanship and maintained a 3.0 grade average throughout their school years, could apply for a scholarship by submitting their resume stating what they wished to accomplish after their college years that would benefit mankind. All resumes were read and those that met all the requirements were included in the lotto drawing once each year. The Foundation met twice each year---once in the month of June to select the winners and once in December to award the scholarships and to honor the parents of the students.

Ten students were chosen each year. Those students each received a $10,000 scholarship to the college of their choice.

The board of directors of the Foundation was as follows:

Jack was CEO
John was President
Sara, Vice President
Patty, Vice President and Secretary
Tom, Vice President and Foundation Chaplin
Bob, Vice President and Assistant to the President
Dominic, Vice President and Sgt. of Arms
Matthew, Vice President, Legal Assistance.

Zack, though not a partner in the original group was nevertheless invited to attend each meeting held by the foundation and he was afforded a vote in all decisions. In his third year of attendance, he was appointed Assistant vice President. His comment upon accepting the appointment was, "I'll hate this job, but I'll do it just this once."

Sam was brought aboard in the foundation to be in charge of all banquets. He then hired Patty's sister Joyce as the kitchen chef, making her in charge of all cooking. Sam was made the Assistant Vice President to the Assistant Vice President, making him and Joyce the only salaried members of the foundation. Zack commented, "Here we go again."

Tom built his church into the largest congregation in California. His Sunday morning services were attended by 1,500 believers. Tom purchased an additional hundred acres to enlarge the orphanage and improve the parking area. A Sunday morning shuttle service was available from the parking lot to the church.

One Sunday morning as the shuttle service was busy coming and going, Tom walked outside to greet families that were arriving. One family was new to Tom and he introduced himself and welcomed them to his church. Tony DeLorenzi introduced his wife Sue Ann, his sons Waylon, Chase and Parker and his daughter Emma.

Tom was smitten by Emma, for she was the most beautiful young lady he had ever seen. She wore very little makeup for it wasn't needed to enhance her beauty. She made eye contact with Tom and Tom was smitten again.

After service that morning, Tom invited the DeLorenzi family to join the other first-time arrivals for lunch in the fellowship hall. After introductions and prayer, Tom made sure he had a seat next to Emma.

After small talk, Tom ask Emma where she normally attended church and was surprised when she said, I only attend church on special occasions. Without missing a beat Tom asked, "Is today a special occasion?" Emma took a moment before answering, "It is now." Tom almost spilled his coffee.

After lunch, Tom went to the front and invited everyone back the next Sunday, all the time looking at Emma. Tom then did something he had never done before. He walked the DeLorenzi family to their car. Tony noticed the extra attention Tom gave his daughter and he was pleased, for his daughter was choosy in accepting attention from men and she seemed to like Tom.

The next Sunday morning Tom again changed his morning schedule so he could greet those arriving, all the time looking for the DeLorenzi family. Time was getting short before service was to start and Tom had to leave the parking area and return to the church. He was disappointed for he was looking forward to seeing Emma again.

As the music started and the worship team approached the platform, the rear door opened and Emma walked in alone. She took the first open seat in the rear of the church, opened her Bible and began to read without looking up.

As Tom rose to approach the front of the platform, Emma looked up from her Bible, smiled and made eye contact with Tom. Tom's heart lost a beat and he was somewhat flustered as he began to speak.

"Brothers and sisters please forgive me this morning if I stumble in presenting God's Word, for a wonderful thing has happened to me and I am not myself. I am in love. Yes, I love my God, but I also love a wonderful and beautiful female whom I just recently met. I will explain all to you at the conclusion of today's service."

Tom began to preach about God's plan for the union of man and woman and the wonderful results being the family. Tom expanded his sermon by explaining the vows taken during the wedding ceremony. The congregation was stunned and pleased, for they had never heard the explanation as Tom presented it.

As Tom approached the ending of his sermon, he paused, bowed his head and began to pray. "Heavenly Father, of that which I am about to do, I ask for your blessing, for it is your plan we do these things. Bless these people this morning Father and especially the one which I feel is your choice, as it is mine. Amen."

"Ladies and Gentlemen, the lady I am in love with is in attendance this morning and with your indulgence I wish to ask her a question."

The congregation was silent for a brief moment before erupting into applause. Tom then walked off the platform and down the walkway to the back of the church. He approached Emma, went down on one knee and began to speak. "Emma, though I have only known you for one week, I deeply love you. I have prayed all this week that you would feel the same about me. I want to marry you, love you and care for you for the remainder of my life. Will you marry me?"

You could have heard a pin drop in the church that morning as 1,500 worshipers sat silent, waiting for Emma's answer. Slowly, Emma rose from her seat and began to speak. "Pastor Tom, I loved you from the moment I saw you. I knew you were to be my husband for the rest of my life. Yes, I will marry you."

The congregation erupted into applause. The organist began to play a short version of the wedding march as Tom led Emma to the front of the church. The congregation rose to their feet as Tom motioned for silence. Holding Emma's hand, Tom began to pray. "Father, as we conclude the service this morning, I thank you for your wonderful choice. Be with us as we prepare for our wedding and the vows we will take. This morning's service is over. Amen."

The wedding was radio-broadcast throughout America. The reception was held in the fellowship hall and Tom made sure his sniper friends had a special location just for them. Emma's parents were honored with a special seating directly in front of the wedding party.

Next to Emma's parents was a table with three empty chairs. One chair was beautifully decorated and upholstered, befitting a King. The table was beautifully roped off.

Best man John rose and had his say and Sara, the matron of honor, had her say. Tom then rose to speak. He began by thanking each of his sniper friends by name, thanking them for the wonderful way they welcomed him and for taking him as a full partner in their enterprise.

Tom then asked everyone to fill their glasses with the apple cider present on each table. Tom proposed a special toast. Tom stood and turned as he gestured toward the empty table.

"Here is to my mom and dad, whoever and wherever they may be. Here also is to my Jesus who I know is here this day, occupying that special chair. Thank you Jesus for this wonderful day."

That my, friends, was the most silent toast I was ever a part of. Everyone drank from their glass without a spoken word, for they were all busy wiping tears from their eyes. Tom then said, "Amen and Amen."

Wedding gifts and donations poured into the church from every state in America. One thing Tom insisted upon---solicitation for funds was never allowed during a broadcast or at any other time. Nevertheless, funds were received every day of the week to compliment Tom's work. Tom and his church board were stunned for they had never seen such a pouring out of love.

Tom made a special radio broadcast to thank the world and to thank his God for the blessings. Tom assured the general public that all funds received would be used to spread the good news of the gospel and that an accounting of all funds spent would be available upon request.

Tom further announced that his salary from the church would remain the same as it always was---one dollar per year, without an expense account.

Jack passed away in 2001, age 90, followed within two days by Sara. They said she died of a broken heart. Tom was senior pastor at their service and those friends and neighbors of Jack and Sara say it was the most reverent funeral service they ever attended. Tom made it known that Jack and Sara were the originators of the "Friends for Life." Though they did not know at the time, it started when they took their vows and decided to move to the mountains so many years ago. Tom further commented, "Jack and Sara will be remembered as the founders of those no-good low-down river snipers of Downieville, credited with many good things in life."

Jack and Sara's mansion was donated to the city of San Jose and today is a fine museum, highlighting the life and times of those people who suffered and those who were successful during the Great Depression.

The End

About The Author

Wiley Joiner is a former military man. After a ten-year naval career he relocated from Miami, Florida to California in 1962, and became hooked on California history. In 1964, he reenlisted in the Army and found himself recruited into the Green Beret Special Forces, serving in a number of overseas locations.

After his discharge from the service, Wiley teamed up with lifetime friend, Robert Jernigan. The two collaborated in the research and writing of Black Bart, The Search is Over. Since then Wiley has written Oakdale, California, California's Golden Glory Days and Cattle, Cards, Barbed Wire and Gold. He is currently working on two other books.

Wiley resides in Oakdale, California with his wife, Glory Ann. They have two sons, Mark and Jeffery, five grandchildren and six great grandchildren.

**For a complete selection of books by
Wiley Joiner and other authors, please
visit our website.**

www.shalakopress.com

Wiley Joiner

CPSIA information can be obtained
at www.ICGtesting.com
Printed in the USA
LVHW020013280319
612094LV00007B/17/P